P9-CLQ-295

SOLDIER OF GOD

FICTION BY DAVID HAGBERG

WRITING AS DAVID HAGBERG

Twister

The Capsule

Last Come the Children

Heartland

Heroes

Without Honor

Countdown

Crossfire

Critical Mass

Desert Fire

High Flight

Assassin

White House

Joshua's Hammer

Eden's Gate

The Kill Zone

By Dawn's Early Light

WRITING AS SEAN FLANNERY

The Kremlin Conspiracy

Eagles Fly

The Trinity Factor

The Hollow Men

False Prophets

Broken Idols

Gulag

Moscow Crossing

The Zebra Network

Crossed Swords

Counterstrike

Moving Targets

Winner Take All

Achilles' Heel

SOLDIER
OF GOD

DAVID HAGBERG

A TOM DOHERTY ASSOCIATES BOOK
NEW YORK

This is a work of fiction. All the characters and events portrayed in this novel are either fictitious or are used fictitiously.

SOLDIER OF GOD

Copyright © 2005 by David Hagberg

"The Only One" by Gina Hagberg-Ballinger is reprinted on page 413 with permission from the author.

All rights reserved, including the right to reproduce this book, or portions thereof, in any form.

This book is printed on acid-free paper.

A Forge Book
Published by Tom Doherty Associates, LLC
175 Fifth Avenue
New York, NY 10010

www.tor.com

Forge® is a registered trademark of Tom Doherty Associates, LLC.

Library of Congress Cataloging-in-Publication Data

Hagberg, David.
    Soldier of God / David Hagberg.
        p.   cm.
    ISBN 0-765-30622-0
    EAN 978-0-765-30622-7
        1. McGarvey, Kirk (Fictitious character)—Fiction.   2. Saudi Arabians—United States—
Fiction.   3. Children—Crimes against—Fiction.   4. Terrorism—Prevention—Fiction.
5. Intelligence officers—Fiction.   6. Suicide bombings—Fiction.   I. Title.

PS3558.A3227 S65 2005
813'.54—dc22

                                                                2005047857

First Edition: November 2005

Printed in the United States of America

0   9   8   7   6   5   4   3   2   1

For Lorrel, as always

I take sanctuary in the Lord of humankind,
the master of humankind,
the God of humankind,
from the evil of insidious intimation
that whispers in human hearts
from satanic and human sources.

When the earth shakes,
in her shock,
and the earth sheds
her burdens,
and the people say,
"What is wrong with her?"
that day she will tell her news,
that your Lord has inspired her.

On that day humankind
will go forth apportioned
to be shown their works.

Thus whoever has done
a iota of good
will see it.

And whoever has done
a iota of evil
will see it.

THE QUR'AN

SOLDIER OF GOD

THE LETTERS

□

"My dearest mother," the letter began, as so many had begun before it. "The day of joy will soon arrive. Send out presents and sweets. Prepare my father and my brother for my wedding to come. My black-eyed wife waits for me in Paradise. Rejoice, O my mother, for we will meet in heaven."

The imam, Mustafa Amir Qasim, who was taking the boy's dictation, looked up and offered a comforting smile. "You may continue. You're doing fine, Muhamed."

The boy was shivering. At nineteen he knew very little of the real world, although he had been raised in the refugee camps of Lebanon, in what was called Hell's Bootcamp, and he had seen at least something of the United States, including the stab in the heart of capitalism where the World Trade Center had once proudly stood. But he was frightened to be away from a place he knew; horrible, a hell on earth, but home nevertheless. He nodded uncertainly.

He was a slightly built boy, narrow-hipped, sloping small shoulders, an almost feminine face except for the intensely dark scraggly beard and deep-set coal black eyes. His name was Muhamed Ali Abdallah, and when he volunteered he had left behind his parents, one brother, two sisters, and many uncles and aunts and cousins, though many more were dead or in the hospital because of the attacks on their homes from the Zionist pigs. He wet his lips with the tip of his tongue.

At four he was already going with his brother and some other boys in a neigborhood in Nablus to throw stones at the armed Israeli soldiers. When his mother found out, she had, for the first time in her life, stood up to her husband. "Rashid you may have. But Muhamed is mine. He will not die on the streets to prove he is a man."

His father had dismissed her with an indifferent wave of his hand. "For now," he said.

Muhamed had not heard this conversation, of course, but he had been told over and over again that his duties, for the moment, lay with the household, with his mother and sisters, and not outside the camps. Read books, he was told. Write dissertations; learn the mysteries of mathematics so that you can go to college and bring back knowledge—and money.

Money was the key to their salvation from the grinding poverty that would kill them all eventually, though such an heretical thought could not be spoken aloud.

He had learned to read and write. He had learned mathematics and physics and even engineering. But since the righteous attacks in New York and Washington, the doors to his education were closed. He was from the West Bank, he was a resident of Lebanon, his family were supporters of the PLO, his father and two uncles were wanted men in the U.S., and there never could be a legitimate visa for Muhamed to any Western country—where the good universities were located.

This now was his only way out, the only way in which he could help his family. To repay their years of love and devotion. This was his duty.

The imam was dressed, as he should be for this occasion, in a black galabiyya and white head covering, but Muhamed wore jeans, an L.A. Lakers sweatshirt, and Nikes. All-American, or at least a Muslim who appeared to have embraced the American ideal. The room they were in was small, without a window, and with only a small, cast-iron light fixture hanging from a plain plastered ceiling. They sat on a carpet facing each other, no furniture or other fixtures in the starkly familiar space.

Muhamed felt a measure of comfort being here, composing his last will and testament, his death letter to his family. And another, deeper part of him even felt a serenity that he would soon die and be transported to Paradise.

The death letter of the martyr Hamdi Yasin, who'd given his life to kill an Israeli officer years ago, had been read to him in Palestine before he left: . . . *It is not correct when some people say that we commit suicide because we do not value life. We love life, but life in dignity.*

Muhamed managed to smile, and the imam nodded his understanding that a sense of holiness had finally descended into the boy.

" 'Our flowers are the sword and the dagger,' " Imam Qasim quoted from Ali ibn Abi Talib as he calculated the profits from his nine 7-Eleven stores that would go to pay the fifty thousand dollars to this boy's family and the families of the other three young men here this afternoon also dictating their death letters to other imams. Financial help would come as usual, but care had to be taken with the money trail.

The boy began to speak again, stealing and changing the lines of his death letter from Yasin because he could not remember them exactly. *"My dearest mother, I cannot allow God's houses to be violated without defending them. I pray to Almighty God that my mission may result in the death of one hundredfold of God's enemies."*

Dictating the letter to an imam, rather than writing it himself, made sure that the words would be closer to Allah's liking.

The boy straightened up a little. *"I profess that there is no God but the One God, and that Muhammed is the messenger of God."*

Imam Qasim finished the flowing script, then passed the paper and pen to the boy for his signature. "It is a fine letter," he said. "You are a soldier of God now."

Muhamed signed his name. "You will make sure that my mother gets this?"

"Yes. As well as the money."

"May Allah bless you," Muhamed said, rising to go.

"And you, my son," Iman Qasim responded. He handed the boy a sealed manila envelope with new identification papers, Greyhound bus tickets, some cash, and instructions.

Muhamed hesitated just a moment, wanting to say something else, but not sure what it was; then he left the room. Down a long corridor he passed a series of arches that opened to the main room of the mosque where a few old men were praying, their heads bowed to the floor. Such a scene had been perfectly familiar to him all of his life, but this afternoon he seemed to see this place as if for the first time, through the eyes of a newborn.

Outside, the noise, swirling colors, movement, and the sheer volume of the traffic on the downtown streets were almost staggering. America was so vast. So alive. So busy. Surreal.

Muhamed walked four blocks to the memorial on the site of what had been the Murrah Federal Office Building, the warmth of an early September Oklahoma afternoon reminding him of Palestine. Unbeknownst to him, the three other martyrs to the cause would make the same pilgrimage from the mosque to this place this afternoon before continuing on to their targets. They were Ibrahim Hablatt, also from the camps of the West Bank; Abbas Adri from the deserts of Algeria; and Iskander Zia from Peshawar near Pakistan's border with Afghanistan.

Insha'allah.

PART
ONE

ONE

No one could help but spot the tall, gangly man with the chocolate brown complexion and ridiculous Hawaiian print shirt at the baggage claim area in Juneau International Airport. Everyone noticed that he retrieved too many leather satchels and overstuffed B4 bags to reasonably carry, and that he wore striped Bermuda shorts when it was in the low forties and drizzling outside. But his broad smile seemed to be genuine and was infectious. He was a man in his mid to late forties, with flashing dark eyes under a sharply defined brow that complimented a sculpted aquiline nose and high cheekbones, who knew that he cut a silly figure but who nevertheless was having a grand time. His laugh was the best of all, a rich deep baritone that boomed across the hall as the last of the luggage off the Air Canada flight from Vancouver came out on the moving carousel.

The man was content to wait his turn with dozens of people, many of them older couples on their way to or from cruise ships up or down the Inside Passage. Everyone was in a holiday mood, and the tall man joked and laughed with the people around him, putting everyone at ease, and making this trip just a little extra special. Characters were rare in these difficult times, and the man's Caribbean British accent was pleasant as was the mellifluous timbre of his voice.

"Of course I know that I'm not dressed for the cold, madam," he told a frail; white-haired old woman waiting in line. His smile widened. "In Trinidad it is never cold."

The woman was puzzled by the man's answer, as was her husband and others around them.

"Don't you see, mum? I want to be cold."

"You do?"

"Yes. It's a new experience."

Her husband smiled and shook his head. "I don't think you'll like it," he said.

"Isherwood?" one of the passengers asked, holding up a duffel bag he'd snagged from the carousel.

"Yes, Thomas Isherwood, and that is my bag, my good man." He retrieved his bag from the passenger, then gathered up his other luggage and with a toothy grin strode across the hall toward the exits, leaving in his wake the scent of Bay Rum cologne and a few good-natured chuckles.

When he was out of sight, he ducked down the corridor that led to the car rental agencies. Alaskan wilderness and wildlife posters adorned its walls. He went into a men's room, where in a stall he changed into jeans, an oiled wool Irish fisherman's sweater, a light jacket, and waffle-soled, lightweight nylon hiking shoes.

The man who emerged still traveled as Thomas Isherwood from Port of Spain, Trinidad, but no one from the Vancouver flight would have recognized him; the Caribbean bonhomie was gone, replaced with the matter-of-fact bland indifference of a well-heeled businessman here to catch fish no matter how much effort or money it cost. The face was the same, but the expression was so completely different it was as if he were wearing a mask.

Isherwood walked past the car rental counters and went outside where he loaded his bags in a cab. A steady cold rain fell from a darkly overcast sky. He ordered the driver to take him to Flights over Alaska Air Charters, then sat back and allowed himself to relax for a few minutes. He'd been on the go for three days, since he left Switzerland, maintaining several different personas, and the effort was draining, though if need be he could continue his charade for weeks or months, even years.

This was nothing new for him. Home was just another word that held little or no real meaning, though his wife and children were in Switzerland for the moment, and his many aunts, uncles, cousins, two sisters, and three brothers were scattered across Saudi Arabia. Over the last nine years, ever since he had received the call, he had spent very little time with his own people.

But that was as it should be, insha'allah. Progress was being made, though even if it weren't he would still move forward if for no other reason than the thrill of the hunt. Osama's *fatwah* was as crystal clear as the Qur'an. If the unbelievers cannot be made to see the error of their ways, if they cannot be converted, then either treat them as slaves by taking away their liberties and their properties, or kill them. All the world was to be converted to Dar el Islam, even if it took one thousand years. The hunt was on. It was the grandest game in the universe, and Isherwood was one of its most successful practitioners. He was alive as never before. He had been born for this. From the desert tents of the Bedouin to the towers of Babel in New York, he was in his element.

It was a little late for the normal tourist season, so the reception area in the Flights Over Alaska Air Charters Operations Building was deserted except for the square-shouldered woman who looked up and smiled when Isherwood walked in.

"May I help you, sir?"

"The name is Thomas Isherwood. I believe you were expecting me." He handed her his passport. Payment for the hundred-mile flight down to Kuiu Island on the Inside Passage had been made with a credit card two weeks earlier.

The woman glanced at the clock. It was coming up on noon. "We weren't expecting you until later this afternoon."

"I caught an earlier flight," Isherwood said. He made it a point to change his schedules whenever it was possible. "Are there an airplane and pilot for me?"

"Of course, sir," the woman said. She glanced at the passport, then handed it back. She picked up the phone and dialed a three-digit number. "Your three o'clock is here. Can you fly now?" She gave Isherwood a reassuring smile, and nodded. "Thanks, Frank. I'll bring Mr. Isherwood right over." She hung up, and came around the counter. "The rain won't bother you none. Should be a smooth flight."

"I appreciate it. I'd like to get down there, have a couple of drinks, and then maybe get a couple hours of fishing in before dark."

"Name's Mary," she said. Outside she tossed his heavy bags in the back of a Toyota Land Cruiser as if they were filled with air, then drove him a half mile across the bumpy concrete apron to a large hangar where several Otters, Beavers, and one DeHavilland floatplane were parked. "I have to tell you that I fell in love with your accent when you called to make the reservation."

Isherwood gave her a warm smile, thinking that killing her would give him a certain pleasure. "I hope my appearance fits your expectations."

She glanced at him to see if he was going along with her good-natured ribbing; then she nodded, the corners of her eyes crinkled in laughter. "Oh, I guess I was expecting someone older." She shook her head. "But don't get me wrong, you'll do just fine——"

Isherwood threw back his head and laughed from the bottom of his feet. He would crush her windpipe with one blow, and then watch her eyes as her life drained away. He especially enjoyed the moment when the person knew that they were going to die and knew with equal certainty that there was nothing they could do about it.

He patted her hand on the steering wheel. "You're a gem, Mary. An absolute jewel."

She blushed openly as no Arab woman would ever dare, but then she didn't know how close to death she was.

The pilot, Frank Sterling, a gray-haired but rugged-looking outdoors type in his early sixties, was finishing his walk-around as Mary tossed Isherwood's bags in the back cargo area of the beefy-looking Otter wheeled floatplane. This, the Beaver, and the DeHavilland were Alaska's workhorses, delivering people, mail, food, and supplies, and doctors to just about every inaccessible spot in the state. And there were a lot of them. The pilots were among the best in the world. They had to be, often operating out of extremely short, muddy fields, or lakes still half-choked with ice, in every weather condition including all-out blizzards. They were generally no-nonsense people who would just as soon haul cargo, or passengers who had the good sense and manners to keep their mouths shut, tourists.

"How long a flight?" Isherwood asked him.

Sterling gave him an appraising look. Not many Caribbean blacks got this far north, and Sterling inspected his passenger as if he were studying a circus oddity. "About an hour, if we can start anytime soon, Mr. Isherwood."

Isherwood's muscles bunched. It would take less than two seconds to remove his belt buckle, slide the razor-sharp lower half open on its hinge pin, and slit the man's throat. Maybe he would see an apology in the eyes. Maybe not. But there would be copious amounts of infidel blood. He forced a faint smile. "Anytime that you're ready, captain."

Mary was obviously embarrassed by an exchange between the two men that she didn't understand. "I hope you have a good week of fishing, Mr. Isherwood. This time of year it should be great."

"Ah, thank you, Mary, my love," Isherwood said, laughing. "You're a terrible flirt, but thank you for the transport over."

He stepped up on the starboard float, climbed in the front right seat, and strapped himself in. Sterling said something to the woman, then got aboard, strapped in, flipped a few switches, and hit the starter switch. The big Pratt & Whitney radial engine roared into life, and once the gauges were all in their nominal ranges, Sterling set the altimeter, released the brake, and eased the throttle forward, sending them trundling out of the hangar and down the sloping apron into the chilly black waters of Stephens Passage, doing his run-up to check the magnetos on the move.

Without a glance at his passenger, Sterling said something into the mike of his headset, then firewalled the throttle as he turned the big plane into the wind. They were airborne within a thousand feet, water stream- ing off the floats, and almost immediately the thick overcast ceiling was just above them. Sterling leveled off, and turned just east of due south to follow the pass all the way down to Entrance Island, where he would swing west to pass Cape Baranof, and then on to Karsten's Fishin' Mission on the northwest bay of Kuiu Island.

Isherwood had studied the air and sea charts of the region, so he knew the area almost as if he had lived there all his life. He prepared for every mission in the same way, with a professional thoroughness that left little or nothing to chance. He was a man who did not like surprises. In his business the unknown could be deadly.

In fact, Isherwood was not his real name. According to Western intel- ligence agencies, he was the international terrorist, possibly Osama bin Laden's operations chief, known only as Khalil. According to the CIA, he was thought to be an Egyptian with a wife and children hidden some- where in Cairo under assumed identities. Supposedly he was a medical doctor who had served with bin Laden in Afghanistan in the eighties fighting Russians, whom he hated almost as deeply as he hated Jews and Americans. No clear photographs of him existed in any Western intel file, nor was there any DNA or fingerprint evidence available that could positively identify him. He was as elusive as the night mists, and as cruel as is possible for a human being to be. In the past fifteen years no one who had come up against him had survived. Rumors were that even bin Laden was respectful—if not frightened—of the depth of the man's savagery.

As the town of Juneau fell away from them, one spot of civilization in the middle of a vast rugged wilderness, Khalil realized how perfect an area this was for the operation he had so meticulously planned. Heavily forested, craggy islands separated the limitless expanse of the Pacific Ocean to the west from the snow and glacier-covered, forbidding mountains to the east. Except for fishing boats heading to or from the passes to the open ocean, cruise ships that traveled the Inside Passage, and the occasional sailboat or recreational trawler, there was nothing below them for as far as the eye could see.

"Empty, isn't it?" Sterling shouted over the roar of the engine.

"No," Khalil replied, mesmerized by the bleak landscape below. "It's filled with opportunities down there." He glanced at the pilot, who was looking at him. "Lots of fish to catch. And I will catch them."

The small fishing resort was invisible from the air until the last moment, when Sterling set down in the long bay as lightly as a feather on a woman's cheek and taxied to the end of the long dock on the south side. Then, except for the dock and two small fishing boats and three canoes, all that could be seen was a gravel footpath that led to a scattering of cabins all but hidden in the dense forest that ran right down to the water's edge.

It was raining harder here than up in Juneau, and it had gotten dark. Sterling held up at the dock, the Otter's engine idling, as Khalil got out and unloaded his own bags.

"I'll be back the same time next week, unless you want to get out sooner," Sterling said. Without waiting for a reply, he reached over and closed the passenger door, then gunned the engine and turned left, the broad wing sweeping over the dock so that Khalil had to step back to avoid getting hit.

There were seven sets of eyes watching from the woods and from the cabins. Khalil could feel them studying him, evaluating his behavior. Some of his soldiers had been here for as long as three days, waiting for their leader to show up. Waiting for the operation to finally begin. Only Zahir al Majid, his second-in-command, had ever worked with him on an operation. The others had heard of him, of course. Kahlil was a living legend, and they would be curious to see how he handled what was obviously an insult.

He gave a thumbs-up to the departing airplane, then walked up to the main lodge completely hidden in the forest, leaving his bags on the dock for someone to fetch.

Zahir, a short squat man with a thick mustache, but nearly bald on top, met Khalil in the rustic lobby. They warmly embraced. A fire burned on the stone hearth. The log walls were adorned with mounted fish, presumably caught by former patrons of the fishing camp.

"I'm glad you have finally arrived safely," Zahir said. "Will you have something to eat? Our people would like to sit with you."

"Soon. Is the equipment we need here?"

"Yes."

"Our other soldiers are in place?"

Zahir checked his watch. "I spoke with Abdul in Juneau this morning. All is as it should be. The vessel will depart in a few hours and begin its southbound cruise."

"The resort staff?"

"The maintenance man, two guides, and the owner are dead, as you ordered. Their bodies were placed in the generator building, safe from the wildlife. The owner's wife and their daughter are being held upstairs, in case a radiotelephone call needs to be answered."

"Cell phones are out of range?"

"Yes."

Khalil nodded in satisfaction. "Give the daughter to the men. When they are finished with her, kill her. The mother can answer the telephone if need be."

"They will like that."

"Now we will go fishing," Khalil said. "Do you know how, Zahir?"

"There is no fishing in the desert."

Khalil laughed. "Then we will learn together."

"In the meantime I will send someone to the dock for your bags."

TWO

Kirk McGarvey got out of the cab into the cold drizzle at the cruise ship dock, and paused for a moment to unlimber his tall, husky body and look up at the bulk of the 192-foot pocket cruise ship *Spirit of '98* that would be his and Katy's home for the next seven days.

He was a man of about fifty, in superb physical condition because of a daily regimen of hard physical exercise overseen by Jim Grassinger, his bodyguard, and the physical trainers and docs at the Central Intelligence Agency. It didn't do to allow the director to get flabby, especially not this director. He wasn't overly handsome, but his face was pleasant, his gray-green eyes honest and direct, and he exuded the quiet self-confidence of a man who was supremely capable of taking care of himself no matter what the situation was. People who got close to him, and who were perceptive enough to understand who he was, felt protected, as if they were under an umbrella where the rain could never reach them.

He had more than twenty-five years' experience working for the government, first in the Air Force as an intelligence and Special Ops officer; next with the CIA as a case officer with assignments everywhere from Vietnam to Berlin and back; then as a freelance working what in those days were called "black operations," which more often than not resulted in the death of one or more bad guys; and finally, reluctantly, back to Langley as the Company's director.

Whenever he had a choice, he opted for a field assignment over a desk job, which was a curious contradiction to his main passion, besides his family: the study of Voltaire, the eighteenth-century French philosopher whose thoughts on everything from religion to government to science he found fascinating.

Otto Rencke, the best friend he'd ever had, who worked for him as special projects director, was fond of telling anyone who'd listen that Voltaire was okay for a Frog, except that he'd never known when to keep his opinions to himself. Which was the same criticism usually thrown at McGarvey. *Common sense is not so common,* Voltaire wrote in 1764, and as far as Mac was concerned, nothing had changed in the intervening two and a half centuries.

The sign on Truman's desk had read that the buck stopped there, but the sign on McGarvey's desk should have warned The Bullshit Stops Here. He hated nothing worse than liars, cheats, and bullies. Tell it like it is, or keep your mouth shut. Don't blow smoke up my ass. Lead, follow, or get out of the way, but don't whine about it. Anything but that.

A knight in shining armor, his wife Katy called him, but almost never to his face, and certainly not in public. He would have been embarrassed.

"Hey, how long are you going to keep me locked up?" Kathleen asked from inside the cab.

McGarvey, realizing he had been wool gathering, took her hand and helped her out. "Sorry about that," he said.

She laughed, the sound light, almost musical. It was her happy, if not contented, noise, a mood he was finally beginning to recognize and understand without having to ask. She was tall for a woman, and slender, with short blond hair that framed a perfectly oval face, high cheekbones, full lips, finely formed nose, and a Nefertiti neck. She was fifty, but it was impossible to tell her age by looking at her, because her complexion was nearly flawless, and she was in almost as good physical shape as her husband, and for some of the same reasons—a lot of exercise and a strict attention to diet. In addition, though she would never admit it, she'd had a couple of brief, but expensive sessions with a plastic surgeon. Katy wasn't denying her age, but she wasn't letting it get the better of her. Not just yet.

"What a beautiful boat," she said with pleasure.

"Ship," McGarvey corrected, automatically. They weren't the first of the ninety-six passengers aboard, but they were not the last, and the dock was busy with cabs, a couple of Cruise West courtesy buses, and people pushing carts with their luggage. No one seemed to mind that it was dark, raining, and in the low forties. The scenery on Alaska's Inside Passage—hundreds if not thousands of islands, mountains, glaciers, and dense, almost primeval, forests—and the wildlife, including whales, would make the holiday worth just about any discomfort. The *Spirit of '98*, a magnificent four-deck cruise ship built in the style of a turn-of-the-century steamer, had actually been used in the Kevin Costner movie *Wyatt Earp*. She had all the modern amenities including diesel engines, a full suite of electronics, lifeboats, a first-class gourmet kitchen and staff, plush upholstery, carved wooden cabinetry, and a player piano in the Grand Salon, but she looked like a gold rush ship. She had a single funnel just aft of the sweeping bridge, sharply vertical bows complete with pennant staff, and fine, old-fashioned lines.

McGarvey paid the cabby for the lift from Juneau's airport as his bodyguard Jim Grassinger took the bags from the trunk. Needing a bodyguard was one of the downsides of the job as DCI. He had been used to taking care of himself for most of his life. But having a bodyguard was in his charter, and he'd already had one killed out from under him, proving the necessity. But he still didn't like it, though he had developed a great deal of respect and trust in Grassinger over the past year.

"I hope it stops raining sometime this week, Jim," McGarvey said. "I'd like to see you work on your tan."

"We're in the wrong part of the world for that, boss," Grassinger replied. He was not a very large man, and almost no one would take a second look at him. He had a round face, pale blue eyes, thinning, sand-colored hair—his mother was Swedish—and in a suit, the jacket always cut large to accommodate his hardware, he could easily pass for the manager of the appliance section at Sears. But behind his bland, pleasant demeanor was a body of hard bar steel and the determination to match. First in hand-to-hand combat at the CIA's training facility in Virginia; first in marksmanship with a whole host of weapons including handguns, foreign and domestic, assault rifles, riot guns, submachineguns, RPGs, and handheld missile launchers such as the Stinger, the Russian Grail, and the LAW; and first in surveillance and countersurveillance methods, he repeatedly turned down offers from the Secret Service to protect the president. He liked working for the CIA. And as far as bosses went, McGarvey was the best in his book.

He never stopped scanning the dock, and his jacket, beneath which he carried a 9mm Glock 17 with a nineteen-round box magazine, was loose as usual. He was doing a job that he would not quit until he was fired, retired, or killed, none of which he figured was going to happen anytime soon.

McGarvey and Katy each took a bag and walked across the covered boarding ramp into the ship. It had begun this cruise last week in Fairbanks, and would head down to Seattle in a few hours.

Normally, Grassinger would have gone ahead to check out the ship, but this time the crew and all the passengers had been vetted by the CIA and by the DoD because the former secretary of defense Donald Shaw and his wife, Karen, were also on board. Both he and McGarvey were significant targets for groups such as Osama bin Laden's al-Quaida, but they both traveled with bodyguards, the Coast Guard was nearby, the ship would be under almost constant satellite surveillance, and Shaw's and McGarvey's names had not been made public. Even their travel arrangements from Washington had been kept strictly under wraps.

Both couples needed the time off, the Shaws because of the continuing strife in Iraq, for which the former SecDef was working in an advisory capacity for State, and the McGarveys because of the horrible ordeal they had gone through less than a year ago in which Katy had been brainwashed into actually attempting to assassinate her husband.

Their only daughter, Elizabeth, who worked for the CIA as a field officer and instructor, had suffered too. She'd been four months pregnant but had lost the baby in an arranged accident. Now she and her husband, CIA combat instructor Todd Van Buren, could not have children. They were in their twenties, head over heels in love with each other, and Elizabeth's hysterectomy had devastated them.

The Shaws and McGarveys were greeted in a receiving line by four ship's officers, including the captain, the purser, the concierge, and the chief steward, who assigned them their accommodations and dinner seatings.

"Mr. and Mrs. James Garwood," the concierge announced.

"Welcome aboard the *Spirit*," Captain Bruce Darling said, shaking hands. "If there's anything I can personally do to make your trip more enjoyable, please, don't stand on ceremony. Just ask."

"Good scenery, good food, and good weather, Captain," Kathleen said, smiling.

Darling chuckled. "How about two out of three, ma'am?"

"Fair enough," she told him, and she and Kirk moved off with a steward's assistant to their first-class cabin, as Grassinger went through the same routine. He would be bunking in a cabin adjacent to the McGarveys'.

The cabins were relatively Spartan compared to those aboard larger cruise ships. But the McGarveys' cabin was equipped with a television, a reasonably sized bathroom, a queen bed, and a killer view from a very large window.

"Just leave the bags," McGarvey told the steward.

"Yes, sir. We sail at five, and there will be a welcoming cocktail party in the Grand Salon at six."

Katy went to the window and looked across the channel at the docks and the processing buildings for the fishing fleet.

"Should we dress?" McGarvey asked.

"No, sir. Casual will be fine," the steward said. He was a slight man with an olive complexion and a ready smile. "There will be a lifeboat drill first."

"Fine," McGarvey said. When the steward was gone, he took off his jacket and tossed it on the bed, revealing a quick-draw holster at the small of his back that contained the 9mm version of the Walther PPK. He seldom went anywhere without the pistol. The German handgun was an old friend that had saved his life on more than one occasion.

"Well, we finally made it," Kathleen said, as if a weight had been lifted from her shoulders.

McGarvey went to her and took her in his arms. She leaned her head back against his shoulder. "How do you feel, Katy?"

She chuckled at the back of her throat. "Pregnant, happy as hell, content, frightened out of my wits, fat, hungry, thirsty." She turned her face up to his.

He kissed her for a long time. "A penny for the laugh."

"You said Katy. I almost corrected you."

"Kathleen. Old habits die hard," McGarvey said.

They watched out the window, in each other's arms, for a few minutes content with the peace and quiet after an extremely contentious year. Of all the places in the world they could have picked for a week's vacation—the Caribbean, Greece, Wales to look up her relatives, Ireland to look up his—they had chosen an Alaskan cruise because of the isolation. They were both peopled out. If truth were to be told, they would almost have preferred a desert island somewhere.

She snuggled a little closer to him, pressing her breasts against his chest. "Hmm."

"Tender?" he asked.

"A little," she answered.

McGarvey felt a sudden surge of doubt. "We're doing the right thing, aren't we?"

She chuckled again. Her everything's-really-okay sound. "If you mean being fifty and getting pregnant, no, we're being reckless. But if you mean getting pregnant with our daughter and son-in-law's fertilized egg because they can no longer have children, we're being foolish, but loving." She looked up at him again, her face open and vulnerable. "Is my knight a little frightened?"

"Yup."

Her eyes filled. "It's okay, because it's you and me, darling. Nothing else counts."

Someone knocked at the door. Kathleen stiffened for a moment, but then settled back. Life went on.

McGarvey gave her a brief kiss, then went to the door. It was Grassinger. McGarvey let him in.

"What's the drill tonight, boss?"

"We're going to the cocktail party, then dinner, and we'll be turning in early," McGarvey said.

"And sleeping in," Katy added.

"What about Shaw's bodyguard?" McGarvey asked.

Grassinger nodded. "Tony Battaglia. He's good man. Ex–Army Special Ops. He's up on the bridge deck in the captain's sea cabin." The Shaws occupied the owner's suite, the only accommodation on that deck, except for the captain's on-duty quarters, which he used only in an emergency when his presence on the bridge was required 24/7.

"I'll talk to him, see if we can coordinate our activities so that you and Battaglia can have a little slack time," McGarvey promised, but he gave Grassinger a stern look. "Let's get something straight from the get-go. I'm here on vacation, which means I'm not going to jump through a lot of security hoops. The ship is secure, the passengers and crew have been vetted—twice—and I'd just as soon not see you until we get to Seattle."

"The passengers and crew have been cleared, but I don't trust anybody, boss."

"Neither do I. But we're here to relax."

"Maybe you are, but I'm not," Grassinger mumbled.

"None of the passengers are going to relax either," Katy said. "Not unless both of you keep your jackets on all the time to cover up your arsenals. Guns make most people twitchy."

McGarvey grinned. "You're right, Katy," he said. He took off his holster and stuffed it and a spare magazine in a side pocket of one of his bags.

"Do you think that's wise?" Grassinger asked, skeptically.

"I'm a tourist on vacation," McGarvey said, though he did feel somewhat naked.

"No, sir, you're the director of Central Intelligence, and fair game for a good number of people who would like to see you become a permanent resident of Arlington National," Grassinger said bluntly. He glanced at Katy. "Sorry, Mrs. M., I didn't mean any offense, just doing my job."

"None taken, Jim," Katy said graciously. "And I would like it very much if you continued to do you job."

McGarvey had been staring intently at his bodyguard. "What's up, Jim, rats in the attic?" Every intelligence officer who survived long enough understood that it was wise to listen to hunches, gut feelings.

Grassinger took a moment to answer. "Not really. It's just that we'll be fairly well isolated for the next few days."

"We'll keep our eyes open," McGarvey said. "What else is new?"

"Part of the business, boss."

THREE

☐

Twenty-nine hours later, a few minutes after eight, the forty-foot fly-bridge sportfisherman *Nancy N.* under the command of Khalil's number two, Zahir al Majid, came out of the lee of Kuiu Island's north bay into the teeth of a strong northwest wind that funneled between Admiralty and Entrance islands. The rain clouds had cleared, and the distant mountains and stark blacks and whites of the glaciers toward Mount Burkett on the mainland stood out in a beauty that was as harsh as the open deserts of the Saudi Arabian peninsula. This time of year, this far north, night came late, but it was twilight, and combined with the fantastic scenery, accurate depth perception beyond a couple of hundred yards was difficult at best. Almost nothing seemed to be in proportion out here.

Khalil's seven soldiers were excited to finally be going into battle. They had been anxious all day. But Khalil appeared indifferent. He had been in battle before, and he expected that he would be in other battles in the coming months and years. He would continue the holy struggle until he was dead, a thought about which he was totally philosophical. His death would be of no more consequence than the death of a common soldier or a president or even an imam. Each man would either get to Paradise or not, according to the earthly life he had led.

Frankly, he was indifferent about any thoughts of an afterlife. His time was here and now. He made meticulous plans for the future, but he lived for the present. Whatever money and worldly goods he could possibly want were his merely for the asking. On the rare occasions he found that he desired female companionship, or a male friend, or even the services of a young boy, he had those pleasures as well.

His only real interest was in the game, what Western intelligence analysts called the *jihad*, which Muslims took to mean holy war, or the struggle, and in the *fatwahs*, or decrees, issued by religious leaders or scholars, who for years had been telling the faithful to kill all Christians and

Jews—men, women, and children—whenever and wherever they were found. He had visions of swimming in rivers of blood wider than the Tigris or Euphrates, wider even than the Jordan or the Mississippi.

Kidnapping the war criminal Donald Shaw, whisking him to a cargo ship one hundred miles offshore, and transporting him eventually to Pakistan, where he would stand trial for crimes against Islam, would be the perfect counterpoint to the supremely arrogant religious war in Iraq.

It would be doubly satisfying to the jihad, because Shaw had repeatedly made public his disdain for the cause, calling al-Quaida's soldiers of God "criminals." The former secretary of defense had been a combat pilot in Vietnam, flying more than one hundred missions before his plane was shot down. He spent the next two and a half years as a POW at the Hanoi Hilton. But the enemy never broke him. He was a genuine American hero. But all that would change when he stood trial and his crimes against humanity were exposed to the world.

No important westerner would ever consider himself safe after this mission, Khalil reflected. Presidents, prime ministers, even kings and queens would not be immune from accounting for their transgressions. Ultimately the effect of such kidnappings and trials would make every leader in the West think twice about supporting Israel or continuing the war against Dar el Islam. The world would become a safer place in which to live.

He braced himself against the control console and raised the motion-damping Steiner mil specs binoculars to study the green-and-white rotating beacon of the small airport at Kake on the big island of Kupreanof a few miles to the northeast. There was no activity over there at this time of the evening, nor would there be any scheduled flights in or out until morning, except for the twin Otter, parked at this moment in the Air West hangar on the south end of the field; it would leave and fly west sometime after midnight tonight. No one at the field would know about the unauthorized flight until it was too late. Nor would the tower be manned, so there would be no one to track the flight on radar out into the ocean where the airplane would be scuttled in water that was a half-mile deep.

Khalil had gone over the details dozens of times, from the initial planning stages three months earlier, when it was first learned that Shaw might be taking an Alaskan Inside Passage cruise, until last night when he had gone over each step of the operation with Zahir and the other six operators. In addition to the eight men already aboard Spirit—four in engineering and four on the steward's staff—they would present an overwhelming force, with superior weapons and the element of surprise.

Shaw traveled with a bodyguard, who would be armed, but his would be the only operational weapon aboard the ship. The one Ruger Mini-14 folding stock rifle and the few Colt .45 pistols in the ship's weapons locker had been disabled, their firing pins removed. Meanwhile Khalil and his people were armed with the suppressed Polish-made 9mm RAK PM-63 machine-pistols, Austrian Steyr GB self-loading pistols modified to take the same Makarov round as the RAKs, several Haley and Weller E182 stun grenades, and a total of forty kilos of Semtex plastic explosive and acid fuses.

The crew and passengers would present no insurmountable problems. Those who did not instantly cooperate would be killed. Nor would communications be a problem once the ship's SSB and VHF radios were disabled, and the comm center's satellite phone rendered inoperative. In this stretch of the Inside Passage between Juneau to the north and Ketchikan to the south, cell phones were out of range. A cross-match of the crew and passenger lists with the FCC's roster of amateur radio operators, to see who might be carrying portable radios or handie-talkies, came up with no hits. And the only other people aboard who might carry a satellite phone would be Shaw or his bodyguard.

Those two men were the primary targets. They would be brought under control so fast that neither of them would have time to react.

He checked the chart again, against what he was viewing through the windshield, and rechecked his weapons. Although he was supremely confident in his own preparations, he wanted the men to see that even he took special care with his equipment. Image had a lot to do with success, and he was a master at presenting the face that he wanted the world to see.

One hour later they finally came abeam of Kake settlement, a town of about seven hundred people, the wind screaming at a full force of at least thirty knots, with viciously steep, two-meter waves that slammed into the bows of the Nancy N. Anything or anyone not tied down or holding on for dear life would be in trouble.

"I have a target," Zahir called out over the shrieking wind.

Khalil turned the binoculars across the pass toward Entrance Island, where he picked up the many lights of the small cruise ship. "I see it," he shouted.

The Spirit was turning southeast into Frederick Sound at about ten or twelve knots, taking the seas in stride at her stern. She was a little early by Khalil's reckoning, but he saw no obstacles to coming around the tip of the big island and catching up with her in the next half hour while most of the passengers would be finishing dinner and awaiting a show in the Grand Salon. He motioned for Zahir to increase their speed, despite the pounding they were taking, until they were practically flying off the tops of the waves.

"As soon as we clear the island, head directly for the ship," Khalil shouted.

"We could broach if we take a big enough wave on our stern," Zahir warned.

Khalil fixed him with a baleful stare. "In that case we would all perish out here. See that you do not allow a broach to happen."

Zahir didn't bother to respond, turning his entire attention back to controlling the boat. Khalil was a man who was not to be disappointed.

Khalil made his way below to where his operators were grimly hanging on. The cabin reeked of vomit, but he was satisfied that not one of them seemed like he was ready to give up. They were competent, if unimaginative, men. "Ten minutes," he told them.

No one had a question.

In the pilothouse Zahir was getting set to turn downwind. He was braced against the console, one hand fighting the wheel, the other trying to feather the engines each time they came off the top of a wave. Water flew from every direction as if they had gotten themselves caught at the base of Niagara Falls.

They were clear of the tip of the big island but not quite abeam of the cruise ship. It took Khalil a moment or two to sort out the situation from the picture being painted on the radar screen. He saw immediately that Zahir was correct not to make the downwind turn until they crossed the cruise ship's track. If they turned now they would almost certainly broach, but if they waited they could steer a zigzag path toward the ship, keeping the waves on their quarters, not square to their stern.

He braced himself next to Zahir. "You steer," he shouted. "I'll take the throttles."

The boat, the seas, and the wind were three separate living things that had to be balanced against each other to avert disaster. Ten seconds after he'd taken over the throttles, his respect for his chief lieutenant soared. But then, he thought, fear was the most powerful of all motivators. Without it Zahir would have turned back by now.

In every operation Khalil made certain that the men feared him more than they feared the mission itself. He had worked with Zahir on previous operations, but for the other men he'd instilled that fear on the very first day of their training by selecting the most battle-hardened of the recruits and challenging him to a hand-to-hand combat exercise. With the same indifferent cruelty that a cat shows for its prey, or that a Bedouin father shows for a physically flawed daughter, Khalil took the man apart piece by piece, until in the end he was reduced to a sobbing, bleeding hulk, begging for mercy.

"I do not reward failure by anyone," Khalil, speaking in a calm, reasonable tone of voice, told the recruits assembled at the desert camp. He grabbed a handful of the man's hair, pulled his head back, and in several deft moves, the cuts so swift and the knife so razor sharp that the man had no time to react, Khalil removed his nose and his lips, and then peeled the skin from his face as if he were skinning a dead animal.

The man reared back suddenly, screaming in abject horror at what was being done to him. Blood flowed from a dozen wounds in his body.

"Go into the desert now and die," Khalil told the man, and he turned to the recruits. "Now we will have a meal together, and you will tell me why you think that you could be loyal soldiers in Allah's struggle for justice."

The wounded man, having nothing left to lose, his eyesight obscured by blood, reared up, stumbled into Khalil's back, pulled a pistol from the holster at the hip of his tormentor, and then stepped back.

Khalil calmly turned to face the man, and looked directly into the muzzle of the gun. "You have two choices now, Achmed. Either shoot me, thus putting an end to our just and godly mission, or turn the pistol to your own head and pull the trigger." Khalil shrugged indifferently. "Of course, no matter what you decide, you will die tonight."

The soldier turned to his comrades, but no one raised a hand to help him. He looked again at Khalil, then stepped back another pace, not at all certain what he should or could do.

As the man hesitated, Khalil pulled a pistol out of his tunic and shot him in the head at point-blank range.

"Never trust in chance," Khalil told his men, and from that moment they were his, body and soul.

That was eleven weeks ago. They would not let him down tonight.

The cruise ship was well aft of their beam now. Zahir glanced at the radar image, then at Khalil, and nodded. He was very frightened, but he looked determined.

"Now," Khalil shouted over the wind. He feathered the props as Zahir hauled the boat into a tight turn to starboard. For several breathless seconds it seemed as if they would be caught with the seas on their beam. The Nancy N. heeled sharply to the right, practically burying her gunwales in the black water of Frederick Sound, but at the last moment Khalil gunned the starboard engine. The prop on the low side bit, and the boat spun around as if it were on a pivot, came upright, and suddenly shot downwind as if it were a lemon pit squeezed out between a thumb and forefinger.

The motion was still lively but they were no longer taking a pounding, and the Spirit of '98's bright stern lights were suddenly very close.

"Good work," Khalil shouted.

"We were lucky," Zahir replied, without breaking his concentration, though the water was getting much calmer in the lee of the island.

The answer was irritating, and Khalil was instantly enraged. But he gently patted his lieutenant on the shoulder of his uniform blouse. "I disagree my old friend; it was not luck, it was your skill. Now take us the rest of the way."

He took a walkie-talkie out of a pocket, and hit the push-to-talk switch. "Charlie, any luck catching fish tonight?"

"I'm checking the bait now," Abdul Adani radioed from where he waited at the stern of the ship. They spoke in English in case the frequency was monitored.

Khalil switched on the *Nancy N.*'s navigation lights for just a moment, then shut them off. "Try the back spinner on about two hundred yards of line."

"Good suggestion. I'll drop the hook in the water now."

Khalil pocketed the walkie-talkie, and as they closed on the cruise ship he could see a boarding ladder being lowered over the stern. He ducked below. "Take your positions," he told his operators.

The six men, all dressed in ship's uniforms, packs and weapons slung over their shoulders, scrambled up on deck. One of them took over the helm for Zahir.

The new man matched the speed of the cruise ship, then nudged the *Nancy N.* to within reach of the boarding ladder and the thick towrope and bridle that had been lowered with it.

Khalil went out on deck, Zahir right behind him. Abdul was looking down at them from the cruise ship's rail fifteen feet above. He gave the all-clear sign, and Khalil clambered up the boarding ladder.

Abdul stepped aside for him, and once Khalil was on deck, six of his operators started up.

"Have you or your men come under any suspicion?" Khalil asked.

"None," Abdul said. He was a slight man, and was dressed in the white jacket and dark trousers of a steward's mate. But he was a fearless and deadly knife fighter from Cairo. "They are all in position, awaiting your signal."

Khalil hesitated a moment as the remainder of his operators came aboard. He could hear music coming from the salon, and the sounds of laughter. All of that was about to come to a very abrupt end.

The last man up the ladder had secured the towrope to a heavy cleat amidships just forward of the pilothouse. The man at the helm would stay with the small boat. He reduced the engines to idle speed and shifted the transmission to neutral. The *Nancy N.* bucked and heaved as if she were a wild horse suddenly put to the bridle, but then she settled in a reasonably docile fashion to be towed by the cruise ship.

Everything was set. Khalil turned back to Abdul. "Now," he said.

FOUR

□

A fine mist rose over Lake Lucerne in the predawn darkness, as if a fire had been lit beneath the bedrock and the expanse of water was coming to a slow simmer. The midnight-blue Mercedes CLK320 cabriolet, its top snuggly up against the chilly morning air, made its way smoothly along the lake road south of the city, Mount Pilatus rising more than two thousand meters from the Swiss plateau off to the west.

An attractive blond woman in her early thirties, with a finely defined face, high narrow cheekbones, and wide, pale blue eyes, was at the wheel, her small shoulders thrown back defiantly. She wore sandals, a short khaki skirt, and a light pullover. Her 7.65mm Walther PPK and her Swiss Federal Police wallet, which identified her as Sergeant Liese Bernadette Fuelm, were in the black leather purse on the seat along with several fat file folders. Her position on the force as a watch officer was hard won because of her sex, something she had been reminded of the previous evening during drinks with her boss, Captain Ernst Gertner, the Kanton Nidwalden Polizei commander. Because of their conversation she had spent a sleepless night, memories piling on memories coming back at her, some of them hurtful, a few of them erotic, but all of them filling her with a crushing sense of loneliness.

"So, *Liebchen*, I'm hearing that you are dissatisfied with your little assignment." Gertner had come directly to the point as if he had read her mind. He was a slick career officer, very nearly a politician in his outlook, and she hated it when he talked to her with his annoying diminutives.

"It's nothing but a simple surveillance operation, captain," she said. "I have more experience than that. Almost twelve years, as a matter of fact."

"For God's sake, we're off duty; you can call me by my Christian name," Gertner blustered. "But you're wrong about your assignment. The good prince is much more than a simple man. In an offhand way, you have a connection with him. It's one of the reasons you were selected, though it's a surprise to all of us at District that your woman's intuition didn't ferret out the clue off the bat."

Liese was confused. "I'm sorry, sir, but I don't know what you're talking about. I've never met Prince Salman. He's a very rich man. We don't run in the same circles, I can assure you."

Gertner chuckled at her little joke. He waggled a finger at her. "But you do have a connection nonetheless, which you might have divined had you done the same homework as I did. I read your file. Your complete file." He rolled his eyes, as if he were a schoolmaster exasperated by the antics of a naughty student. "I'm surprised."

In Liese's estimation Gertner was a smarmy, sexist bastard; many Swiss males were, but at least he was a capable administrator even if he had forgotten what it was like to be in the field. He had four brutish children and a fat wife who worshipped the ground he walked on, giving him the confidence to actually think that he was dashing with the ladies. "Then I've evidently missed something; please fill me in."

So far as Liese knew, the assignment she'd been handed—to conduct an in-detail and in situ surveillance of Prince Abdul Hasim ibn Salman, a Saudi Arabian national—had to do with politics and Swiss banking laws. The man was a multibillionaire playboy who as often as not left his wife and staff at their palatial lakeside compound while he jetted off to London, Paris, Monaco, even Las Vegas to play games with his royal-family oil money and with his many mistresses, all supposedly forbidden by the Saudi adherence to the Muslim fundamentalist sect of Wahhabism.

Her initial brief, which had been handed to her along with the order of personnel and equipment and her budget lines, suggested the possibility of a financial connection between the prince and Osama bin Laden's al-Quaida. Normally a blind eye would have been turned to such financial dealings, as long as no banking laws were being violated. But since 9/11, and the second Gulf War waged by the U.S. and Britain against Iraq, and the "New World Order," many formerly aloof countries such as Switzerland had taken a more cautious attitude about doing business with organizations and individuals who might have terrorist ambitions.

The prince had been born in the tiny settlement of Bi'r Fardan in the vast Ar Rub' al-Khali desert south of Riyadh, and had been educated primarily at King Abdul Aziz University in the Saudi coastal city of Jeddah. Since he was a member of the royal family, he'd gotten his start in business the easy way, with a great deal of money and all the right connections. But he was a brilliant and ruthless businessman and a savvy politician, so as soon as his education was completed he'd been sent to Saudi embassies, first in London, then Mexico City, Moscow, Beijing, and finally Washington.

Suddenly, ten years ago, he had all but dropped out of active Saudi politics and turned his talents to deal-making. Like the legendary Adnan Khashoggi before him, Prince Salman seemed to be in the middle of every hundred-million-dollar-plus deal between the Saudis and the rest of the world. He'd been a frequent guest at the White House, at 10 Downing Street, at the most palatial estates, and aboard the yachts of every influential, wealthy player in the world, and he seemed to be connected with nearly every beautiful woman at the height of her desirability.

"The prince was involved with Kirk McGarvey eleven years ago when you were beginning your career with the service," Gertner said, and his words hit her like a ton of bricks. "Fascinating reading, I must say."

She was floating a couple of centimeters off her seat in the Gasthaus, the sounds of the conversations around her fading as if she were hearing them from the end of a long tunnel.

"We thought perhaps McGarvey might have mentioned the name to you at the time. Or perhaps later," Gertner said.

His words flowed over and around Liese. But she was brought back so completely that she could see every line on Kirk's face, hear his laugh, smell his clean, masculine, American odors. *Verdammt*. Had it been all that long since she had first fallen in love with him?

"Or might Marta have said something to you?" Gertner was asking. "Just anything at all, some little phrase, or little word that might give us a clue?"

Kirk, who had been a CIA assassin, had suddenly quit the agency under a cloud of some sort that was never adequately explained to the Swiss police. But he had been allowed to settle in Lucerne providing he never went active. As long as he never picked up his gun and never made contact with anyone in the business, he was welcome in Switzerland. Marta

Fredericks had been sent to his bed to keep a close watch on him. And Liese Fuelm and a few other Swiss police officers were also assigned to keep an eye on him. No one ever considered that first Marta and then Liese would fall in love with him.

But they had. And Liese could still remember some of the erotic dreams she had about Kirk: tasting him, feeling his body on top of hers, inside of her, kissing her breasts, her thighs.

But then Kirk had gone for his gun, and he had left Switzerland for good. A year or so later Marta quit the force and chased him to Paris, where she was killed in the destruction of a Swiss Air flight, leaving Liese with nothing other than her bitter memories. She and Marta had not only been rivals; they had been close friends.

But Prince Salman's name had never come up, and Liese told Gertner as much. "I think I would have remembered."

"It's been a long time, and you were young and impressionable." Gertner let the comment hang.

Liese shook her head, still off balance.

"Well, for goodness sake, you were in love with the man. Certainly you must have talked."

Gertner had nothing; he was on a fishing expedition, but Liese resigned herself to stick out the assignment. There was no way she would be pulled off. "I was in love with Mr. McGarvey, as was Marta, but if you will look at the record you will see that he wasn't in love with either of us."

"It must have hurt," Gertner observed mildly, almost fatherly. "Does it still, Liese? Hurt, I mean? Carrying any old torches, are we? Perhaps even a grudge or two? Just the tiniest bit of resentment? It could have been you, the wife of the director of Central Intelligence."

"Fond memories, no grudges," Liese said. "What was the connection between the prince and Kirk—Mr. McGarvey?"

"It was a tenuous one, but we have to consider all the aspects, don't we?" Gertner said. He fiddled with his glass of wine, a characteristic gesture of his when he felt he was skating on thin ice. He smoked a pipe, and when he was unsure of himself he cleaned it, or filled it to draw attention away from what he was saying. "The prince, as a young man, was one of Darby Yarnell's hangers-on. The same Yarnell who had an affair with Mc-Garvey's then ex-wife, and the same Yarnell whom your Mr. McGarvey shot to death in the CIA director's driveway." Gertner couldn't contain himself. "They're all cowboys over there. The lot of them are raving lunatics, in my book."

"This is the first I've heard of the prince's involvement," Liese said. "I'm sorry, but I don't know how much help I can be."

Gertner dismissed her objections with a wave of his hand. "The point quite simply is that you know more about Kirk McGarvey than does anyone else in Switzerland. We would very much like to know if there continues to be a connection between Mr. McGarvey and the prince and therefore the Saudi royal family."

"I can't imagine such an alliance."

Gertner threw up his hands in exasperation. "Goodness gracious, are all women, even Swiss women, so thickheaded that they cannot see the mountains for the glare of the glaciers?"

"What are you talking about?"

"Have you thought about who was behind the attacks in New York and Washington?"

"You're talking about September eleventh? The World Trade Center and the Pentagon?"

"Yes, of course."

"Al-Quaida," Liese said. "What are you driving at?"

"Indulge me. What was the purpose of those attacks?"

"Terrorism," Liese replied offhandedly. "Militant Islamics striking at the infidel as they have been doing for a lot of years now."

"Splendid. And the result, in practical terms? Have the Muslims won their war?"

"No, so far it's backfired," Liese said. But then it dawned on her what Gertner was getting at. She'd heard the view mentioned in roundabout terms, but she thought it was a minority opinion. Now she wasn't so sure. "You think that the Israelis engineered the attacks. Mossad, to focus America's attention on the Muslims."

"It makes sense to me," Gertner said. "And I am not alone in this thinking." He gave Liese a shrewd look. "But the current point, so far as you're concerned, is learning if there is any connection, no matter how slight, between Prince Salman and Kirk McGarvey, and therefore the American intelligence establishment."

"You're crazy," Liese said. "Salman is a Saudi not an Israeli."

"Perhaps he is, but then Mossad is devilishly clever with its cover stories. We Swiss have been victim to more than one of their operations. I expect you'll do your best with this assignment, especially now that you and I have come to a clear understanding that this is not a simple job of surveillance."

"I'll tell you this, Ernst: I'll do everything within my power to prove that Kirk is not in some sort of collusion with the prince, and that the attacks were just as they seemed, engineered and carried out by al-Quaida."

"Good," Gertner said. "I merely ask that your prejudices do not blind you to the truth, even if the truth should fall unfavorably on Mr. McGarvey."

Liese reached the narrow gravel road, where she switched off her headlights and went the rest of the way to the small chalet in starlight. The simple A-frame lodge was owned by a Bern businessman who sometimes cheated on his taxes, and was very cooperative when the Federal Police asked for his help. The lodge was perched on the hill of a finger directly across a small bay from the five-hectare palatial compound of Prince Salman.

There were only a few security lights on over there at this hour of the morning. She telephoned the chalet as she came up the long driveway. "It's me."

"We have you," Claude LeFevre, answered. He was one of two men who had pulled the morning shift.

Liese had been given a total of eight men, which was a luxury for this kind of operation. Everybody was getting plenty of sleep, and their thinking was still sharp. No one had gotten bored yet, though boredom would come. Most cops hated surveillance, no matter how important the subject. Unless, of course, it was a beautiful woman who liked to take off her clothes in front of windows. Then the pigs would line up as if at the trough.

And most Swiss cops hated being bossed by a woman. But that was just too bad, Liese thought, getting out of her car as the sky in the east began to lighten. They had a job to do, and they were going to do it right. Marta would have expected nothing less for Kirk.

The chalet was dark except for the fire on the hearth in the middle of the great room, and the soft green glow of the communications and sur-veillance equipment set up on a low table a couple of meters back from the main windows that opened toward the bay.

LeFevre was finishing breakfast, a sausage and black-bread sandwich, and Detective Tomas Ziegler was looking at the compound through a set of powerful Zeiss image-intensifying binoculars set on a sturdy tripod.

Liese laid her purse on the table. "Are they up and about at this hour?"

"I saw a light, but it was in the staff wing," Ziegler said.

"One of them had to take a pee then," LeFevre suggested. They were both very young and very superior, though Ziegler had already tried to hit on her.

"Any telephone calls overnight?" Liese asked, heading into the tiny kitchen to heat the pot for some tea.

"Just the school," LeFevre said. "About nine."

"One of the kids sick?" The prince had a wife and four children—three girls and a boy, all away at boarding school outside Zurich.

"The school didn't call; the Prince's wife called them," LeFevre said.

Liese stopped what she was doing and went back into the great room. "That was late for her to call the school. Who did she talk to? What did she want?"

"The headmaster. She wants her kiddies back home with her. And she sounded as if she was in a great hurry—"

"*Verdammt,*" Liese said, going for her phone. "The prince is coming home—either that, or something is about to go bad for them, and they're circling the wagons. Either way we're going to need some intercept peo-ple up here."

LeFevre was confused. "What do you mean?"

"It's the start of term, you idiot. They were supposed to stay there un-til December break. If she's called them home, it means she's talked to her husband." The operations officer at Nidwalden came on the line, and Liese began issuing her instructions.

FIVE

☐

On the bridge of the *Spirit of '98* First Officer Matt LaBlanc studied the overhead multifunction monitor, his pale blue eyes narrowed with puzzlement. He was an excellent, if unimaginative officer, who did everything strictly by the book.

He picked up the ship's phone and called engineering. "We're losing speed over the bottom; is there a problem?"

Sterling Granger, the engineering officer on duty, came to the phone. "RPMs are steady at seven hundred. We might have picked up something on one of the props. Stand by."

Besides LeBlanc, the only other crew on the bridge were Officer-in-Training Scott Abfalter and the helmsperson, Able-Bodied Seaman Nina Lane, who was so tiny she was barely able to see over the top of the ship's wheel. The weather tonight wasn't much different than it normally was at this time of year. The *Spirit* was taking the seas in her stride; she was built for these waters, but a couple of minutes earlier she had suddenly lost a half knot of speed over the bottom as registered by their bottom-sounding sonar. The present weather was a known, as were the tidal and wind-driven currents, but none of those factors could explain the loss in speed. It was almost as if they were towing a sea anchor.

Granger, whose real name was Babrak Pahlawan, came back. "I'm showing the same thing here. We may have picked up some debris on one of the props."

"Wouldn't we be able to feel the vibration if the shafts were out of balance?" LeBlanc asked. This was the first trip he'd made with Granger, and he didn't have a measure of the man yet.

"Not necessarily. It depends on what we've picked up and how it's streaming, if that's the problem," Granger said. "Stand by."

Something wasn't right to LeBlanc, who'd been with the company for ten years. He had the hours for the Master of the Oceans certificate, and he would be taking the test in a couple of months. Granger's explanation didn't make any sense to him. "How's the helm feel?" he asked Lane. "Have you noticed any change in the past few minutes?"

The young woman hesitated a moment. "I'm not sure, sir."

"You have the wheel; you're the only one who can tell me," LeBlanc said, trying to be as reassuring as he could be.

"It feels sluggish," she said, diffidently, "like there's something wrong with the steering gear, or the rudder or something."

Granger came back to the phone. "The shafts are balanced."

"Could one of our rudders be out of alignment, somehow, or maybe bent?"

"It's possible," Granger said, "but there've been no collision reports. Give me a couple of minutes and I'll check on it."

"Right," LeBlanc said. He hung up the phone and stood for several long moments staring at the multifunction display. The numbers he was reading and what Granger told him simply did not add up.

The sweeping view from the bridge was nothing short of magnificent during the day, but at night very little could be seen beyond the reflections of the various instruments in the windows and the cast of the ship's running lights on the waters. They had passed the small settlement of Kake to their starboard several minutes ago. Its airfield beacon was very prominent. Forty minutes earlier they had left the lights of the even smaller settlement of Fanshaw to their port. Out ahead there was nothing except for the occasional blinking green or red channel marker, and the village and airfield of Petersburg fifty miles to the south where they would put in tonight. On moonlit nights the glaciers glowed with an eerie violet cast, and on some special evenings in the fall the aurora borealis flashed and wavered from horizon to horizon as if the entire world were on fire. But tonight all was flat twilight outside the windows of the bridge, and First Officer LeBlanc was concerned, though he couldn't put his finger on exactly why.

The intercom phone buzzed. It was Granger in engineering. "There may be a slight drag on the starboard rudder post. But it's nothing serious, and certainly there's nothing we can do about it until we get to Seattle."

LeBlanc glanced at the multifunction display. Their speed had increased slightly, but the RPMs had climbed by ten revolutions. That wasn't right. "Keep an eye on it," he told the engineering officer. "If there's any change let me know."

"Roger."

LeBlanc stepped over to the helm. "Excuse me," he told the young AB. He took the wheel, and slowly moved it a quarter turn to starboard. The ship's head came right, but sluggishly. He turned the wheel back to port until the ship swung to its original course, and then he neutralized the helm.

Something was definitely amiss. "The helm is yours," he told Lane and she took the wheel from him.

The captain's strict rule was that if something appeared to be out of order, he was to be called, no matter the time of day or night, no matter what he was doing. LeBlanc called the chief steward's alcove adjacent to the Grand Salon.

"With my compliments, ask the captain to come to the bridge."

"Is there a problem, Mr. LeBlanc?" Chief Steward Tony Bianco asked. LeBlanc had shipped with the man for the past five years. Bianco was a dynamo of an officer whose proudest achievement was serving as number four on the steward's staff of the *Queen Elizabeth II.*

"No. And it wouldn't do to alarm the passengers."

"Yes, sir."

LeBlanc hung up the intercom phone and glanced up at the multifunction display. Their speed had crept up a little higher, but so had the RPMs.

"Is something wrong, sir?" Abfalter asked. He had come to the *Spirit* right out of the Merchant Marine Academy.

"If it's anything at all, it's just a minor problem in engineering that somebody doesn't want to answer for," LeBlanc said. But that didn't seem right to him.

Captain Bruce Darling, all six feet six of him, arrived a couple of minutes later, his summer white uniform incredibly crisp. He was an even greater stickler for details than his first officer. He took in his bridge crew and the ship's instruments in one sweep, his gaze lingering for just an extra moment on the multifunction monitor.

"What's the problem?"

LeBlanc explained his misgivings and the steps he had taken to isolate the problem. Darling took the helm, moving the wheel to starboard and then back to port exactly as his first officer had done. "We're towing something," he said. "Maybe one of the life rafts came adrift, or the stern anchor. Go aft and check it out."

LeBlanc felt foolish that he had not suggested it. He resolved not to forget the feel of the helm. "Just be a minute, sir," he said.

He left the bridge, hurried past the owner's suite, which was occupied by former secretary of defense Shaw and his wife, and took the elevator down three levels to the main deck just forward of the galley. Out on the promenade deck he hurried past the Klondike Dining Room, empty now that dinner was over except for the cleanup crew. The passengers had moved to the Grand Salon forward and up one deck for the evening's entertainment, but even this far aft, LeBlanc could hear the music and laughing. The beasts, as passengers were called, though never to their faces, were having a good time. But then for the money they paid for these cruises they ought to be having a good time.

The blinds were drawn on Soapy's Parlor, the farthest aft passenger space, where on nights like these there was usually a poker game going that would last well into the wee hours of the morning. Technically, gambling was not allowed within three miles of the shoreline, but even though the stakes were usually high—often in the thousands of dollars—the ship's officers were encouraged by the company to turn a blind eye, though that bothered LeBlanc. It would be different once he had his own ship.

As soon as he came around the curve of the aft bulkhead, he knew there was a problem. A one-inch line, leading overboard beneath the lowest rung of the rail, was secured to a port cleat. They were indeed towing something. He crossed the afterdeck and peered over the stern. A fairly large sportfisherman, but with a low-slung bridge deck, its VHF whips laid flat, wallowed in Spirit's wake. It was no wonder their speed had dropped and steering was sluggish. Whatever fool had set up the towing rig had not used a proper three-point bridle, nor had he given the towline enough scope. Though what the boat was doing attached to them was anyone's guess, at this point LeBlanc was more curious than alarmed.

He turned to call the bridge from one of the deck intercom phones when a dark figure, clad in the dress uniform of a cruise ship captain, stepped out of the deeper shadows. "Who are you—"

A thunderclap burst in LeBlanc's head, and he did not feel his body fall into the water because he was already dead.

Khalil stood at the open doorway to the darkened Soapy's Parlor. The five elderly gentlemen who had been playing poker had been shot to death, their bodies hidden out of sight in storage lockers just minutes ago. Two of his operators had just tossed the officer's body overboard.

"Who was he?" Khalil asked.

"LeBlanc, the first officer," Adani said. "We're well rid of him; he could have caused trouble."

"Who else will be trouble?"

"The captain and the chief engineer. But both of them will be in the Grand Salon—" Adani hesitated. He stared at the stern rail, as if something had just occurred to him. "We might have a slight problem," he said, turning to Khalil.

"What is it?

"LeBlanc was on the bridge tonight. The only thing that would bring him back here is if he suspected there was a problem. They might have detected the tow. But before he left the bridge, he would have called Captain Darling."

"Where's the problem?"

"The captain carries a satphone wherever he goes."

Khalil had considered the problem of the satellite phone in the communications shack, and the likelihood that Shaw or his bodyguard would be carrying one. The comm center and the bodyguard were the main preliminary targets. They never guessed that the captain would have a satphone. They figured that they would catch him in the Grand Salon. Once they had control of him, the psychological effect on the crew and passengers would make their jobs much easier. But that was no longer likely.

"We will kill him," Khalil said, the decision easy. Automatic weapons in the hands of a determined force were all the psychological effect they would need. He glanced at his watch. It was 10:10 P.M. They were dead on schedule.

"Shall I give the word?" Adani asked.

"No, I'll do it," Khalil said. "Go back to your station in the Grand Salon, and prepare your people. We strike in five minutes."

Adani's eyes were bright with excitement. He nodded to Khalil and the others. "*Insha'allah*," he said, *God's will*, and he headed forward.

One man would make his way to the communications shack and disable the radio gear; three would make a quick but thorough sweep of the crew's quarters and kill any crewmen still in their bunks; and the last man would go with Khalil and Zahir to the bridge, where they would kill all the crew except for the helmsman and disable the captain's satphone.

When the ship was secure, which Khalil estimated should take no more than four or five minutes, one man would remain on the bridge, one in the communications center, and two in engineering. Everyone else would converge on the Grand Salon and their final objective.

Khalil keyed his walkie-talkie. "Granger, phase one, five minutes."

Pahlawan, in the engine room, came back at once: "Roger."

Khalil pocketed his walkie-talkie, checked the load on his Steyr pistol, and looked up at his men, his dark eyes narrowed malevolently. "I want to be off this boat with our prisoner in H-plus-thirty minutes. Do not fail me."

"*Insha'allah*," they muttered and melted into the darkness.

Khalil led the way forward, past the Klondike Room where two of his operators had already gunned down the four steward's assistants who'd been cleaning up after dinner. He held up just a moment at the door to the thwartships corridor adjacent to the galley. A man dressed in a steward's uniform emerged from the intersecting corridor and went into the galley. He was one of Adani's people. He carried a RAK machine pistol with a large suppressor attached to the end of the short barrel.

Already crewmen all over the ship were dying in their bunks or at their duty stations, while none of the passengers had any idea that the *Spirit* was under attack. Long before any alarm could be raised, it would be too late. Within a few minutes the ship would no longer be under Cruise West's control, and Khalil was certain that no power on earth could change the inevitable outcome that was already set in motion.

The only sounds were those of the ship's engines, the wind in the rigging, and the music and laughter coming from the Grand Salon.

Khalil and his two operators, their machine pistols at the ready, slipped into the corridor, hurried noiselessly to the stairway next to the elevator, and went up three flights to the bridge deck.

The covered area and the sundeck aft were empty, as were the passageways. Zahir quickly checked the owner's suite to make sure that Shaw hadn't come back to his cabin for some reason. He came out, shaking his head, and they proceeded down the starboard passageway and up the stairs to the bridge.

Khalil was first. He threw open the door, went inside, and stepped left to allow Zahir and Hasan to come in right behind him.

Captain Darling turned around, and seeing the weapons realized in a split instant that something was drastically wrong. He held a cup of hot coffee in his left hand. He tossed it at the intruders, hoping for a moment's distraction, and sprang for the weapons locker.

Khalil easily sidestepped the cup and fired three shots, the first two hitting the captain in the shoulder, but the third plowing into the side of his head, killing him instantly.

Zahir put three shots into Abfalter's chest, knocking the officer-in-training off his feet; he struggled to breathe for almost three seconds before he too died.

The young woman at the helm released the wheel and stepped back, her hands going to her face. She was shaking, and she appeared ready to faint. Khalil lowered his weapon and went to her. He took her arm and guided her back to the wheel.

"Someone has to steer the boat, my dear," he said pleasantly. "It wouldn't do to run us aground. Might upset the passengers."

She was frightened out of her mind, but she did as she was told, bringing the Spirit, which had drifted only a few degrees to starboard, back on course.

"The captain's satphone," Khalil reminded Zahir. He keyed his walkie-talkie. "One is secure," he radioed.

SIX

□

Shortly after ten Katy realized that she'd lost an earring, and she leaned over to her husband. "Could you fetch something for me from our cabin, like a good boy?" They were having after-dinner drinks at one of the tables at the edge of the dance floor. It was the second night out, and most of the ninety-six passengers were enjoying themselves in the Gay Nineties, plush, floral-upholstered, and hand-carved-wood ambiance of the *Spirit's* Grand Salon.

They were tablemates with Don Shaw and his wife, Karen. The two couples had agreed at the boarding cocktail reception not to talk shop, and the ship's crew had been instructed not to recognize the former secretary. He and his wife were to be treated as ordinary passengers.

"I hope it's nothing heavy," McGarvey told his wife under his breath. "It's been a long day and I'm tired."

"Would you believe an earring?"

McGarvey gave her a smile. "I don't suppose it would do me any good to say that you look beautiful without it."

"You'd earn points, but other than that—" She gave him a contented, warm smile. "Small, blue velvet, zippered pouch in one of the pockets of my brown leather hanging bag."

Their drink order arrived, and their steward seemed a bit nervous. He spilled some of Shaw's martini on the napkin and clumsily started to wipe it up, but the former SecDef waved him off. "It's all right."

Captain Darling had been seated with them, but he'd been called away by the chief steward a few minutes ago. "What happened to the captain?" Karen Shaw asked, pleasantly. Darling had been regaling them with hilarious stories about some of the gaffes he had committed with passengers when he was a young, inexperienced officer just out of the Merchant Marine Academy.

The steward, a young, dark-complexioned man with long, delicate fingers glanced across the dance floor toward the door. "He was called to the bridge, ma'am, though I'm sure I don't know why."

"Will he be long?"

"I don't know, ma'am," the steward said, and he turned abruptly and hurried across to the service alcove, where he disappeared behind the screen.

The hairs at the base of McGarvey's neck prickled, and his eyes narrowed. He resisted the urge to follow the steward and ask what was bothering him. This was supposed to be a vacation. It was the first one he and Katy had taken since the trouble, and they needed the time away from Washington. Jim Grassinger was seated at a table by the door with Shaw's bodyguard, Tony Battaglia. Both of them sipped soda water. Their heads were on swivels, but turning slowly, as if they were nonchalantly people watching. Nothing could have been further from the truth. McGarvey caught Grassinger's eye and nodded toward the door. Grassinger got to his feet, said something to Battaglia who surreptitiously glanced over at his boss's table, and then Grassinger stepped out into the passageway.

"Duty calls," McGarvey told the Shaws, and he got up.

The former SecDef looked up, questioningly, but McGarvey gave him a reassuring nod.

"Be just a minute," he said, and he left the Grand Salon. Grassinger was waiting out in the passageway, very alert.

"What's up, boss?"

"Mission of mercy. Katy lost an earring." They headed to the starboard stairs one deck up and forward to the McGarveys' inside-corridor deluxe stateroom. The wind was screaming outside now, but they were sailing in protected waters and the cruise liner rode easily.

This part of the ship seemed very quiet. They could hear music from downstairs, but nothing else in the inside passageway. There were no stewards, no crewmen, no engineers doing maintenance. But then perhaps nothing was broken and needed fixing.

McGarvey forced his dire feelings to the back of his mind. Pretty soon he would be looking for bogeymen under his bed. It was just a case of overwrought nerves brought on by the constant pressures of the seventh floor at Langley and the events of the past year. He smiled, and chuckled to himself. Hell, considering the life he had led, the people he'd killed, and the ones who had made very serious efforts to kill him, it was a wonder he wasn't a basket case.

"Something I said?" Grassinger asked.

"I'm going to give it another half hour or so, and then I'm going to pull the pin," McGarvey said, stifling a yawn. "I'm so tired I'm starting to imagine all sorts of stuff."

Grassinger reacted as if he had just sucked on a lemon. "Jeez, don't say that, Mac; I'm already spooked as it is."

"You too?"

"Yeah."

McGarvey had to laugh. "It's one of the perks of the business. Things will look up tomorrow."

Khalil's people finished their sweep of the upper deck, silently killing two crewmen—one on steward's duty and one repairing a jammed door lock—and three passengers who had the misfortune to miss the night's entertainment and retire early.

They assembled in the port stairwell that led down to the lounge deck, six operators plus Khalil, who keyed his walkie-talkie. "Engine room."

"Secure," Granger reported.

"Bridge."

"Secure," Karin replied.

"Communications."

"Secure," Muhamed came back.

"Abdul," Khalil radioed.

For several seconds there was no reply, but then Adani finally came back. "Two of the male passengers left about three minutes ago. They took the stairs to the upper deck. Did you run into them?"

"No. Who are they?"

"I haven't had time to check. But they must have cabins on that deck; there's nothing else up there."

"We just took care of three passengers up there," Khalil said. "It must have been them." He considered sending two of his people back to make sure, but in another four or five minutes they would have Shaw in custody and would be off this ship. "Is our target still there?"

"Yes."

"What about the rest of our people?" Khalil asked. Besides Adani and two others on the steward's staff in the Grand Salon, there were three from engineering.

"They're in place on the bow viewing area, ready to strike on your command," Adani said, and it was clear from his voice that he was excited.

"We're coming down. The time is now T-minus-thirty seconds."

"*Insha'allah*," Adani radioed.

Yes, *insha'allah*, Khalil thought, and he led his people downstairs to the lounge deck, in the corridor just aft of the Grand Salon. The combo was doing a good job with "In the Mood," and he could hear people talking and laughing, having a good time. After the events of this evening, however, the handful of passengers and crew who might survive, if they were lucky, would forever have second thoughts about the true meaning of happiness.

Of the sixteen operators, Khalil's was the only face not in the photographic files of any intelligence or law enforcement agency somewhere in the world. One of his strengths was his anonymity. He pulled a black nylon mesh balaclava over his head, checked his RAK machine pistol's silencer, and motioned for his people to do the same. They had made little or no noise to this point, and he wanted to keep it that way. There were still crewmen on duty in various parts of the ship. Alerting them at this stage would merely complicate things. They all would die in due course, but for the moment Khalil wanted to maintain his tight schedule. In approximately sixty minutes, the *Spirit* would be in range of one of the cell-phone towers that served the Ketchikan area. They had to be well away long before that time, because there was no possibility of finding all the cell phones that might be aboard.

Khalil watched the numerals of his digital watch count down the last five seconds to 22:15. He keyed his walkie-talkie, and spoke one word: "Now."

The four men from engineering who waited on the bow were first inside the Grand Salon. Without warning they opened fire on the tiny stage, killing the four musicians. They quickly took positions along the starboard wall.

Adani and his two stewards snatched their weapons, hidden under towels on serving trolleys, and opened fire on the eight officers seated at various tables throughout the salon, moving in from the pantry and serving stations along the port wall.

Even before the first woman let out an ear-piercing scream, Khalil and his six operators stormed in from the aft corridor, and closed the watertight double doors, cutting off sounds from the rest of the ship.

The passengers reacted in stunned disbelief. Some of them ducked under their tables, while others shouted for the crew, for anyone, to do something.

Khalil's men took up positions across the back wall, completing the encirclement of the Grand Salon. As the noise slowly began to subside, Khalil nonchalantly walked toward the front of the room, stopping next to the woman who was still crying and screaming, her eyes wide, her hands to her mouth. She was in her late sixties or early seventies, and frightened beyond control. Nothing like this had ever happened to her or any of her friends in Waterloo, Iowa.

She looked up into his eyes, suddenly rearing back as if she'd looked into the eyes of a hooded cobra ready to strike. "My God—"

Khalil raised his machine pistol and put one round in the middle of her forehead. She was shoved backward, onto the deck. An older man, probably her husband, dressed in a tuxedo, started to get to his feet, when Khalil calmly switched aim and fired one shot into his face at point-blank range, killing him instantly.

"The next person who utters a sound, any sound, will suffer the same fate," Khalil told the passengers and those of the crew who were still alive.

A deathly silence descended upon the big room, as if someone had dropped a funeral shroud from the ceiling.

"Appreciate the gravity of the situation that you now find yourselves in," Khalil told them. "You have my word as a gentleman that once we have accomplished our task this evening, we will leave the ship, and no further harm will come to any of you."

"Just go away!" a teenaged girl seated with her parents cried, and her mother tried to hush her.

Khalil reached their table on three strides. "Which of your parents do you want me to kill, little girl?" he demanded.

The teenager looked up at him and shook her head, unable to speak.

"Make another sound, and I shall kill them both." Khalil held her eye for several long moments, until the mother pulled her daughter away and protectively cradled her.

He looked at them with contempt. If it had been a defiant son who had made the challenge, he would have enjoyed the killing. But a daughter was not worth the effort of pulling the trigger.

Only five minutes had elapsed since they had come aboard, but already the cruise ship was under their control.

Khalil stepped back, then turned and walked to the tables in the front of the room at the edge of the dance floor. Shaw and his wife, plus another, very attractive, woman sat together. The seat next to the attractive woman was empty, as was the one at the head of the table.

"Mr. Secretary of Defense, what a pleasure to see you this evening," Khalil said.

Shaw looked up over his glasses at Khalil, but said nothing.

Khalil motioned toward the empty chairs. "Where are the individuals who were seated with you?"

"They're gone," Kathleen answered quickly.

Khalil turned his bland, almost dreamy eyes to her. "One of them was your husband?"

"No. It was Captain Darling and one of his officers. The chief steward called them away a few minutes ago."

Khalil considered her answer. The captain had come to the bridge, but he'd been alone. "Where is your husband?"

"I'm a widow."

Khalil resisted the urge to tell her that she would soon be joining her husband. Instead he turned back to Shaw. "On your feet, Mr. Secretary, you are coming with us. Someone wishes to speak to you."

Karen Shaw was clutching her husband's arm. "Who?" the former SecDef asked.

"Why, Osama bin Laden, of course—"

An unsilenced pistol shot rang out at the back of the salon, immediately followed by the rapid putt-putting of at least two machine pistols. Khalil spun around in time to see that one of his operators was down, as was one of the male passengers. Blood was splattered all over the paneled wall, and was pooling under the two bodies.

"He had a gun," one of the operators said.

Khalil turned again to Shaw. "Was he your bodyguard?"

The former SecDef nodded tightly. "However long it takes, we will hunt you down; you and the scum bastards you work with. Make no mistake."

"It is you who have made a mistake by coming on this trip," Khalil said, calming himself. "Get to your feet now, or I will kill your wife."

Shaw stood up, disengaging himself from his wife's grasp. "First Afghanistan, then Iraq. You and al-Quaida are next."

"You will have plenty of time to practice your speech," Khalil said. "Where we are going there will be many people most interested in your words." He laughed. "Very interested indeed."

He turned to his operators at the door. "The man has a satphone. Destroy it," he ordered. Without warning, he slashed the machine pistol's heavy butt across the side of Shaw's head, nearly knocking the former SecDef off his feet, a six-inch gash opening from his cheek to the hairline above his ear.

SEVEN

McGarvey and Grassinger reached the inside corridor cabin assigned to Mr. and Mrs. James Garwood without seeing any other passenger or crewman. Once again the hairs at the back of McGarvey's neck prickled, though he couldn't say why. It was some inner sense, some inner early-warning system kicking in. But like an overused smoke detector, he sometimes got false alarms.

He unlocked the door with his key, and eased it open with the toe of his shoe. They'd left one of the lights over the bed on, and it provided enough illumination for him to see that nothing had been disturbed.

Grassinger pulled his pistol, glanced both ways up the corridor, and then eased McGarvey to one side, and looked inside the cabin. "Okay, boss, what's going on?"

"Probably nothing," McGarvey said. He went to the closet, where he found Katy's blue velvet zippered pouch in one of the side pockets.

"I don't like that word *probably*," Grassinger said. He looked inside the tiny bathroom tucked in the forward corner, then checked under the bed and took a look out the big window. But there was nothing to be seen except for the reflection of the ship's running lights in the water rushing past.

"Like I said, I'm tired," McGarvey answered absently. His mind was elsewhere. There was something he was missing. Something at some unconscious level of his awareness. Something he was hearing, or feeling, or even smelling that wasn't registering. Yet it was there.

He found the gold hoop earrings Katy wanted, and slipped them into his jacket pocket.

Grassinger went to the door and looked out into the corridor. "It's too quiet," he said softly, as if he didn't want to disturb the silence by raising his voice.

"Everybody's in the Grand Salon."

"Most of the crew aren't," Grassinger said.

"That's right. They're on the bridge, in the radio room, down in the galley, or in engineering doing their jobs. The ones off duty are either in their bunks or in whatever common room they have aboard, not up here wandering around in the corridors."

"Let's stop by the bridge and see what's holding up the captain."

"He's probably already back in the Grand Salon wondering what's taking me so long," McGarvey said. He opened one of the side pockets in his hanging bag where he'd stuffed his gun, holster, and spare magazines. He debated rearming himself, but then he had to ask why. He was supposed to be on vacation. He had an armed guard with him, and the CIA and DoD had vetted the crew and passengers.

"I can call and ask," Grassinger suggested.

McGarvey zippered the side pocket, and shut the closet door. "This is only the second night out, Jim. And if we keep going like this, we'll probably end up shooting each other." He forced a grin. "We're going to start having a good time around here, and that's an order."

Grassinger reluctantly put his gun away. "You're right. But it doesn't mean I'm going to stop doing my job."

McGarvey looked at him. "I don't expect that you will. But we have to ease up a little. And that goes for me as well as for you."

Grassinger chuckled. "It's a deal, boss, as long as you don't use the word *probably* again. Gives me the creeps."

"Right. Katy and I are going to have a last dance, and then we're coming up to bed. It's been a long day."

"That it has," Grassinger said.

Getting out of Washington unnoticed yesterday had been an exercise in subterfuge. Ever since McGarvey's contentious Senate subcommittee hearings to confirm his appointment as director of Central Intelligence, the media had practically camped on the CIA's doorstep, and down the block from his house in Chevy Chase when he was in residence. Every time his limousine made a move, the press was on his tail. It was almost as bad as being chased by the paparazzi. One of the security people drove Katy and their bags out to an Air Force VIP Gulfstream at Andrews, while McGarvey was taken to FBI headquarters in the J. Edgar Hoover Building on Pennsylvania Avenue. He transferred to an unmarked, windowless surveillance van and was finally driven out to Andrews, where he was given immediate clearance to take off.

The flight was bumpy all the way out to Ellsworth Air Force Base in Rapid City, South Dakota, where they were forced to land in a blinding rainstorm with high winds because one of the control system's trouble lights indicated they were losing hydraulic fluid. It turned out to be a false alarm, but they refueled and then took off again during a brief break in the weather. An hour out of Ellsworth, Katy got airsick, but refused to let them set down or turn back.

After that, the weather improved a little until they finally landed at

Juneau in a cold drizzle, and Katy immediately perked up. She had looked forward to this trip for several months, and absolutely nothing was going to stop her from having a good time; once they got back to Washington, her obstetrician promised to be on her back 24/7, and she would have to start behaving herself.

Katy and Kirk would have to get a good night's sleep, because they would be busy again the next day, hiking on glaciers, kayaking to chase whales, otter spotting, maybe salmon fishing or oyster hunting, white-water rafting, and even hiking through the Sitka forests to see elaborately carved totem poles. They wanted to see and do as much as they possibly could while Katy was still in the earliest stages of her pregnancy. The toughest part would be complying with the strict order her doctor had given to Mac: "Slow her down, Mr. Director; she's not a twenty-five-year-old girl."

"Did you tell her that?" McGarvey asked.

Her doctor had smiled faintly. "All except the part about not being twenty-five. But she'll be just fine as long as you don't let her overdo it."

McGarvey followed his bodyguard back down to the lounge deck. The doors to the Grand Salon were closed, but the corridor was ice cold, as if a hatch or something was open to the outside.

Grassinger shoved open the door and stepped inside, McGarvey right behind him. Almost immediately, Grassinger pivoted, danced to the left, and went for his gun.

McGarvey caught a snapshot glimpse of the passengers seated at their tables, a lot of bodies lying in pools of blood on the floor and up on the stage, and eight or ten men armed with what looked like compact sub-machine guns, big silencers on the ends of the barrels, positioned along the walls. Katy and Karen Shaw were seated at their table, but the former SecDef stood next to a man dressed in what could have been a ship's officer's white jacket, a black balaclava over his head.

Grassinger only just got his gun hand inside his jacket when he was violently cast sideways off his feet by a hail of gunfire from a silenced submachine gun, which stitched a half dozen or more wounds from the side of his head to his hip.

The man in the black balaclava next to Shaw started to turn toward the commotion, as did the other terrorists.

The passengers were slower to react, but already several of them had jumped up and were attempting to escape, while a few others were diving for the floor to get out of the line of fire.

Within the next few seconds the situation would get completely out of hand unless the terrorists were too busy dealing with an immediate threat to their own safety to take their rage out on the helpless passengers. It was obvious that they were here to take the former secretary of defense hostage. It meant that they might be open to some form of negotiation, especially if they weren't sure that they were in total control.

All that went through McGarvey's head at the speed of light, and to an observer it seemed as if he reacted the instant Grassinger reached for his pistol.

The shooter, just behind the door to the right, moved forward toward his target as he fired, as most shooters do. The silencer and muzzle of the RAK submachine pistol poked around the edge of the door. Mindless of the hot metal, McGarvey grabbed the barrel with his bare hand, and twisting it sharply to the left as he deflected it upward and away from himself as well as the passengers, he pulled the gunman half out into the corridor.

McGarvey's instant impression was that the shooter was a young kid, maybe in his early twenties, most likely a Saudi or perhaps an Iranian or an Iraqi. He forced the muzzle of the silencer under the terrorist's chin, and then yanked the gun upward, causing it to fire. The one round took the top of the shooter's head off. His grip slackened as he went down. McGarvey snatched the RAK, and fired one controlled burst of three rounds over the heads of the panicking passengers.

The terrorists dove for cover, and before they could react Mac stepped back into the corridor and out of sight. He didn't want to further endanger the passengers by drawing fire.

He could have taken out several of the terrorists, but they not only had the firepower advantage over him, they also had the passengers as shields. Katy was at the Shaws' table, and although it didn't appear as if the terrorists knew who she was, that might not last.

It was likely that the terrorists had already taken control of the ship. It's why he and Grassinger had not bumped into anyone on the upper deck when they'd gone back for Katy's earrings. The rest of the crew was probably dead, or incapacitated.

Grassinger's blood was spreading through the doors out into the corridor, a shocking red against the pale green carpeting.

The entire Grand Salon could very well become a killing field soon unless McGarvey did something. Katy had turned toward the door when the firing started. She'd had just a split second to see what was going on, and to see who was there, before he ducked out of sight. She knew that he would not leave her there.

Hang on, Katy, he said to himself, as he turned and sprinted down the corridor to the starboard stairs, and took them two at a time up to the bridge deck.

First he would see if the radio room could be salvaged so that an SOS could be sent. Next he would check the bridge to see if the terrorists had put someone at the helm. And then he would start isolating them and taking them down, one or two at a time. Keep them so busy and so much on the defensive that they would be forced to forget about their primary mission.

They would pay, not only for killing Jim Grassinger and for placing the passengers in such great danger, but for putting Katy in harm's way. After this night they would rue the day they ever heard of the *Spirit of '98*.

EIGHT

□

Ernst Gertner's call to the chalet did not come as a surprise.

Detective Ziegler held his hand over the mouthpiece. "It's the captain, and he doesn't sound happy." He handed the phone to Liese. This was supposed to be a stealthy surveillance, which in Swiss parlance meant that no one was to know anything about it; neither the prince's family nor anyone official at Nidwalden HQ. When she'd called the Kanton operations officer for telephone records of the Thalwil Boarding School near Zurich, the ball had been sent up. Questions of an official nature were raised because they had to be raised. Wealthy, powerful men such as the prince were to be treated with extreme care. So long as they broke no Swiss laws, they were not to be interfered with under any circumstance. Now that was the official policy. In actuality men such as the prince simply could not be left entirely to their own devices. They had to be monitored. Especially in this day and age. But quietly, unofficially.

A lot of eyes at headquarters in Bern were looking at Liese as if under a microscope. If she continued to do her job with intelligence and self-control, she would be considered for promotion to lieutenant. She would be the first woman in the history of the Swiss Federal Police to hold such a lofty position. But if she made a mistake, any mistake, it would be blamed on her sex, and she would remain a sergeant until she finally got disgusted enough to resign, which is exactly what half of the force wanted to happen.

"Goodness gracious, why didn't you call me first?" Gertner demanded angrily. "I could have made quiet inquiries."

Liese bit her tongue to hold back a sharp retort. She had merely been doing her job. "It was five in the morning, captain. I didn't think you wished to be disturbed at that hour."

"I was disturbed twenty minutes later, from Bern."

"I don't see the point—"

"Bad news travels fast," Gertner replied brusquely. "The president is scheduled to meet with the Saudi ambassador this noon. What would happen at that meeting if word got out of what you were doing down here?"

"What, spying on a member of the royal family?" Liese asked sharply. Who were they trying to kid? This assignment had not been her idea.

Gertner did not catch her sarcasm. "Exactly."

"We're to watch the prince, without appearing to watch him. Is that correct, captain?"

This time he did catch it. "That's exactly what is required, Sergeant Fuelm," Gertner said. He lowered his voice, his tone guarded. "Are you within earshot of your men?"

She looked at Ziegler, who was sitting at the equipment table an arm's length away. "No," she lied. Her father had called her his little vixen, and Kirk had called her a spoiled brat. Nobody had ever faulted her intelligence, however.

"Considering the importance of this operation, we are prepared to give you a certain amount of, shall we say, latitude."

"I'm grateful for that, sir," Liese said.

"I have the transcript of the brief telephone conversation that occurred between Princess Sofia Salman and Dr. Junger, the headmaster at Thalwil. I have also listened to the digital recording. You were absolutely correct to assume that the woman, for whatever reason, was in a great hurry to have her children prepared to leave the school this very morning."

For as long as she could remember, Liese had a great deal of impatience with people who took a long time to get to the point. She wanted to jump in and finish their sentences for them. Hurry them along. It was one of her least charming attributes. Sometimes she came across as arrogant.

"Did she give the headmaster a reason?"

"A family matter of some importance, though she was not specific. Nor was she precise about when the children would be returning to school."

"They've done it at least once before," Liese said. She had the Thalwil file open. The four Salman children had attended the private school for three years. This was the start of their fourth.

The line was suddenly very quiet, until Gertner came back. "Yes, we know that."

"The prince was gone almost three months that time. And his wife took the children out of school on the third of September. For ten days. 2001."

"The prince was at the Saudi UN Delegation office in New York."

Law enforcement in Switzerland was much the same as anywhere else in the world. It was departmentalized. Division chiefs tended to guard their own turfs, sometimes to the detriment of ongoing investigations. In this case what Liese had not been told about the prince constituted a greater volume than what she *had* been told.

"Have there been other incidences—"

"A few," Gertner answered too quickly.

"I meant other times when the prince's absences matched other al-Quaida attacks?"

"On the surface there could have been other incidences."

"What does that mean?" Liese shouted angrily. The thing she hated worst, even worse than being discriminated against because she was a woman, was being lied to.

"It means the timing was there, but his absences could have been co-incidental."

"Come on, Ernst."

"No, you *come on*, as you put it. There were many, many incidences when the prince was gone during which there were no terrorist attacks anywhere that could be attributed to al-Quaida. He was simply conduct-ing business, or gone on one of his gambling jaunts. Can we say with equal authority in those cases that he was ensuring the peace?"

"No, of course not," Liese conceded. "But I would not have been handed this assignment unless you thought there might be a connection."

"Continue," Gertner said.

"Assuming that there is a financial connection between the prince—and therefore the Saudi royal family—and assuming that it wasn't simply a coincidence that he ordered his wife and children to hunker down be-fore 9/11, then something is about to happen again, and the prince knows about it because he's the moneyman."

"Those are very large and, I must say, dangerous assumptions."

"Especially if it were to come out that Switzerland harbored such a criminal, and Switzerland's banks were the conduit."

"He may have heard rumors—men in his position are often privy to such information. In such a case he would not be guilty of violating any Swiss laws."

"He has a house staff across the lake."

"Cooks, gardeners, drivers."

"Them too, Ernst. But also some very large men." The sun was up, form-ing a bright halo over the Salman compound. "Supply me with a search warrant, and I can almost guarantee that we will find weapons over there."

"If that was the only crime the prince or his staff was guilty of—considering his position—we would take no issue."

"If he was merely a man who listened to rumors, an international playboy and multimillionaire, why would he need armed guards?" Liese asked. "Only men who are hiding something, or are afraid of something, hire bodyguards."

"Or men protecting something. Their families."

God, she hated this roundabout way of getting to a point. "I want to see the prince's file. The *complete* file. You can e-mail it to me."

"I'll send it by courier. The computer is too dangerous."

"Fine, I'll wait here then until it arrives," Liese promised. "But tell me, Ernst, what am I going to find out? What is it you saw fit not to tell me yesterday?"

"I'll include my notes in the file."

"What is the problem, Ernst?" Liese demanded, her voice rising. "I'm trying to do a job down here, and you see fit to play your silly little bureaucratic games with me. If you believe that Prince Salman is funding terrorists, and you believe that somehow he might have a connection to Kirk McGarvey that I might be able to unravel for you because of my brief encounter years ago, then so be it. But give me a chance to succeed. Don't tie my hands behind my back."

Gertner took a moment to reply, and when he did it was clear that he too was angry. "Don't push us on this, Liese," he said. "There are very good reasons for our caution that have nothing to do with you or your investigation. But do let me give you a word of fatherly advice. For the moment we need you, and as I said, we are willing to give you a certain amount of latitude. But that need will not last forever."

Liese felt cold. She walked to the tiny kitchen, her back to her surveillance team who were undoubtedly eating this up. "If you're threatening me, then you will have my resignation on your desk before your courier arrives. I am an experienced Federal Police officer, and I demand the same treatment as any male officer is given."

"But, my dear, you aren't a male officer; you are a female who needs to attend to the business of following orders. And something else. You are bright and capable, but you are not a genius for whom we would be willing to make exceptions."

Gertner tapped his pipe on an ashtray to empty the bowl. Liese could hear it. He was stalling as he tried to marshal his thoughts.

"I'll do my best, as I always do," Liese said. Her mother told her that her beauty would attract any man she looked at, but her big mouth would drive away any man she wanted.

"We have good intelligence that Prince Salman was in Washington as of two days ago. But then he disappeared. The problem for us is that since yesterday Kirk McGarvey has also dropped out of sight. One coincidence is acceptable; two are not."

"You thought that the prince might be back by now?" Liese asked.

"Yes."

"But combined with the call to Thalwil there may be something," Liese went on. She did have a big mouth, but beyond that she was carrying a feminist grudge that was getting her absolutely nowhere. "I'm sorry, captain; I was out of line. But I was merely trying to do my job."

"I appreciate that," Gertner said, and he sounded smug, as if once again he had stepped into the breach and solved a difficult personnel problem. He fancied himself to be a brilliant administrator.

"We will continue our surveillance operation here, of course, but what else is it that you would like me to do?" Liese asked. She knew what he was going to tell her, but she didn't care. She did not want to be pulled off this assignment so long as it involved Kirk.

"I would like you to place a telephone call to Mr. McGarvey. You are an old friend who is somewhat nostalgic for the old days. Maybe you called simply to chat. You are lonely, and have been handed a very troubling assignment."

You bastard, Liese thought. To them she was nothing but a pain-in-the-ass woman, a thing to be tolerated, no more. But they were afraid of Kirk. And as they had done with Marta, they wanted to provide him with another Swiss whore. A man would say anything when he was in bed with his lover, or nearly anything if the prospect of going to bed with a young woman was dangled in front of his nose.

But they didn't know Kirk. Nor did they know her.

"It's midnight in Washington," she pointed out.

"If he's not out and about somewhere, he's sure to be at home and not at his office."

"I'll make that call now, sir," Liese said.

"Liese?"

"Yes, sir."

"Record the call, please," Gertner instructed. "All of it." He hung up the phone.

Liese was seething. Never in her life had she been treated this way, though she'd been expecting something like this to happen. But now that they had used her sex as a lever against her, she had no idea how to fight back. She looked up at the ceiling for a moment and closed her eyes. God help her, but after all these years she was still in love with Kirk McGarvey. There never was another man like him, nor could there ever be. The thought that somehow he was involved in the 9/11 attacks and was in collusion with Prince Salman was ludicrous. But if Gertner thought such a thing were possible, then others would think so too. It was up to her to prove them wrong.

She dialed Kirk's home number in Chevy Chase from memory, though it was the first time she'd ever let it go through. It rang twice before it was rolled over to what Liese thought would be an answering machine. She was about to hang up when a man with an oddly pitched voice, as if he were lifting something very heavy, answered.

"Oh, boy, what could the Swiss police be wanting at this hour? Especially calling from Lake Lucerne. Are you in a house or on a boat?"

"I'm sorry; I must have the wrong number," Liese said, and she tried to break the connection, but could not; the line had been seized.

"I don't think you have a wrong number, so don't leave. And you have a pretty voice."

"Who are you?"

"Otto Rencke. Does that name tinkle any little bells in your head? I'll bet you're pretty too. Odd for a Swiss cop."

Liese checked the number showing on her phone's display. It was Kirk's home phone, which meant her call had been rolled over, probably to an operations officer at Langley who had the CIA's computer system at his fingertips.

"No, your name isn't familiar to me. I'm trying to reach Kirk McGarvey. He's an old friend. I thought I might catch him at home."

The line was dead for a moment. "Oh, boy, you're Liese Fuelm," Rencke said. "Am I right or what?"

A fist clutched at her heart, but she recovered fast. "If that makes you happy, sure," Liese said. "Can you tell me how I could reach Mr. McGarvey?"

"Oh, don't get mad. I'm an old friend, just like you," Rencke said, apologetically. He sounded like a big kid. "But Mac is out of town right now; it's why his number showed up here."

It's not what she wanted to hear. She closed her eyes again. Everything seemed so screwed up. "Can I get a message to him?"

"Nope, he's on vacation, and I wouldn't bother him even if it was the second coming, ya know," Rencke told her. "But listen, is there something you need? Maybe I can help. I'm Mac's special assistant, ya know. I can find out things."

Talking to Rencke was like dealing with an overgrown, exuberant puppy. It had to be an act, but the number she'd called was correct, and only an organization such as the CIA could trace and seize her line so quickly, and then come up with her name. "Just say hello when he gets back."

"Who are you surveilling?"

"I have to go now. Release my line, please."

"I can find out, you know. You're at the lake house owned by Heide Rothberg. I've got that much; though his name doesn't come up in any of my serious databases, I'm sure I can get something on him. And I can take some good angle satellite shots of your location within twenty minutes that should give me some line-of-sights. That'd probably eliminate all but a few nearby locations. Somebody in one of those spots is of interest not only to the Swiss Federal Police, but maybe to the director of Central Intelligence. A blast from the past. Is that it?"

"Look, Mr. Rencke, I can't tell you that—"

"Otto," Rencke said. "Please. We're practically family. He still wonders about Marta Fredericks from time to time, ya know."

"How are you coming up with this information? It's nobody's business."

"I won't say anything to anybody, nohow, never, except Mac. Honest Injun!"

"Prince Abdul Salman, he's a—"

"I know who he is," Rencke said, his aw-shucks manner suddenly gone. "What do you have on him?"

"I can't tell you that."

"Why did you call the director of Central Intelligence to ask about him?"

"I didn't call the DCI; I called an old friend," Liese shouted. She was frustrated *and* frightened now. She was getting in over her head. "Release my line."

"Give me what you have, and I'll pass it along to Mac," Rencke said, gently. "Look, if it's any comfort to you, we're interested in the man too. Mac will probably want to share intel on this one."

"The prince spent some time in Washington about ten years ago. He was one of Darby Yarnell's crowd."

"I see," Rencke said after a beat, and he seemed almost sad. "I'll have Mac call you. And in the meantime I'll take a quick peek at what we have. I might be able to come up with something."

"Thanks."

"Don't let them get to you, Liese. They can be bastards, sometimes, but mostly we're all on the same side."

There was no need to ask who *they* were, or what he was talking about. He had figured out who had suggested she make the call and why. "Just say hello," Liese said, "and give him a hug."

"Sure," Rencke said, and he released her line.

Liese realized that she had not pushed the Record button, but she didn't care. "Hell," she said, softly, and she began to cry.

NINE

The expression on Kirk's face was caught like a photographic flash image in Katy's head.

She got up and helped Karen Shaw get her husband seated. He was nearly out on his feet, and for the moment, at least, he didn't seem to know what was going on around him. The terrorists had all dived for cover, except for the one wearing the balaclava who'd struck Donald Shaw in the head. He seemed to be the leader, but he apparently hadn't counted on meeting any resistance because he was exhorting his men to get to their feet. Or at least that's what it sounded like to Katy. She thought he was speaking Arabic, which was no surprise. But how they had gotten aboard the cruise ship without detection was a mystery. According to Kirk, the ship's crew and passengers had passed complete background checks.

Shaw's bodyguard was down, as was poor Jim Grassinger, both of them presumably dead; but Kirk was alive, he was armed, he was free, and he knew the situation. She'd never approved of his profession, of the spying and especially the killing, although she understood that such things were necessary in the real world. But at this moment, aside from her love and respect for him, she wouldn't have traded him for all the bank presidents, artists, CEOs, or scientists in the world.

She was frightened out of her wits. Already there were bodies all over the Grand Salon. Most of them were crewmen or entertainers, but two of the passengers had been brutally murdered in cold blood, and she thought that some of the people remaining would not survive the night. Yet she had to suppress a bitter smile of satisfaction. The bad guys had no idea what they had gotten themselves into. If she hadn't lost an earring, they would have caught Kirk, seated here, unarmed, and she didn't know how that could have turned out for the good. But now, she thought, anything was possible. She had seen her husband in action, and he was a sight to behold.

The former SecDef sat with his head hanging, his eyes fluttering as he tried to catch his breath and regain his balance. Blood oozed from a long gash at his temple, and it was obvious that he would need medical help soon. At the very least he had probably suffered a concussion. For a man of his age the blow could well be fatal.

"My God, Don, are you all right?" Karen Shaw whispered to her husband. She had her arms around his shoulders, trying to protect him and hold him up.

Katy scooped the ice from her water glass and wrapped it in her linen napkin. "Try this," she offered. She placed the cold pack on Don Shaw's head. He reared back, but his wife held him still.

"Easy, darling, this should help."

The terrorist with the balaclava had gone to the back of the Grand Salon and positioned himself to the left of the door. One of his men, his weapon up and at the ready, was on the right. On a signal he yanked open the door, and the leader poked his machine pistol out into the corridor and fired off two quick bursts, then ducked back.

There was no return fire.

Shaw jerked as if he'd been hit, and he looked up out of his daze, his eyes finally coming back into focus. He looked at his wife. "Where's Tony?"

"They shot him," Karen said. "But he got one of them."

Shaw glanced at Katy and the vacant seat next to her, then surreptitiously made a quick survey of the carnage around the Grand Salon. The passengers were completely subdued. No one dared to move so much as a muscle for fear of getting shot. "What happened to Kirk and his bodyguard?" he asked softly.

Katy looked over at the terrorist leader and two of his men at the door. For the moment their attention was directed toward the corridor. "Jim is dead, but Kirk managed to kill one of the terrorists and grab his gun."

"Has he got a cell phone?"

"Yes, but I don't think they work out here," Katy said, careful to keep her voice low and her eye on the terrorist leader. "He'll think of something. They won't get away with this."

"But he's only one man," Karen said. She was a brave woman, but amidst all this carnage and with her husband as the terrorists' target, she was just hanging on by her fingernails.

"That's true," Katy said. "But just hold on; he'll come back."

"The radio room," the former SecDef mumbled. "Kirk can get a message out. The Coast Guard is listening."

"I'm sure he's already thought of that," Katy said. She was watching the terrorists at the door.

The leader stationed two of his people to guard the corridor, then turned, looked down at his two dead operators as if they were nothing more than pieces of trash cluttering up the floor, then looked up and surveyed the room. He was obviously in a hurry, but he was being methodical.

A deathly silence fell over the Grand Salon. The air was hazy with gun smoke and the metallic odor of fresh blood. Every passenger thought about 9/11 with a sense of total helplessness. There were just too many terrorists with guns. Any sort of resistance was less than futile. It was dangerous.

"One brave, but foolish man among you," Khalil said. He took a few steps away from the door, and stopped. "I don't believe that he was a member of the ship's crew. He wasn't dressed in a uniform. So he was a passenger. Who was he?"

No one answered, and Katy held her silence. Kirk should have reached the radio room by now, and unless the terrorists had destroyed the equipment, he would be sending out the SOS. Help would be arriving soon. They just had to hang on until then.

"Who knows where the purser's office is?"

One of the terrorists who'd masqueraded as a steward stepped for-ward. "It's on the main deck below us."

"Go there now and get the passenger list," Khalil ordered. "But watch out for our mystery man; he's armed. If you see him, kill him."

The man nodded and went to the door at the rear of the Grand Salon. He stopped for just a moment to make sure the corridor was clear and then left.

The terrorists had come to kidnap Shaw, but Katy had no idea how they were going to pull it off. The Spirit was too big to hide for very long, even in the thousands of backwaters and fjords along the Inside Passage. And unless there were a lot more of them, defending a ship this size from an assault by a team of Special Forces would be impossible. Which left an escape by air—perhaps a helicopter or a floatplane—or a pickup from a boat standing by off their stern. Either way they would have to be concerned with a loose cannon, such as Kirk, running around the ship armed with a submachine gun, who could spoil every-thing with one well-placed shot. And time could not be on the side of the terrorists.

Khalil walked over to a young couple seated at one of the tables lo-cated next to a serving station. The woman held a baby, perhaps eight or nine months old, in her arms. Coming into the Grand Salon earlier, Katy had been surprised to see that the couple had brought their child, not only on the cruise, but also to this evening's entertainment. But then when Elizabeth was a child, Katy hadn't trusted babysitters either. An older man and woman seated with them seemed to be the grandparents.

"Does anyone here know who that man was?" Khalil asked, reasonably.

"No, we don't. What do you want?" the older man asked.

"We've come to arrest Secretary Shaw," Khalil replied matter-of-factly. He could have been discussing the weather.

"Then take him and go," the older man ordered. "Leave us alone. We've done nothing to you or your cause, whatever that might be this time."

"*Shut your stupid mouth*," Katy muttered under her breath. She wanted to go over and strangle the man. There were bodies lying in pools of blood all over the Grand Salon, and this guy was probably grandstanding for his wife, and maybe his son-in-law.

"Where were you on 9/11?" Khalil asked, conversationally. But the question was bizarre, like the warning rumble of a volcano on the verge of erupting.

"Minding my own business," the man shot back. "Which I suggest that you do if you want to survive. You know what happened in Afghanistan and Iraq."

"Mind my own business?" Khalil asked. "Very well." He smashed the butt of his machine pistol into the head of the young father, sending him crashing to the floor.

"Johnathan," the woman with the baby screamed. She lunged for her husband, but the older woman grabbed her arm.

"You bastard—" the older man shouted, and he started to get up.

The young man, dazed, reached a hand to the bloody wound in his head, and looked up as Khalil calmly fired one shot into his forehead at point-blank range, killing him instantly.

The young mother opened her mouth but made no sound, completely unable to comprehend what had just happened in front of her. She shook her head, and held her baby close to her breast. The older man's jaw dropped, and he slowly sat down, the color draining from his face.

"I need to know the identity of the man who attacked us," Khalil said.

"We don't know who he is," the older woman cried. "Please, can't you have mercy on us?"

Shaw, realizing what would happen next if someone didn't intervene, started to get to his feet, but his wife held him back, a look of terror on her face. Katy could not take her eyes away from the unfolding scene. The terrorist was going to kill the young woman and her child next. Katy could see it coming. Everyone in the room knew it was about to happen. But there was nothing any of them could do. If they moved, they would be shot down like the others.

Khalil pointed his machine pistol at the back of the baby's head. If he fired, the shot would certainly kill the infant and most likely the mother as well. The young woman held her breath and closed her eyes.

"Who is the man who attacked us?" Khalil asked, patiently.

Katy got to her feet. She did not take her eyes off the terrorist pointing the gun at the mother and child, but she was aware that some of the others had swung their guns in her direction.

"He's my husband," she said, in a loud, clear voice. Karen Shaw reached over and gave Katy's hand a squeeze.

Khalil turned toward her, hesitated just a moment, and then walked over to her. "Your husband?"

"Yes," Katy said. She could see his eyes behind the mask. They were coal black and inhumanly emotionless, like those of a wild animal, a jungle animal.

"Who might you be?"

"I'm Kathleen McGarvey."

For a brief instant the terrorist seemed to be taken aback, almost rocked on his heels. But he recovered immediately. "Your husband is Kirk McGarvey? The director of the Central Intelligence Agency?"

"That's correct," Katy said. She let that sink in for several seconds, and then she looked at the other terrorists positioned around the room. "If you want to live, I suggest that you get off this ship while you can," she said in a loud, perfectly steady voice. "Otherwise my husband will kill you." She turned back to the terrorist behind the balaclava. "Count on it," she told him.

T E N

□

Moments after one of the terrorists had fired the short burst down the corridor, McGarvey had made his way up to the bridge deck taking the stairs two at a time. Except for the faint sounds of the powerful diesel engines in the distance, the ship was deathly quiet. Normally there would be passengers in the corridors, or stewards delivering room-service orders. But the Spirit seemed to be deserted.

It was out of the ordinary. He had picked up on it earlier, but he had put it off as nothing more than a combination of fatigue and the paranoia that accompanied his kind of work. He always listened to his inner voices. But this time he had ignored his instincts. He was supposed to be on vacation.

The ship was unnaturally quiet because the crew and passengers not in the Grand Salon were probably already dead. The terrorists had to be well organized. They'd probably masqueraded as crewmen, which meant they had a professional organization behind them; otherwise they couldn't have passed the extensive background checks the DoD and CIA had carried out. Either that or they had transferred aboard from a smaller boat following in the Spirit's wake. But even then it would have been necessary to have someone aboard to make sure the way was clear.

If they were professionals and not fanatics, it would make defeating them much more difficult, but on the plus side a professional understood logic. He would recognize when it was time to cut his losses and run, whereas a fanatic would rather die, taking everyone with him, than give up.

McGarvey was used to dealing with professionals. He had been in the business for more than twenty-five years, starting with the Office of Special Investigations in the Air Force before signing on with the CIA as a field officer. Most of his early career had been spent in black operations. He had been a killer. An assassin. It was a job that had very nearly destroyed him, and had caused the deaths of a number of people who had been very close to him.

His job had even destroyed his marriage, until he and Katy had both finally come to their senses and realized that they loved each other, and could deal with whatever was separating them. He'd risen quickly then from assistant deputy director of operations all the way up to his present appointment as director of the CIA. It was a position he'd promised the president that he would stick with for three years. But 9/11 had put everything on hold for him. And this attack now, which was directed at the former secretary of defense, was probably just the next step for bin Laden, a man McGarvey knew better than anyone in the West. If this were a bin Laden–directed operation, then it would have been exquisitely planned. And it would be ruthless.

He held up at the head of the stairs. The owner's suite, which the Shaws had occupied, was directly across the corridor from him. Just aft was the funnel, and beyond it the open sundeck. Forward of the suite were the bridge, radio room, and captain's sea quarters.

The weapon he'd taken from the terrorist was a Polish-made RAK PM-63 machine pistol that fired a 9mm Makarov cartridge at six hundred rounds per minute. A long suppressor was screwed to the end of the barrel, but even with the degradation of accuracy that most silencers caused, the Wz-63, in its Polish designation, was a deadly weapon. The trouble was its suppressor got very hot when the weapon was fired, and McGarvey's right palm had a waffle-pattern burn from grabbing the gun out of the terrorist's hands.

The RAK was the weapon of choice for many Eastern European terrorists, so it was taught to field officers at the Farm, the CIA's training facility outside Williamsburg, and McGarvey knew it well. He released the catch at the bottom of the pistol grip, popping out the twenty-five-round magazine. Only six bullets remained.

Three-fourths of the bullets in the magazine had been fired. The kid had probably murdered one or more crewmen or passengers before he had gunned down Grassinger, and he would have almost certainly done more killing tonight unless he and the others were stopped.

There wasn't time for McGarvey to return to his cabin for his pistol and spare magazines, so six rounds would have to be enough for now.

He drove the magazine home with the heel of his hand, then stepped out of the stairwell, ducked across to the owner's suite, and sprinted down the corridor to the radio room.

The bridge itself was raised a few feet above the level of the main part of the uppermost deck. Access was gained up a short flight of stairs on each side of the ship. There was no other way up. From where he stood, poised next to the radio room door, he could not see up into the bridge. Nor could anyone up there see him unless they came out onto one of the lookout wings and peered through a window.

He felt guilty about leaving Katy in the hands of the terrorists and for allowing Jim Gassinger to be shot to death. In the old days he would have blamed himself for allowing people to get so close to him that their lives would be placed in danger. But now he felt bad because he wasn't fast enough, not quick enough on the uptake to thwart the determined gunman. But this time the terrorists had made a mistake. They had failed to make a complete sweep of the ship before they took over the Grand Salon. They had missed him, and he was determined to bring the fight back to them in an up close and very personal way.

The radio-room door was ajar. Each time the ship yawed when a wave hit the starboard quarter, the door would swing open a few inches, then swing back almost but not quite hard enough to latch.

From where he stood, McGarvey could see a young man with short cropped black hair and narrow shoulders, his back to the door, seated in front of a rack of radio equipment, most of which had been shot up or smashed beyond repair. The man was dressed as a ship's officer, but an RAK machine pistol was at his elbow on the desk. He was listening to a portable VHF transceiver of the kind used for ship-to-ship and ship-to-shore communications. Probably the U.S. Coast Guard channel to make sure that no one from the *Spirit* had managed to send a distress signal.

McGarvey waited until the door started to swing out, then yanked it all the way open and stepped inside. "I'd like to send a message, if you don't mind."

The terrorist was startled. He looked over his shoulder, his eyes going wide at the sight of one of the passengers standing there with a weapon in hand. He shouted something in Arabic, wildly flung the VHF radio, and snatched his gun.

McGarvey reached for the radio with one hand, but missed it. The transceiver smashed against the steel door frame as the terrorist brought his gun up over his shoulder and started to fire even before he was on target, spraying the overhead with bullets, deadly shrapnel flying all over the place.

The terrorist had left him no choice. McGarvey brought his weapon up and squeezed off two shots, one catching the young man in his left shoulder and the second in the side of his head just behind his ear, sending him sprawling across the desk in a bloody heap.

McGarvey ducked back out into the corridor to make sure no one had heard the commotion and was coming to investigate; then he stooped down and picked up the VHF radio. A big piece of the plastic case had cracked open and fell off, exposing the main circuit board, which had also broken in two. The radio was as useless as the ship's communications equipment. Whatever happened aboard now was up to him.

The terrorist carried no wallet or identification or anything else in his pockets except for a 9mm Steyr GB self-loading pistol, with one eighteen-round magazine, plus two extra twenty-five-round magazines for the RAK. A digital watch was strapped to his right wrist, but he wore no rings or other jewelry.

McGarvey took off his dinner jacket and tossed it aside, then stuffed the pistol in his belt, ejected the nearly spent magazine from his RAK, replacing it with one of the spares. Then he pocketed the second, all the while listening for someone to come up the corridor.

The bridge crew was probably dead, but the ship was still moving, which meant that someone had to be at the helm because running on autopilot in these confined waters would be a dicey business. The same was likely true down in the engine room. The regular crew was probably dead, and one or more of the terrorists were taking care of business.

He cycled the RAK's slide to cock the weapon and turned to go, but then stopped. Something bothered him. Something about the terrorist's wristwatch. He went back to the body and lifted the kid's lifeless arm. The watch was in countdown mode with a few seconds more than seventeen minutes left. But seventeen minutes until what? Until they got off the ship? Or was it something else? McGarvey had a very bad feeling that he was missing something important. He took the watch.

The wind was screaming when McGarvey stepped outside and quickly made his way forward and mounted the port stairs up to the bridge. He flattened himself against the upright and cautiously took a brief peek in the window. A slightly built young woman was at the big wheel. Captain Darling lay on his side by the starboard door in a pool of blood, his eyes open and sightless. Two other officers were down and presumably dead, one at the radar and navigation position to the left of the helm and the other in a crumpled heap beside the chart table aft of the helm.

The woman was frightened. That was obvious from the grimace on her face and the stiff way she stood. But there was no one on the bridge to threaten her, to force her to remain at her post. Unless she was one of the terrorists. For some reason he didn't think that was the case. The terrorists were almost certainly Muslims, and most Islamic fundamentalist operational cells did not send women out on missions. The major exception was the military wing of Hamas, which sometimes sent women as suicide bombers to Israeli-occupied areas. But this was not a Hamas operation; it wasn't the organization's style.

McGarvey looked through the window again. Nothing had changed, and there was no place for anyone to hide. Even if the girl was one of the terrorists, she didn't appear to be armed. And time was running short. Every second Katy was under the terrorists' control in the Grand Salon increased her chances of getting shot to death.

He yanked the door open and stepped onto the bridge. The girl at the helm practically jumped out of her skin.

"I'm a friend," McGarvey said. "Are you okay?"

The girl urgently looked over her shoulder toward the officer lying next to the chart table, at the same time a walkie-talkie lying on a shelf beneath one of the forward windows hissed.

"*Achmed, keyf heh'lik?*"

McGarvey turned toward the sound, and almost immediately he realized he'd been set up, and that the young helmsman had tried to warn him. He dove for the deck as he swiveled in his tracks and brought his gun to bear on the man dressed as a ship's officer lying in a heap beside the chart table. The terrorist opened fire with his Steyr GB, the heavy 9mm Makarov rounds starring the forward windows, smashing one of the digital radar displays, striking the already destroyed SSB radio, and plowing into the overhead before McGarvey got three shots off, all of them hitting the man in the back below his left shoulder blade, knocking him down.

McGarvey picked himself up, keeping his weapon trained on the terrorist, but the man was dead. And so was the young woman at the helm, the back of her head a bloody mess where she'd taken one round.

He went to her, but there was nothing he could do. She was gone, and no power on earth could bring her back. He wanted to go over to the bastard he'd just shot and kick his body down the stairs to the Grand Salon and dump it at the feet of whoever was leading this attack.

If it was death they wanted, he was going to give it to them in a very large, and very personal, way.

ELEVEN

□

With fifteen minutes remaining to zero hour, Khalil was forced to consider his options. Although he had never come face-to-face with Kirk McGarvey, the man was a legend in the intelligence business. No one on the outside would ever know the full extent of the former CIA assassin's entire career, but there were so many stories about him that if even one-tenth of them were true, McGarvey would have to be a superman.

The one story that was absolutely true was his encounter with Osama bin Laden. Khalil knew it was a fact because he got it from bin Laden himself, and Osama never lied. McGarvey had actually come to Afghanistan to seek out bin Laden a couple of years before 9/11. Al-Quaida had managed to purchase a one-kiloton nuclear suitcase demolitions device that was to be used in a strike on the U.S. McGarvey had come to make a trade: the bomb for American concessions in the region, especially on the Saudi Arabian peninsula.

Khalil had met with bin Laden one month before 9/11 to discuss the probable reaction from the U.S., and Mac's name had come up.

"I looked into his eyes, and what I saw made me wish that he was a friend and not an enemy," bin Laden said.

"An infidel?" Khalil suggested, testing bin Laden's depth of respect for the American.

McGarvey had stopped the nuclear attack two years earlier, and there was some concern among bin Laden's advisers that he might somehow get wind of the plans for the attacks on the World Trade Center, Pentagon, and White House.

Bin Laden nodded. "Kirk McGarvey is a man among men. If you ever come up against him, kill him immediately. Doing so will be your only chance of survival."

Khalil stared at Kathleen McGarvey as if he could see through her skin and bone right into her brain, and into her soul. He wanted to have a real measure of her before he ended her life. One bullet into her head, or one quick slash of his knife across her throat, severing not only her windpipe, but both of her carotid arteries, and he would see whatever that measure was.

It wasn't the mechanical act of killing that enticed Khalil; he'd had his fill of those kinds of thrills, and he was no longer satisfied by simple body counts. Now he had the insane idea that if he were quick enough, his perceptions agile enough, he would be able to catch the exact moment when a person's soul actually left the body.

It would be just like the green flash on the horizon at sunset, a sight never to be forgotten.

But that pleasure would have to wait. Kirk McGarvey was loose aboard the ship, and he could interfere with their plans if he was allowed to continue unabated. Shaw would come back with them to Pakistan, but so would Kathleen McGarvey.

He stepped back and took the walkie-talkie from his pocket. Everyone in the lounge was looking at him—the passengers waiting for him to make a mistake, his operators waiting for his next order. Everyone wanted to get off the ship, and he was going to accommodate all of them.

There were fourteen minutes left.

He keyed the walkie-talkie. "Bridge, report." The ship had not altered its course, so far as Khalil could tell, so whatever else McGarvey had tried he'd not gotten there.

But there was no answer.

"Bridge, what is your situation? Report now."

A slight smile came to Kathleen McGarvey's lips. Kahlil resisted the nearly overpowering urge to shoot her.

"Radio room, what is your situation?"

Some woman across the lounge started to cry, a moist snuffling that grated Khalil's nerves, raising his gorge. If McGarvey had already taken out his operators on the bridge and in the radio room, he would still be up there. There wouldn't have been enough time to reach the third vital point on the ship—the engine room—yet, but that's where he was probably heading.

"Purser's office, report."

"Here," the operator radioed back immediately. "The passenger manifest was on the desk. But there's no listing for Kirk McGarvey."

"Never mind the list," Khalil ordered, relieved that at least one of his people was answering. "He's taken out the bridge and radio room, so he'll probably try for the engine room next, which means he'll have to come past you. "If you see him, kill him."

"Yes, sir."

The woman's sobs were getting louder. Khalil was having trouble hearing much of anything else. He keyed the walkie-talkie, and called the engine room. "Granger, what is your situation?"

"The crew has been neutralized, and we're just about set here. Give me five minutes."

Khalil breathed a silent thanks to Allah. "You may have some trouble coming your way. One of the passengers is on the loose, and he's armed."

Pahlawan chuckled. "We'll give him a warm reception if he pokes his nose down here."

"Listen, you idiot," Khalil practically shouted. "This one is a professional. He is dangerous, so don't take any chances. Post a lookout."

"Very well," Pahlawan said. He was a veteran of numerous terrorist operations in Afghanistan and India. He was a fearless mujahideen.

"You're forgetting something," Kathleen interjected, softly.

Khalil turned his gaze to her. He was fascinated despite himself. She was an extraordinary woman of very great courage. "What is that?" he asked, mildly, though he wanted to lash out at something, at anyone. At the stupid woman making all the noise on the other side of the lounge.

"My husband has already killed your men in the radio room and on the bridge. At the very least it means that he has already taken partial control of this ship."

"Make your point."

Kathleen's smile turned vicious, as if she were a shark coming in for the kill. "He has one of the walkie-talkies. He's heard everything that you told your men."

Khalil's rage spiked, but he caught himself before he raised his pistol and put a round into her face. He wanted to take her back to Pakistan, to personally teach her the true meaning of humility. But more importantly for the moment, there was a very good chance that he would need her as an additional hostage.

He keyed the walkie-talkie. "Mr. McGarvey, I would like to propose a truce."

There was no answer. The sobbing woman was getting louder.

"I know that you can hear me, Mr. McGarvey. We don't want to hurt anyone else aboard this ship. Our operation is a political one. We have come to arrest Mr. Shaw and take him to the World Court at The Hague, where he will be put on trial for crimes against humanity. You know that there have been calls for just such a trial. We are merely acting as the policemen."

Khalil figured that there were two possibilities: Either McGarvey was not listening, or he was ignoring them.

They were running out of time.

"Your bodyguard is dead, as is the secretary's bodyguard. They were brave men, but their only chance would have been to lay down their weapons. It's your only chance. You are outnumbered and outgunned. Come down to the passageway aft of the lounge, unarmed and with your hands in plain sight. Once you have been secured, we will leave with Shaw."

There was no answer.

Khalil stuffed his pistol in his jacket, walked over to Kathleen, grabbed her by the arm, keyed the walkie-talkie, and shoved it in her face. "Tell your husband to give himself up or we will kill you."

Kathleen did not hesitate. "There are at least seven here, all armed with submachine guns—"

Khalil shoved Kathleen aside. He yanked out his pistol, strode across the room, and fired five shots into the head of the woman who was crying, driving her backward off her chair and onto the deck in a spray of blood.

TWELVE

□

Up on the bridge McGarvey heard the sounds of gunfire transmitted over the terrorist's walkie-talkie, and then the transmission stopped.

There wasn't another word from Katy, which could have meant that the terrorist had simply cut her off in midsentence when he realized she was shouting a warning. But the gunfire could also mean that the terrorist had murdered her in cold blood as he warned he would.

McGarvey stood flat-footed for two seconds, the walkie-talkie in one hand, the RAK machine pistol in the other, a feeling of utter despair threatening to consume him. The thought of his wife lying dead in a pool of her own blood was more than he could bear.

The terrorist had *allowed* him to hear the gunshots. The bastard was sending a sick message. We have your wife down here, and we may—or may not—have murdered her in cold blood. Why don't you come down and see with your own eyes?

They were stalling for time. *Because they're not ready to get off this ship yet,* McGarvey thought. The watch from the wrist of the terrorist in the radio room was in countdown mode, with less than seventeen minutes to go. Seventeen minutes for what?

He raised the walkie-talkie and started to depress the Push-to-Talk switch but then held up. Somehow the terrorists knew who he was. They had to know what he was capable of doing. That being the case, they would need Katy as a hostage.

Katy was alive.

Nothing else mattered except freeing her. But in order to do that, he would have to kill or disable a significant number of the hijackers. Now, before they got off the ship. There wasn't enough time to find a radio, call for help, then wait for the cavalry to arrive.

He looked up out of his daze and surveyed the blood and gore in the confines of the relatively small bridge. Blood was pooled in several spots on the deck, splashed up on the bulkheads and overhead, on the windows, and on the faces of the dials and electronic equipment. This place had become a killing field.

The entire ship was a killing field.

A flashing red light directly ahead of the ship caught his eye. It was one of the buoys that marked the channel. With no one at the helm, the ship was slowly drifting off course to the left. If they went aground on the rocks at this speed, there was a very good chance they would punch a hole in the bottom and sink. The water was very near freezing. If somebody went overboard, they wouldn't survive more than a few minutes.

He laid the walkie-talkie and machine pistol aside, and turned the wheel to starboard. It took several seconds for the ship to respond before the bows slowly came right, bringing them back into the navigation channel, the red buoy on their port side where it belonged.

All the communications and navigation equipment had been smashed beyond repair, but McGarvey was able to tighten the wheel lock, so at least for the moment the Spirit would continue on its present heading. That would be good only as long as the channel was straight, and didn't take a jog to the left or right, but for now he didn't have any other choice.

The engine telegraph lever was mounted on a console to the right of the wheel. It was in the All Ahead Full position. McGarvey disengaged the lock, and shoved it up to the All Ahead Stop position.

He waited for a few moments, but so far as he could tell nothing happened. The ship was not slowing down. The terrorists had also taken over the engine room and its functions which didn't come as a surprise. Except for steering, the controls on the bridge were useless.

He couldn't stop the ship's engines, nor could he lock the wheel hard over to port or starboard, for fear that the channel was too narrow and he would end up ripping the bottom out of the ship after all.

Time was running out for him. He couldn't leave the bridge for fear of sinking the ship, nor could he leave Katy or the other passengers under the guns of the terrorists. They'd already shown their utter lack of regard for human life. They'd already murdered in cold blood more than just crew members and his and Shaw's bodyguards. He had spotted at least one of the passengers, a woman, lying in a pool of blood in the Grand Salon.

His eyes lit on another control panel. Two sets of buttons marked Up and Down—one for starboard, the other for port—controlled the ship's anchors. If he couldn't stop the engines, perhaps he could stop the ship.

He hit both Down buttons, then braced himself against the helm's binnacle rail. Immediately a tremendous, deep-throated metallic clatter came from low in the bows as the two massive anchors dropped into the icy waters, dragging with them the heavy chains.

The din seemed to go on forever, until the Spirit gave a tentative lurch to starboard, and a high-pitched squeal of metal-on-metal rose from somewhere below.

The ship straightened her head, hesitated for a second or two, and then both anchors caught at the same time. The bows came sharply around to starboard, the ship listed about fifteen degrees, and then the stern followed.

At first McGarvey thought that the engines driving the ship forward would sail the boat around her anchors and break free, but it didn't happen. Instead the Spirit came to a new heading, nearly back the way they had come, and then shuddered as she balanced between the anchors dug into port and starboard somewhere aft.

McGarvey pocketed the walkie-talkie, grabbed the machine pistol, and then started for the door. But he stopped. The bridge communications and navigation equipment had been destroyed, but a telephone-type handset hanging from a clip above the helm seemed to be intact. The panel beside it contained a small digital display with a selection switch beside it. The display showed Grand Salon. The phone was the ship's intercom.

He went back and dialed through the selections to Public Address, pulled the phone down from the hook, and pressed the Push-to-Talk switch. He wanted everybody aboard the ship to hear him.

"I'm coming," he said. He could hear his amplified voice somewhere aft. "I'm coming right now, and no one will help you. Not bin Laden, not even Allah."

McGarvey put the phone back, then raised his gun to the anchor control panel and fired two short bursts, totally destroying the mechanism. The anchors were down, and they would stay down long enough for him to do his job.

THIRTEEN

□

People throughout the Grand Salon were still picking themselves up after the ship suddenly lurched and heeled to starboard when McGarvey's warning came over the public address system.

The instant he'd heard the anchors dropping, Khalil braced himself in anticipation that people and things would get tossed around when the ship came to an abrupt stop, her engines still producing full power. He glanced over at where Kathleen McGarvey had also braced herself, helping Shaw and his wife to hold on as well. Khalil's eyes met Katy's, and she offered him another grim smile, as if to say she had warned them.

Khalil's rage threatened to rise up and blot out all sanity, but he returned her smile instead, the almost inhuman effort causing sweat to pop out on his forehead. He had been raised to accept the Muslim fundamentalist philosophy that although women were not second-class citizens as they were portrayed to be by the West, they occupied a different place in Allah's scheme for the world. Women organized and ran the home, while men organized and ran the world. It was a simple division of labor set down more than ten centuries ago by Allah's prophet Muhammad.

Men were strong, and women were silent. Sons were of inestimable value, while daughters were a burden upon a family. Especially if they grew up not knowing or understanding their place.

Like Western women. Especially American women. Especially this woman.

Khalil raised his pistol and pointed it directly at Katy's face. She didn't flinch, nor did she avert her eyes. It was as if she was almost daring him to fire.

Taunting him with failure in front of his men.

Khalil lowered his pistol, turned, threw his head back, and laughed out loud as if he had heard the most amusing thing in his life. "One man," he said in English for the benefit of the passengers. "Apparently he has delusions of grandeur." He shook his head. "Well, I for one can scarcely wait until he shows up here. If he has the courage. Although we've already seen what his real mettle is. After he killed young Ismal, he did not stay to fight. Instead, he turned and ran away like a mouse."

Some of Khalil's operators laughed uncertainly, but their eyes kept darting to the door as if they expected McGarvey to burst into the Grand Salon spraying the room with gunfire.

Khalil looked at his watch. There were less than thirteen minutes remaining. He used his walkie-talkie to call the engine room. "The anchors have been released. Can you raise them from there?"

"I don't think so," Pahlawan came back. "The motors are forward behind the chain lockers. What happened?"

"It doesn't matter," Khalil said. "Never mind the anchors; we are leaving on schedule. Is everything in readiness down there?"

"We'll shut down the engines and set the switches."

"Be quick about it," Khalil said. "When you're finished, we'll meet on the aft deck But keep alert. Our uninvited troublemaker is armed."

Pahlawan laughed. "He is just one man. If you do not want to shoot him, I will."

Khalil's rage rose up again like a tidal wave. One of his operators, a worried look on his young, narrow face, came across the salon, passing the Shaws' table.

"Get back to your position," Khalil told him.

"We need to leave now, Khalil," the young man said. He was frightened.

Kathleen McGarvey heard the exchange; though she tried to hide it, Khalil could see her sudden understanding. She knew his name.

He raised his pistol and shot the operator in the forehead at point-blank range. The young man's head snapped back, and he crumpled dead to the floor.

"*Coward*," Khalil said in Arabic, loudly enough for his operators to hear, but he looked at Kathleen. Still she didn't avert her eyes.

He keyed his walkie-talkie and called the purser's office. "McGarvey is on the bridge. Go up there and kill him. You have twelve minutes to do that and get back of the aft deck."

"*Insha'allah*," the operator said.

"McGarvey can listen to my orders because he has one of our walkie-talkies," Khalil told his people genially, as if nothing had happened. He made a hand motion to a pair of his men. "But he cannot hear what is being said in this room as I speak now. He knows that someone is coming up from the purser's office to kill him, and he will set a trap. What he cannot know is that Said and Achmed will be waiting for him in the starboard and port stairwells just below the sundeck. When he shows himself, he will die."

The two men Khalil named went to the salon doors, held up for just a moment to make sure that the corridor was clear, and then slipped out.

"Do not fail," Khalil called after them.

He turned again to face Kathleen and the others. An ominous silence had fallen over the Grand Salon. There wasn't a person in the room who believed that the terrorist was sane, but everyone had a great deal of fear of him. He could see it in their eyes, and in the way they held themselves in postures of respect and deference.

Except for McGarvey's wife, who continued to defy him. But once she was safely aboard the cargo vessel steaming away from the West Coast, she would begin to learn a very bitter lesson: Even the high and mighty were vulnerable.

Khalil's plan, which had been worked out in detail over the past nine months, was perfect. It even took into account a whole host of unpredictable factors, such as the weather, mechanical breakdowns, accidents, even the heroics of a crew-member or passenger as they were faced with now. McGarvey was a dangerous man, but he was only one man after all.

"You're getting a little low on troops, aren't you?" Kathleen said.

Khalil couldn't figure her out. Was she actually trying to goad him into shooting her? Or did his promise that he was taking her with Shaw make her feel so safe that she thought she was invulnerable? Was she trying to make him angry so that he would start making stupid, spur-of-the-moment decisions?

There had been many women in his life: mother, sisters, aunts, cousins, lovers. But none like this singular female. In truth he might be doing McGarvey a favor by killing her.

He glanced around the salon. He had five men left up here. Thin, but not dangerously so.

"Be thankful that I do not agree with you. If I did, I would order my men to kill some of the passengers to even the odds."

Kathleen's lips started to form a word, but then she shook her head, finally turning away.

Khalil turned on his heel, strode across to the table where the older couple and their daughter with the infant were seated. He dragged the younger woman, who was still clutching her child, to her feet.

"All passengers will be taken belowdecks, where you will be locked up. If you cooperate, no one else will get hurt. Within an hour or so the Coast Guard will come around to see why this ship has stopped in mid-channel, and you will be rescued."

"What about our daughter and granddaughter?" the old man asked with none of his earlier arrogance.

"She and the child will be killed if you and the others do not cooperate," Khalil replied with cold indifference, and he led the unresisting woman back to the Shaws' table. "On your feet," he told them. Kathleen took the young mother and child in hand, as Karen Shaw helped her husband get up.

Khalil motioned for Zahir Majiid and Abdul Adani, who came to him. "Zahir and I will take these four and the infant to the aft deck. As soon as we're out of here, Abdul will take the passengers below. If anyone resists, kill them. But be quick about it."

Adani nodded. This was part of the carefully rehearsed plan.

Zahir went first to the doors and checked the corridor. He turned back and gave the all-clear sign, and Khalil herded the former SecDef, Kathleen, and the others across the Grand Salon and out into the corridor; it was frigidly cold because the port and starboard doors out to the deck had been left open.

"Unless you mean to freeze us to death, we'll need coats or at least blankets," Kathleen said.

Khalil ignored her.

Zahir checked the starboard door, and again gave the all-clear sign. Khalil prodded Kathleen in her back with the muzzle of his machine pistol. "Move."

Kathleen turned on her heel and glared up at him. "Do not poke me with that thing again," she warned through clenched teeth.

"I would like to use you as a hostage, but believe me, you are not necessary to my plans," Khalil told her. "Move, or I will shoot you."

She was stalling, of course, to give her husband time to come to her rescue. But it wouldn't work.

Behind them in the Grand Salon, Adani or one of the other terrorists fired a short burst. Several people screamed or shouted in fear, and there was a great deal of commotion as one of the terrorists stepped out into the corridor and the seventy-plus passengers began jostling out after him.

Kathleen wanted to go back to help comfort them, especially some of the elderly passengers for whom this was a horrible nightmare that they simply could not comprehend. But the baby in the young mother's arms began to cry, and Khalil shoved the woman toward the open door to the starboard passageway where the wind was howling fiercely.

Suddenly Kathleen was no longer sure how this was going to turn out. Her husband was very good, but he was only one man.

She slowly turned away from the unfolding drama behind her, and allowed herself to be herded out on deck into the gale, and then aft toward the back of the ship and whatever awaited them there.

Like animals to the slaughter.

FOURTEEN

☐

McGarvey waited around the corner from the starboard stairwell on the bridge deck just aft of the Shaws' stateroom.

One man was coming up from the purser's office to take him out. But the terrorist leader had given the order via walkie-talkie, which he knew McGarvey was monitoring. It was crude, but obviously they were trying to set a trap for him.

If he took out the lone terrorist, at least two others would be waiting somewhere between here and the Grand Salon for him to show up. They meant to catch him in a crossfire.

But he kept thinking about the elapsing time on the terrorist's watch. The countdown to whatever was about to happen was under twelve minutes now.

And he kept thinking about Katy.

Time was on nobody's side. Especially not his.

On top of that the terrorists had several other advantages: their superior numbers and weaponry, and the passengers as shields and hostages.

But they had targeted Katy, and that was a very large mistake.

He crossed the corridor to the stairwell where he held up. Someone was coming up the steps in a big hurry, his footfalls heavy. The man from the purser's office. The one who was supposed to die so that the trap could be sprung.

McGarvey flattened against the bulkhead behind the door and waited until the terrorist reached the landing and stopped. He could imagine the man peering through the window in the door to make sure the corridor was empty. The terrorist might not want to go up against an armed man; unarmed passengers were much easier to deal with. But he had his orders.

The door slowly came open, and the terrorist stepped out into the corridor, sweeping his machine pistol to the left, when McGarvey took one step forward and popped the young man at the base of his skull with the butt of the RAK. The terrorist dropped to the floor like a felled ox.

For just a second McGarvey could feel hatred rise up from his gut, like bitter bile at the back of his throat. It would be so easy to fire one round into the back of the young man's head and end his miserable life here and now. If the terrorist wanted to reach Paradise as a martyr, why not help him along?

Who would know what really happened up here? And who would care?

McGarvey hurriedly dragged the unconscious man around the corner, out of sight from anyone emerging from the stairwell. Then he took the terrorist's weapons and walkie-talkie, and turned and sprinted back down the corridor, where he let himself out onto the open deck, closing and latching the door behind him with as little noise as possible.

It would take the hijackers only a minute or two to figure out that the terrorist from the purser's office was taking too long to report back. But by the time someone realized that McGarvey had made an end run, it would be too late.

He slung his RAK muzzle down by its strap over his shoulder so that it was centered on his back, then went to the starboard rail and tossed the terrorist's weapons and walkie-talkie overboard. Although it had mercifully stopped raining, the wind was on their starboard quarter, blowing at least twenty-five knots and bitterly cold. The sky was cloud-covered, and there was almost nothing to see except for the flashing red buoy bouncing around about a hundred yards ahead.

The Spirit, whose motion was lively as it balanced under full power between the two anchors, suddenly steadied out, as if it had broken free. Almost immediately McGarvey realized that the engines had been shut down. He could no longer feel the deep, low-frequency vibration on the soles of his feet.

The terrorists were getting set to abandon ship. Some of them might have already been aboard when the Spirit left Juneau but some of them must have come aboard earlier this evening. Probably from a chase boat that had been waiting in some cove along the Inside Passage; an approaching floatplane or helicopter would have made too much noise. Somebody would have heard it. Boarding a moving ship in this kind of weather would have been dicey. Getting off would be no worse, even though the ship was bucking and heaving against her anchors.

He leaned well out over the rail, but he couldn't see anything aft. If there was a chase boat, it was either standing off in the darkness, or it was hidden by the bulk of the hull at the stern.

But they were taking Shaw with them and he was precious cargo, so they had shut down the engines to steady out the motion. They didn't want to lose him.

The problem was, who else were they taking off the ship?

And the other problem was his nearly uncontrollable anger. He could see the expression in bin Laden's eyes, hear the tone of his voice saying that every non-Muslim—men, women, children—were fair game for murder.

McGarvey climbed over the rail, dangled there for just a moment, then swung himself inward and dropped down to the upper deck, landing off-balance with more noise than he'd wanted to make.

He pulled out the Steyr pistol he'd taken from the terrorist in the radio room and scrambled into the deeper shadows to see if someone would come to investigate. He almost wished that someone would come.

Except for the wind there were no noises.

He eased around the corner and made his way to the forward extremity of the upper deck. Directly above was the bridge; below were the Grand Salon and the open-bow viewing area where on good days passengers gathered to watch the passing scenery and wildlife.

Big windows in the Grand Salon's forward bulkhead opened onto the viewing area. Anyone jumping from the deck above would be visible for just a moment as they dropped. But the bow area was in darkness, and the terrorists' attention would be directed toward the passengers.

In any event there was no time to consider any other alternative.

McGarvey climbed over the rail and jumped. This time he landed solidly, but without making a sound. He ducked below the level of the windows, unslung the RAK, switched the safety lever to off, and crab-walked the five feet to the starboard door. He rose up, intending only to take a quick peek through the window and to then duck down. But he stopped.

The Grand Salon was apparently empty of any living thing. The room had become a killing ground, as he feared it would.

He yanked open the door and rushed in, sweeping his weapon left to right in case any of the hijackers had anticipated his arrival, but stopped again. There was nothing here except for corpses and blood—blood in pools under the dozen or more bodies, splashed across tables, some of which had been overturned, up against the bulkheads, and along the buffet serving line and service bar.

Katy wasn't among the bodies, nor were the Shaws, but there was some blood on the tablecloth at the former SecDef's place.

McGarvey almost turned to go when he spotted a tiny pencil with a gold cap lying beside Katy's napkin. He went back and picked it up. It was her eyebrow pencil. She had left it on the table for some reason.

She'd been trying to tell him something.

He lifted the napkin. Beneath it, written on the tablecloth was one word: KHALIL.

Like Carlos the Jackal in the sixties and seventies, Khalil was just a work name. He was a man who the Western intelligence agencies considered to be the real brains behind most of the successful Islamic fundamentalist attacks against the West. No photographs of him existed in the West, nor were the CIA, FBI, or British SIS even sure of his nationality.

What everyone did agree upon, however, was that Khalil was as deadly and merciless as he was elusive. No one who had ever come up against him lived to tell about the encounter. The attacks of 9/11 were probably his doing, but they were only the most recent and most infamous of his operations, which stretched back at least twenty years.

Currently the U.S. was offering a twenty-five-million-dollar reward for his capture dead or alive. In the two years since the reward had been posted, there had been no takers; in fact, there hadn't even been one inquiry.

Except for Katy's earring this operation would probably have gone off exactly the way Khalil had planned it. No one knew that the director of Central Intelligence would be aboard, nor could anyone have predicted the business with one passenger's earring. It was nothing but pure, dumb luck.

And McGarvey planned on telling Khalil that his luck had run out. Nothing would give him more pleasure.

Where were the passengers?

McGarvey went to the back of the room and checked Grassinger's pulse. His bodyguard was dead, as was Shaw's. They had tried to do their jobs, but they'd simply been outnumbered.

Their deaths he could understand. And Shaw's kidnapping made sense from the terrorists' viewpoint. But why kill passengers? Innocent men and women?

Osama bin Laden had tried to explain that reasoning to him in a cave in Afghanistan before 9/11. But what he said about no one being innocent made no more sense now than it did then. In McGarvey's estimation, Islamic fundamentalists by very definition were little more than rabid animals snapping at anything that moved, trying to tear down anything that didn't square with their own brand of radicalism, their own horribly misguided take on a fine religion.

He stood up and took a quick look into the corridor. There was no one there, but the starboard door to the outside passageway was open.

He ducked back for a second. Khalil had taken Shaw and possibly Katy as hostages and was holding them in the stern of the ship. There were outside stairs down to the main deck, where a small boat was probably waiting to take them off. In the meantime the passengers had most likely been led below and locked in the galley, or possibly the dry-storage pantries, to keep them out of the way. For the moment then Khalil's forces were divided.

But it was the countdown that bothered him. There were less than ten minutes remaining. *For what?* He had a lot of ideas, but none of them were very comforting.

McGarvey checked the load on his RAK and stepped out of the Grand Salon, intending to cross the corridor and take the inside stairs down to the main deck, when someone fired from the door to the men's bathroom ten feet to the right, spraying the deck and bulkheads.

Instinctively, McGarvey fell back while firing a short burst down the corridor in the general direction of the shooter. The terrorists were a lot smarter than he thought they were. They'd expected him to return to the Grand Salon, and they'd simply waited for him to show up.

All that went through his brain in a flash. Dropping to the deck as he spun around, he fired toward the front of the room as one of Khalil's men came through the portside door from the bow viewing area, where he had apparently been waiting to catch McGarvey in a crossfire.

The man shouted something in Arabic and fired another long burst toward the back of the room, the bullets smacking into the bulkhead.

McGarvey rose up on one knee and fired two single shots, both catching the man squarely in the chest, knocking him backward into the piano.

The RAK was out of ammunition. McGarvey ejected the spent magazine, pulled the spare out of his belt, and was about to shove it into the pistol grip when the terrorist who'd fired down the corridor rushed into the Grand Salon.

He didn't see McGarvey crouched against the bulkhead to his right. His attention was directed toward his dead comrade at the front of the room.

It was all the opening that McGarvey needed. He dove forward, catching the younger man at hip level, bowling the hijacker over, the man's head bouncing off the carpeted deck. McGarvey had dropped his RAK, and he pulled the Steyr pistol out of his belt, cocked the hammer, and jammed the muzzle into the man's neck just below his chin.

"What happens in ten minutes?" McGarvey demanded.

The terrorist's eyes were bulging. He shook his head.

"Ten minutes. There's a countdown. What's going to happen—"

The terrorist got one hand free. He grasped for the pistol, and McGarvey fired one shot, the bullet spiraling up from beneath the man's chin and plowing into his brain.

There was no time. The single thought crystallized in McGarvey's head as he got to his feet, crossed the corridor, and started downstairs to the stern observation area on the main deck.

FIFTEEN

At the stern rail, Khalil cocked an ear to listen to what he thought sounded like gunfire from somewhere forward and above. But he wasn't sure. Although the ship's engines were silent, the wind howling around the superstructure was almost as loud as a jet engine.

A full gale was developing, and he was beginning to worry about getting back to the island airport, and about the ability of their bush pilot to lift off.

He peered over the rail. Mohamed had eased the *Nancy N.* close enough so that the boarding ladder reached the foredeck. She rode fairly easily in the lee of the *Spirit*.

But time was running out.

Shaw and his wife were huddled together, and Kathleen McGarvey was holding the young woman and infant closely to conserve body heat in the sharp cold.

Pahlawan and his assistant had come up from the engine room without spotting McGarvey. Abdul Adani and his three people came up the aft stairs a minute later.

"The passengers are securely locked below," Adani reported. "*They were as so many sheep,*" he added in Arabic, which drew a few chuckles from the men.

"What will happen to them?" Katy demanded.

"Why nothing at all, if your husband does not interfere with our orderly departure," Khalil told her. He thought of the things that he would teach her once they were away from here. She would not be happy, but she would be amazed.

In addition to the one man who'd been standing lookout in Soapy's Parlor with the dead poker players, Khalil had a force of eight operators back here, plus Mohamed aboard the *Nancy N.*, out of the fifteen he'd started with. But every mission had its casualties. It was to be expected. And in the end, McGarvey was just one man, for whom time had just about expired.

Khalil could not remember the name of the boy he'd sent to the purser's office and then to the bridge deck to intercept McGarvey. But there was a much better than even chance he was already dead.

He had served his purpose, as all of Allah's soldiers of God must.

He keyed the walkie-talkie. "Achmed, it is time."

With the boy from the purser's office to draw him off, McGarvey would have walked into a trap in the vicinity of the Grand Salon. Khalil almost wished he could have been up there to participate in the killing. But there were other more interesting pleasures to contemplate.

Impatiently he keyed the walkie-talkie again. "Achmed, report. It is time to leave the ship."

There was no answer.

He and Said should have dealt with McGarvey by now. The first glimmerings of doubt began to enter Khalil's mind. He worked out in his head what McGarvey could have deduced given the information at hand and the man's experience.

"Have you misplaced even more of your toy soldiers?" Katy asked, sweetly. "I did warn you." She turned to the other hijackers. "Release us, and then get out of here while you still can."

Khalil resisted the nearly overpowering urge to smash a fist into her face, to wipe away the smug *Western* expression he'd seen on so many other faces, especially on those of intelligence officers who thought they were coming in for the arrest when in fact they were coming to their deaths.

McGarvey knew that a trap had been set for him. He knew they would expect him to return to the Grand Salon, where he had last seen his wife.

Khalil suddenly knew. McGarvey was right here, probably within a couple of meters.

He drew his Steyr pistol, grabbed Katy away from the young woman and child, and placed the muzzle of his pistol against Katy's temple. "Mr. McGarvey, won't you come out and join us?" he called out over the shriek of the wind.

"Kirk, no!" Katy shouted.

"I can't miss from here," McGarvey said from the darkness somewhere above.

Pahlawan spotted him first, on the stern viewing area one deck up. He raised his RAK, but Khalil stopped him with a head gesture.

"Neither can I miss at this distance," Khalil said, pulling Katy closer.

"Frankly, what do we have to lose?" McGarvey asked. "If I lay down my weapon and surrender, you will kill me and my wife. My way, we have a chance."

"What if I give you my word that no harm will come to either of you?" Khalil countered. "We only took your wife as hostage to neutralize you. All we want is Shaw."

"Get on your boat, just you and your men; get away from here, and I will let you live. For now. There has been enough killing tonight. These are innocent people—"

"There are no innocents," Khalil said. "Toss the woman and child overboard," he told Pahlawan.

"You bastard, no!" Katy cried. She tried to pull away from him, but he was much stronger than she was, and he held her very close, the muzzle of the pistol jammed into her temple.

"Don't you do it!" McGarvey admonished.

"Watch me," Khalil shot back.

Pahlawan pulled the young woman and child to the rail. Shaw tried to break away from his wife to go to their aid, but one of the terrorists butted him in the gut with a RAK, knocking him back.

The young woman had no idea what was going on, but she was very frightened and she tried to pull away from the bull-like hijacker. But it was no use. Pahlawan scooped her and the infant up in his arms, lifted them over the rail, and dropped them the seven or eight feet into the freezing black water.

"No!" Katy screamed.

"Next will be Mrs. Shaw," Khalil called up to McGarvey. "Then, if need be, your wife will go into the water. After that we will hunt you down." Khalil shrugged, as if he were merely discussing tomorrow's weather. "It is your choice. But we will prevail."

SIXTEEN

□

McGarvey raced forward along the starboard walkway out of sight of Khalil and his people, kicked off his shoes, laid the RAK on the deck, climbed over the rail, and jumped.

The water was unbelievably cold. The shock took his breath away as he plunged several feet under the surface, and he came back up sputtering. Within a few minutes anyone in the water would start to lose their ability to kick or move their arms so that they could keep afloat. A few minutes after that, hypothermia would be so advanced that the swimmer would lose consciousness. And finally their heart would stop.

The effects came much faster for someone with a small body mass, such as a young, slender woman or, worse yet, an infant.

Staying within reach of the hull, McGarvey set out for the stern of the ship, where the mother and child had gone overboard. The angle of the ship's hard chine offered him some protection from a shooter on deck, but not from someone on the bow of the smaller boat that was attached to the Spirit's stern by a towing bridle.

If the cruise ship had not been resting at anchor, any rescue attempt would have been futile. As it was, a fairly fast tidal current was running, only slightly counteracted by the strong northerly wind, and a vicious two-foot chop marched whitecaps down the narrow Frederick Sound.

A woman's weak voice cried out in the darkness ten yards or so off to McGarvey's right. It was the young mother. She had drifted away from the stern and away from the protection of the flaring hull.

He could not see her, but he struck out in the direction of her cries.

Someone shouted something in Arabic from above on the starboard lounge deck where McGarvey had left his shoes and the RAK.

Now they knew that he was in the water.

The ship still showed all her running lights, so Khalil and his men on the stern platform were at a disadvantage for seeing anyone in the water. They were lit as if onstage. McGarvey looked back over his shoulder. There were a lot of people up there. He spotted Shaw and his wife, and Katy, who had gone to them. The tallest of the terrorists was Khalil. He was giving orders to his people, some of whom were starting down the ladder that dangled onto the bow of the small fishing boat.

McGarvey considered using the Steyr pistol stuck in his belt to try for a headshot on Khalil. If he could take out the terrorist leader, perhaps the others would fold their tents and get the hell out.

But considering his precarious position, there was the very real possibility that he would miss, and the further possibility that no matter what happened, Katy, Shaw, and the former SecDef's wife would be gunned down in retaliation for a mission spoiled by the director of Central Intelligence.

The young mother's screams were already becoming weaker as the cold water affected her. She was crying a name, "Brian" or perhaps "baby"; it was very difficult to understand her.

One of the hijackers from the ship suddenly opened fire in the general direction of the woman's feeble cries. The bullets peppered the water a few yards ahead and to the left of McGarvey. The poor woman did not realize that the terrorists could not see her; they were shooting in the blind. If she stopped crying, they would have no idea where she was.

They had thrown the woman and child overboard, and now they were shooting at them. What manner of animals were they?

The cold was beginning to seep into McGarvey's bones. He could feel that his coordination was falling apart, and already he was having trouble thinking straight. He would not last long in the water.

The woman was suddenly there to his right. He could see her blond hair floating on the water. She was splashing with her hands, as if she were shooing away flies, but slowly, aimlessly.

McGarvey had nearly reached her when the yellow beam of a powerful small light slashed across the water from aft of the bow of the small fishing boat. Whoever was aboard had switched on a handheld halogen spotlight and was searching the water.

The woman looked up, desperately hoping that someone was coming to her rescue. She managed to raise her right hand in the air when the spotlight found her and stopped.

"Brian," she cried, her voice so low as to be nothing more than a whisper.

McGarvey could see that she no longer had the infant with her. She'd probably lost her hold on the child when she'd first hit the water. At this point there was absolutely no hope for the baby.

The bastards. This fight had become personal the moment they'd manhandled Katy. But now, seeing what depths they were capable of sinking to, his resolve to hit back rose ten thousand percent.

"There she is, Mr. McGarvey," Khalil's voice came across the water.

The stern was in the lee of the waves, the bulk of the cruise liner creating a wind shadow of relative calm.

McGarvey was within a few strokes of the woman as she began to flail weakly, her head sinking beneath the surface. She popped back up, but just for a moment. She was on the verge of drowning.

"Come to her rescue, Mr. McGarvey," Khalil called.

"Kirk," Katy screamed.

One of the terrorists opened fire on the young woman.

McGarvey dove beneath the surface, and in a couple of powerful strokes came up behind the young mother, bullets splashing the water all around them. He clamped his left hand over her nose and mouth, dragged her beneath the surface, and swam directly toward the stern of the boat.

For the first few feet she fought against him, but then her body went slack. He couldn't tell if she had lost consciousness or had simply given up the fight, given up the will to live. But with bullets smacking into the water above, he could not risk surfacing. Not until they had come under the flare of the ship's hull.

After that he had only a vague idea about getting the woman back aboard the ship and stashing her someplace out of the wind and out of harm's way so that he could continue his fight to save his wife.

It was becoming increasingly difficult to keep on track.

The ship's hull loomed up in front of him like a huge black wall, and McGarvey surfaced, willing himself to stay focused. He took his hand away from the woman's mouth and nose. She took a deep, blubbering breath and then another and another.

He held her head above water by the collar of her sodden blouse, while he tried to figure out where they'd come up. They were about thirty feet forward of the stern. He could just make out the starboard anchor chain angling away from the bow, an impossibly long way forward against the wind-driven chop. But at this point it was the only way aboard.

The woman slipped away from his grasp. He turned but she was gone. At first he thought she had lost consciousness and slipped under the water, and he dove for her. But when he came up, he heard her feeble voice already fifteen or twenty yards back the way they had come.

"Brian," she cried. She was going back for her baby.

The hijackers at the stern heard her cries the same moment McGarvey did. The beam of the halogen spotlight from the small fishing boat stabbed the water to her left. It swept right and had her almost immediately.

She stopped and looked up into the light. "Brian?" she cried.

Someone on the stern of the cruise ship opened fire. At least half a dozen bullets slammed into the poor woman, killing her instantly, driving her riddled body beneath the whitecaps.

Even before the beam of the spotlight started a grid pattern search, centered on where the young woman went down, McGarvey had turned and headed forward toward the starboard anchor chain.

Revenge, pure, sweet, and simple, like the bright flame of a blast furnace, flared deep within his soul. Only Khalil's death would quench the fire.

SEVENTEEN

"Is there any sign of him?" Kahlil called down to the bow of the *Nancy N.*

"No, just the woman. But he's out there, I can feel it," Zahir warned. "It's time to leave."

Khalil glanced at his wristwatch.

It was *past* their time to leave. In less than four minutes the explosives that Pahlawan and his people had placed in strategic locations deep in the ship's bilges would automatically arm themselves. From that moment the *Spirit* would be a gigantic bomb waiting for a hair trigger to send her to the bottom.

According to his chief engineer almost anything could set the charges off: a stray electrical current, a radio signal from a nearby ship or an airplane passing overhead. There were safeties on the triggers. But nothing was perfect.

The moment the explosives were armed, anyone left aboard the cruise ship would be in immediate danger.

All because of one man.

"No one could survive that long in this water," Pahlawan said. "At the very least the motherless whore is incapacitated."

"You'd better hope he's dead or incapacitated," Katy said softly. She was shivering violently, in part from the cold and in part because she'd witnessed the brutal murders of the young mother and her infant son.

Khalil looked at Katy. She was still defiant, against all odds, and he found that he could almost admire her mujahideen strength and courage. She was unlike any woman he'd ever known. Fascinating and dangerous.

The sooner she was dead and her body destroyed so that it would never be found, the sooner he would breathe easy.

"Very well. We'll start them down now," he told Pahlawan. "Mr. Shaw first." He leaned over the rail to Zahir. "Keep a sharp watch. I want no further surprises."

Katy was staring intently at him, as if something had just occurred to her. "You're speaking in English." She looked at the other terrorists. "Why?"

Shaw stopped at the rail and turned back, a look of defiance on his face. "They're trying to prove they're not as stupid as we know they are."

Khalil raised his pistol to smash the former SecDef in the head, and Katy stepped away from Karen Shaw before any of the terrorists could stop her. She grabbed Khalil's gun hand, and pulled him around.

"Try me, you bastard," she shouted.

Khalil looked down at her like he might have been seeing a disagreeable bug at his feet.

"You like to beat up helpless people. Kill innocent women and children," Katy said into his face. "Try me; why don't you?"

He reached out with his free hand and took her throat. Before he could squeeze the life out of her, she drove her knee into his groin with every ounce of her strength.

All the air left him in an explosive gasp. He released his hold on her neck and stepped back a pace. His face was red in the dim illumination of the stern observation deck. All his men watched him. Looking for a sign of weakness. Looking for a lack of resolve.

Harden your heart if you wish to avenge the sacrilege. The gates of Paradise are not for the weak of spirit.

The sharp pain deep inside his body between his hips was not as unbearable as the thought of failure.

"Now, go ahead and do your thing if it makes you feel like a man," Katy said. There was a great deal of fear in her eyes, but even more resolve in her voice.

Before Khalil could raise his pistol, the engineer Pahlawan shoved Shaw aside and came for Katy.

"Over the side with you—" he said, when a pistol shot came from the darkness one deck above. A small black hole appeared in his forehead, and he fell back dead.

Before anyone could react, another shot came from above, the bullet ricocheting off the deck inches from where Khalil stood.

"Everyone settle down," McGarvey's authoritative voice called out from one deck up.

One of the terrorists broke left, trying for the protection of the overhang.

"Yu'af," stop, McGarvey shouted in Arabic.

The man started to raise his RAK when McGarvey fired one shot, catching him in the side of his head, knocking him to the deck.

Everyone on deck stopped in his tracks.

"No one else except for Khalil need die tonight," McGarvey said. "But everyone else must leave right now."

To every operation came the dénouement, as the French called it, the moment at which the operation's success or failure was assured. Beyond that point it became fruitless to try to change the inevitable outcome. In the case of failure the only option was an orderly retreat, with covering fire if possible.

From his pocket Khalil took a small electronic device—what looked like a cell phone or a television remote control—and held it up for McGarvey to see. "I push the button, and the bottom of the ship blows out. All the passengers locked below will die." His voice was strained because of the pain in his groin.

"Jesus, Mary, and Joseph," Katy said softly, "you're nuts."

"Dedicated," Khalil corrected her. "What do you say, Mr. McGarvey: the lives of the passengers, including your wife, for the safe passage off this ship for myself, my operators, and Secretary Shaw?"

"No hostages. Get off this ship now."

"You won't risk the lives of the passengers—"

McGarvey fired two shots in rapid succession, one buzzing off the deck a few inches to Khalil's left, the other to his right. "Don't tempt me, because I sincerely want to meet you again. Soon."

Khalil didn't think the CIA director had it in him, but McGarvey had to play it up for the sake of his wife, who was an extraordinary woman. "Very well," Khalil said, "it is a fair trade, for now. But you're right; we will meet again, and I will kill you."

"Go."

Khalil turned to Katy and gave her a polite nod. "You will look good in black, madam."

He turned and climbed down the boarding ladder to the bow of the *Nancy N.*, where he brushed aside Zahir's helping hand. "As soon as the rest of our people are aboard, get us out of here," he said, and he made his way aft and below.

EIGHTEEN

McGarvey appeared on the aft observation platform at the same moment the small fishing boat peeled away from the *Spirit*, and Katy flew into his arms. She shivered almost uncontrollably from the cold, from the horror she had witnessed, and now from the sudden letdown.

"I thought they had killed you in the water," she sobbed. "My God, I didn't know how I could go on."

For several long seconds McGarvey stared at the retreating fishing boat. He wouldn't put it past them to circle around and attack again. They had come for Shaw, and they had not only left without him, but they had also lost a significant number of their people. But he felt as if he had failed here tonight, because a lot of the passengers and probably most of the crew had been gunned down in cold blood.

Worst of all was the young mother and her infant son. The woman's screams would never leave that dark corner of his brain where his most terrible memories lived.

"Are you okay, Katy?" McGarvey asked, afraid to give voice to his worst fear. "Is the baby all right?"

"I think so," she said, looking up at him in wide-eyed wonderment.

"You have to be strong for just a little while longer," he told her. "I have to go below and get the passengers out."

"What can we do?" Donald Shaw asked. He was too old for this, and his injuries were slowing him down, but he was tough and he hadn't given up.

"Find the controls for the lifeboats, pull off as many of the covers as you can, and get ready to abandon ship."

Shaw's lips compressed to a thin line. "You think he's going to push the button?"

"Yes," McGarvey said. He gave his wife a last, reassuring look, then turned and headed belowdecks, not sure how much time remained. But the count on the terrorist's wristwatch in the radio shack was at zero. Whatever was going to happen would happen at any moment.

Compromising with the terrorists, allowing them to leave the cruise ship alive, had gone against nearly every fiber of McGarvey's being. He'd told himself that Khalil would push the button once he was in the clear, but in the delay perhaps some of the passengers' lives could be saved. Had he put a bullet into Khalil's brain there was a very good possibility the man would have pushed the button as his last dying act.

Time was all they needed. Just a few minutes . . . five minutes and he would have the passengers topside.

Provided he could find them.

McGarvey stood on the catwalk at the head of the stairs that led down to the engine room, the big diesels quiet now. Only the auxiliary generators one compartment forward were still operating, supplying electrical power to the ship.

But the engine room, where he thought the passengers might have been locked up, was empty except for the bodies of at least three of the legitimate crew.

Adding these to the passengers and crew the terrorists had killed in the Grand Salon, plus those on the bridge and in the radio room, and probably in the galley and crew's quarters, there were about fifty corpses littering the ship. In addition, there were the mother and her infant son in the water.

That left at least one hundred passengers and crew members still unaccounted for, and there weren't that many spaces aboard the *Spirit* that were large enough to accommodate them all. The Grand Salon, the Klondike Dining Room, here in the engine room. Or the crew's mess, which was probably somewhere forward, most likely below the galley.

McGarvey turned. Standing on the catwalk above the engine room, he was two levels below the main deck. He raced back the way he had come, taking the stairs two at a time to the next deck up. Emerging from the stairwell, he found himself in a long, dimly lit, narrow corridor that ran forward at least one-third the length of the ship, ending at a T intersection. Doors along the length of the corridor indicated that it was probably the crew's quarters.

Superconscious of the ticking clock, he raced past them to the intersection where the corridor split left and right. He hesitated for only a moment before he took the right passageway. The bulkheads here were plain painted steel with firefighting equipment in alcoves, and the overhead was laced with tubing and electrical conduits, all marked with stenciled legends, much the same as aboard a naval vessel.

The corridor jogged left: then thirty feet farther, it opened to a broad intersection with stairs leading up, and corridors branching forward and port. Double steel doors marked Crew's Mess were across from the stairs. A steel chain was looped around the door handles and secured with a stout padlock.

McGarvey banged on the door with the butt of his pistol. "Is anyone in there?"

He thought he heard a sound, as if someone were standing just on the other side of the door.

"The hijackers are gone. My name is McGarvey. I'm a friend."

"We're here," a man called from within. "I'm Third Officer Mark Hansen. Both doors seemed to be jammed."

"This one's chained and padlocked. How many are you?"

"One hundred eighteen, passengers and crew. Some of them are in bad shape."

"Hold on, Mr. Hansen, I'm going to get you out of there. But we have to get to the lifeboats as quickly as possible. Get your people organized. And see if you can find some flashlights, life jackets, anything else you can use."

"Yes, sir."

McGarvey had one bullet left in the Steyr, but even a 9mm round would have little or no effect on the padlock.

He stuffed the pistol in his belt, then turned and hurried back the way he had come, to the first fire-emergency alcove. He broke the glass with his elbow, grabbed the fire ax from its brackets, and rushed back to the crew's mess.

A thump somewhere forward sounded as if the ship had bumped into something. But they were resting at anchor, and the engines were shut down.

Unless a log or some other bit of heavy flotsam had come down on the current and hit the hull.

McGarvey held his breath waiting. A second later another thump came from somewhere deep within the bowels of the ship, followed by a third and fourth. The bastard had triggered the explosives after all.

He swung the ax, sparks flying from the chain holding the doors. He swung again and again, trying to hit the same link.

Already the ship was beginning to sink by the bow, and settle slightly to port.

He swung again, and the ax handle shattered, the heavy steel blade flying off down the corridor. The chain, though damaged, was still intact.

"Hold on, Mr. Hansen, we're almost there," McGarvey shouted. He sprinted back down the corridor toward the engine room, the deck steadily canting forward and to the left.

The next fire-equipment alcove was nearly all the way aft. He busted the glass, this time cutting a good-sized gash in his elbow, grabbed the fire ax from its bracket, and headed back to the crew's mess in a dead run. Downhill now.

He could hear a lot of water rushing into the ship one deck below, and even before he attacked the chain again, water appeared just a few feet down the stairwell.

This time the chain parted on the second blow. He tossed the ax aside, freed the latches, and yanked the doors open.

A young man in the uniform of a ship's officer, his hair disheveled, dried blood on the side of his head, stood there, a grim but determined expression on his narrow features. The room was crammed with people, many of them on the verge of panic, but he and several other officers and crewmen had gotten things well in hand.

"We're sinking," the officer said.

"That's right, Mr. Hansen. Get your people out of here to the starboard deck. Someone's getting the lifeboats ready."

"Somebody will have to stay behind to see to the stragglers."

"I will," McGarvey said. "Now get the hell out of here!"

Hansen handed him a big flashlight. "Someone has tampered with the emergency lights in here," he said. "All right, folks, step smartly now," he shouted to the passengers. "You remember your abandon ship drill. To-night it'll be the starboard boats." He gave McGarvey a last glance. "Good luck, sir."

"I'll be right behind you," McGarvey said.

The deck was down by the bow so steeply that many of the older passengers had to be helped, lest they lose their balance and fall. Third Officer Hansen had his remaining crew people well organized so that the evacuation out of the crew's mess, across the corridor, and up the stairs to the starboard deck proceeded rapidly. No one protested, and best of all there was very little panic, even when water spilled out of the stairwell and began to cover the deck ankle deep.

A big crash somewhere aft was followed immediately by the loss of their electricity. All the lights went out, plunging them into total darkness.

A woman screamed in abject terror, and several people clutched at McGarvey until he got his flashlight on. There were emergency lights in the stairwell leading up, and two of the crewmen with flashlights were out in the corridor directing the passengers through what had rapidly become knee-deep water.

"Calm down!" McGarvey shouted sternly. "There's plenty of time to get to the lifeboats. Just keep moving."

He remained by the doors, herding the people out of the crew's mess and into the waiting hands of the crewmen in the corridor, who handed them off in turn to men on the stairs, like a bucket brigade, only with humans instead of water.

The ship seemed to come back upright on her keel as the downward angle on her bow increased. There hadn't been time to manually close the watertight doors throughout the ship, and apparently the terrorists had sabotaged the automatic controls. In addition to kidnapping Shaw, they'd wanted to kill all the passengers because they could have acted as witnesses. The simplest, most economical way to do that was to lock them belowdecks and sink the ship.

Not this time, McGarvey told himself. *This was not going to be another 9/11.*

The water was chest deep by the time McGarvey handed the last passenger, a man in his early fifties, out to the waiting crewmen; they immediately hustled him upstairs.

A tremendous crash from somewhere aft, probably in the engine room, shook the entire ship as if she were ready to come apart at the seams.

The angle on the bow increased even faster.

"Come on!" the last crewman on the stairs called back, desperately. "She's going."

"Right behind you!" McGarvey shouted. He stopped long enough to sweep the beam of his flashlight around the almost completely submerged crew's mess for any sign of life.

There was no one. He turned and started for the stairs when he heard a faint cry from behind, which was immediately cut off when the level of the water reached the top of the door frame, leaving less than two feet of airspace below the ceiling.

He had to fight his way back, duck under the water, and come up inside the crew's mess.

"Who's here?" he shouted, swinging the beam of his flashlight across the surface of the water, which was choked with floating debris.

"Help me," an old woman cried off to the right.

McGarvey found her in the beam of his flashlight, clinging to a lifejacket, her white hair plastered to her head, her eyes wide with fright. He reached her in a couple of strokes, grabbed her roughly by the back of her dress, and hauled her back to the doorway as the last of the airspace above their heads disappeared.

There was no time to be kind or considerate. The ship was going down right now, and either she would survive the short swim across the corridor and up the stairs to the surface of the water or McGarvey figured he would probably drown with her.

He'd lost his flashlight, and the corridor was in total darkness until he started up the stairwell, when he saw several lights above.

He redoubled his efforts, and seconds later a pair of waiting crewmen dragged him and the old woman out on the starboard main deck, now awash.

They were helped across to the last lifeboat, which immediately backed away from the rapidly sinking cruise ship. Six men manning the oars pulled hard to get them away from the side of the ship that was threatening to roll.

Someone put a blanket over McGarvey's shoulders, and Katy suddenly was there in his arms. "That's twice tonight I thought I'd lost you."

"Not a chance," McGarvey said.

The old woman he'd pulled out of the crew's mess at the last reached over, patted his hand, then gave Katy a weak smile. "Hold on to him, sweetie; otherwise I'll grab him."

Everyone within earshot chuckled.

"It's a deal," Kathleen said.

"She's going," someone said in awe.

Everyone watched in silence as the *Spirit of '98* slipped beneath the black surface of the water—everyone except McGarvey, whose gray-green eyes were turned toward the south, the direction in which the small fishing boat had disappeared into the night.

THE MISSION

Muhamed Abdallah's first view of the wall of mountains rising up behind Denver came that night at sunset, and he pressed the fingers of his right hand against the window glass as if he could reach out and touch the snow-capped peaks that seemed so near and yet so distant.

His bus approached from the east on I-70 after crossing the other-worldly, barren rolling hills of Kansas in the hot afternoon. He had dozed fitfully, waking often in a cold sweat, seeing the Israeli tank that killed his uncle Rafiq, seeing the blood erupting from his body as the heavy-caliber machine-gun bullets tore into his flesh.

On that day the fourteen-year-old Muhamed became a man in the family. Although he did not abandon his studies as his mother feared he would, he did leave her side. The tank attack had sealed his future with more finality than had his inability to secure a student visa to study abroad.

As a young man fighting the Israeli occupation of the West Bank, Muhamed had dreamed of the mountains of Afghanistan where the mujahideen—the real soldiers of God—were trained by Osama bin Laden himself. He never got there. But seeing the American Rockies was almost as inspiring. In some ways they were even more inspiring than the Hindu Kush, because it was here that he would martyr himself for the greater glory of Allah.

It was a weekday and late, but traffic on the interstate was busy, especially the closer they got into the city, so it was midnight by the time they pulled into the large, modern Greyhound Bus depot on Nineteenth Street within blocks of the state capitol building.

Denver was different than Oklahoma City; the streets were narrower here, the air cooler and drier and the ever-present Front Range loomed like a wall on the horizon.

Muhamed carried only a small packsack with a change of socks and underwear, a clean shirt, and his toothbrush and tooth powder, plus the manila envelope with his papers and money. When he got off the bus, he did exactly as he had been instructed. He walked directly through the brightly lit terminal and out onto the street, where he turned left. One block later a dark blue Toyota SUV with tinted windows pulled up to the curb and the back door opened.

It was as if he were drifting through a dreamscape, not the nightmare of his uncle, but rather a waking dream in which the entire world seemed to be in soft focus. All the colors were pastels; all the sounds, even the bass thump of a stereo system in a passing car, were like sweet music;

the air was perfume, the breeze a zephyr, the clouds streaming off the mountaintops like the flowing hair of angels.

Muhamed was a happy boy. He was a soldier of God, one among the truly blessed, and soon his would be the kingdom of Paradise. His father would be proud of him, and his mother would weep tears of joy for his passing.

He climbed in the backseat of the Toyota, and the man in the front passenger seat reached back, closed the door, and stared at him as if he was seeing a god. The driver immediately took off, but his eyes kept darting to Muhamed's image in the rearview mirror, with the same look of respect as the man in the passenger seat.

When Muhamed didn't speak, the passenger cleared his throat. "Welcome to America. We are proud to be of assistance."

He spoke Egyptian Arabic, the most common dialect, and one understood by just about any Arabic speaker. It was flowery by Western standards, but there was a comfort in the rhythms of the ancient language.

"Thank you. How far must thou drive to reach Fort Collins?"

"About one hour," the passenger said. He and the driver were members of the London-based Advice and Reformation Committee that had been created by Osama bin Laden to supposedly further al-Quaida's goal of protecting the holy shrines at Mecca and Medina. The real reason for its existence was to raise money for al-Quaida operations worldwide.

These two men were the fund-raisers and bureaucrats of the organization, not the genuine article like Muhamed, who had actually done battle against the Zionists on the streets of Nablus and in Hell's Bootcamp. And certainly they were not of the material that martyrs were made of.

Muhamed was boss as long as he was here. No matter want he wanted, his word was law. Their instructions were to obey his every command without a single question, without hesitation, no matter how young he was.

"We have a trailer in the hills above the town, near a place called the Horsetooth Reservoir—"

"I would first like to see the target, and then my equipment. Has it arrived?"

The passenger, Seyoum Noufal, like the driver, Mustafa Maghawri, was a man in his late thirties. He'd led a reasonably comfortable life in Cairo as a small-time electrical contractor until he began to feel guilty about the great jihad that was passing him by. Allah's righteous work was being done in America. Besides, Seyoum's wife was a shrew, his business was failing, and his twenty-year-old Chevrolet Citation was disintegrating.

The past three years in the United States, even during the post-9/11 paranoia, had been comfortable. Until now. What the young martyr was suggesting was dangerous. Police were profiling suspects even though they denied doing so. Three Arab males driving around Fort Collins, Colorado, in the middle of the night would generate some interest. If they were stopped, they would be hard-pressed to explain what they were doing.

But the young man's orders were to be obeyed.

Seyoum nodded for Mustafa to do as they were told, and they headed for I-25 North, the sky clearing of smog as they got out of Denver, horizon to horizon filled with stars that had been named millennia ago by Arab astronomers.

Muhamed tightly gripped his pack as the lights of the big city fell behind, and traffic on the highway thinned out. There was a darkness here that was frightening, and yet he knew that the light was waiting for him.

No more suffering. No more struggle or uncertainty. And best of all, his family would be taken care of.

He smiled, his young face that of an angel at peace, and he did not notice Seyoum watching from the front seat, his expression a mixture of fear and awe.

PART
TWO

ПIПЕТЕЕП

□

The U.S. Coast Guard cutter *Storis* eased alongside the Harris Harbor cruise-ship docks in downtown Juneau just before dark, and within minutes the 230-foot warship was secured by a young, highly charged crew. They had rescued 122 people from four overloaded lifeboats that were in immediate danger of swamping in the high winds and large seas.

They had also retrieved the bodies of nineteen of the *Spirit's* crew and passengers from the frigid waters. Black plastic bags were lined up on the aft deck.

The wind had calmed down, but the overcast had lowered and the cold rain had started again. Despite the bad weather, police had to cordon off a large area of the dock to hold back a crowd of more than a thousand people. Media trucks ringed the fringes of the crowd, and dozens of reporters and cameramen jockeyed for positions in front. More newspeople were on their way from the lower forty-eight and from nearly every news organization in the world.

Word had leaked that the director of the CIA and the former secretary of defense were both aboard. To top it all off, it was the DCI who had apparently saved not only Shaw but more than half the passengers and crew. He was with the U.S. government *and* he was a hero. It was an oxymoron, and the media were buying into it. Washington had been taking a lot of criticism internationally and at home, so a story like this was front-page news.

So far, nothing official had been told to the media about the hijacking, the shooting, and the cause of the sinking. But once the *Storis* had come into the range of a cell-phone system, more than a dozen passengers called friends and loved ones with the story. It was picked up by a radio station in Juneau, which immediately broadcast a bulletin, even doing several live interviews with survivors aboard the cutter before the captain announced on the IMC that the FBI was requesting they be stopped until the passengers were debriefed.

That had been five hours earlier, and already the entire world knew that terrorists had attempted to kidnap the former American secretary of defense Donald Shaw to take him back to Pakistan where he would have been put on trial for war crimes.

Nothing so big had happened since 9/11.

Also gathered on the dock were six FBI special agents who made up the lead investigative team. A high school lunchroom had been set up as a processing and debriefing center for the Spirit's crew and passengers. A triage system had been put in place, and first aboard would be doctors and nurses from the hospital who would evaluate the survivors and assign them to one of three groups. Those who required immediate medical attention, such as for heart conditions or injuries, would be taken directly to the hospital. Those needing only a bandage or a tranquilizer would be treated aboard the Coast Guard cutter and then transported over to the high school. The final group, those needing no medical attention, would be the first off the ship.

However, the media would be allowed only very limited access to the survivors until after they gave their statements to the FBI. The killings and the sinking of the cruise liner, as bad as those events had been, were secondary to the attempted kidnapping of Donald Shaw, who had been one of the driving forces behind the war on terrorism.

Shaw was big news, not only because the kidnapping had failed, but also because of Washington's likely response. The war on terrorism would be stepped up a serious notch because of last night, and the entire world held its breath waiting to see what would happen next.

The FBI's first task would be to extract as much information from the survivors as possible. Though the search, centered at the position where the Spirit had gone down, had been in full swing since dawn, no sign of the fishing boat or the terrorists had been found. The Bureau was looking for clues anywhere it could.

Katy McGarvey and Karen Shaw were below helping with the survivors, while the former SecDef finished briefing his people in Washington via encrypted satellite coms from the cutter's CIC.

McGarvey was on the bridge watching the activity on the dock and on the cutter's decks. The Coast Guard medic aboard had bandaged McGarvey's burned hand and had put a couple of stitches in his arm where he had gashed it getting an ax from the firefighting alcove aboard the *Spirit*. He had already spoken with his deputy DCI, Dick Adkins, and with his special projects director, Otto Rencke, assuring them that he and Katy were fine, and getting them up and running on what was being called "Project Alpha," a plan to identify, find, and kill the terrorist Khalil.

The project had become personal last night. Not only had they manhandled McGarvey's wife, but they had killed innocent passengers and crew as well. Worst of all they had cold-bloodedly tossed the young woman and her child into the water, and then had shot her to death.

He would never get that image out of his head, not if he lived a thousand years.

But Otto had also told him about Liese Fuelm's call, which got him wondering what the hell the Swiss were doing watching the comings and goings of a Saudi prince. And why had Liese tried to reach him at home? Was it something out of his past catching up with him? Such things had happened before, with unhappy consequences. He did not want to go through that kind of pain again.

But there it was: the nagging at the back of his head, impossible to ignore.

The cutter's skipper, Commander Tom Gallagher, was speaking via walkie-talkie to his first officer down on the main deck, when Don Shaw, who was dressed like McGarvey and the other survivors in Coast Guard utilities, walked in. The captain looked up. "Stand by," he told his first officer. "Did my people provide what you needed, sir?" Gallagher, with his square features and ruddy outdoors complexion, looked like a high school football coach. He was a sharp officer with an ace crew.

Shaw was obviously hurting. The ship's medic had bandaged his head wound, bound up his ribs, and given him a mild painkiller, but the former SecDef had refused anything else, preferring to keep his head on straight for the moment. A team of Navy doctors was coming up from

Seattle aboard the C-130 Hercules that would take Shaw back to Washington, and they would conduct a thorough examination of him in flight.

He nodded tiredly. "You have a good crew," he said. "Thank them for me, would you?"

"Will do, sir," the skipper said. He glanced down at the crowd on the docks. "What would you like to do about security, Mr. Secretary?"

"My ride is about a half-hour out, so if you can provide it, I'll need a detail and transportation out to the airport."

"That'll be no problem, sir," Gallagher promised. "But what about the media? Would you like us to do something about them?"

Shaw smiled, even though he was tired and beat up, and he patted the Coast Guard officer on the shoulder. "I'll take care of that part, if you'll just send someone down to tell them I'll conduct a very brief news conference on the dock as soon as all the passengers are taken care of."

"Yes, sir," the captain said, and he turned back to his walkie-talkie as Shaw took McGarvey aside.

"I suggest that you hitch a ride back to Washington with me. It'll make security easier."

"If you don't mind the company, Don."

Shaw got a distant look in his eyes for just a second. Then he shook his head as if he was having trouble believing what had happened during the night even though he had been right there and had lived through it. "I think you have become a man impossible to ignore. Hell of a job, last night, Mac. You saved a lot of lives."

McGarvey's jaw tightened. "Not enough."

Shaw nodded knowingly. "It's never enough. How many lives could we have saved if we had continued into Baghdad the first time, or if we had picked up on the signals leading to 9/11. They were there."

"The leads are there again," McGarvey said. As badly as he felt, he wasn't going to beat himself up this time. He had a job to do. A terrorist to catch and kill. "Kidnapping you was just a prelude to—"

"My trial and the humiliation of America."

"Something else," McGarvey said. He'd felt something last night, watching Khalil, listening to the man's words, evaluating his attitude and the almost fatalistic attitudes of his men.

Katy had picked up on the man's subtly odd behavior too.

He was restrained, as if someone or something were holding him back, deterring him from doing what he wanted to do, and that was going on a frenzy of killing.

He would rather have murdered Shaw than try to take him captive.

Khalil had been saving himself for something even bigger than the kidnapping of the former SecDef.

"What are you thinking?" Shaw asked, concerned. "Another 9/11? Something like that?"

"It won't be the same thing," McGarvey said. "But we're not out of the woods yet."

Shaw looked away momentarily, an expression of sadness mingling with pain on his face. He shook his head. "We're in this for the long haul," he said, and he gave McGarvey a bleak look. "Especially you. It doesn't end here for you, does it?"

"No, it doesn't," McGarvey said.

Shaw nodded his understanding. He glanced at the crowd on the dock. The media was setting up a stand for microphones across from the cutter's boarding ladder, where the news conference would be held. "Do you want to talk to them?"

"I wouldn't know what to say."

"You'll have to sooner or later, you know. The president will probably insist on it. You're a national hero, something we rather desperately need just now."

"I'll deal with that issue if and when it comes up. In the meantime I have a job to do that could get impossible if I have the media on my back."

Shaw nodded toward the crowd. "How are you going to get past them?"

McGarvey had to smile. "I am a spy, Mr. Secretary; I think I can manage something like that."

Shaw smiled too. "I'll bet you can." He turned back to the captain. "Okay, let's get this over with. I have a plane to catch."

"Yes, sir," Gallagher replied. He said something into his walkie-talkie, and ten seconds later a four-man security team carrying sidearms showed up to escort the SecDef down to the dock. Along with the local authorities, who would provide a police escort, the Coasties would stick with him and Mrs. Shaw until they were safely aboard their transport aircraft.

"See you at the airport," Shaw said, and he left the bridge with his armed escort.

When the SecDef was gone, the captain gave McGarvey an expectant look. "How can I help, Mr. Director?" he asked.

"Have somebody fetch my wife up here, if you would. We'll have to borrow jackets and hats and sidearms. She and I will be joining the secretary's escort detail."

The skipper suppressed a grin, but he nodded. "Will do, Mr. Director."

TWENTY

☐

The Ritz-Carlton, Doha rose from the shores of the Persian Gulf in the capital city's prestigious West Bay Lagoon like a beacon in the night for the newly enfranchised rich—the rich of not only the Arab world, but also the West, especially the U.S., Japan, and Germany. The Ritz, the Inter-Continental adjacent to the Aladdin's Kingdom that was Qatar's only amusement park, and the fantastic Sheraton known as the "Pyramid of the Gulf," were new, as was just about everything else in the small nation of only eight hundred thousand people.

Beneath a barren, hostile terrain of sand, rock, and gravel bordering Saudi Arabia lay untold wealth in oil reserves, as well as one-eighth of the world's known natural gas. Technically there were no poor people here. But less than seventy-five years earlier, almost everyone on the tiny peninsula was a Bedouin—a nomadic person of the desert whose only possessions were his camels, his tents, his family, and his honor. Little or nothing of that past remained to be seen; all traces had been obliterated by buildings, by pavement, or by the shifting sands.

Lights from the hotels and other tall buildings reflected in the still waters of the bay in multicolored profusion, but the narrow rocky beach was empty except for two men, one of them dressed in a business suit and waiting near a jet black Mercedes E350 parked beneath a palm tree at the downtown marina. Huge multimillion-dollar yachts were tied up at the docks, and the only sounds were from the distant traffic at the Arch Roundabout. The night was warm and humid, a slight haze softening the stars overhead.

The other man, Imad Najjar, sat in the darkness on his Vespa beside an advertising kiosk fifty meters away from the car, watching the man he was supposed to meet. He was young, only nineteen, and until an hour earlier when he had begun smoking hash, he had been filled with fear. But now he was flying, like a bird with wings, far above even the range of a Kalashnikov rifle. He was dressed in blue jeans, a UCLA Dept. of Athletics tee shirt, and Air Jordans. His hair was cut very short, and a four-day stubble darkened his narrow face that was all planes and angles.

His eyes were alive, and he could see for ten million kilometers with perfect clarity. He could even see his own death, and it was as if a great joy awaited him in Paradise.

Imad had to laugh. That was the line they had fed him and the others last year in the training camp outside Drosh in the mountains of northwestern Pakistan. But he had been westernized by his father to expect— and feel comfortable with—money and the gadgets and comforts it could buy, so he never bought into the Muslim fundamentalist mumbo jumbo.

Bin Laden had not been up there in the camps, and the rumor was that the Americans had killed him in one of the first raids in the war in Afghanistan. But the mujahideen instructors had been filled with the holy zeal; this was a jihad, a striving against the Western infidels.

Some of the students had swallowed the idea, but they were mostly the losers. West Bank Palestinians, Cairo slum kids, a few spoiled Saudis, angry Iranis, and the odd lot that included one seriously screwed-up kid from Chicago or Seattle or someplace like that.

But there were women in the camps, and good hash, and the promise of money to the right boy or girl doing the right thing for the cause, at the right time and against the right enemy. A suicide bombing on an Israeli target—say, a bus in downtown Jerusalem or even Tel Aviv—would net the bomber's family thirty-five thousand dollars or more—paid in U.S hundred-dollar bills, which Imad thought was ironic as hell.

He checked his wristwatch. He was five minutes early. The bastard could wait for him. Nobody was going to say that Imad was an ignorant

Bedouin, anxious to prove his conviction to the cause. Tonight was nothing more than another simple delivery, for not much money.

His parents had immigrated to Saudi Arabia in the seventies, and his father had gone to work for Bin Laden Construction, working on the holy places at Mecca and Medina, and becoming wealthy in the process. Imad went to the best private schools, first in Riyadh and then the King Abdul Aziz University in Jeddah, where Osama bin Laden himself had gotten a degree.

Imad was one of the rich kids who flew up to London or Paris whenever the urge struck them. After graduation, their parents told them, things would change. So while in university they were expected to study as well as have fun.

He took another toke on his bomber joint, cupping the glowing tip in his palm.

Construction was boring. Acting the part of the international terrorist was exciting. So long as his father's money continued to flow, Imad figured he could attend classes from time to time; go on sabbaticals, as he thought of them, to places like Pakistan and Iran; and run the occasional mission when it was convenient and interesting.

Having a little extra money he'd earned himself was a plus. And when he returned to school from one of his missions, he got a lot more respect, not only from his professors, but from the liberated girls.

Life was good. Insha'allah.

He took another hit, then carefully snuffed out the glowing tip, pinched the end, and stuffed the roach in a side pocket of his backpack, before he started the rental motor scooter and slowly putt-putted to his contact.

The man at the Mercedes was much older and much better dressed than Imad was. He was slightly built, sloping shoulders and long legs. And he was intense; his eyes continually darted toward the marina entrance as if he expected someone to show up at any moment.

"My name is Achmed."

"I am Imad. And before you ask, no, I was not followed. I made sure of it."

Imad had worked with a different cutout each time, but they all seemed to be alike in their nervousness, as if they expected the CIA to jump out of the shadows, guns blazing. This one was no different.

He had seen the change in practically everyone since the September eleventh attack on the U.S., and the American invasion of Afghanistan and Iraq. Iran was probably next because of Tehran's defiance over the nuclear question. Pakistan was coming under increasing fire from the West, and North Korea was skirting the edge of disaster.

On top of all that, the rumor on the street was that al-Quaida was preparing another spectacular strike on the U.S. mainland. This time it would be more personal than 9/11.

"Americans should never feel safe anywhere in the world, especially not in their own homes," his professor of economics had emotionally told his class two weeks ago.

The feeling that Damocles' sword was about to fall had infected the entire region. In cities from Riyadh to Islamabad ordinary people were stockpiling food and water. Hospitals were hoarding medicines. Police units were sticking close to their barracks. And the Arab press in general was less strident in its attacks on Westerners.

But watching CNN and some other Western media outlets, Imad couldn't see that anyone in Washington or London was picking up on the obvious signals that the Muslim world was holding its collective breath.

"This is not a game," Achmed warned sharply. He took a VHS tape from the car and handed it to Imad. "People's lives, including your own, will depend on how well you do tonight. We have long memories of who our friends and our enemies are."

Imad realized that the man was frightened. "I've done these things for the cause before. Nothing will go wrong tonight. I'll deliver this to the Al Jazeera studio, and in the morning I'll be on the first flight back to Jeddah."

"I was told to expect someone older."

"I think they wanted someone like me—someone anonymous—for this kind of delivery," Imad said.

"You're a rich man's son."

Imad looked pointedly at his cutout's Mercedes. "Exactly," he said. "Which here in Qatar makes us anonymous."

Achmed's expression darkened, and his eyes darted to the highway as a noisy diesel truck passed. "If you fail, your body will be identified, and there will be unnecessary attention."

Imad laughed. "No chance of that happening. My father would disown me, just like Osama's family disowned him. We're both criminals."

It was the wrong thing to say. Osama bin Laden was like a god.

Achmed held out his hand. "I've changed my mind. Give me back the tape. I will get someone else to deliver it."

Imad stuffed the tape in the waistband of his jeans. "I'll do it, no problem."

"It is important."

"What about my money?"

Achmed slowly shook his head. "Make the delivery first; then come here. I'll wait for you."

"I'm not doing this for my health, man."

Achmed laughed disdainfully. "That's *exactly* what all of us are doing. You will either be a part of the jihad or you will be one of its targets. The choice is yours."

Through his drug-induced haze Imad realized that he might have gone a little too far. He nodded modestly. "Just be here when I get back."

"Someone will be waiting for you at the east entrance. Do not talk to him. Do not look him in the eye. Just hand him the tape, turn around, and leave. Do you understand?"

Imad nodded again, and he took off without looking back. This whole gig was starting to feel bad in his mind. For the first time since he had started dabbling in the struggle, his fears were not being suppressed by the hash. Achmed was one of the crazy ones. Imad saw it in his eyes. Mujahideen, they called themselves: warriors for God. Those types would just as soon kill you as look at you.

Tonight he was backed into a corner. He had to deliver the tape to the television network. There was no turning back. But he didn't have to go back for his money, nor did he have to accept any other missions. It'd be his luck that next time they would want him to be a suicide bomber.

Learn by example, his father said. Either take up the construction business and become a multimillionaire. Or take up arms and live in a cave in Afghanistan.

Imad decided that he was claustrophobic after all.

He followed the broad Corniche Boulevard as it gracefully curved away from the waterfront toward the Bin Omran District where the U.S. Embassy had put up its new building. To the right was the upscale New District, where the American new chancery was located, and farther out the city's tall buildings quickly gave way to residential neighborhoods, and suddenly, as if cut off by a switch, the city ended and the desert began.

Traffic was light, with only the occasional delivery truck or private car, but Imad was getting spooked. He was convinced that someone was watching him. Unseen eyes somewhere in the darkness were monitoring his progress to make sure he didn't screw up.

He wanted to be anywhere else except here in Doha. But he could not turn back. They would kill him if he did.

He decided that when he got back home he would go up to Riyadh and tell his father everything. Together they would figure out how to get him out of the mess that he was in.

The Al Jazeera studios were in a small, nondescript building on a tree-lined street in one of Doha's more fashionable districts of professional offices and expensive homes set behind painted walls. Qatar was safe, but these days everyone in the Middle East felt more comfortable sleeping nights behind tall walls.

The only outward signs that betrayed the studio's purpose were a rooftop bristling with satellite dishes and a Qatar Army Humvee parked in front. The studio's front and side entrances were barricaded by sandbags.

Imad couldn't see any soldiers when he made his first pass and turned the corner at the end of the block, but he knew they were there. Watching. Waiting. Over the past few years there had been a number of attacks on Al Jazeera bureaus and its correspondents.

The television network was underwritten in part by the Qatari government, so the army had placed guards at the home studios. If there was going to be any further trouble, it would not be here in Doha.

The problem, as Imad saw it, was that if he stopped at the east entrance and tried to deliver the tape, the army guards would first demand to see his identification. That was something he did not want to happen. He did not want his name listed on some roster of suspected terrorists when it was discovered he had delivered a tape for al-Quaida to the studio.

Yet he could not toss the tape in a trash can and go home. Al-Quaida would find him and kill him.

He turned around in the middle of the block and stopped. The Vespa idled softly in the balmy night air. How had he gotten himself into this situation? What had once seemed like a lark now seemed to be a terribly dangerous enterprise. He wanted to be done with it and get out of there.

The tape was like a brick of hot lead against his belly. Achmed said to hand it to a man who would be waiting at the east entrance. But there were soldiers there, behind the sandbags.

Imad suddenly gunned the Vespa and accelerated down the street. He had to slow down for the corner, but then he accelerated again.

A soldier stepped out from behind the Humvee and raised his hand.

Imad cranked the throttle full open, the Vespa's engine buzzing like a million bees. At the last possible moment, he maneuvered around the soldier and yanked the videotape out of his jeans. As he passed the east entrance, he caught a fleeting glimpse of a shadowy figure in the doorway six or seven meters away.

He threw the tape toward the figure at the same instant the soldier behind him shouted, "Halt!"

Twenty meters from the corner, something like a bee sting, but with the power of a sledgehammer, slammed into his back, lifting him off his motor scooter.

He grunted as all the breath was knocked out of him, and the night went black as he smashed face-first into the pavement.

TWENTY-ONE

Kelley Conley got to her desk on the second floor of the U.S. Embassy in Doha at 8:00 A.M. sharp as she did every morning, six days per week. She was a slightly built, attractive woman, who at thirty-two was the youngest assistant to any U.S. ambassador in the world. Divorced three years earlier, she had to send her two children to live with her parents in Waterloo, Iowa, until she was either reassigned to Washington or given a post in what she believed was a more stable part of the world.

As a result she was ambitious and earnest almost to a fault. And she was almost always nervous, expecting the Islamic struggle against the West to blow up in her face at any moment.

As far as she was concerned, all Americans living and working in the Middle East were on borrowed time.

Ambassador Peter Sorensen was in Washington this week, so all problems facing American interests in Qatar ended up on her desk. This morning the first two items were a reported shooting the night before in front of the Al Jazeera studios, less than a half-mile from where she sat. And the second was the arrival of Kamal Isomil, a senior news editor with the Arab television network.

It didn't take a genius to figure out that the two things were related.

And all of that was in addition to the attempted kidnapping yesterday of Secretary of Defense Shaw. Every U.S. embassy and consulate in the world was on high alert. Everyone was jumpy.

"Did he say why he's here?" she asked the receptionist downstairs at the security desk.

"No, ma'am. Just that it was a matter of some importance."

"Very well. Have someone escort him up," she told the receptionist.

She buzzed her secretary to say that Isomil was on the way, and two minutes later the Al Jazeera senior editor showed up with a plain padded envelope, which presumably had been checked by the Marine guards and bomb-sniffing dogs outside at Post One, the gate to the compound.

"Thank you for agreeing to see me on such short notice and at this early hour," Isomil said, graciously, in English. He was a short, somewhat paunchy man with wavy gray hair, dark eyes, and a ready smile. This morning, however, he was serious.

Kelley had gotten to her feet when he came in. "You have piqued my curiosity." She motioned him to sit down.

"It's not necessary, Mrs. Conley. I've only come to deliver this." He handed her the padded envelope. "It's a copy of a videotape that was delivered to our studios last night." He seemed relieved to be rid of it.

"There was a shooting."

Isomil nodded gravely. "The messenger did not stop when he was ordered to by the army, and unfortunately he was shot to death."

"Good heavens," Kelley said.

"It's another message to the United States," Isomil said.

Kelley stared at him. "From whom?"

"Osama bin Laden. And it's very recent. He holds up a New York Times for June sixth."

A tight fist clutched at her stomach. "Last week?"

"Yes," Isomil said. "We must broadcast this, of course. But we are giving you twenty-four hours."

It wasn't the first time that a video or an audiotape from bin Laden had been delivered to the Arab network, nor was it the first time that someone from Al Jazeera had brought a copy of the tape to the embassy. But never had such a senior network executive played the role of delivery boy, nor had any messenger before appeared so solemn.

Bin Laden's last message had come nearly a year ago. "What'd he say this time?"

Isomil looked as if he felt sorry for her. He shook his head. "View the tape, Mrs. Conley, and then get it to Washington as quickly as possible. We can only give you twenty-four hours, as I said."

After the Marine guard escorted the Al Jazeera editor downstairs, Kelley brought the tape across the hall to Neal Stannard's cluttered office. Stannard, the CIA's chief of mission in Qatar, was just getting off the phone. He looked up, his round face, horn-rimmed glasses, and polished complexion making him look like an eager contestant on a quiz show.

Kelley handed him the padded envelope. "Al Jazeera just brought this by. It's bin Laden."

Like Kelley, Stannard was young for his posting, but unlike her he *wanted* to be in the Middle East, where the action was. "Close the door," he told her.

While she was doing that, he took the tape out of the envelope and checked to see if there was a message of any sort, which there wasn't. Then he turned on his portable television/tape player and started the tape.

Bin Laden looked ill. His face was gaunt, his cheeks hollow, his long beard mostly white. His hands shook with a slight palsy when he held up a copy of *The New York Times* close enough for the camera to catch the date. He was seated on a Persian rug in a nondescript room, which had no furnishings whatsoever. When he started to speak, in Arabic, his voice was low and ragged as if he needed to clear his throat.

"I want this translated—" Kelley started.

Stannard held up his hand. "I speak Arabic."

The recording was less than three minutes long, but it was of good quality and the sound was clear. Stannard made some notes, and when the message ended he rewound the tape and started it again, this time translating for Kelley.

When it was finished for the second time, Kelley's legs felt shaky. "Jesus," she said softly, "he's a monster."

"And then some," Stannard said. He picked up his secure phone and dialed a number. "I'm taking this to Riyadh this morning. They have the equipment to digitize the tape so we can send it via satellite to Langley and to NSA. They'll need to get on it right away. Has this been broadcast yet?"

"No. They're giving us twenty-four hours," Kelley said.

"Has anyone else seen it?"

"They didn't say."

Stannard glanced at the clock on his desk. "It's a little after eleven in Washington. You should try to reach Peter. State will need a heads-up."

Kelley nodded, sick at heart, and suddenly she felt very naïve. "Do you think he'll get the people to do it?"

Stannard shrugged. "Why not? He got the guys for 9/11, and that op was a big success for them." His call went through. "Charlie, it's Neal Stannard in Doha. I'm coming over this morning. We got a new bin Laden tape, and this one is definitely flash traffic."

Dennis Berndt, the president's adviser on national security affairs, arrived at his White House office a few minutes before 7 A.M. He was in a highly charged mood because of the stunning events of the past twenty-four hours.

First was the hijacking of a cruise liner, the murder of dozens of innocent people, among them an infant child, the attempted kidnapping of the former secretary of defense, and finally his dramatic rescue by the director of the CIA.

Then late last night was the call from Peter Sorensen, the ambassador to Qatar, about the videotape from bin Laden and the hint about its disturbing contents.

And finally the call just after midnight that the Navy plane transporting Shaw and McGarvey to Washington had made an unscheduled stop in Denver. The SecDef had suffered a mild heart attack, and his medical team needed the use of an MRI machine. Shaw would be okay, but the unscheduled stop was delaying his and McGarvey's return by several hours.

Berndt had come to Washington from a professorship in international law at Harvard. Within the first year he had shed his academic persona and had reverted to his more comfortable background as a midwest lawyer. The media classified him as "one of the most laid-back presidential advisers in recent memory."

He was a large, amiable man with a warm smile, but this morning he was worried. His mother used to say that troubles came in threes, each one worse than the one before it. He'd seen that very thing happen. And if that old saw held any water, God only knew what was coming that would top the hijacking of the Spirit of '98 and bin Laden's new warning.

His secretary hadn't arrived yet, but the messenger from the CIA's Directorate of Intelligence was waiting in his outer office with an attaché case. Berndt signed a release form, and the messenger handed over the tape.

"Thank you, sir," the young woman said. "I was instructed by Mr. Doyle to tell you that a translation line was added by us to the bottom of the screen, and that NSA analysts have a ninety-eight percent confidence that the message is authentic."

Berndt had almost hoped for a hoax. "Have Mr. Shaw and Mr. McGarvey arrived at Andrews yet?"

The messenger glanced at her wristwatch. "Any minute now, sir."

"Good."

Berndt's charged-up mood had turned dark and somber by the time he finished viewing the three-minute tape for the second time. He took no notes; it wasn't necessary. Bin Laden's message was as simple and straight-forward as it was chilling. When Al Jazeera broadcast this to the world in another fifteen or sixteen hours, there were going to be a lot of nervous Americans.

He ejected the tape from the player and took it down the West Wing hall to the Oval Office.

The door was open, and already this morning the usual people were gathering: secretaries, chief of staff, speechwriters, and others in prepara-tion for the usual 9 A.M. CIA briefing to the president. Three telephone conversations were going on at once, and four television monitors were tuned to the three major network news shows plus CNN. All of them were using the attempted kidnapping of Shaw as their lead story.

President Lawrence Haynes, a cup of coffee in hand, seemingly obliv-ious to the turmoil around him, stood next to his desk watching ABC's Charles Gibson give his spin on what the event meant in the war on ter-rorism. Gibson, like the other news anchors, was making a big deal out of McGarvey's daring *Die Hard* rescue. Finally someone was willing to step up to the plate and strike back one-on-one. America had a new hero who had saved the day.

Haynes was built like a Green Bay Packer linebacker, with broad shoul-ders, bulging muscles, and a flat stomach. Despite his hectic schedule he managed to keep on a strict diet and maintain an exercise routine every day except Sunday. He was a family man, with a deeply rooted sense of honor; he knew the difference between right and wrong, and even his enemies could not fault him in that respect.

He looked up when Berndt walked in. "Good morning, Dennis. Have you been watching this?"

"Good morning, Mr. President," Berndt said. "I saw it on *Fox and Friends* on the way in." He stepped in front of the president, switched the televi-sion to channel three, and popped the cassette in the player.

"What is it?" Haynes asked.

"Watch," Berndt said, and he pushed the Play button.

Everyone in the room stopped what they were doing as the image of Osama bin Laden came up. The Saudi terrorist picked up a copy of the front section of *The New York Times* and held it for the camera to home in on the date.

He began to speak, in Arabic, and two lines of script scrolled across the bottom of the screen, one in Arabic and the other in English.

"*The great (jihad) struggle against the Western infidel has been in its infancy. Despite the many valiant and courageous successes by our brothers and sisters around the world; despite the triumph in the nest of thieves on eleventh of September 2001; despite the strike at the heart of the warmongers' headquarters; despite the righteous blows against the embassies, barracks, warships, and even the buses and shopping centers of our enemies, of the blasphemers against Allah; despite the virtuous pain caused to show the unbeliever the correct path to Paradise, we are not finished.*

"*We are at the dawning of a new chapter of our book of just causes.*

"*The infidel has learned to pay attention. But they have only taken the first halting steps; as a child would upon leaving its mother . . .*"

"When did we get this?" the president asked.

"It showed up at our embassy in Doha about eleven o'clock our time last night," Berndt said. "CIA Riyadh digitized it and sent it by secure satellite link early this morning, and NSA's people are saying it's really him."

"*. . . time now to continue in earnest the battle we have only just begun.*"

Bin Laden carefully laid the newspaper on the floor next to him. He moved slowly and deliberately, as if he were in pain. It looked as if he was having trouble with his back or the muscles in his flanks. When he turned again to face the camera, he was still grimacing, but his facial muscles slowly relaxed and he smiled again; he was a man who was extremely sad, but who was at peace with himself and his terrible decisions.

Seeing the tape for the third time, Berndt was suddenly struck by the notion that bin Laden was not only a man at peace, but he was also a man who had made peace with his maker.

Bin Laden was dying, or preparing to die.

"*No infidel should feel safe in his own home. No woman doing her household duties should feel protected. No man at work should feel sure his family will not die very soon. No person anywhere in the U.S. should feel secure that his children will reach their destination— unless their destination is Paradise, and then only if they have made amends with Allah.*"

Berndt's flesh began to crawl, the hairs at the nape of his neck stood up, and he had a bad taste in his mouth. When this next part was broadcast, no one in America would get a good night's sleep, and tomorrow would be a day of panic and chaos.

"*We will strike in America's heartland. We will deliver a blow that the infidel will never* forget. This time we will send our arrow of justice into the heart of the evil ones. We will prove that there are truly no innocents among the evildoers.

"By now our soldiers of God are ready to strike the very nests where the children of the infidels lay their heads each evening to sleep; where they dream in peace certain that their parents are near to protect them; where they first learn the heretical words that cause them to wrongly believe that there are gods other than the One God.

"Infidels, send your children to bed, but do not expect them to wake in the morning."

One of the president's staff stifled a sob.

"There will be no further compromise. Insha'allah."

Bin Laden looked away and made a gesture to someone off camera, and the tape went to snow.

The president and the others in the Oval Office, struck with the enormity of bin Laden's message, did not move at first. Always before the warnings were vague, calling for terrorist strikes against the U.S. and our interests. This time he had specified the targets: America's children in their homes.

"Al Jazeera is giving us another fifteen hours before they broadcast it," Berndt said. "Shall I play it again?"

The president tore his eyes away from the television and shook his head. "No need to ask if he means it, or if he has the resources to carry out his threat."

"No, sir."

"Is McGarvey back yet?"

"He should be arriving about now. I expect his people will be bringing him up to speed right away."

The president's jaw tightened. He glanced again at the blank screen, then nodded as if he had made a tough decision. Everyone in the office was looking at him, waiting for him to say something, to let them know how they should react.

"This attack will not happen," he told his people. "I am putting every resource available to me for the single purpose of finding bin Laden and killing him." His expression hardened. "He will not be offered amnesty, nor will an attempt be made to arrest him and bring him to trial. Any possible collateral damage will not become a consideration. I want to be very clear on those points. No deal making. We're going to get that bastard once and for all."

It was the reaction Berndt had expected. Haynes was slow to get angry, but once there he became an unstoppable force.

"I'll meet my National Security Council at noon. That should give Mac time enough to get fully briefed and up to speed." He gave his staff a reassuring look. "I'll speak to the nation tonight at eight, *before* the tape is broadcast. There will be a lot of panicky parents who'll want to know that we're doing something to stop the monster."

No one challenged the president, who had already broken several laws by ordering an assassination, nor did Berndt think that the Democrats would do so. The current mood of the country was one of subdued anger at the al-Quaida terrorists and frustration with Washington for not having gotten rid of bin Laden. Once this tape hit the airwaves, all that would change. The entire country would be behind the president.

TWENTY-TWO

□

At that moment it was 6 P.M. in Karachi, Pakistan's largest city and arguably one of the most dangerous spots on the planet, when a Gulfstream bizjet with British tail numbers touched down at Jinnah International Airport. Ground control directed the pilot to taxi to a private boarding gate on the west side of the field, which serviced Pakistan International Airlines' diplomatic and VIP passengers.

When the jet was parked and the engines were spooling down, the steward, a young Bangladeshi man supplied by the air-leasing service, opened the door and lowered the stairs, then stepped aside politely as the lone passenger got up and exited the aircraft without a word.

Khalil, who had traveled from Vancouver via Montreal, London, and Cairo under the name of Thomas Powers, walked over to a waiting Mercedes sedan and got into the backseat. He was dressed in a stylish linen suit, with a white silk shirt, a pale blue cravat loosely tied around his neck, and hand-sewn tan Brazilian loafers.

Even something more than a casual glance would not connect him with Thomas Isherwood or with the terrorist who had hijacked the *Spirit of '98* thirty hours ago. He was a completely different man now. His facial expression was different, the way he carried himself was not the same, and the color of his eyes and hair, which had both been dark, were now light brown.

The major change was the look in his eyes. On the cruise liner he had been a man on a carefully controlled military mission, but now he was a wild animal, scarcely in control of himself, poised to strike at anything that crossed his path. A Bengal tiger who was disappointed and angry because he had missed his kill, he was extremely dangerous as a result.

A minute later the steward came over with two pieces of matched Louis Vuitton luggage and placed them in the trunk.

The solidly built, capable-looking driver, dressed in a Western business suit, handed a sealed manila envelope—addressed to Ibn Rashid care of the Sheraton Karachi—over the seat to Khalil, who accepted it without a word. Inside were Khalil's new passport, stamped by Pakistan customs, as well as several other identity and credit documents.

Thomas Isherwood, who had traveled to and from Alaska, and Thomas Powers, who had made his perfect escape here to Karachi, no longer existed. Those identities were as false as the Rashid persona.

In fact, Khalil thought, he sometimes had trouble remembering his real identity, his real background. Since he received the call fifteen years ago and slipped underground, he had become a man with no name and no past.

The name "Khalil" had been assigned by the CIA simply as a code word, a way to identify him. He had found out about it from a source in the Egyptian Embassy in Washington and had adopted it as his own.

Very few people outside the business even knew that code name.

All that would change when the director of the Central Intelligence Agency lay at his feet, the rich, red American blood flowing like a river. What sights would be seen in McGarvey's eyes at the time of his passing.

The car was waved through the airport security gate, and Khalil settled back, not noticing the slums they had to pass through to get into the city proper. Most people in Karachi were desperately poor and filled with a religious fervor. They were a dangerous force, like dynamite near an open flame, ready for one spark to set them off.

He was in a very dark mood this evening, mostly because of his failure, but also because of his impatience to get on with the task he had set himself to do: kill Kirk McGarvey.

Impatience was rare for him, and whenever the mood arose, like now, he stopped to closely examine its cause. In his business inattention to detail could get you killed.

On the desert, where the nearest oasis might be one hundred kilometers away, and where noontime temperatures might reach fifty-five degrees Celsius, to make an error in judgment because the wanderer was in a hurry was a sentence of death.

He had never failed before, nor had he ever been bested by anyone. Bin Laden had warned him that if he ever came up against McGarvey to kill the man immediately. He had been unable to do that, and the only reason had been his own weakness, his lack of ability. He was desperate to right that wrong.

He looked at his reflection in the window. Perhaps he had lost his edge. Perhaps he had been away from the desert for too long.

Not yet, not yet. There was at least one more battle to be won.

His real age was nearer to fifty than the CIA guessed, but he looked thirty-five. Tall, with an olive complexion, dark flashing eyes, and a feline grace, Khalil could project an intimate warmth if the circumstances dictated it, but could in an instant become as cold, indifferent, and deadly as a king cobra ready to strike.

His family had been Bedouin, wanderers on the open deserts of the Arabian Peninsula. They had a tradition of being tough, heartless people who had to be that way in order to survive the harsh conditions, not only of the desert, but also of the constant internecine fighting of the royal family, of which they were a minor branch.

It was a way of living that had been bred into them over the generations. And like the Tikritis of Iraq, which spawned such warriors as Saddam Hussein, Khalil's family had been exceedingly strong and close knit, in contrast to the modern Saudi family that was as often as not dysfunctional and scattered.

Since the oil boom many of the royals had spent untold billions of dollars on hedonistic pleasures around the world—yachts, jets, mistresses.

All that time Khalil's family believed that the royals needed to pay more attention to their internal affairs and to the principles of Wahhabism, the strictest and harshest form of Islam.

Only through Allah will the world be saved.

As a child growing up in the late sixties and early seventies, Khalil was trained to be a true Bedouin. A hard, religious fundamentalism was beaten into him by his masters. He learned to be heartless when it was needed, cruel when it was called for.

The Bedouins' philosophy, and Khalil's, was a stern obedience to the fatalism of a harsh environment.

Even in this modern age a true Bedouin is able to harden his heart in order to kill his own daughter as an offering to Allah. The refinements of modern life are nothing more than the effeminate devices of degenerate men.

Khalil had never been able to think in any other way, though he could easily slip into the role of the playboy if and when the need arose.

And during the rare times he went home, he acted the role of a kind, loving husband to his wife, and a compassionate father to his children.

To his house staff and servants, he was by all accounts a considerate man. His third cousin, Prince Faisal, once told him that a man could be judged by how he treated his inferiors.

It was important that a man do the correct things when important people were observing, and do the necessary things when important principles were at stake.

Khalil looked up out of his thoughts long enough to realize they had already driven past the Chaukhandi Tombs, because they made the turn on Shahrah-e-Faisal Road directly into the heart of the modern city with its luxury hotels and high-rise commercial buildings. Away from the outlying districts, Karachi could be a large city almost anywhere in the world.

Yet it was here, right in the capitalistic heart of Pakistan, and not in some mountain hideaway as Western intelligence thought, where the real planning for the jihad had taken place well before 9/11.

President Musharraf and his National Command Authority were happy to cooperate with the American CIA's hunt for terrorists in the remote mountains of Drosh, Chitral, and Shoghot on the far north border of Pakistan and Afghanistan. It was an open secret among Muslims that only the bandits and Kashmir rebels were left up there. But it occupied the Americans, who thought they were making real progress in their "war on terrorism," and Pakistan benefited because American aid was starting to flow.

The faint trace of a smile briefly crossed Khalil's face. The early days of the movement in the mountains of Afghanistan had been a wild adventure. Khalil, like many Saudis, longed to go back to nature. It was no different than Americans who camp in the woods. For many Saudis, including Khalil, it was going back to the desert to a simpler time when religion and a respect for the land were important.

If the oil were to be permanently shut off, the West would be forced to return to its roots, just as the Saudis would have to return to the desert.

It was an intriguing thought.

Downtown on M. R. Kayani Road near the red sandstone pile of brick cupolas and balconies that housed the Sind Provincial Assembly, the driver slowed the Mercedes and entered a parking-garage ramp beneath the modern glass-and-steel, forty-eight-story M. A. Jinnah Commercial Centre.

"Were we followed?" Khalil asked, softly.

"No," the driver replied succinctly. Karachi was his city. The suggestion that he had been careless in his duties coming from anyone other than Khalil would have angered him. As it was, he took it to be a reasonable question from a professional.

He pushed a button on a remote control, and a steel gate rolled back allowing them entry. Five levels down, at the far southeastern corner of the ramp, he stopped in front of a single elevator, its doors open.

"Leave my bags in the trunk, and remain here. I won't be long," Khalil said. He got out of the car and walked across to the elevator. The doors automatically shut and the car started up.

The floor-selection panel was locked out, and a miniature closed-circuit television camera was mounted in the ceiling. Security was unobtrusive but tight. Wealthy men conducted their business in this building. It was expected that security measures would be in place.

In order to hide the lizard, change his color to red and place him in a rose garden.

The elevator stopped at the twenty-fifth floor. Across a thickly carpeted hall, a plain wooden door opened as Khalil approached. An old man in evening clothes, whom Khalil had known all his life, nodded pleasantly. "Good evening, Mr. Rashid. I trust your trip was a productive one."

Khalil preferred the mountains, although this place was a more secure hideout. "I'm in a hurry."

The old man smiled indulgently. "If you will just go straight through, Mr. bin Laden is waiting."

Khalil passed through the small, plainly furnished receptionist's office, into a dimly lit, plushly decorated corridor right out of an English manor house, to a small windowless room at the end. The walls were plain plaster, and the only furnishing was a Persian rug in the middle of a plain tiled floor. A single light in the ceiling cast a pale yellow glow.

He slipped off his loafers and sat down at one end of the carpet to wait, but it was only a minute or two before the door opened and Osama bin Laden, dressed in a British tailored business suit, but with an open collar, a gentle smile on his clean-shaven face, walked in. Khalil started to rise, but bin Laden waved him down.

"Please, do not arise for me, my friend." He spoke in Arabic, his voice strong and clear. He took off his shoes and sat down on the rug. "You had a safe journey. Would you like refreshments?"

Khalil looked for a sign in bin Laden's eyes that he was disappointed or angry because of the failure to kidnap Shaw. But there was nothing to be seen except for the pleasure of seeing an old and trusted lieutenant.

"No, thank you, my brother. In fact, it is not my intention to stay with thee for long this evening. I have further urgent business elsewhere." The Arabic language was more formal than English; rightly so, in Khail's mind.

"All of us have urgent business to attend to now," bin Laden said. "I have ordered the next phase in the war against the infidels to begin. I have rereleased the message."

Khalil let his surprise show. The tape was not to have been made until after Shaw had been safely brought to Pakistan, put on public trial, and convicted for the world to see. "The timing is perhaps incorrect?"

"In fact, the timing is perfect," bin Laden replied mildly. "My message was delivered to Al Jazeera last night, and as I suspected would come to pass, a copy of the tape was handed over to the CIA in Doha and transmitted to Washington. By now the criminals in the White House believe they know what they are faced with."

"We have lost the element of surprise that made the September attacks so successful," Khalil pointed out. He had come to Karachi expecting to be chastised for his failure. Instead he was being told the next attack on American soil was going ahead

"We will strike fear into their hearts," bin Laden said. His voice was still mild, but he was angry. His mouth was set, his eyes narrowed. This was bin Laden just before a battle.

Khalil knew that he had to choose his words with care. "Yes, my brother, but their law enforcement agencies will be watching for our soldiers."

Bin Laden's expression darkened. "They are already in place."

"The necessary supplies are there?" Khalil blurted. He had trained some of the boys who would provide the support network in the States. It did not matter to him if they died in battle, but he did not want them to give their lives for no reason.

Bin Laden's broad nostrils flared. "Everything was moved into position over the past two months."

Khalil felt the first hint of trouble. He had dropped out of sight for the past two months in order to have the time to validate his Trinidad identity. He had left the real work, bin Laden was telling him, to someone else while he went about the business of conducting a doomed mission.

Bin Laden took four envelopes out of a breast pocket and laid them on the carpet beside Khalil. "These are the four death letters from our martyrs. You will personally deliver them along with fifty thousand dollars in cash to each family after they succeed. Then our cause will have more righteous converts. Money will come to us as it did after the September attacks. As it would have had you not blundered your very nearly foolproof task."

Every muscle in Khalil's body stiffened. Any man other than bin Laden who spoke to him like that would die now. But he gave no outward sign of his almost overwhelming rage. "It will be as you ordered. When will the attacks take place?"

"Very soon, my brother. You will keep yourself in readiness to make the deliveries. And you will remain out of reach of Western intelligence."

"I have a most important task to—"

"Yes, killing Kirk McGarvey. Someone else will do it."

"He is mine," Khalil blurted.

Bin Laden's gaze turned ice cold. "You have another mission," he said. "See that you do it well. When the moment comes, there will be a great outpouring of fear and anger. It will be a dangerous time. There will certainly be reprisals, and we all must be ready for them. The families of our heroes must be made to know that our hearts are with them in Paradise."

Khalil calmed himself by shear force of will, an artery in his neck throbbing. He would not be denied what was rightly his. No power on earth, not even his loyalty to bin Laden, would stop him.

Bin Laden got to his feet. "Go to your family now, and make peace with Allah. The time will be soon."

Khalil picked up the envelopes. "How do you wish me to get the cash?"

"You are a wealthy man. You supply the money. Take it from one of your bank accounts. The ones in the Cayman Islands, or perhaps the ones in the Jersey banks. It is of no matter to me."

When bin Laden left the room, Khalil pocketed the envelopes and settled back. He was no longer angry. He knew what he had to do, and he had a good idea how he would do it.

McGarvey was a man without a future.

TWENTY—THREE

Ten time zones to the west, a Navy C-130 Hercules fitted out as a hospital transport, carrying SecDef Shaw, DCI McGarvey, and their wives, touched down at Andrews Air Force Base and taxied directly over to one of the alert hangars on the far west side of the base.

A number of people were gathered on the ramp, several of them high-ranking brass, presumably from the Pentagon, waiting for their boss. In addition to several military staff cars and four windowless vans with CIA series tags, there was an ambulance and a Cadillac limousine.

Watching from a window, McGarvey picked out his deputy director Dick Adkins, who stood near the limo, his hands in his pockets, his slight shoulders slumped, and his thinning, sand-colored hair ruffled in the breeze. Next to him, by contrast, was a mountain of a man who looked like a heavyweight prizefighter. McGarvey figured the muscle would be his new bodyguard; number three—after Dick Yemm and Jim Grassinger—in less than eighteen months. It didn't say much for job security.

Even before the big airplane came to a complete halt, a dozen armed Air Force security troops formed a perimeter around the aircraft.

McGarvey had insisted on remaining in Denver until Shaw was cleared to travel, in part because the delay was only a couple of hours, and in part because he and Katy needed the rest. Overnight, Adkins had briefed him on the bin Laden tape. He suspected that the coming days were going to be intense.

The hijacking of the *Spirit* and the attempted kidnapping of Shaw were only the tip of the iceberg. And no one at Langley expected the threatened terrorist attacks to be the end of it unless bin Laden and the rest of his fanatical al-Quaida planners were bagged.

The president was going to speak to the nation at 8 P.M. Eastern. Before then, the CIA would have to coordinate the development of the latest National Intelligence Estimate and the Watch Report, both of which detailed the current and expected future threats to the U.S. Then the president would have to be briefed; he needed to know his options, which could range from all-out war to a purely political move such as demanding UN sanctions against whatever country or countries harbored terrorists.

A one-on-one surgical strike, of the variety that McGarvey was intimately familiar with, would be included in the list of possible actions.

So far as McGarvey was concerned, it was the only option.

He could see Khalil's hands on Katy, his pistol pointed at her head. He could hear the cries of the young mother desperately searching for her baby in the water. He could hear the screams of panic as the cruise ship was sinking.

Bin Laden's taped message had been downloaded to McGarvey's PDA very early this morning, even before it had been hand-carried to the White House, and he'd watched it several times.

There was no doubt in his mind that the tape was authentic and had been recorded last week, but there was something about bin Laden that didn't set right with McGarvey. He had met the man several years ago, and had spent enough time with him to form a vivid impression of how he looked, how he acted, how he spoke.

The man in the tape was bin Laden, but there was something wrong with him. It was something that seemed wrong to McGarvey. He had been turning it over in his mind for the past couple of hours without being able to put his finger on exactly what it was that bothered him. But it was something.

He had spent several hours on a secure phone link with Adkins and with Otto Rencke, his director of special projects as well as with his daughter Elizabeth and her husband Todd Van Buren, both of whom were currently instructors for the CIA's internal operations course at the Farm.

Priority one was finding out who Khalil was and where he was hiding. He was bin Laden's right-hand man and chief planner, which meant he had not only been responsible for the attempted hijacking, but he had also had a hand in setting up the new round of threatened terrorist attacks in the U.S.

Get to Khalil soon enough, and we might be able to stop them once and for all.

"How's mother?" Elizabeth had asked at one point.

It was around three in the morning, and McGarvey had just finished watching bin Laden's monstrous tape for the fourth or fifth time. "She's sleeping. But she came out of it okay."

"Promise?"

"Scout's honor," McGarvey said, feeling a wave of love and protectiveness for his daughter and for his wife. Both of them, along with Elizabeth's unborn baby, the baby her mother was carrying, were legitimate targets in bin Laden's world.

The bastard and his henchmen were going to die. And their deaths would not be pleasant. No trumpets, no angels on gossamer wings transporting them to Paradise, only pain and then lights out.

One hour out, Katy had touched up her makeup and fixed her hair, but now as a crewman opened the forward door she still looked tired and worried. She squeezed her husband's hand. "Will we be able to stop them before they hit us this time?" They were dressed in the Coast Guard utilities that they'd been given after they'd been rescued from the sound by the *Storis*.

Of all the people McGarvey wanted to reassure, his wife was at the top of the list. But he had to give her the same answer that he would have to give the president: "It's not likely. But no matter what happens, it's over for them now, for sure."

Katy's eyes filled, and she turned away momentarily to look out the window. "Nobody will trust anybody. It'll be worse than after 9/11," she said, a bitter edge to her voice.

McGarvey had considered that possibility, and he thought that Katy was probably right. "Once the tape is broadcast, no parent is going to feel safe anywhere, not even in their own home."

Katy shook her head. "It's the worst thing that's ever happened to us."

"Yes, it is."

Shaw was still sedated, but Karen gave them a hug; then she gave McGarvey a searching look. "Thank you for what you did for us. But this time let's finish the job."

"You can count on it," McGarvey told her. He looked down at the SecDef lying on the stretcher. Shaw was pale, but he did not seem to be in any distress. "Take care of him; he's a good man."

Karen nodded, a sudden look of fierce determination on her pleasant face. "You can count on it."

McGarvey shook hands with the medical crew, then handed over the sidearms he and Katy had borrowed in Juneau to one of the aircrew. "See that these get back to the *Storis*."

He helped his wife off the aircraft, shook a few more hands, and accepted what he figured was probably just the start of a lot of tiresome congratulations for simply doing his job. Then Adkins hustled them into the backseat of the limo, after first introducing Neal Julien, McGarvey's new bodyguard.

"Pleased to meet you, sir," Julien said. He was a sturdy, chocolate-skinned man with a warm smile, a round nearly bald head, and a mellifluous voice that held a hint of a Bermudan accent. His manner was pleasant but professional.

"Watching over me has become a dangerous job," McGarvey told him.

"Yes, it has, Mr. Director," Julien said.

The SecDef was being carried off the aircraft when the DCI's limo, with two vans in front and two in the rear, headed up to Chevy Chase, Julien in constant radio contact with the two dozen Office of Security operators in the four vans. They had no police escort, but McGarvey figured there would be at least one chase helicopter armed with air-to-ground missiles somewhere in the vicinity. The bad guys might bag a DCI elsewhere, but it wouldn't happen here on his home territory.

"What's the drill this morning?" McGarvey asked his deputy director.

"I went through your list overnight, and everybody's up to speed," Adkins said. Since his wife died the previous year, he had no one at home, so he had thrown himself into his work. He was content to remain the DDCI, putting McGarvey's orders into effect and sometimes smoothing over his boss's administrative rough edges when needed. "We'll get you home first so that you can change clothes. We've swept your house and grounds, and set up a solid perimeter, so Mrs. McGarvey will be okay for the time being. But I still think you should get to the safe house."

"They weren't after me," McGarvey said. The last couple of times they had run to ground had not been very successful anyway.

Adkins shrugged, knowing it was the answer he would receive. "The staff meeting is set up for ten-thirty, and the full National Security Council meets at noon at the White House. We should have the NIE and Watch Report pretty well cobbled together by then."

"What about this business in Switzerland?"

Adkins glanced pointedly at Katy, but McGarvey nodded for him to continue. It had always been an unwritten understanding that what the DCI's wife was told or not told was up to the DCI's discretion.

"Ms. Fuelm's call was evidently a back-burner request by Zurich for information on the prince. Otto figures they used her because of her . . . history with you. Anyway, Otto's working on it, but of course he won't tell the rest of us what he's doing. Apparently the Swiss are interested in his comings and goings, and they put Liese Fuelm in charge of the investigation."

Katy had caught the history reference, and she gave her husband a questioning look, which he caught.

"Liese was one of the cops, along with Marta Fredericks, watching me when I lived in Lucerne. Her people probably figured to use the contact, see if there were any sparks still smoldering somewhere."

Sometimes when Katy was tired or particularly stressed out she became brittle, and the old, sharp-tongued, suspicious Katy emerged. Her dark moods had always been about a lack of self-confidence and a low self-esteem. "Are there?" she asked.

"I doubt it," McGarvey told her, but secretly he wouldn't be surprised. Liese had been in love with him, and she had fallen hard when he left, and even harder when Marta, her best friend and McGarvey's lover, had been killed. "Why do they think I'd know anything about Prince Salman?" he asked Adkins.

"I don't know if Otto knows, but he's working on it."

At the mention of Salman's name, Katy stiffened slightly, but neither man caught her reaction. She turned and looked out the window, apparently no longer interested in the briefing.

Morning traffic was heavy on I-95 but moved well, so it was just a couple of minutes after nine when the driver pulled up at the McGarveys' sprawling colonial at the end of a cul-de-sac on the fifteenth fairway of the Chevy Chase Country Club. The somewhat exclusive neighborhood was quiet, except for a couple of lawn-service people at work two houses down. They were legitimate; otherwise, the Office of Security would not have let them come within five miles of the place. After the screw-up with the Spirit's passenger and crew list, no one at Langley or the Pentagon or downtown at the FBI was taking any chances.

By this afternoon, after the president met with the National Security Council, all the major players in Washington would know about the latest bin Laden threat. And by tonight, after the president spoke to the nation, the same fear and paranoia that everyone felt after 9/11 would be back in full force.

The attempted kidnapping of the former secretary of defense wouldn't exactly become yesterday's news, but the story would be eclipsed by the bin Laden tape. Not many people would get much sleep tonight.

Two teams of security operators would remain on-site, the vans parked in the cul-de-sac and on Lenox. Four agents would remain inside the house, and would rotate in shifts with those stationed outside in the vans, and at several strategic locations on the golf course.

No one liked the arrangements; they were too loose, but it was the

best they could do under the circumstances. The safest place for the director and his family would be the DCI's residence at the Farm, but he was
needed in Washington.

The house was quiet. The security officers were keeping watch from
the upstairs front and back spare bedrooms. When McGarvey and Katy
went up, they appeared briefly at the doorways like curious ghosts and
then disappeared.

"This is starting to get real old," Katy said, but before McGarvey could
say anything, she touched a finger to his lips. "It's not your fault, darling.
You're a cop, and it's your job to deal with the bad people in the world."
She looked at him with a wave of love and admiration. "Thank God for
you, and all the people you work with."

McGarvey's throat was suddenly a little thick. "Thank you," he told his
wife, and he took her in his arms, glad that they were here like this together. Yet another part of him was already at Langley—and wherever this
business would take him.

It was after ten when they reached the sprawling CIA headquarters across
the river, the parking lot full, a steady stream of traffic coming and going.
Since 9/11, recruitment had risen to an all-time high. The Company was
finally able to screen for the kind of people it wanted, rather than just accepting any warm body that walked in the door.

McGarvey's secretary, Dhalia Swanson, dressed as usual in a conservative suit, her gray hair up in a customary bun, got up when McGarvey
and Adkins walked in. "We didn't expect you back so soon," she said. She
was obviously relieved. "Mrs. McGarvey is well?"

"Just fine; thanks for asking," McGarvey said, giving her a reassuring
smile. "We got lucky this time." He walked through to his office, Ms.
Swanson right behind him.

She shook her head emphatically. "Oh no, sir, luck had nothing to do
with it. Your presence did."

"I'll start getting the staff together," Adkins said, heading for his own
office.

"Ten-thirty, sharp," McGarvey called after him.

Ms. Swanson got McGarvey a cup of coffee. "I worked up a tentative agenda for you, not knowing until yesterday when you would be back, and of course not knowing about the bin Laden tape until early this morning. I've weeded out most of the mail, and rescheduled most of your routine appointments and telephone calls. The president would like to speak with you as soon as possible this morning, and Senators Harms, Bingham, Wilson, Daggert, and Stowe want to talk to you, as do all the usual media." She looked up from her notes, a pinched look of disapproval on her narrow face. She was protective of her DCI.

"Liz and Todd?"

"They'll finish up at the Farm this afternoon and be at the house by eight."

For just a moment McGarvey was back in the water, swimming in the brutally cold Sound toward the woman and her child, knowing that he could not save them, and yet having to try. In his mind's eye it was Elizabeth out there crying for help, and the baby was his grandchild.

"We'll do the letters and calls this afternoon. The congressmen will have to wait. I'll leave it up to Herb to set up a news conference, but I want it coordinated with Carleton's office. We're going to conduct this operation by the numbers." Carleton Patterson was the CIA's general counsel. Since the war in Iraq, anyone who had access to the media had questioned the legality of both the U.S. search for weapons of mass destruction and the ouster of Saddam Hussein. Word had come directly from the White House that every move the CIA made would have to have a solid legal basis.

Or at least appear to, because it's not possible to fight terrorists on any terms except theirs. Sometimes some laws would have to be bent. That's just the way it is in the real world.

"Shall I call the president for you?"

"Yes," McGarvey said, already up to speed. "Then have Otto come up. I'd like to talk to him before the staff meeting. And ask Dick to bring over the draft NIE and Watch Report. I want to see those before the meeting."

Ms. Swanson's eyes softened. "All those people . . . ," she said. She focused. "It's not just religion, is it?"

Like everyone else in the nation, she had been trying to get a handle on the issue ever since 9/11. The Osama bin Ladens of the world, and their organizations—al-Quaida, al-Nida, Hamas, hundreds of others—

were incomprehensible to the average American, who simply could not grasp the terrorist's concept that *no one was an innocent*.

"It's never had anything to do with religion," McGarvey said. "It's always been about money."

TWENTY-FOUR

□

McGarvey wasn't the least surprised that President Haynes was brusque on the telephone. Word had already leaked about the bin Laden tape and the latest threat to the U.S. and at least one network was attributing the leak to a *senior employee within the administration*. Haynes had gone through his share of major crises during his administration, and he was a president who was very dangerous to cross. He had a long memory and an even longer reach.

"I'm glad you're back in one piece. You did a damned fine job up there. In the meantime, I assume that you've seen the tape. What do you think?'

"It's authentic, if that's what you mean, Mr. President," McGarvey said. "But beyond that I don't know."

"What are you talking about?" Haynes demanded. Right now he didn't want ambiguities, especially not from his intelligence chief.

"He's been coming across like he's a sick man. Like he's dying. But I'm beginning to think that it's been a ruse to throw us off."

"Does the CIA have any direct evidence of that?"

"No," McGarvey had to admit. "It's just a gut feeling I got from watching the tape." It wasn't until the third time through that he had begun to notice the little signs: the forced slump of the shoulders, the moves too slow, too studied, as if the man were an amateur actor playing a difficult role. Bin Laden was no longer convincing.

President Haynes wasn't deterred. "Unless you think his faking it affects the current situation, we'll put it on a back burner for now. We have to deal with the bastard's warning. Is it real or is he merely trying to shake us up? And we have to deal with the leak. I'm going to personally cut them off at the knees when I find out who did this to us. We're already getting more than one thousand calls every hour. By this afternoon, I'm told, that number will rise one hundredfold, and I have none of the answers, because all I've seen is the tape. No analysis. No facts. No details."

Sitting at his desk, looking out the window over the pleasant early fall morning toward the Potomac, McGarvey felt unsettled to hear a president of the United States speak with fear in his voice, even though he had cause to be afraid.

If bin Laden had issued a warning before 9/11 that suicide squads were going to hijack airplanes and fly them into buildings, nothing could have been done in the short run. Air traffic could not have been grounded, every tall building could not have been closed, and even with armed air marshals aboard at the last minute, the attacks probably couldn't have been prevented.

There wouldn't have been enough time.

Nor was there enough time now. The task of guarding every single home in the nation was impossible, if those were the targets that bin Laden warned al-Quaida was going to hit. Parents could not keep their children safe, so they were turning to their government to do what it had not been able to do in September 2001, and what it probably could not do now.

In a free society with relatively open borders, no thought police, no unreasonable searches and seizures, no real way of listening in on every single telephone conversation, bad things could and would happen to good people.

Until the bad guys were hunted down and shot to death like rabid animals.

McGarvey could do nothing more than his job, and that was to give his support to the president. It was all that the job of DCI had ever been. "I'll have the NIE and Watch Report for the NSC at noon. My people are still working on the problem. But I will have some ideas and some options for you to consider."

"I should hope so," Haynes said. "Now what about the leak? Could somebody over there have talked to Jennings?"

The first McGarvey had heard of it was just minutes ago from the president. "It's possible."

"I want a full investigation immediately—"

McGarvey interrupted. "No, sir."

Haynes was never one to bluster. When he got angry, his voice lowered in pitch and volume. He practically whispered now. "What was it you said, Mac?"

"I'm not going to hamstring my people by chasing after someone who might have shot off his mouth," McGarvey said. "A least not right now. I don't give a damn who leaked the warning; it was going to come out this evening in any event. My only concern is finding out when and where the attacks are going to take place—which I think is a long shot—and finding out who's directing the show, and then getting to them."

"Do you mean to say the CIA believes they cannot be stopped?"

"The Israelis have much tighter security than we do, and they can't prevent terrorist attacks."

These were things that the president did not want to hear. "This country cannot stand another 9/11," he said coldly. "Maybe it's time to broaden the emergency powers provisions of the Patriot Act."

It was a chilling idea, but McGarvey thought there was a better than even chance that Haynes would get away with it. Parents wanted to make sure their children were safe. After events like the Murrah Federal Building, Columbine, and 9/11, the nation was traumatized. This latest warning from bin Laden could very well be the last bit to tip the balance even further toward a police state.

There was little or no street crime in Nazi Germany that wasn't committed by the Brown Shirts.

"I'll provide you with your options as the CIA sees them," McGarvey said. "After that it'll be up to you how we should proceed. But I am with you, Mr. President. One hundred percent. We will stop these bastards once and for all this time. You can count on it."

The president was only slightly mollified. "I'll hold you to that promise, Mac. We're going all the way. There'll be no holding back. I don't care what Congress or the media have to say, we're past that. When we make our attack, collateral damage will not be a consideration. Do I make myself clear?"

"Perfectly clear, Mr. President," McGarvey said.

. . .

Dick Adkins came over with a dark blue leatherette folder. He handed it to McGarvey with a rueful look. "The NIE and Watch Report. You're not going to like them."

"What's the upshot?" McGarvey hadn't expected that he would.

Adkins shrugged like a teacher who had been asked to explain the obvious. "Assuming bin Laden's people are already in place, and that the attacks could come from any direction at any time, our only options are to mobilize every cop and National Guardsman in the country to take criminal-suspect profiling to new heights, and to station air marshals aboard every commercial aircraft and at every airfield private or public, at every bus station and train depot, outside every mosque, and any other place you might expect to find young Arab males."

It was something the president would understand perfectly.

"All that's on the FBI's turf," McGarvey said. "What's our role?"

Adkins pursed his lips. "Well, if we found bin Laden and brought him to trial, the attacks would probably escalate. If we found him and put a bullet in his head, there's no predicting what the immediate reaction would be. But it's my guess that a significant portion of the Muslims on the planet would take up arms against us."

Something else was on Adkins's mind. McGarvey had worked with the man long enough to know when something was bothering him. Most of the time the DDCI was a monotone presence in his office next door. That wasn't a negative attribute; it was just Adkins's way of dealing with the incredibly complex real-world problems that the CIA was supposed to unravel every day. Right now though, he seemed to be preoccupied and a little agitated, as if he had jumped into a situation that was over his head. "What else have we come up with?" McGarvey asked.

"It's not in the Watch Report," Adkins said reluctantly. "It's too far-fetched. But one of our photo interpreters downstairs in Imagery Analysis thinks that bin Laden might be playing games with us."

"What are you talking about? Isn't the tape authentic?"

Adkins shook his head. "It's real all right. Or at least we think it is. But the analyst has convinced herself that there's something fishy about bin Laden's appearance."

There it was. A little chill raised the hairs at the nape of McGarvey's neck. He'd come to the same conclusion after watching the tape, but he had not been able to put his finger on exactly what bothered him. A photo analyst had apparently seen something too.

"She thinks bin Laden is wearing makeup," Adkins said, almost sorry he had brought it up. "It's something we've not seen before. But she spotted something funny, and pulled up several of the other recent tapes he made for comparison."

"He's gotten vain in his old age."

Adkins shook his head. "The makeup made him look sick. And she thinks that he's wearing a hairpiece."

"There were rumors that he had kidney problems. Maybe he's developed cancer. Could be that he's on chemotherapy and lost his hair."

"His beard's a fake too," Adkins said. "Now if our analyst is right, why do you suppose that bin Laden has to dress up in stage makeup and a costume to send us a message? What's he playing at this time?"

Adkins had just walked back into his office, leaving McGarvey to wonder exactly what it was that bin Laden was playing at, when Ms. Swanson buzzed to say that Rencke was on his way. Before McGarvey could hang up, Otto Rencke, all out of breath, his face flushed, burst into the office.

"Oh, wow, Mac, am I ever glad to see you."

McGarvey looked up as his director of special projects bounded across the room. Rencke was all arms and legs attached to a gaunt frame. His head seemed to be too large for his body, in part because of his wide green eyes and long, out-of-control, frizzy red hair, and in part because of his long, broad forehead. He was dressed in dirty sneakers, faded jeans, and a Moscow State University sweatshirt. He was in his early forties, a Jesuit-trained mathematician, and yet he looked and acted like a college kid or, McGarvey sometimes thought, like an overwrought, exuberant puppy.

But it was obvious even to someone meeting Rencke for the first time that he was either an idiot savant or a genius. He knew more about computers, computer systems, and information gathering, collation, and analysis than did any man alive.

Adkins once said that there were only two possible places on the planet where Rencke should be: either working for the CIA, where he could be watched very closely, or buried deep underground in a cell with absolutely no access to the outside world. There was little doubt that no computer on the planet was safe from his hacking.

The saving grace was that except for his genius, Rencke was just a baby boy who wanted someone to love him. All his life he'd only ever wanted one thing: to be part of a family. And he had found one with Mc-Garvey, Kathleen, and Liz, and with his wife, Louise Horn, who was chief of a technical means section of the National Security Agency.

Rencke had discovered his niche and he was a truly happy man, except when his people were in harm's way and then he became a mother grizzly defending her cubs.

McGarvey had to grin when Rencke came around the desk and grabbed him in a bear hug. "Oh, wow, you're back, and you did it again, and you saved a whole bunch of folks who would have gone down with the ship." When he was excited, he said everything in a rush. "Kinda hard to hide a hero."

McGarvey patted him on the back, and it brought back a poignant memory of talking with Katy a few months before their separation and divorce about having a second child, perhaps a boy.

"Glug, glug," Rencke said straightening up. "Ya gotta take a swim if you want to find the clues, ya know. But that takes time and concentration."

"Do you think that the hijacking was a diversion—"

"Yeah, but not the way everybody thinks." Rencke looked off into space for a few seconds, the animation leaving his face. When he came back, he frowned. "It's going reddish, did you know that?" He hopped up and down, one foot to the other, as he talked. "Lots of things to consider now, ya know. But they all point toward desperation with a capital D. Last-ditch stand. The Titanic is going down, and the captain himself is grabbing for a life jacket."

Years ago Rencke had figured out a way to teach a friend of his, who had been blind from birth, about color. Rencke wanted his friend to actually see the spectrum, the reds and blues and greens and yellows. He was able to do it with a series of complicated tensor calculus equations—the same mathematics that Einstein used in his theories of relativity.

And it worked because Rencke's friend was a gifted mathematician. But the same mathematical approach could also be used to reduce concepts, so complicated they were invisible, into colors. The pastels, in Rencke's analytical models, were akin to mild problems brewing in some distant future. The deeper colors meant trouble was just around the corner. And as Rencke would say, the *baddest* of all colors was red, which meant that something awful was on the verge of happening.

"Okay, tell me what you're seeing," McGarvey said. When Rencke got this way, he was never wrong.

"I don't know yet, Mac. Honest Injun. Snatching Shaw was only supposed to be the opening salvo. But you put the kibosh on that plan—" He gave McGarvey an odd look, almost as if he were a drowning man desperately gazing up from the bottom of the pool toward his rescuer, and wondering what was taking so long. "Last night you said something about Khalil that got to me. And Mrs. M. said the same thing. He was in a hurry. Right?"

"He had something else on his mind; I saw that much," McGarvey said. "He wanted to get the kidnapping over with and bug out of there as soon as possible so that he could get back to whatever it was he was really after. At the time I thought it was taking Shaw back to Pakistan to stand trial."

"That was supposed to be a diversion," Rencke said. "The kidnapping and trial were supposed to keep us looking in one direction while the main event was gearing up."

"In that case, bin Laden's tape could be just another diversion. But for what?"

Rencke stopped hopping. "The sixty-four dollar question, kemo sabe. Mighty big diversions for what he says he wants to do."

Unless something else was going to happen. Something bigger.

"Divers are already down on the wreck to recover bodies. Soon as we get DNA results, we should be able to track some of the hijackers back to their origins. Even just one positive ID should give us a direction."

"Saudis," McGarvey said.

Rencke nodded solemnly. Osama bin Laden was a Saudi, and although the royal family officially denounced him and his al-Quaida followers, it was openly known that Saudi money was at the heart of a great many Islamic fundamentalist groups. But no U.S. administration had been willing to take the Saudis to task, for the simple reason of Saudi Arabian oil.

Oil dollars for lives.

"But Pakistanis too," Rencke said. "Maybe ISI." Interservice Intelligence was Pakistan's powerful intelligence service, which General Pervez Musharraf used to control the country. Pakistan was where bin Laden and others had set up Taliban training camps, and where al-Quaida put the finishing touches on its recruits.

"The Saudis supply most of the money," McGarvey said.

"The man your friend Liese is watching is a Saudi prince," Rencke said, turning away. It was as if he couldn't look McGarvey in the eye. "I did some checking. Just before every al-Quaida attack—Kenya, Riyadh, the *Cole*, 9/11—the prince disappeared. He and Khalil are of the same general description. And Salman has the perfect cover. He's a megarich jet-setter. A deal maker. Who would think he's one of the bad guys who want to pull us down?"

What Otto was saying made sense, but McGarvey wanted to make sure they weren't snatching at straws because of the pressure to come up with answers. "Okay, assuming for the moment that you're right, and Salman is Khalil, why are the Swiss watching him, and why do they think I'd personally know something about him?"

"I don't know what they have on him, but they turned to you because there's a connection between him and you and Mrs. M. That's why they sicced Liese on you."

McGarvey was confused. "I never met the man in my life."

Rencke was agitated. He started hopping again. "Oh wow, Mac, you didn't; you didn't, honest Injun. But Salman was one of Darby Yarnell's crowd when you and Mrs. M. were divorced. He was right there in the middle at Yarnell's house when Mrs. M. was there and when Powers was brought down. He was one of Baranov's recruits."

McGarvey closed his eyes for a second, all those very bad days coming back to him in full color. General Valentin Baranov was one of the most brilliant KGB officers the Soviets produced during the entire period of the cold war. Among his most spectacular operations was one in which the equally brilliant Donald Powers, the CIA's director at the time, was assassinated. Key to the complicated plot was a former CIA officer, Darby

Yarnell, whom everybody, including McGarvey, was led to believe was a spy. In the end Yarnell was maneuvered into pulling the trigger on Powers, and McGarvey was maneuvered into killing Yarnell, drawn to the man because Katy was sleeping with him.

Katy was in Yarnell's arms plain as day in the lens of the spotting scope they'd set up in the apartment across the street.

"There were a lot of guys like Salman in Darby's mob," McGarvey said. "What's Liese trying to find out? Why from me—?" But all of a sudden he knew, and his stomach did a slow roll.

Rencke could see that McGarvey had made the connection, and his face sagged. He stopped hopping. "Bad dog, bad dog," he said. "They probably think that Mrs. M slept with the prince, too."

TWENTY-FIVE

☐

When McGarvey walked across the hall to the director's conference room, his staff was already gathered, glad to see their boss back in one piece but mad as hell that the bin Laden problem would not go away. They got to their feet when he came in, and as he went around the table to his seat he shook hands with each of them.

Besides Dick Adkins and Otto Rencke, the CIA's senior officers included the deputy director of operations, David Whittaker, who was one of the most moral men McGarvey had ever met; the brilliant, dapper-dressed deputy director of intelligence, Tommy Doyle; the Company's equally bright but ponderous deputy director of science and technology, Jared Kraus; the deputy director of management and services, Felicia Quinones, whose warm heart was only outshone by her absolutely spot-on management abilities; and the patrician general counsel, Carleton Patterson.

Over McGarvey's two-year tenure as DCI the group had become a well-oiled machine, fiercely loyal not only to their boss but also to the organization and what it stood for. They considered themselves to be the frontline troops against America's enemies.

"The bastards didn't know they'd be running into a buzz saw when they tried to take that cruise ship," Kraus smirked. He pumped his right fist. "Way to kick ass, Mr. Director."

McGarvey gave him a sharp look. "A lot of good people lost their lives up there, including Jim Grassinger who was just doing his job." Shaw might have been right that Americans needed a hero right now, but McGarvey wasn't going to step up to that plate. "If there's any celebrating to do, let's wait until we've shut the bastard down once and for all."

"As soon as Jim's body is recovered, we'll set funeral services at Arlington," Felicia said. "I spoke with his wife last night; she's holding up."

"I'll talk to her later today," McGarvey said, taking his seat. "In the meantime we have a job to do, so let's get on with it. Priority one is Project Alpha, because I think there is a very real possibility that Khalil not only put together the kidnapping attempt, but is also the mastermind behind bin Laden's latest threat. If we can find and eliminate him, we might solve the bigger problem, because without Khalil I think al-Quaida will fold up its tents and fade away. So how do we proceed?"

"Along six lines of investigation," Rencke was the first to answer. He had the bit in his teeth and he was impatient to begin. "First we need to find out what went wrong over at the FBI, the Department of Defense, and right here on our own turf. The entire crew and all the passengers aboard the Spirit were vetted by all three of our organizations, and yet a fair number of the crew were bad guys."

"That'll be my Office of Security," Felicia said. "We've already set up an internal affairs team to figure out what went wrong at this end. I'll get with the Bureau and DoD right away."

"While you're at it, find out how Shaw's travel plans were leaked," Rencke said.

"Are you looking for one source?" Felicia asked. "I mean, if that's your thinking, we'll have to add White House security to the list. Paul Hogue is kind of sensitive at the moment, so we'll have to use a little finesse."

Hogue was chief of the president's and first family's security operation. Less than two years earlier President Haynes, his wife, and their daughter almost lost their lives in an al-Quaida–sponsored attack in San Francisco. If it hadn't been for McGarvey, the president and his family would be dead. Hogue had not forgotten that the Secret Service had very nearly blown it.

"Doesn't matter," McGarvey said. "Nothing's off-limits for this one. If we step on toes now, we can apologize later. What next?"

"Canada," Rencke said. "We need to find out how Khalil and the men who left the *Spirit* with him got out of the country without leaving a trace, other than the sportfishing boat that was found last night washed up on one of the small islands in the sound."

"I'm working with RCMP's Secret Intelligence Service chief for western Canada," Adkins said. "At least some of the terrorists flew a DeHavilland Otter out of Kake, just north of where the cruise ship went down. No trace has been found of the aircraft."

"What about the pilot?" McGarvey asked.

"He's missing too, but so far as the RCMP knows, the guy's a longtime local. Our Coast Guard is working with the Canadian Coast Guard and a private salvage company from Seattle hired by Cruise West to bring up whatever they can from the wreck. The bodies have top priority, of course, in addition to any forensic evidence. I passed along your incident report so the salvors would have something to shoot for."

It would be cold and dark, the current swift, the wreck possibly unstable and dangerous. And there would be many bodies. Too many bodies.

"Lean on them, Dick," McGarvey said. "We're going to need whatever they can come up with—anything—as soon as possible." This was not going to get away from them like 9/11. "I don't think we have much time."

"I think you're right," Tommy Doyle agreed. It was one of his analysts who had come up with the notion that bin Laden was wearing a disguise. "His warnings in the past have always been vague, but this time he's being a lot more specific, almost as if he's taunting us." Doyle fiddled with his tie, a gesture of his when he was nervous. "Hell, they don't have to do anything else, and they've already won. Trading on the New York Stock Exchange was suspended ten minutes ago, because the market was taking a nosedive. Airlines are canceling flights in nearly every market because people are afraid to fly and are simply not showing up at the airports. Just before I left my office, I got the news that GM was declaring a holiday at its Detroit headquarters. Two-thirds of all their junior and midlevel managers called in sick. No one's left to run the company." Doyle looked away as if he hated to be the bearer of such bad news. "That's just the start. By tonight the entire country will be all but shut down, unless the president makes one hell of a good speech at eight."

"It's up to us to give the man what he needs," McGarvey said.

"Bin Laden's head on a platter," Whittaker stated the obvious. "Because even if we do nail this Khalil character, bin Laden is going to find another chief planner. You can count on it. Some very bright people over there are standing in line for the job."

"Killing Khalil would at least buy us some time," Rencke said. "Look, guys, if Uncle Osama is faking being sick, it has to mean that somebody was getting too close for comfort. He's come down out of the mountains like Moses, and he's living right in the middle of his tribes." He looked to the others for support, but no one said a word.

"What are you thinking?" McGarvey asked him.

"My guess is that he's hiding out in the open, maybe Riyadh, maybe Karachi, maybe Tehran, posing as an ordinary businessman, like he's done before, ya know." Rencke was getting agitated because no one was catching his drift.

"We have a twenty-five-million-dollar reward on his head," Adkins said. "Do you think if he's out in the open now somebody is going to lead us to him?"

"Exactamundo, kemo sabe. And we even know who's going to do it!" Rencke waved his hands as if he were trying to pull the others along. "Khalil, who just might be a Saudi prince by the name of Abdul Hasim ibn Salman. He's going to be the super rat fink."

Tommy Doyle sat forward, scowling. "We've not come up with anything other than a string of concidences to tie the two men together." He turned to McGarvey. "We've got no DNA, no fingerprints, not even a voiceprint of Khalil. There's nothing linking them. And the prince is such a big name internationally that he can't kiss a woman's hand in Paris without the tabloids picking up on it." Doyle shook his head, completely dismissing the idea. "Salman is a member of the Saudi royal family, and lest we forget, bin Laden and the royal family aren't exactly on friendly terms. The man wants to overthrow the government, for Christ's sake."

"Being an international playboy is pretty poor cover for someone who doesn't want his true identity known," Whittaker suggested.

"Bzzz. Wrong answer, recruit. What about James Bond?" Rencke demanded. "He did okay."

McGarvey thought it would be the ultimate irony if Khalil and Salman were one and the same. It conjured up images of one of General Baranov's old operations. Brilliant, deadly, and loaded with unexpected twists and turns. "Okay, Salman is apparently living in Switzerland at the moment, and the Federal Police are taking a look at him for some reason they haven't shared with us yet. They've asked for our help."

Whittaker looked confused. "I haven't heard anything about this. Did it come through my COS in Zurich?"

McGarvey shook his head. "It came as a personal request from an old friend of mine. I want a records search done ASAP to see what we have on him." He did not elaborate any further. At the moment there was no need. "In the meantime we might get lucky with something from the wreck of the *Spirit* or the sportfisherman they used to make their escape. For now I want a complete search of every database anywhere in the world for anything and everything on Khalil: his past operations, eyewitness reports including mine and my wife's, along with all the other crew and passengers who had contact with him. Send someone to interview Secretary Shaw and his wife, and I want two of our people up in Juneau right now to work with the Bureau. Khalil and at least some of his people got aboard the *Spirit* in the middle of nowhere. They didn't simply materialize out of thin air. I want to know how they got to Frederick Sound from the Middle East. Someone, somewhere, saw something, and I want to know about it."

"We're grabbing at straws," Carleton Patterson mused. He was a lawyer and a pessimist by nature. He had hired on as the CIA's temporary general counsel six years ago and had not gotten around to leaving yet. He thought of himself as a voice of reason in a nuthouse.

"You're right, but it's all we have at the moment," McGarvey said. "Khalil has made a mistake somewhere in his past, and we will find it."

"Why haven't we done so earlier?"

"We weren't looking hard enough," McGarvey said.

.   .   .

In the few short hours since the message on bin Laden's latest tape had been leaked to the public, Washington had become a city under siege. Riding over to the White House in his Cadillac limousine, the first thing McGarvey noticed was how much emptier the streets were than normal. People were staying home, glued to their television sets to find out what was going on, waiting for someone to tell them what to do.

Police or National Guard units were stationed at every major intersection from the Roosevelt Bridge all the way up to the White House. Air Force fighter/interceptor jets circled overhead, and Air Force One was crewed and powered up at Andrews in case the president needed to be evacuated from the city.

The Pentagon had declared a DEFCON Three, which placed all U.S. forces anywhere in the world on a heightened state of alert, and the Department of Homeland Security was expected to issue a red alert after the president's address to the nation tonight.

Unlike bin Laden's other warning messages, this one had gotten to Americans. The majority of the country was frightened that another 9/11 was about to happen and that no one in Washington knew what to do.

Tommy Doyle was right. Even if there was no attack, bin Laden had already won an important victory. If the role of a terrorist was to terrorize, the deed had been accomplished.

But it would not go unpunished. Khalil would die and then so would Osama bin Laden. No delays this time. No excuses. No mistakes. No international deal making to put together a coalition. Just a bullet in each man's brain.

McGarvey called his house on his cell phone. "How are you holding up?" he asked when Katy answered.

"I'm watching television. It's like 9/11 all over again." Katy's voice sounded strained. She hadn't gotten a decent night's sleep since the hijacking, but she was holding together. "How about you?"

"I'm too busy to worry," he told her, which was a lie. He couldn't get out of his mind Otto's conjecture that Prince Salman and Khalil were one and the same, which was why the Swiss had resorted to using Liese Fuelm to get personal information from him.

"Will you be home at a reasonable hour? Elizabeth and Todd are coming over."

McGarvey had a feeling that tonight might be one of his last early nights at home until this business was settled once and for all. After the ordeal in Alaska, Katy deserved at least that much. "I'd like a bourbon and water, one cube, on the kitchen counter at precisely seven."

"Aye, aye, skipper," Katy said warmly. "Love."

"Love," McGarvey responded.

The president's press secretary, Lucille Rugowski, met McGarvey at the security post just inside the west portico. She was a short, sturdy brunette from Gary, Indiana, who the media loved to hate. She was fair but extremely tough. In the nine months she'd been on the job, she'd developed a reputation for being one of the brightest people ever to hold the pressure-cooker job. On top of that she was married and had four children, all of whom were strictly off-limits. It was her aloofness that had early on earned her the nickname "the Snob."

"You'll be joining the president for a brief ceremony and a photo op in the Rose Garden, Mr. Director," she said, as they headed to the Oval Office. "The NSC will meet directly afterward in the Cabinet Room."

She had caught McGarvey flat-footed, though he should have suspected that something like this would happen. Shaw *had* warned him that the nation needed a hero. But he didn't have to like it. "I'd like to have a word with the president first."

Rugowski shook her head. "He thought you might say that. But he's not going to give you the chance to try to talk your way out of it." She gave him a faint smile. "When's the last time the media considered a CIA director to be a great guy? Just go with the flow, Mr. McGarvey, and it'll be over in a few minutes."

"It's not a good idea."

"It's the president's idea, and he would like your cooperation," Rugowski said. "What you did up there—saving lives, stopping the kidnapping— was nothing short of magnificent. He wants to thank you publicly."

TWENTY-SIX

☐

Liese Fuelm watched out the chalet's window a few minutes past one in the afternoon as the black Mercedes sped up the driveway. She was trying desperately to get control of her emotions.

The last twenty-four hours had passed in a blur. Kirk had actually been aboard the Alaskan cruise liner when the terrorist Khalil had tried to kidnap the former American secretary of defense. He was being hailed as a hero, his face plastered on every newspaper and television screen in the world. And then came the fantastic warning by bin Laden, a man whom Kirk had come face-to-face with a couple of years before 9/11.

There were too many coincidences, too many improbabilities, one piling atop the other, coming faster and faster, centering on Kirk McGarvey, a man suspect in the eyes of the Swiss Federal Police, to be ignored any longer.

Captain Gertner had been on the verge of firing Liese after she had failed to record her telephone conversation with Otto Rencke at the CIA, and in fact she had expected to be drummed out of the service and blocked from ever working in Swiss law enforcement ever again. But then the kidnapping occurred and right on its heels the bin Laden tape.

"Everything has changed," Gertner said on the telephone a few hours ago. "You can see that, finally, can't you, *Liebchen?*"

She was off-balance, and she felt stupid. "He was a hero."

"Surely you can appreciate the absurdity of what you are trying to maintain." Gertner was practically shouting. His legendary temper could be incendiary. "One man against what apparently was a well-organized force? And why wasn't the terrorist Khalil unmasked as Prince Salman? Why is it your McGarvey maintains his silence?"

Liese felt battered. What Gertner was suggesting simply could not be true. Kirk McGarvey was not a traitor. "I don't know," she said weakly.

"For heaven's sake, why hasn't he returned your call?" Gertner shouted. She imagined his spittle flying all over the place. "For heaven's sake, you two were practically lovers. Even now, if you put your heart into it, I can imagine you seducing the man."

She could imagine such a thing. In fact, that's all she had been imagining for the past forty-eight hours.

"We would be doing the world a favor," Gertner said, suddenly calm, even friendly. "Think about it, *Liebchen*, with your head and not your heart. McGarvey single-handedly stops a terrorist attack on the Golden Gate Bridge that would have killed his president, and yet he fails to notice terrorists being trained to hijack four airliners and crash them into buildings. Under his direction the CIA has failed to find bin Laden, and yet he just happens to be in the right place at the right time to stop a spectacular kidnapping attempt?"

Liese could not raise her voice above a whisper. "If he's a traitor, who does he work for? What is his purpose?"

"Why, that's simple. Kirk McGarvey has not changed one whit since his days here in bed with poor Marta. Now, as then, he works for himself. Now, as then, he was a bitter man who was turned out of his own country for merely doing what he thought was his job. Now, as then, his agenda is his alone, and it is revenge."

"No—"

"Listen to me, Liese. Your Herr McGarvey is an assassin who has never bothered with a license for his killing sprees. He is possibly the most dangerous man in America."

Liese closed her eyes and laid her head against the wall. "It's silly—"

"Not silly, *Liebchen*. And you and I will expose him for what he really is, once and for all, because we finally have the means at hand. Prince Salman is his tool, and you, my dear, will once again become his weakness."

Liese watched as the Mercedes pulled up next to her car. Two men got out and came around to the side entrance. One of them was Gertner, and the other much larger man she thought she might have seen at the Nidwalden headquarters the previous week, but she didn't know who he was. She didn't know what to do, except that she couldn't leave the investigation to men such as Gertner who were not looking for the truth, but simply looking for facts that would fit their own personal theories.

Nor was Gertner doing this for simple justice. She was convinced that there was more than simple justice to his desire to expose Kirk McGarvey as a traitor. The Swiss never did favors for anyone, especially not the U.S.

Gertner's was one of the faces Liese remembered from Marta's funeral. There'd been two dozen Federal Polizei in attendance, but Gertner stood out in her memory because he was the only man there with tears streaming down his cheeks.

"Look sharp, gentlemen," she told Tomas Ziegler and Claude LeFevre, who were pulling duty with her again this afternoon. "Himself has arrived with reinforcements. Heads could roll." One part of her wished it were so. She wanted out.

"We're with you, Sergeant," Ziegler said, looking up from the spotting scope. He gave her the thumbs-up. "Besides, as long as they think you have the inside track at the CIA, they won't get rid of you."

LeFevre opened the door for Gertner and the other man, who brushed past him and stormed into the chalet's great room.

"Has he arrived yet?" Gertner shouted.

LeFevre was right behind him. "Has who arrived, Captain? Unless you mean the children, in which case they're over there."

Gertner gave him a withering look and, without glancing in Liese's direction, went across to the scope and motioned Ziegler aside. "The prince landed in Bern over an hour ago." He bent down and peered through the powerful scope that was trained on the big house across the lagoon. The afternoon was cloudy. One or two dim lights were on inside, and several security lights illuminated the front gate and the area of the dock and boathouse. But there didn't seem to be anyone out or about.

For a moment Liese entertained the idea of demanding why the hell Gertner had put her in charge up here if he was going to barge in and take over when the supposed subject of their surveillance operation was apparently on the verge of showing up. But such an outburst wouldn't accomplish much. McGarvey didn't need her to defend him from the ravings of a lunatic Swiss cop. She was just thinking through her heart instead of her head.

"The last arrival was a delivery van from a dry-cleaning service at eight this morning," Liese said. "Perhaps the prince has business in the city?"

Gertner looked up. "No, he's on his way here. But I wasn't informed until forty minutes ago." He motioned for the other man to sit down at the sound and electronic surveillance equipment. "I brought Sergeant Hoenecker, who is an Arab speaker, with me since Corporal Miller is not available."

Willi Miller was the only person on Liese's team who understood Arabic. She'd been out sick since the previous morning, and Liese's call to Gertner asking for an immediate replacement had gone unanswered until now.

Liese put a lid on her anger. "It was good of you to personally drive my replacement translator out here, Captain."

"There is a car approaching the compound's gate," LeFevre announced. He was watching across the lagoon through a pair of binoculars.

An expression that looked like fear to Liese briefly crossed Gertner's face. He glanced at her for just a moment, but it was long enough to know that he *was* frightened. All at once she realized what was happening. Gertner had been in love with Marta Fredericks, and it must have torn his heart out when she'd fallen in love with Kirk McGarvey. After McGarvey left Switzerland, and Marta was killed following him to Paris in an effort to win him back, Gertner's heartbreak had transformed itself into hate, hate for the American assassin who had stolen the woman he loved. But it wasn't until now, with his fantastic theory, that he saw a way of getting revenge.

But the stakes were very high. Gertner's career rested on at least casting a shadow of doubt on McGarvey. That much would be enough because very few people in Bern had any love lost for the director of the CIA, who, in the government's estimation, had never been a friend of Switzerland.

Since Liese had been and was still in love with Kirk McGarvey, she was a part of Gertner's plot whether she wanted to be or not. He would not fire her, nor would she be allowed to quit.

Lights started to come on throughout the prince's compound and inside the house. Even to the naked eye it was clear that something was going on over there. The car passed through the gate and headed up the long driveway, its headlights flashing through the gloomy trees, until it disappeared around the front of the house.

"Put the entry hall on the loudspeaker," Gertner ordered.

Ziegler reached past Sergeant Hoenecker, typed a brief command on the electronic surveillance computer keyboard, and suddenly they were hearing what was going on inside the prince's house.

Every piece of electrical and electronic equipment inside the Salman compound—everything from the electrical wiring itself, the lamps and other fixtures, the microwave, the telephones, the television, and of course the computers—had been compromised in one fashion or another over the past few years since the prince and his family had taken up residence.

The entire compound was targeted by ultraviolet and infrared laser beams, which could pick up minute vibrations of the windows, walls, and even the roof tiles caused by any noise inside. If someone walked across a room, the sounds would be detected, washed through a sophisticated series of computer-directed filters, and identified for whose footfalls were being heard. If someone spoke, the exceedingly faint mechanical vibrations that the sound waves made on windows or doors were picked up, amplified, filtered, and sent over to the surveillance equipment.

Liese had always known that her countrymen were paranoid. She was that way herself, to an extent. But she'd not realized just what a national mania it was until she'd become a cop. Nobody really trusted anyone.

The sounds of someone walking across the tile floor in the entry hall came over the speakers. "Two men, heavy," Ziegler said. "House-security. There're six of them over there."

Hoenecker held up a hand for silence as the front door was opened. A man spoke in Arabic, and Hoenecker translated.

"Welcome home, *ya Hagg*."

Ziegler cocked his head. "That's one of the guards."

There was something that sounded like a confused shuffling in the hall, but then a different man said something. He sounded tired, and perhaps angry.

"Everything is in order here?" Hoenecker translated.

"There have been no disturbances. The children arrived yesterday afternoon. Shall we summon madam?"

"No, do not disturb her yet," Prince Salman said. "My bags are in the car. Bring them to my quarters, please; then put the car away and make double sure that our perimeter is secure. I have some work to attend to."

"Pardon me, sir, but may we know how long you plan to be in residence?" one of the guards asked, politely.

The prince had apparently started up the stairs because his voice was distorted, echoing off the ceiling and perhaps the walls in the corridor above. "Three days."

"Shall we make plans to move the family home?"

"Not this time—" Salman's voice trailed off. He said something else, and Hoenecker shook his head. "I didn't catch it."

Ziegler backed up the digital recording, adjusted the filters, and replayed the snippet of voice.

"Not this time," Hoenecker said. "I won't be as long."

Liese was suddenly galvanized with fear. "Follow him," she told Ziegler.

"No, stay with the guards," Gertner countermanded her order. "They might say something that we can use."

"Don't lose him, Tomas," Liese said urgently. "Stay on him."

"You forget who is in charge here, Sergeant," Gertner shouted.

Liese wanted to throttle the bastard. She turned on him. "Don't be as stupid as you usually are. If the prince is Khalil, it means that he's just flown halfway around the world after botching a mission in which half his men were killed. He'll be angry, disappointed, and tired. If he's going to make a mistake, it'll be right now, when he thinks that he's safe in his own home in the middle of what he and the rest of the world believe is a neutral nation. Didn't you hear him? He said he has some work to attend to. I think he's going to phone someone."

She turned back to Ziegler, who pulled up a chair next to the translator and shifted the computer's search-and-recognize program to the upper corridor, and then more specifically the prince's private apartment on the southeast end of the house. His wife and children occupied a separate suite of rooms in another wing.

"We might miss something important," Gertner said. He completely ignored the gross insult.

"Everything that goes on over there is recorded," Liese told him. "We can come back to the guards later."

The computer was picking up the very faint sounds of Arabic music playing somewhere in the house, over the noise of Salman's muffled footfalls on the carpeted floor in the upper corridor. The prince would also be hearing the music, and Liese briefly wondered if he preferred that kind of music over Western tunes. He was an international playboy. Or at least that's the role he played. He went to operas and concerts.

A man said something, and Prince Salman replied. "*Shukran.*"

"The first was one of the security people, I think," Ziegler said.

"He welcomed the prince home, and Salman thanked him," Hoenecker translated.

Salman entered his apartment, and Ziegler made sure that the computer stayed with him. Salman sighed deeply, as any man might after returning home from a tiring trip. He went into the bathroom where he relieved himself, then washed his hands before going across to his office, which occupied a very large room overlooking the lake toward the towns of Weggis and Brunnen on the far shore.

There were no sounds for a long time, perhaps three minutes. Liese imagined that the prince was standing in front of the windows looking out across the lake. A dozen small sailboats were in the middle of a club race, and their colorful spinnakers looked like exotic birds skimming the surface of the water.

Someone knocked once at the corridor door, and the computer picked up the steps of one of the guards, who set two items down, perhaps on a stand or possibly a low table. It was the luggage. The man called out to the prince.

"Shall I unpack for you, sir?" Hoenecker translated.

"*La',*" the prince replied. No.

The guard left. A half minute later the computer picked up the first of a series of soft tones, and immediately a box dropped down on a monitor showing that the prince was using a cell phone to make a call. Their sensors were picking it off the Lucerne-west-seven tower a few kilometers north.

The first three digits were 966, the country code for Saudia Arabia; the second two were 01, the area code for Riyadh; and the final seven were the phone number itself. As the call went through and the connection was made, the computer searched its databases for an identification, but came up blank.

After two rings a man answered. "*Ahlan!*" Hello.

"Good afternoon, cousin, I trust Allah that you are well." Hoenecker translated Salman's words.

"I am very well, praise God. And thou art well?"

"I'm back in Lucerne, but I will be in Monaco on Friday."

"For how long?"

"I don't know yet," Salman said. "It will depend on the events of the coming week. Afterward I might have to go to Washington."

The prince's cousin in Riyadh was silent for a moment, and Liese was worried that somehow he had detected that the call was being monitored. "We live again in a dangerous period."

"'*Aywa*," Salman replied. Yes.

Again there was a longish silence. When Salman's cousin spoke, he sounded sad, as if he was resigned to the likelihood that something bad was going to happen and there was nothing he could do about it. "Go with God."

"You as well."

The connection was broken, and Gertner clapped his hands in delight. "That's it then."

Liese was suddenly angry. "Their conversation proved nothing."

"For once I agree with you, *Liebchen*."

"Then what are you talking about?"

"The prince is merely half of the equation. Your Mr. McGarvey is the other half." He looked to the other officers to make sure they got his point. "Would anyone care to hazard a guess where Mr. McGarvey will be three days from now?"

"You're crazy," Liese said, her stomach hollow now with fear. "Kirk McGarvey is anything but a traitor."

TWENTY-SEVEN

McGarvey got home at seven on the dot, because he'd promised Katy he'd be home on time, despite the work left to be done. The CIA was on a 24/7 emergency footing now until the latest bin Laden threat was dealt with. Everyone was putting in long hours. After tonight that would include the DCI.

All the way in from Langley, McGarvey was lost in his thoughts in the backseat of the armored limousine. Even though he was distracted, he was aware that traffic on the Beltway was sparse compared to what it normally was at this hour on a weekday. The president would be on television at eight, and the uncertain nation was at home waiting by their TV sets, as they had been after the 9/11 attacks and every other disaster.

Otto's theory that Khalil and the Saudi multimillionaire deal maker Prince Abdul Salman were the same man would answer a number of questions about how the Saudis funneled money into organizations such as al-Quaida, and why they were doing it when bin Laden was targeting his own country as well as the U.S. It was just possible that the Salman branch of the royal family wanted to take the crown. The prince was using al-Quaida and bin Laden's name to act as a kingmaker.

All afternoon McGarvey had been trying to pick the idea apart; find its inconsistencies, the impossibilities; find out that when the prince was attending some public function, Khalil could be positively placed elsewhere. So far, Otto's search had produced nothing but the opposite, though proving that the two men were never seen at the same time did not prove they were the same person.

Security at McGarvey's house was obvious but not blatant. A van with silvered windows was parked at the entrance to the cul-de-sac, a second van was parked at the curb across the street from the house, and as the limo approached the driveway Julien checked with the detail inside to make sure it was safe to come in.

"Is everything okay?" McGarvey asked.

"Yes, it is, Mr. Director," Julien said, pulling into the driveway. He stopped. "Just one moment, sir." He took the MAC-10 submachine gun from its bracket in front of the center console and got out of the limo. He was speaking to someone via radio as he did a three-sixty, looking for something or someone who shouldn't be there. But the neighborhood could have been abandoned.

He came back and opened the door, and McGarvey got out.

"Will you be needing me tonight?" Julien asked.

"Not unless something comes up," McGarvey told him. "Wish your wife happy birthday from me."

Julien looked startled for just a moment, but then he grinned. "Your secretary is a sharp lady."

"That she is," McGarvey said. "See you in the morning."

"Yes, sir."

McGarvey let himself into the house, resetting the code on the security keypad in the front hall. One of his stern rules was that any security detail inside was to be as unobtrusive as possible. They were CIA Office of Security experts, not upstairs maids or butlers.

There were no sounds.

For just an instant McGarvey thought about reaching for his pistol. He'd drawn a 9mm version of the Walther PPK from the armory to replace the one that had gone down with the Spirit. It was comfortable in the quick-draw holster beneath his jacket at the small of his back.

But then one of the security officers appeared at the head of the stairs. "Everything okay, then, Mr. McGarvey?" he asked. He looked like a Marine—young, square jaw, short hair, a big Heckler & Koch SOCOM pistol in a shoulder holster.

"Just fine. Where's my wife?"

"Downstairs, sir."

"Here," Kathleen said, from McGarvey's right. She was in the study at the front windows, an odd expression on her face. She'd evidently seen Julien get out of the limo and do a three-sixty with his weapon before letting Mac get out.

The guard melted away, and McGarvey went to Katy and took her in his arms. "Get any sleep?"

"Couple of hours," she said. She was shivering, but it wasn't from cold. "Should you be at work?"

"Yes, but my people are working on the problem. We've got a shot at stopping them."

She pulled away and searched his eyes to make sure he was telling the truth. She was just like the rest of the country, looking to someone in charge to tell her that everything would be okay. "Honest Injun?"

McGarvey smiled at her. "Been thinking about Otto?"

"I asked Louise and him to come for dinner tonight. She's working, but he'll try. Do you mind terribly?"

McGarvey knew that Katy wanted to gather her family around her, as any mother would when her world was being threatened. "No," he said. "It's probably a good idea anyway, because it's going to get hectic after the president's speech tonight."

"Do you know what he's going to say?"

McGarvey had a fair idea what Haynes was going to tell the nation, but he wasn't at all sure it would do any good.

"Is he going to tell us not to worry?" Katy asked, breathlessly. "We won't have to endure another 9/11?"

"I don't know, sweetheart."

Her lips compressed.

"He's going to say that everything possible is being done. This time bin Laden and his people are not going to get away. No matter what it takes, we will get them."

"That means you," Katy said.

McGarvey nodded. The president was going to say a lot more than that. He was going to tell the American people that a lot of their civil liberties would have to be curtailed until all the bad guys were destroyed. What he wouldn't tell them was how many of those rights, such as Miranda, speedy trials, writs of habeas corpus, search and seizure, wiretapping, mail intercepts, or computer monitoring without court orders, would be waived. Nor would he be able to say how long the Constitution would be all but suspended.

Desperate measures for desperate times.

And who was to say that if some of those measures had been put in place before 9/11 the attacks might have been prevented?

The CIA, under his watch, had been asleep at the switch. In no small measure 9/11 had been as much McGarvey's fault as anyone's.

Katy smiled. "Bourbon and water, one rock, will be on the kitchen counter as soon as you grab a quick shower."

TWENTY-EIGHT

□

Liese straightened up from where she'd been leaning against the porch rail at the side of the veranda as Gertner came from around back. She'd come out to get some air, away from the stifling man-smells. "Has the prince made another telephone call?"

"No. It would appear that he is settling in for a day with his wife and kiddies," Gertner said. "Domestic bliss and all of that."

"There's something to be said for that," Liese replied. Her parents were divorced when she was a child. She went to live with her father, who was a drunk and a womanizer, but he was a respected barrister so he was very busy and spent little time at home. Liese had been forced to endure a miserable, lonely childhood. Mac had a wife and child, Gertner had his family, and even the prince was married. "You want to speak to me?"

"We have half of the equation. Now we need the other half."

Liese looked across the lake. All the little sailboats were heading back to their docks a few kilometers away at the yacht club in Horw. "He's in Washington, a national hero. Waiting there like everyone for the president's speech."

"But not us. We have other work to do, and we have less than seventy-two hours in which to prepare."

"What are you talking about?"

"I don't think that I have to spell it out for you like a schoolmaster for his student. The prince is leaving for Monaco in three days, where he will remain for some already predetermined time, after which he may have to go to Washington."

"Go ahead and spell it out for me, sir."

Gertner ignored her sarcastic tone. "The prince came back to make certain that his family was secure, and to get himself noticed. Out in the open. Nice and tidy. He'll do the same in Monaco. Play his role as international playboy in plain view of the entire world. At some point, while he is there gambling and womanizing, al-Quaida will make its strike, after which his presence will be required in Washington to once again make certain that nothing stands in the way of U.S.-Saudi relations."

"The same as he did in September 2001," Liese said. She'd read the prince's file that Gertner had sent down.

"September fifteenth. He was in Paris on the eleventh. And so was Mr. McGarvey."

Liese looked out across the lake again. There were only a few gaily-colored spinnakers up now; the rest had been doused. The crews would have a party tonight. Prizes would be handed out. Some of them would get too drunk to drive, but they would be important men, and the traffic cops would look the other way. It was so damned unfair. The entire bloody world was so damned unfair. She turned back. "What do you want me to do, Captain?"

The expression on Gertner's face softened for just a second. Almost, Liese thought, as if he had a soul. "I think you know, *Liebchen.* I'll give your Mr. McGarvey twenty-four hours to telephone you about the prince. After that, if he hasn't called, you will place another telephone call to him. At his home. We need to know when he will be coming to Monaco."

"Why should I do that?" She looked up. "Is that an order?" she asked defiantly.

"If you wish it to be," Gertner said. "But you will call him because you *must.* Heavens, you are in love with the man."

TWENTY-NINE

McGarvey's daughter Elizabeth and her husband Todd had already arrived and were in the kitchen when he came down from his shower. He could hear them talking with Katy. He stopped just around the corner from the kitchen door to gird himself for the inevitable spate of questions about Alaska and about bin Laden's latest threat.

In his mind the time for talk was done. If they could prove that Khalil and prince Salman were one and the same man, McGarvey would find him and kill him. It was all that mattered at this moment. It was all he was focused on.

The president's Rose Garden photo op that afternoon and all the media requests for interviews with America's latest hero could do nothing but slow him down. And even now he was reverting to an old mindset in which his family would hinder him too.

Excess baggage was the bane of the special operator, and most especially of the assassin.

That was a role he had played for almost all of his life in the service, a role he had tried without luck to quit over and over again. Since the Soviet Union had disintegrated, threats to Americans had popped up all over a world that had once been held in a delicate balance between the two superpowers, but was now fractured into hundreds if not thousands of factions all with one common enemy: the United States.

Neither the war in Afghanistan nor the war in Iraq put a stop to bin Laden's al-Quaida. And until this moment the administration had only paid lip service to the goal of finding and killing the man. Now the country was on the verge of paying again for that lack of resolve.

And it was just as much the CIA's and McGarvey's fault that the U.S. hadn't run the man to ground.

That was going to change. Once again he was going to pick up his gun and go hunting, no matter what the cost.

He put all that at the back of his mind, smiled, and went into the kitchen. Katy was putting a basket of cut potatoes into the deep fryer, Todd was grinding pepper onto a platter of thick steaks, and Liz was tearing lettuce into a large wooden salad bowl.

For just a moment they didn't notice him standing in the doorway. They seemed happy to be here together, despite what had happened in the past couple of days and the new bin Laden threat. At twenty-four, Liz was the spitting image of her mother at that age: long graceful body, tiny oval face, wide, beautiful green eyes, and a frank, direct manner that had been only slightly clouded by the fact she could never carry a child. The same sadness rode on Todd's sturdy shoulders like the world on Hercules', but it was something he never talked about with anyone. He simply went about his job with his usual steady-handed competence, but minus some small little spark that in the old days had showed up in his eyes or at the corners of his mouth when he thought something was funny. A little bit of his lightness had gone out.

Liz looked up first. Her face lit up. "Daddy," she said, and she came around the counter into his arms, holding him tightly and burrowing her face into his neck like she'd done ever since she was a child.

McGarvey patted her back, and when she looked up he kissed her forehead. "How're you doing, sweetheart?"

"Fine." She studied his eyes. "Was it bad up there?"

McGarvey nodded. "A lot of good people lost their lives."

"There would have been more if it hadn't been for you," Liz said. "Mother told us all about it." She shook her head, a look of adoration mixed with amazement on her face. In her eyes her father could never do wrong. He was the most important man in her life, which was another of the unspoken issues between her and her husband. "But you had such a terrible scowl on your face when the president was thanking you in the Rose Garden."

"Makes me glad I never ran for office," McGarvey said.

Katy was grinning, like she did lately whenever she and Liz had one of their mother-daughter talks. "It would have made for some interesting campaigns, especially when you started shooting at your opponents."

Todd chuckled, but there was little humor in it. "Good work up there, Mac. Was it Khalil? Are we sure this time?"

"Ninety-nine percent."

Todd nodded, and glanced at Liz and her mother. "Someone will have to go after him."

All the joy left the room, even though all of them knew what was coming, as surely as they knew the sun would rise in the morning. It's what McGarvey did. It was, or had been, his job. And at the moment there was no one in the Company better qualified to go after the terrorist.

"Maybe not," Liz said, and she looked away almost as if she were ashamed of suggesting that her father not go back into the field. "It's getting weird out there. Driving over, there was almost no one else on the roads. Even the radio shock jocks are being nice. Howard Stern was talking about Pearl Harbor and 9/11, wondering how the people who died would have turned out. Maybe there were some artists, or scientists, or poets."

"I'm pretty sure that the Shaw thing was just supposed to be a diversion for the main act," McGarvey said. "If they had pulled it off, we would have had our hands full trying to rescue him. And then right in the middle of that op, they would have hit us with this warning. It would have been worse than it is right now."

"So why did bin Laden release the tape?" Todd asked.

McGarvey figured there were two reasons. The first was to keep us off-balance, to prove to the world that no matter what happened in Alaska, al-Quaida was still a power to be reckoned with. That the *jihad* against America was still in full swing. But the second, more subtle, reason was that there might be a power struggle going on between bin Laden and Khalil. Bin Laden went public with his threat because he hoped it would force McGarvey into leaving Langley to personally hunt for Khalil. Alaska was an embarrassment, and McGarvey had been a thorn in bin Laden's side since before 9/11. No matter the outcome of a confrontation between McGarvey and Khalil, bin Laden would come out the winner.

In the meantime, the new threat, even if it was never carried out, was already having the desired effect. America was in a collective terror. "Could be he's just taunting us."

"But you don't believe that, do you, Mac?" Todd asked.

McGarvey shook his head.

"You came head-to-head with Khalil, and now they're daring you to come out and face him again."

"That's a possibility." McGarvey went to the counter and got his drink from Katy. They looked at each other for just an instant, and he could see that she understood completely what he was setting himself to do. And she was okay with it finally, because of Alaska and more importantly because of the continuing aftermath of 9/11. To have it happen all over again would be a horror beyond imagining.

"It would take you away from Langley just when you're needed the most," Todd said. But he was just playing devil's advocate. "Maybe you need to send somebody else."

The problem with being a spy, especially a spymaster, was that the job came with its own set of vulnerabilities. Give a spy a good puzzle, and he would be compelled to chase after it like a mouse after cheese in a trap. This time the spymaster was none other than the director of the U.S. Central Intelligence Agency, and the bait was Khalil, the number two terrormaster behind Osama bin Laden himself. At risk were the lives of innocent American men, women, and this time, children.

"I might have a personal stake in this," McGarvey said. He took a drink, then held the cool glass against his forehead. It had been a very long day, and it wasn't over yet. "There's a possibility that Khalil might be a Saudi prince who I had a brief contact with during an op about eight or ten years ago."

"Who is it?" Liz asked.

"His name is Salman. He's rich, well connected; in fact, he's stayed at the White House. He's one of the Saudis we rely on to broker some pretty big deals, holding OPEC in line, keeping an open channel with Tehran, shipping us extra oil when we're faced with a crunch. He was one of the people behind convincing Riyadh to allow us basing privileges during the first Gulf War."

"Doesn't sound like a terrorist," Todd said.

"No, he doesn't," McGarvey said, but then neither had Carlos in the seventies and eighties. He too had been a rich international playboy. His flamboyant life out in the open had provided him with the perfect cover.

"Can we prove it?" Todd asked.

"Otto's working on it, and the Swiss government is investigating him. He's got some banking interests there, and his wife and children live in Lucerne. Someone over there is trying to make the connection between him and Khalil."

Katy winced, but no one except Mac noticed. There was nothing he could do to help ease her painful memories, except be here for her.

Todd was having trouble accepting the possibility. "I hate to say this, Mac, but are we talking wishful thinking?" He looked to his wife for support, but she shrugged. She had no idea where he was going. "It's counterintuitive to think that a Saudi prince would be working against his own government. Bin Laden's been after the royals since right after Afghanistan. And there's just too much money at stake for a man like Salman to risk it all. For what?"

If Otto could nail the connection, it was one of the questions McGarvey wanted to ask the prince in person.

"Ego," Katy said, quietly.

"That was Khalil, in Alaska," Todd said. "I still don't see a guy like Salman risking his life working as a terrorist."

"I'm talking about Abdul Salman," Katy said. "I knew him."

Liz was bewildered. "When? From where?"

McGarvey shook his head, but Katy gave him her "It's okay" look.

"It was a few years ago, when your father and I were still divorced. The prince was doing something big here in Washington for his government, although none of us knew exactly what it was, but he was suddenly on everybody's A-list. He was popping up all over the place, especially the embassy parties. His English was perfect, his manners and dress were impeccable, and he knew his way around a wine list every bit as well as Darby did."

"Still sounds like a playboy and not a terrorist," Todd said. If he or Liz caught the significance of the name Darby or the fact that Katy did not elaborate, they gave no sign of it. "I'm sorry, but I'm having trouble buying the likelihood that Salman and Khalil are the same man."

"It sounds absurd, I know." Katy hesitated for a moment. She gave Mac a little shrug. "But trust me, Todd, I got to know the prince well enough to know for certain that there were very few men that he could work for. At the time it was a Russian KGB general, and now it's bin Laden."

Now Liz and Todd were on the same page. They knew about Baranov and Darby Yarnell and the operation that had ended with the deaths of Yarnell and Donald Powers, the director of the CIA at the time. They also understood how incredibly difficult it was for Katy to speak up.

Katy looked as if she wanted to crawl into a hole and bury herself. But she squared her shoulders. "There was something about Khalil aboard the ship that bothered me. But it hasn't struck me until now. He and the prince are the same man, and I know it for a fact."

"But how, Mother?" Liz blurted.

Katy did not lower her eyes. "Because I had an affair with him."

THIRTY

☐

Liz's mouth dropped open. She looked at her father, trying to gauge his reaction, then turned back to her mother. It was obvious that she wanted to be angry, but she was too stunned. "Mother?"

Katy lowered her eyes. "Sorry, but none of us is ever as perfect as you think."

McGarvey nodded. "We were divorced, and I was living with a woman in Lucerne."

He gave his wife a reassuring look. "We knew about each other's lives, and it made our own that much tougher because we still loved each other."

"Do the Swiss know about this?" Todd asked.

"Probably. Otto took a call from one of the federal cops who watched after me when I lived over there. They wanted to know if there was still a connection between Salman and me."

"What'd you tell them, Daddy?" Liz asked.

McGarvey wanted to help his daughter understand. But there were some things that were better left unexplained. "Nothing yet, but the Swiss might be sitting on something that we need. I'll call in the morning."

One of the security people appeared at the kitchen door. "Mr. Rencke is here, Mr. Director," he said. He was listening to something in his earpiece. "Copy," he said softly. "He's alone, sir."

"We're expecting him for dinner," Katy said.

McGarvey nodded, and the agent turned and disappeared down the hall. He glanced at the clock in the microwave. It was nearly 7:30 P.M. "Put the steaks on, Todd. We have a half hour before the president comes on. I'll be just a minute." He put his drink down and went out to the front stair hall just as Otto was coming in.

His special projects director pulled up short; his eyes were wide, his frizzy long red hair in even more disarray than usual, and his sweatshirt with the KGB sword and shield emblem filthy dirty. He'd brought a laptop with him. "Oh boy, Mac, this is the big enchilada this time," he gushed. He hopped from one foot to the other, something he did only when he was excited. "We can get the bastard."

"When have you been home last?"

Rencke stopped all of a sudden, the idiot look leaving his face. "Mrs. M. will make me clean up before supper, but right now you gotta look at something."

They went into the study and closed the door. The room was electronically swept every twelve hours, so it was reasonably secure. Otto put the laptop on the desk and booted it up. Two columns of dates and places appeared on the screen. One was headed *Khalil*, the other *Salman*. They were nearly a perfect match, date for date, place for place.

"These go back eight and a half years," Otto said. "Now even you've gotta admit that this shit goes way beyond coincidence."

McGarvey had already seen some of this, and he had to agree with Rencke. "Are there any mismatches? Any times when Khalil and Salman weren't at the same place and time?"

Rencke thought about the question for a split second. "No way of telling for sure, 'cause most of the Khalil sightings are inferences. He's only been nailed solid four times, including your encounter three days ago."

"Where was Salman this last time?"

An evil grin spread across Rencke's face. "Victoria, BC, in a private meeting with Thomas Malcovich, the Canadian oil minister. After which he picked up a leased Gulfstream in Vancouver under the name Thomas Powers, which took him to London, where he promptly disappeared for twenty-four hours. He just showed up in Switzerland a couple hours ago."

"Why the cover name?"

"Salman has used it at least twice before when he brokered deals in secret. Once in 1997 between Moscow and Tehran over maintenance contracts for their Kilo subs, and again in June 2000 between Pyongyang and Beijing over high-pressure pumps, presumably for their nuclear program."

McGarvey wanted as solid a case as possible before he went into the field. "Okay, so we've got Salman and Khalil in the same part of the world on the same days. Not proof enough. Not even with all the other coincidences. What else?"

"I worked out their most logical escape route," Otto said. He pulled up a map of coastal Alaska and Canada from Juneau to Vancouver on the laptop's screen. Overlaid were several red lines. "You said that Khalil left with somewhere between five and ten of his operators aboard a small sportfisherman. Canadian Coast Guard found the boat abandoned on Kupreanof Island a half mile from the airport at the town of Kake. That's less than thirty miles from where the Spirit went down. The boat belonged to a family who ran a fishing resort a few miles farther south. Their bodies were found this morning. And there was evidence that a dozen or more people had been at the resort for as long as five days. They even did target practice." Rencke looked up, his eyes owlish. "Nine-millimeter rounds, according to the Canadians. Fits with what weapons you say they carried."

"Polish-made RAKs and Steyr GBs," McGarvey said. "Old-fashioned but effective."

"They had some of their people on the cruise ship, probably as early as Seattle, and the rest of them took over the fishing resort a few days ahead of time. They used one of the boats from the resort to rendezvous with the Spirit, and when you screwed up their plans they went to the airport at Kake, where they left aboard a twin Otto floatplane." Rencke highlighted one of the red lines that reached out into the Pacific from Kake. "If they had snatched Shaw, they were going to ditch the Otter at sea and a cargo ship was going to pick them up. There are three possibilities, all of them Liberian registry. Our Coast Guard is heading out to them right now."

"Okay."

Rencke highlighted a spot four hundred miles south of Kake on the northeast coast of Graham Island just across Hecate Strait from the town of Prince Rupert on the mainland. "A fishing crew spotted what they thought was a small explosion in midair about the time the Coast Guard was rescuing you and the survivors. A Canadian search-and-rescue team finally found the wreckage of the Otter three hours ago. At least six bodies, possibly one or two more. One of them has already been identified as Rupert Thompson, a contract pilot working for Airways North. All of the others were male, and none of them carried any identification, though at least two of them were armed with Steyr pistols."

"What were they doing so far south?" McGarvey asked.

"The same question I asked myself," Rencke said. "The times of Salman's meetings with the Canadian oil minister are all before the hijacking. Several days before. After which Powers disappeared, as if he flew back to Switzerland. But of course he didn't show up anywhere outside of Canada until *after* the hijacking."

"There weren't supposed to be any survivors from the *Spirit*," McGarvey said.

"That's right," Rencke said. "But with you in the picture Khalil had to figure that someone would have made it off the ship before it went down, and then it'd be just a matter of time before we put it together and boarded every cargo ship in the vicinity. So he had the pilot take him down to Vancouver or some out-of-the-way spot nearby, and he sent his people back. But he somehow sabotaged the plane to blow up hopefully over the open water, and *voilà*, he disappeared back into the limelight as Prince Salman, and all the evidence aboard the Otter was supposed to disappear into the sea."

McGarvey wanted to believe it, because if Salman and Khalil were the same man, it would unravel a ten-year-old mystery of how the international terrorist had been able to move around under the noses of every law enforcement and intelligence agency in the world and never be caught. The world was focused on Prince Salman and never saw Khalil.

But it was too easy. The answers were too pat.

"Did you know that the Bureau investigated Salman after 9/11?" Rencke said. "He was one of the Saudis who took flight training in Florida the year before, and then in June he went up to Minneapolis where he did flight simulator time on the 747."

McGarvey smiled grimly. "Let me guess. The investigation was dropped because Salman was a friend of the White House."

Rencke clapped his hands together in glee. "Give that man the Kewpie doll. But it's not just the White House and not just this administration, Mac; it's everybody who's anybody inside the Beltway. Salman is a Saudi, the Saudis give us oil, and the prince is the chief broker of some of the most important deals around. He's a holy cow."

"Maybe he's just that," McGarvey said, softly. "A holy cow. A megarich prima donna who's innocent of everything except being a wheeler-dealer."

Rencke was suddenly subdued. He averted his eyes. "What about Mrs. M?" he asked, hesitantly. "She knows."

They'd been through so much. So many heartaches. So many troubles. They didn't need this.

"Maybe she's mistaken."

Rencke looked at him, his long face sad. He shook his head. "She's not."

Down in Washington the president of the United States was going over the finishing touches of the speech he would give to the nation in a few minutes. He still wasn't one hundred percent sure what he was going to propose. But he could think of no other course of action that made any sense. Nor had his advisers been much help. *God help us all,* he thought. *And God help the Republic.*

THIRTY-ONE

Liese stood in the deeper shadows beside the large window that looked across the bay toward the Salman compound, lit now only by the outside lights. The prince had spent the last two hours with his wife and children in the east wing of the main house, but a couple of minutes ago he had returned to his own quarters, where he turned on a television set. It was one in the morning here, but eight in the evening in Washington.

Almost every person on the planet would be watching or listening to president Haynes's speech to his people.

Tomas Ziegler had plugged in a portable television set under Gertner's instructions, and he switched it to CNN. A pair of news analysts, one a man and the other a pretty brunette, were in the middle of discussing the president's upcoming speech.

At that moment, the same audio came from the surveillance microphone in Salman's quarters. The prince was tuned to the same television channel. "It would seem that the good prince is also interested in what Haynes will have to say," Gertner said.

"Filter out as much of the television audio as you can," Liese told Ziegler. "Salman might be the type who talks back to his television set. I want to hear what he has to say."

The telephone in the prince's apartment rang. Ziegler was on it immediately. "It's from out of the country."

The telephone rang a second time.

"Saudi Arabia," Ziegler said, excitedly. "Riyadh."

Salman answered on the third ring. *"Oui?"*

A man said something in Arabic, and Hoenecker translated. "Will you watch the president, nephew?"

"I have the television on now, my esteemed uncle." Hoenecker translated Salman's words.

Ziegler looked up from his monitor. "It's the royal palace. That's Crown Prince Abdullah."

"Turn it off," Gertner ordered.

"Why?" Liese demanded. "If Prince Salman and Khalil are one and the same man, this could mean that the Saudi royals, all the way to the top, are in the terror business."

Gertner shot her a bleak look. "That's exactly why, *Liebchen.* We don't need that trouble, you and I. Turn it off."

At that moment it was five in the morning in Karachi, Pakistan, and a thirteen-inch black-and-white television set on a small table in a featureless room was tuned to Al Jazeera. Osama bin Laden came in, turned the sound up, settled down on a Persian rug, and leaned casually on a large brocaded pillow. His English was good so he did not have to wait for the words of the commentators in Washington to be translated.

The picture cut to an image of a podium with the great seal of the U.S. "Ladies and gentlemen, the President of the United States."

Lawrence Haynes entered the East Room and went to the podium. He'd not brought his speech or any notes. His adviser on national security affairs, Dennis Berndt; the chairman of the Joint Chiefs, Admiral Paul Wilcox; and the director of the FBI, Herbert Weissman, took positions on either side of him.

"Good evening," the president began, his famous smile missing this evening. This was a president come to tell his nation something serious. "Directly following my comments tonight we will show you the latest taped message from the terrorist Osama bin Laden. Many of you have already seen the tape. Many of you have unfortunately have already assumed the worst, that once again an unspeakable evil will be unleashed by monsters on America."

The president slowly shook his head. "Nothing could be further from the truth. Even now units of our naval and air forces are on standby to strike at the very heart of the terrorist's operations. The Central Intelligence Agency is engaged in a massive worldwide manhunt, using every asset and technical means at its command, as are the National Security Agency and National Reconnaissance Office. At home I have instructed the Federal Bureau of Investigation to coordinate a nationwide search not only for the henchmen of bin Laden's al-Quaida organization, but also for any group or individual planning to do us harm."

The president's lips compressed as he seemed to gird himself for what he would say next. "We will capture bin Laden and his lieutenants just as we captured Saddam Hussein and his staff. There will not be another tragic day such as September eleventh! But in order to effectively carry on with our work of eliminating the evil that would attempt to destroy our freedom, our very way of life, drastic measures must and will be taken."

A slow smile spread across bin Laden's harsh features.

"Effective immediately, and to last until we can confirm the capture or the death of Osama bin Laden and his principal lieutenant, the terrorist known as Khalil, I am declaring that a state of martial law exists in the United States and our territories and protectorates."

Bin Laden rose languorously to his feet, no longer interested in the president's feeble speech, then switched off the television set and went to compose a personal letter to each of the four boys who would soon be entering the gates of Paradise as martyrs.

THIRTY-TWO

□

McGarvey had Julien take him directly over to the White House first thing in the morning. On the way over he called Calvin Beckett, the president's chief of staff, to see if he could be fit in early. The morning's national intelligence briefing was usually held at 9 A.M., but McGarvey was an hour early.

"Do you have something for us already?" Beckett asked, hopefully. The man had left a job as head of IBM's legal department to join the administration shortly after Haynes took office. He was an avid skier, skydiver, and acrobatic pilot, who was not afraid to take chances. Decisions came easily for him, and as a result he and McGarvey had developed a good working relationship.

"We might have an identification on Khalil," McGarvey said, "but I don't think your boss is going to like it."

"Can we get to him?"

"I don't think that'll be a problem."

"Then I don't care if he's the pope. If the CIA knows who he is and where we can get him, the president will order it. I can practically guarantee it, Mac," Beckett said. "You heard his speech last night. There won't be another 9/11. Whatever it takes, we're going to nail the bastards this time *before* they hit us. If your people have a lead, he's going to give you the green light for any action that you want to take."

Beckett hesitated, and McGarvey could almost hear him weighing his next words. Their telephone conversation was encrypted, but in Washington once a thought was spoken it could never be taken back. And the wrong kinds of words could take on a life of their own, which had the power to devastate even a solid career.

"The president doesn't want to negotiate this time."

McGarvey knew exactly what Beckett was going to say. He'd heard other men skirt around the very same issue with him more times than he'd care to count. He wasn't going to make it easy by assuring Beckett that he knew what he was supposed to do. He wanted the administration to tell him.

"There'll be no trial, understand?" Beckett said. "If you can get to Khalil, kill him. The same goes for bin Laden."

The White House, McGarvey figured, was operating under the same siege mentality that the rest of Washington was struggling with. Bin Laden's threat was already having a serious effect on the nation. People across the country were calling in sick, keeping their children home from school, all but barricading themselves in their houses with what Fox News was calling the "9/11 flu."

Any building over four or five stories tall was all but deserted. Almost every office in Washington was operating with a skeleton staff. The DOW and NASDAQ were sharply down. And traffic on the interstate system, even the normally crammed-to-capacity I-95 along the eastern seaboard, had less volume than on an average Sunday.

Americans were frightened.

"That's what I'm coming to talk about," McGarvey said.

Beckett sounded relieved. "The president will be glad to hear that, Mr. Director. I'll clear the deck for you. This is priority one. Nothing is more important."

McGarvey looked out the window as they crossed K Street and skirted the greenery of Farragut Square just a couple of blocks from the White House.

"The president is taking a lot of heat over his martial law decision. He'll be meeting with a bipartisan group from the Hill at ten, and we just found out that they're bringing Emmet Sampson with them." Sampson had taken over the ACLU in the aftermath of 9/11, and he had become the most vocal critic of the White House and especially of the Justice Department and Homeland Security.

McGarvey could just guess what the California Democrat would say to Haynes. "There are going to be a lot of people who'll agree with him."

Beckett was suddenly cool. "We want you with us on this one, Mac. The president needs all his people to stand up and be counted."

McGarvey hated bullshit in any variety. "I know. I got a taste of it in the Rose Garden yesterday."

His limo crossed H Street on the light and headed past the Renwick Gallery and Blair House to the west gate. Almost no one was on Pennsylvania Avenue in front of the White House's iron fence. McGarvey almost expected to hear air-raid sirens. The street reminded him of the scene outside the Presidential Palace in Santiago the morning after he'd assassinated army general August Pinar and his wife at their coastal retreat near San Francisco. All of Chile had been thrown on the defensive. It was generally known that the CIA had made the hit, and if a towering figure such as Pinar could be reached, then everybody was vulnerable.

September eleventh had proved that America was not an invulnerable island nation.

"That was a very necessary ceremony that has nothing to do with the problem staring us in the face now," Beckett said.

The president's chief of staff wanted to be belligerent, McGarvey thought, because no one over there knew what to do. We'd been caught flat-footed by just about every act of terrorism ever committed against us, including the Murrah Federal Building, the USS Cole, and both attacks on the World Trade Center. And it was happening again.

Declaring martial law wouldn't do a thing to stop whatever bin Laden was going to do. The only sure cure was finding and killing the men responsible, like we should have done long before 9/11.

Assassination.

"I wouldn't have advised martial law," McGarvey said.

"You weren't asked, Mr. Director," Beckett said, bleakly.

McGarvey broke the connection as his limo was passed through the west gate. He hadn't been at all sure how the president was going to react, and after talking with Beckett he was even less sure. Becoming president did not make a man immune from fear. For a lot of them, from the moment they took up residence in the White House until the day they left, they never got a decent night's sleep. And a frightened man who wasn't sleeping well could make some very bad decisions. Like Truman had when he'd given away our nuclear advantage by promising the world we would never again be the first to drop the bomb. Or like Kennedy, ordering the Bay of Pigs fiasco, then later promising the Russians we would never again attack the island. Or like Nixon, denying he knew anything about the Watergate break-in. And now Haynes declaring martial law.

McGarvey felt a great foreboding as he got out of the car and entered the west wing. Beckett was waiting for him, and wordlessly they walked down the corridor to the Oval Office.

A pair of Marines, dressed in BDUs and armed with Colt Commando assault rifles, were stationed just inside the entrance. They had replaced the usual White House security detail. September eleventh had changed everyone, just as Pearl Harbor had, only this time the changes were happening even *before* the next event.

A harried Lawrence Haynes stood at his desk talking to someone on the telephone, while aides and advisers scurried in and out. This was the beginning of an extremely busy day, typical of any before it except for the threat hanging over the nation. As McGarvey followed Beckett in, he wondered why anyone in his right mind would want the job, because in the final analysis being president had nothing whatsoever to do with power. It had to do with administration, organization, politics, and most of all stamina and the ability to make decisions and to truly believe that they were the best ones possible under the circumstances.

Haynes looked presidential this morning. It was something about him that the American public loved. When the nation needed a leader he was there. Two years ago he and his wife and daughter had almost been assassinated. He'd come out of the ordeal as the most popular president since FDR. His jacket was off, his tie already loose, his shirtsleeves rolled up. Here was a president getting down to the business of leading his country through a difficult time.

He looked over at McGarvey with something akin to relief, then turned away. Whoever he was talking to wasn't an ally. The president did not sound pleased. He had his detractors who were waiting in the wings ready to pounce the moment he made a mistake. The martial law thing could very well lose him the next election, and everyone in Washington was already taking sides.

It was politics in its rawest form.

Beckett herded everyone else out, then motioned for McGarvey to have a seat on the couch. "Coffee?"

"I won't be that long," McGarvey said. "I'm going to lay out what we've come up with, and the president will have to make a decision. The ball's in his court."

"Yes, it is."

Beckett called Dennis Berndt to come over, and the national security adviser showed up a minute later just as Haynes was hanging up. Like Beckett and the president he looked hopeful when he saw that McGarvey was here.

"Mr. Director," Berndt said. He glanced over at Haynes.

"Good morning, Dennis," McGarvey said. "Mr. President. I think we know who Khalil is."

Haynes was direct and to the point. He was obviously in no mood to play games. "Can we get to him?"

It was the same question Beckett had asked. Anybody could be *got*, if that was the sole consideration. But at what price? That was the second, unasked, half of the question. "I don't think there'll be a problem getting close to him. In fact, we'll have to do that first before we can be one hundred percent sure we're right about who he is."

Haynes nodded with satisfaction. "Now we're getting somewhere."

"But it won't be that easy killing him," McGarvey warned. "He's masquerading as an important figure."

"I don't care who it is," Haynes countered. "He damned near snatched Don Shaw, and in the process he murdered nearly fifty innocent people. Most likely he was the brains behind 9/11, and he's probably behind this new threat." Haynes looked at Berndt and Beckett for backup, then shook his head. "I don't give a damn who he is. You find him, prove you're right, then take him down. If you want, I'll put that in writing."

"He's a member of the Saudi royal family," McGarvey told them. "Prince Abdul Hasim ibn Salman."

Haynes exchanged a look with his NSA and chief of staff; then his eyes narrowed in anger. "That's not possible."

It was the reaction McGarvey had expected. He had considered going after the prince first and explaining the CIA's suspicions to the White House later, but this president deserved the unvarnished truth, especially now. Until recently the CIA, like a lot of other agencies in Washington, tended to tell the administration it served only what the administration *wanted* to hear, even if it didn't square with reality. More than one president had made a bad call because of faulty intelligence.

"We've come up with credible evidence linking the two men," McGarvey said, "including at least one eyewitness."

Haynes shook his head. "A man such as Salman has enemies. Witnesses lie."

"Not this one," McGarvey countered, a little too sharply.

"For Christ's sake, Mac—" Beckett warned, but the president held him off with a gesture.

"Just a minute ago you said you wanted to get close to him first because you weren't one hundred percent sure."

In his heart of hearts McGarvey didn't want Salman, the man who had once made love to his wife, to be the terrorist Khalil, because he would not be able to separate revenge from justice. "Not sure enough to put a bullet in his brain."

"You want to set up a surveillance operation to watch him, is that it?" Haynes demanded. "But that'll take time, which we don't have."

"I got within twenty feet of the man aboard the cruise ship. I talked to him. If I get close again, I'll know it's him."

The president was beyond anger; he was puzzled. "I can't believe it, Mac. The fact of the matter is that Prince Salman is an important member of the Saudi royal family. The fact of the matter is that the Saudis still allow us to maintain a military presence there. The fact of the matter—the real fact of the matter—is that Saudi Arabia sits on one trillion dollars in oil reserves. And until we become a hydrogen economy, which I'm told won't happen for at least another twenty years, we need that oil." He shook his head. "The prince is a very important friend to American business. Like Adnan Khashoggi before him, he's brokered a bunch of international deals that we've needed. Some of them critical. Goodwill for us at a time we badly need it."

"I know, Mr. President."

The president's anger was returning. "What would he have to gain by attacking us? He'd be cutting his own throat. It doesn't make any sense from the standpoint of business."

"He's made deals with other countries."

"Yes, Canada," Beckett said, angrily. "At the same time he was supposedly trying to kidnap Don Shaw."

"The times match," McGarvey shot back. "And he's also brokered deals with North Korea, Iran, Iraq, Libya, Syria, and China, sometimes with money from us and the British, and at other times with Saudi money." McGarvey hesitated. "The Saudis want to sell their trillion dollars of oil to us, but at their own pace, because once their oil reserves run dry they'll have nothing. So if they can keep us seriously off-balance with attacks like 9/11, or with military actions in Somalia, Afghanistan, and Iraq, maybe it'll take us longer to get off the fossil-fuel bandwagon. It's going to take a president willing to go out on a limb, like Kennedy did by putting an American on the moon, to fire up the nation to make the switch to hydrogen."

"Continue."

"With all due respect, Mr. President, that's not likely to happen very soon because too much money is being made from oil. And it's people like Salman, if he is Khalil, who are doing whatever it takes to keep us off-balance." One of the reasons the CIA had tended to tell the administration what it wanted to hear was that presidents often got angry if they were proved to be mistaken. So instead of telling Lyndon Johnson that bombing Haiphong wouldn't work, the CIA helped the Air Force work out targets. "We have all the evidence we need to suggest that Saudi money is behind al-Quaida and more than two dozen other Islamic fundamentalist and terrorist groups."

"The Saudis have their dissident factions, just as we do," Haynes conceded. "But men such as Salman, whose family is an integral part of the government, do not become terrorists. What sense does it make?"

"Salman's family were Bedouins," McGarvey said.

Haynes brushed it off. "So what?"

"They want Saudi Arabia cleared of everyone except true believers. If they had their way, all the oil wells would be shut down, and the country would revert to the old ways. The same thing the Taliban tried in Afghanistan."

"They failed miserably," Beckett said.

McGarvey shrugged. "It's not finished yet."

Beckett started to protest, but the president held him off again. "All right, Mac, give me proof that the prince and Khalil are the same man, and we will take action," he said. "But the CIA will not, must not, allow the Saudi government, the prince himself, or anyone else for that matter to get so much of a hint that such suspicions exist. Are you clear on this point?"

It was exactly opposite of what McGarvey wanted to try. Khalil was an arrogant man who had not hesitated to kill anyone who got in his way—men, women, children, it apparently did not matter to him. If he and the prince were the same man, then putting pressure on Salman might force him to make a mistake and reveal his true identity.

"Yes, sir."

"In the meantime, the CIA needs to work with the FBI and the military to come up with a solid plan to make sure that the transition into martial law goes without a hitch. The whole idea is to make attacking us a very risky proposition. Once we have the bastards, then we can get back to the rightful business of the nation. I want to know what the CIA will do."

It was the wrong thing to do, McGarvey thought. But he couldn't really blame the president and his advisers for reacting this way. Saudi Arabia was very important to U.S. interests. Gas lines hadn't been all that long ago, and the American public hadn't forgotten them. And more than ever before, we depended upon foreign oil. Without it America would all but grind to a halt. On the other hand, the president had to do something about al-Quaida's latest threat. September eleventh was still very fresh in everyone's mind.

"All our stations and missions have been buttoned up, and every reliable asset is being pushed to the limit for information," McGarvey replied. "But there isn't much we can do domestically, except continue to provide INS and the Bureau with warnings about people trying to get in who we believe have ties to terrorist groups. The same as we've been doing all along."

"Very well. What about bin Laden himself?"

"We have nothing new about his whereabouts, but we have come up with something that might be helpful. It's possible that he was wearing a disguise in his latest video."

"What do you mean?" Berndt asked.

"His beard may have been fake, and he may have been wearing makeup to make us think that he's sick. If that's the case, it could mean he's not in the mountains between Afghanistan and Pakistan. He could be almost anywhere."

"That's just great," President Haynes grumbled. "What you're saying is that we may never find him."

"Not without finding Khalil first."

Haynes's eyes locked onto McGarvey's. "That'll have to wait. For now we need to do whatever it takes to stop the next attack." He shook his head. "That does not include going after innocent people."

The past couple of years had been something of a journey of discovery for McGarvey. He had discovered what was most important to him, and it was not worrying about the past; it was about helping people. Making things right, as simple as that sounded. Stopping the bad guys from hurting the innocents. When he met bin Laden face-to-face in the mountains of Afghanistan, before 9/11, the man maintained that there were no innocents in this war. It was the same garbage that spewed out of Khalil's mouth when he killed the woman and her infant child.

But there were innocents, and they had to be protected at all costs. That was what civilization was all about.

"I'll send a courier over this afternoon with my letter of resignation," McGarvey said. "I suggest you appoint Dick Adkins as acting DCI; he's done the job before, and he's a good man."

The president stepped back as if he had been physically staggered by what he'd just heard. "What are you talking about?"

"I quit."

Haynes shook his head. "I won't accept your resignation. This country needs you. I need you."

"I'm sorry, Mr. President; I truly am. But it's time for me to take care of my family. It's a duty I've neglected for too long."

"You can't be serious, Mac," Beckett said. "If you want out, okay, no one blames you. But wait until we get past this mess we're in. You can't bail out now."

McGarvey had no idea this would happen this morning. But it seemed to be the only move he could make. As director of the CIA he was too visible a presence. He had no real freedom of movement. Too many people were answerable to him. If being president had more to do with administration and grand visions than with power, then being DCI had more to do with administration and less with spying. Spies, by their very nature, had to be under the radar.

Assassins had to be chameleons, invisible to what they really were.

"Martial law is not the answer, Mr. President," McGarvey said. "We won't stop them that way."

The president's face was hard. "As a private citizen you will not pursue your investigation of Prince Salman. That, Mr. McGarvey, is a direct order from me. One that I shall put into writing. If you take it upon yourself to continue despite my warning, you will be arrested and prosecuted for treason. Are you clear on this?"

"Yes, Mr. President," McGarvey said. He was in pain. He'd given his entire life in service to his government, and now he was defying the president.

Treason was a powerful concept to McGarvey. But the murder of innocents was worse.

He nodded to the president and the others, then turned and left the Oval Office, his mind already on the steps he would have to take to protect his family, to ensure that the CIA did not miss a beat by his departure, and then to find Khalil and bin Laden and kill them.

Berndt was the first to recover, although the resignation of Kirk McGarvey now, of all times, had hit him like a pistol shot between the eyes. It would be interpreted by the public as cowardice, yet no one could possibly accuse Mac of treason. Overstepping his charter. Disregard of direct orders. Arrogance. Conceit. All those, but not treason.

"What do you want to do, Mr. President?" he asked.

Haynes gave his NSA a bleak look. "Get Herb Weissman over here on the double."

THIRTY-THREE

□

The Lake Lucerne chalet had two small bedrooms and a bathroom in the loft over the kitchen and master bedroom. Liese had taken the east bedroom for herself because of its skylight that looked toward Salman's compound. She'd only managed to get a few hours sleep in the past forty-eight, but she was so keyed up that each time she lay down and closed her eyes she saw Kirk McGarvey in a Swiss jail cell, pacing back and forth like a caged wild animal. The vision was so intolerable that she couldn't sleep.

She was supposedly chief of this operation, which meant that she needed to oversee her mission staff. It did not mean she had to remain here 24/7, though in practical terms either she stayed or the operation would be taken away from her.

It was 3:30 in the afternoon, and Liese was lying fully clothed on the narrow daybed, trying to get some rest when Gertner came to the door, his face puffy and red. Ever since President Haynes's martial law speech the night before, Gertner had been beside himself. *They're all cowboys. The lot of them.*

"*Liebchen*, it's him. He's on the phone for you."

Liese's heart skipped a beat. Shakily she opened her eyes and sat up in bed. "Who is it?"

"Your Herr McGarvey."

Liese got up, slipped on her shoes, and followed Gertner down to the great room where LeFevre handed her a cup of tea, black with lemon just as she preferred it. She hated that all of a sudden they were treating her with kid gloves, but Gertner was afraid of her. They all were. The trouble was that she was just as frightened of what Gertner and the people in Bern were capable of doing. They had finally backed her into a trap that she didn't know how to evade.

Ziegler seemed impressed as he held out the chalet's encrypted phone to her. "He asked for an encrypted channel."

"He knows what we're doing here," Liese said. She took the phone, then turned away and looked out the window toward the Salman compound across the narrow bay. The weather was overcast and too windy for sailboats today. "Hello, Kirk. Thanks for calling—" She almost said, "my darling."

"Hello, Liese, it's good to hear your voice again," McGarvey said, and she could hear the stress in his voice. "How are you?"

"It's I who should be asking you that, after Alaska and then President Haynes's speech last night. It's happening again for you." She could see Gertner's reflection in the window glass. He was wearing a headset, listening to every word. What Kirk could not say was that he was going to be in Monaco, because the only way he had of knowing that Salman would be there in two days was if they were working together, as Gertner was mad to prove. It was Gertner's stupid contention that McGarvey would try to throw off the Swiss investigation into Salman's activities. Almost anything he said now would be twisted in one way or another to prove the case. But Monaco would practically be the coup de grâce.

"My people told me that you called while I was away," McGarvey said, no warmth whatsoever in his voice. "You wanted whatever we had on Abdul Salman. Why?"

Liese's heart was breaking. This was nothing more than the director of American intelligence wanting to know what the hell a Swiss cop was doing bothering him. But there was nothing for Gertner to use. "We're investigating the prince—"

"For what?"

"I can't say at this moment, except that it has to do with national security."

"*Swiss* national security," Kirk responded, sharply. "But you mentioned Darby Yarnell, which tells me that someone in Bern has gotten to you. Why, Liese? Because you were once in love with me?"

Liese turned and looked at Gertner, who had the good grace to at least lower his eyes. "Something like that," she told McGarvey. "But it was my superiors who came up with the connection, not me. They thought that you would remember me as a . . . friend."

"Is he there now?"

"Yes."

"Liese, this is important. Was he there all last week?"

Liese got an immediate lift. If Kirk had to ask about Salman's whereabouts last week, then he could not be working with the man. But her spirits immediately sank when she realized that Gertner would simply take Kirk's question as a sign that the CIA director was trying to throw them off.

"No, he wasn't here," she said. "As a matter of fact he's been gone for the better part of three months. We wanted to know if the CIA had been tracking his movements."

"Why, Liese?"

Liese shook her head. "I'm sorry, but I'm not authorized to say. This is nothing more than a personal request."

"I'm coming over. I can be there first thing in the morning."

Gertner frowned. He shook his head.

"You wouldn't be allowed to enter the country."

"Okay, I'll send my daughter. She works for us."

Liese was frustrated and frightened. She didn't know what to do or what to ask him, because whatever he was going to say would be damning in Gertner's eyes. "What do you want here, Kirk?" she asked in desperation. "What is the prince to you?"

"We have a very high confidence that Salman is the al-Quaida terrorist Khalil. He was in Alaska to grab Shaw, and now we think he's behind bin Laden's latest threat."

A look of triumph crossed Gertner's face. He motioned for Liese to cover the phone.

"Just a moment," she said, and she held a shaky hand over the phone.

"Tell him that there has been a change in policy that you just learned about. He can come here after all."

"So that you can arrest him?" she demanded, shrilly. She shook her head. "This proves nothing." She turned back to the phone. "We think you might be right," she blurted. "But sending your daughter here would be a moot point. Salman is leaving for Monaco the day after—"

The connection was cut.

Love or loyalty?

She had asked herself the same question ten years ago when Kirk was here in Switzerland and she had fallen in love with him while working as a Swiss undercover cop whose duty it was to spy on him. Her answer now was the same as it had been then.

THIRTY — FOUR

McGarvey walked into the director's conference room at 10 A.M., and took his place at the head of the long mahogany table. All seven of his senior staff had already gathered, and Dick Adkins had started the Special National Intelligence Estimate briefing that would be ready to transmit to the White House by four this afternoon. The nation was in crisis. The CIA was on emergency footing and would stay that way 24/7 until the threat level dropped from red. For the duration, SNIEs would be generated every eight hours to keep the president and his advisers up to speed on the situation.

After his unsettling talk with Liese Fuelm, McGarvey had written his letter of resignation, printed it, and sealed it in an envelope. It would go by courier to the White House this afternoon sometime after lunch. But he'd not been able to get Liese out of his mind. It was obvious that she was still in love with him after all these years. And it was equally obvious that someone was using her feelings to get to him. The only reason he could think of was that the Swiss also suspected Prince Salman of doing something wrong, probably breaking Swiss banking laws, and they wanted the CIA's input. They could have simply asked through normal channels. The CIA often worked with the Swiss Bureau of Federal Police and their department of external affairs, which operated as an intelligence service.

But they had sent Liese to make contact because of the connection between the prince and the CIA director's wife. It was through the back alley, so very typically Swiss.

He felt a sense of urgency. The countdown to disaster had started, and they had very little time to stop the madness from occurring again.

Adkins handed McGarvey a buff file folder with a pair of diagonal orange stripes indicating that the material it contained was top secret. "This is the latest from Fort Meade on the bin Laden tape. I thought we'd start there."

McGarvey, sitting with his staff around him, could see that all of them were ready to point their directorates, on his orders, in whatever direction was necessary to counter the bin Laden threat. But less than two hours ago the president of the United States had all but called him a traitor. No one person, no matter how dedicated, could be placed above the interests of the nation. Yet in this case McGarvey was convinced that we were selling our safety for the sake of Saudi oil. If that made him a traitor, then so be it. But it was a burden that only he would carry. It was the reason he'd resigned so abruptly, with no notice to give the president time to appoint his successor.

This was a working meeting. Everyone had open file folders or bound reports in front of them. Photographs and maps were spread out over the long table, along with current satellite and other technical schedules and positions, and the location and battle readiness of every asset in the armed forces, along with the current status of the military units of all our allies. Everyone was concentrating on the materials in front of them, except for Rencke, who was staring at McGarvey.

"It's bin Laden's voice all right, but NSA's analysts are just as convinced as ours are that he's wearing a disguise," Adkins said. He was in shirtsleeves, his collar open, his tie loose. "His beard is fake, and he's wearing stage makeup." Like the others, Adkins hadn't been getting much sleep the last few days, and although he was animated, he looked and sounded tired.

"Osama's probably gotten tired of hiding out in the mountains, with the Pakistanis after him," McGarvey said. "Do we have anything on the whereabouts of his wives and children?" He wanted to get them headed in the right direction before he sprung his news.

"We think they might be in Khartoum," Adkins said. He turned to the CIA's general counsel. "Carleton has something on that."

"I got a call this morning from Raul Himanez, an old friend of mine from the Third Judicial Circuit who's teaching law at Harvard now," Carleton Patterson said. "He got a request from a lawyer in the Sudan who has handled bin Laden family matters in the past, about a point of international law concerning repatriation of the families of criminals convicted in absentia." Patterson, who never took off his suit coat or loosened his tie, smiled. "Raul thought I would be interested since the point the lawyer was most interested in concerned Saudi Arabian law."

"Could be that bin Laden is trying to get his family back into the good graces of the Saudi royal family," Adkins said.

"I've asked Jeff Cook to beat the bushes in Riyadh to see if he can pick up anything at all," David Whittaker said. He was the deputy director of operations, a stern, upright man who could have played the part of a Presbyterian minister on any pulpit and be convincing. "But that might take a day or two."

"Keep on it," Adkins said. "In the meantime, we'll have to beef up our liaison staff with the FBI and INS. We can pull them from Security, but they should be Ops people. Any odd bods you can spare, Dave?"

"We're stretched to the limit as it is," Whittaker said. "Except for trainees."

"We could put the Farm on hold, and use the instructors," Adkins suggested, looking to McGarvey for approval since the move would involve the DCI's daughter and son-in-law.

McGarvey nodded. They were good people, and they deserved the truth from him every bit as much as he demanded it from them. Yet he could not involve his people in what the White House might consider a personal vendetta. An operation strictly forbidden by the president himself. "Pair a couple of trainees with each instructor, and if you need more, pull them from Management and Security. But I'll be assigning my daughter and her husband to a special operation."

Rencke, who had not said a word, suddenly sat up straight as if something had just occurred to him. "Oh wow, Mac, you quit," he blurted.

McGarvey was almost glad that Rencke had guessed the truth and had brought it up first. It would save time. "Yes, I have," he said. "I told the president this morning, and I'm telling all of you now. My resignation is effective immediately. This morning."

There was a stunned silence around the table. No one knew what to say. What McGarvey had sprung on them was unthinkable under the circumstances.

"There'll be no media releases from here. That'll be up to the White House. In the interim, Dick will take over as DCI, and Dave can double up as his number two."

"Bullshit," Adkins said. "You're not just walking out, not now of all times. What's going on?"

"You don't want to know—"

"You're going hunting," Rencke interrupted. "Bang-bang, shot in the head. Bang-bang, you're dead. Look out Mr. Khalil."

Everyone started talking at once, and McGarvey let their voices roll around him. Their reactions were the same as the president's. It was as if the general decided to quit in the middle of a crucial battle. He was letting his people down. It was something they would never forget, or forgive him for.

Adkins held up a hand for silence, and the clamor died down. "Is Otto right? Are you going after Khalil?"

McGarvey tried to think of a way out for his people. He owed them that much. But he also could not lie. It was a fine line. "I don't want the Company involved. What I'm going to do will be as a private citizen. Do you understand?"

"No, I don't," Adkins replied angrily. "None of us do. But if you've identified Khalil and you mean to grab your pistol and go back out in the field after him, one-on-one, mano a mano, I'm telling you that you're wasting your time and talents. You're needed right here. If we know who the bastard is, we have any number of teams we can send after him. If you don't want him arrested because of what he did to your wife in Alaska, we'll understand—" Adkins looked to the others for approval. "We won't even try to arrest him. We'll find him and kill him on the spot." Adkins spread his hands. "Whatever you want, Mac. You call the shots, and we're here for you." Again he looked to the others for approval, and they all were nodding. They were behind their director no matter what. "But you can't walk out the door on a personal vendetta. You can't."

McGarvey took a good look around the table. It seemed as if he'd spent half his life turning his back on the people who most needed him, but this time was different, he told himself. This time his departure was necessary. He closed the bin Laden folder, shoved it across the table to Adkins, and got up.

"I'm sorry, but there's no way around it for me. I'm assigning my daughter and son-in-law to help take care of my wife for the next few days. I don't think the situation will last much longer. I'll keep in contact as much as possible through Rencke's office, but I don't want anyone trying to track my movements. I've had my GPS tracker removed."

Adkins was beside himself with anger. "For Christ's sake, Mac, don't do this to us."

"The president will want to see you this afternoon. Try to stall him until morning if you can; I'll be clear by then. But don't put your neck on the block. He'll want to know where I've gone, and you won't have to lie to him about not knowing. He may ask you to find me, and that decision will be up to you. But the Company has its hands full. Your top priority still is to find bin Laden."

McGarvey reflected for a moment on what else he could say to his people to ease their burden before he walked out the door. But there was nothing that he could tell them, except that he had changed his mind and would stay on as DCI. That was no longer a possibility. He was going after Khalil, and nothing on this earth could stop him.

He turned to Rencke. "Have you come up with anything new?"

Rencke shook his head. "Not since last night."

"I'll keep in touch then," he told them. "Work the problem, people. It's what you do."

He left the conference room and went back to his office to break the news to his secretary.

THIRTY-FIVE

McGarvey could sense the change within himself as he rode home in the back of the DCI's limousine. His staff's reaction had been troublesome—they felt he was deserting them—but his secretary had not seemed surprised that he was quitting as DCI so he could have the freedom of movement to return to the field. He'd told his staff to work the problem because that's what they did. His secretary understood his decision because, in her words, *It was what he did.*

National Guard troops were stationed at the Beltway's entrance and exit ramps. A national hysteria was tightening its hold on Americans. Nobody wanted another 9/11, and they were willing to accept whatever it took to stop the terrorists once and for all.

Already he was transforming from a deskbound administrator/politician to a field officer. A greatly heightened sense of perceptions. Accepting the possibility that every situation he found himself in had the potential to be deadly. Trusting no one. Carrying no excess baggage. Accepting that in the end it would be only his finger on the trigger.

The limo pulled into McGarvey's driveway a couple minutes before noon. Julien came around and opened the back door. "We're home, Mr. Director."

McGarvey looked up at his bodyguard, and he had a fleeting thought about Jim Grassinger, whose funeral he would miss, and about Dick Yemm before him, who was killed out on the street just a few yards from here.

His heart slowly emptied of nearly every emotion except the almost overwhelming drive to kill the terrorist Kahlil.

It had been the same when he'd been hunting VC officers in the jungles of South Vietnam.

Outside Santiago when he killed the Butcher of Chile and his wife.

Again in the flooding tunnels beneath a castle in Portugal.

In Japan.

In Moscow.

In San Francisco.

Even here in Washington.

"Are you going back to the office this afternoon, sir?" Julien asked. "Should I stick around?"

"No, I won't be needing you today," McGarvey said, getting out. "In fact, you're being reassigned. I expect Dick Adkins will be needing you. As of now he's the new DCI."

Julien nodded tightly; his round face and serious eyes displayed no surprise. "It's true then; you've resigned?"

McGarvey wasn't surprised either. "It's a hell of a note if even the CIA can't keep a secret."

"Yes, sir," Julien said. He cracked a slight smile. "Good hunting, Mr. Director."

"Thanks," McGarvey told him. They shook hands, and he looked his bodyguard in the eye. "Be careful over the next few days about who you mention that to. Some serious shit is probably going to come down around our heads."

Julien nodded again. "Like I said, Mr. Director, good hunting. We'll take care of the shop for you while you're gone."

The chief of security had notified the house detail of McGarvey's new status, so no one was surprised when he showed up at home early, least of all Kathleen. She came to the head of the stairs when he walked in and reset the alarm. He looked up at her. She seemed brittle.

"I've started to pack for you, but I need to know where you're jetting off to before I can finish," she said, sharply. "Switzerland, for starters, I'm assuming."

McGarvey hadn't expected this coolness from her. She'd been moody during her pregnancy, but never sharp-tongued like in the old days. But suddenly it connected in his mind. His leaving all of a sudden and possibly going to Switzerland. She had admitted that she'd had an affair with Prince Salman, the man her husband suspected of being a terrorist. And now he was rushing off to Switzerland to be with a woman from the old days who had been in love with him. Rekindling an old flame? He'd even asked himself that same question last night. How far would he go to track down Khalil?

All the way, he'd decided. And Katy had evidently sensed something of that resolution in him. This morning she was jealous.

"I suppose it's only fair," Katy said. "Or is it just a part of the business that husbands don't discuss with their wives?"

The Company shrink, Dr. Norman Stenzel, once told McGarvey that the divorce rate among CIA field officers was the highest of any profession. What spouse could hope to compete with a mate who kept odd hours, had questionable friends, and lied every day as a matter of course. It was hard on everybody, especially the wives who sooner or later developed inferiority complexes; low self-esteem made normally reasonable people sometimes say and do horrific things. The suicide rate among agents and their spouses was nineteen times the national average. Much higher even than among cops. "Don't do this now, Katy . . ."

"Your tradecraft was a trifle weak," Katy said. "Her name is Liese Fuelm. She called you when we were on the cruise, but Otto picked it up and talked to her. Of course, you know all that. The problem is Otto wasn't quick enough, because the entire conversation was recorded on the machine in your study. It was actually quite sweet, her calling you at home instead of your office. She's obviously concerned about you."

McGarvey had listened to Otto's recording of the brief conversation, and he too had heard the concern in her voice. But like Otto he'd also heard Liese's anger and frustration. Her people were using her friendship, and possibly even love, for the CIA director to get information they thought they wouldn't otherwise get because the prince had been a good and useful friend to the last three administrations. But in the aftermath of the kidnapping attempt and then the bin Laden tape, McGarvey had forgotten to check his answering machine.

Katy's voice was rising. "She said to say hello. Give you a hug. How sweet is that? But she mentioned Darby and the old days."

McGarvey started up the stairs to her.

"Goodness gracious, I'm beginning to wonder how many people don't know about Darby and the prince and . . . me." She stepped back, as if she wanted to distance herself from her husband. She looked frightened and angry and ashamed all at once.

McGarvey reached the head of the stairs and gathered her in his arms. For just a moment she resisted, but then she melted into him. "It's not like that, Katy," he said, stroking her hair. "It never was."

"She sounded young."

"She is. And she *was* in love with me, or thought she was. And she might still be in love with me, which the Swiss police are using to make her come to me for help."

Katy looked up into his eyes. It was clear that she wanted to believe him, but she was frightened. She was pregnant, and she did not want to be alone again.

"Otto picked up on it, from how she sounded. You must have heard it too."

"I sent you out of my life once; I won't allow it to happen again."

McGarvey wanted to turn his back on everything and simply run away with her. He'd lived for a short while on the Greek island of Serifos; he could easily live there again. He and Katy could have a simple life, happy together, in peace.

"I'm afraid, Kirk. Alaska was nothing compared to this." She shook her head. "I don't know how it can turn out for us . . . for everybody."

"I'm not going to Switzerland. At least not now."

"But you are leaving?"

"I'm going to Monaco."

Katy studied his face. "He'll be there, and you're going to confront him. Is that it?" Her mouth twisted into a grimace. "You're going to find him and kill him. Is that what you're going to do?" She glanced down the hall toward the front bedroom where their security detail had set up its operational center. "You resigned and they weren't surprised. And they're not going away." She turned back. "How did you find out he'd be in Monaco?"

"The Swiss are investigating him. I talked to Liese this morning. She told me where he'd be."

Katy flared again. "Two spies exchanging secrets, or was it chums catching up on the good old days?"

There was nothing McGarvey could say.

Katy started to cry. "Well, get your story straight, because your daughter called a half hour ago all upset, wanting to know what the hell was going on. You'll have to tell her something. She and Todd are coming for dinner again. Unless you're leaving this afternoon."

"Not until morning."

"That's something, at least."

"I'm reassigning them to watch you," McGarvey said. "If I miss the prince, there's a good chance he'll come after you again."

Her mood suddenly swung the other way, and she almost laughed out loud. "There's not much chance of you missing him, is there? I saw you in action on the boat." She shook her head. "Oh no, darling, you'll get him."

He brushed a kiss on her cheek. "Let me help you pack. I'll need my tux—"

"I'll finish it," Katy said. "Go get yourself a drink, and then gather up whatever else you're going to need."

"You won't be able to reach me, so don't try," McGarvey told her. "If something comes up that Liz or Todd can't handle, go to Otto; he'll know how to get to me."

She suddenly looked like a deer caught in some headlights. "You're getting a second chance, Kirk. And I think this might be the most important thing you've ever had to do. So go . . . do it, and when it's over come back to me in one piece."

It was after midnight and the house was quiet, though lying in bed McGarvey could sense the presence of the four-man security team, awake, watchful, ready for whatever trouble might happen. Liz and Todd had agreed to move out of their carriage house and bunk here for the duration, though Liz wanted to go to Monaco with her father.

"You're awake," Kathleen said softly beside him. "Can't you sleep?"

McGarvey turned his head to look at her. "I was just about to drop off."

She smiled. "Liar." She reached over and brushed her fingertips lightly across his eyes, his nose, and his lips. "Make love to me, Kirk."

THIRTY-SIX

□

There should have been no reason for him to come here.

Khalil was irritated as he fell in line with the passengers departing the Palma-Algiers ferryboat the MV *Pierre Égout*, the night air heavy with the odors of rotting garbage, broken sewers, and bunker oil from the numerous cargo ships in the filthy harbor. But there were times when the firm hand of a strong leader was required.

The operation was so close now that any loose end could not be tolerated.

From a distance the harborfront and downtown Algiers looked like any normal port city. But once off the ferry and away from the sounds of the boat's diesel engines, the noise of traffic was punctuated with the not-so-distant sounds of gunfire. All of Algeria was a nation at war with itself. At least three hundred thousand people had been slaughtered in just the last ten years. More had died before that, and more were dying every day.

It was a perfect place for al-Quaida's primary training camps; Afghanistan and western Pakistan had become too hot. By comparison to Algiers, those countries were peaceful paradises on earth, with coalition patrols penetrating even the most remote mountain strongholds. The move had been made necessary in the aftermath of 9/11, and Khalil had little doubt that al-Quaida would be on the move again after the next attack.

After he'd cleared customs and immigration on an Algerian passport, he gathered his robes around him and stopped just inside the terminal exit, out of the flow of pedestrian traffic coming off the ferry, to study the situation on the street. Two buses, one of them the airport shuttle, were parked directly in front. Several taxicabs were lined up at the stand to the left, and across the departing/arriving passenger lanes was a black Mercedes SUV with the DGSN national police emblem on its door and a light-bar on the roof. One man in uniform was seated behind the wheel, staring straight ahead.

The message had come to him in code on the old Groupe Islamique Armé (GIA) Web site maintained by *Al Hayat*, a Saudi newspaper in London.

We have a leak. But he is probably SDECE. Advise. It was the French intelligence service. After their difficulties with the U.S. over the Iraq War, they had become anxious to prove they were friends.

Will arrive, Khalil had responded, with instructions. Now he walked outside and went across to the Mercedes.

Like the days before 9/11, they were on a path that had a life of its own and could no longer be controlled by mortal man.

Insha'allah. God's will.

He reached the Mercedes, opened the door, and climbed up into the passenger seat.

The driver, camp commandant Ziad Amar, turned to him and, after a beat, smiled. *"Welcome, my brother,"* he said in Arabic. *"I am truly blessed that thou art here."* He was nervous.

"As I am, my brother," Khalil responded, though his mind was elsewhere.

Since 1830, when the French began their conquest of the country, Algeria had become a killing ground. Nothing had changed in the interim. People were still dying in droves, and the country attracted killers. Abdelkader, who was a *sherif*, which meant he was a descendant of Muhammed, had fought the French for nearly sixteen years before his defeat. Ever since then the mountain passes and desert sands of Algeria had run red with blood. With a dozen different terrorist groups, not all of them sympathetic to Osama bin Laden's al-Quaida, and with bandits mostly in the south, charismatic leaders seemed to lurk around every bend.

Except for the motorized traffic and electric lights, Algiers had not changed in principle for two hundred years. As they headed away from the ferryboat terminal, Kahlil felt a connection with all the warrior chiefs before and since Abdelkader. He had come here on a matter of blood honor. He would leave with a clear conscience.

Insha'allah.

"You had a good trip?" Amar asked respectfully. He was a slightly built man, with narrow sloping shoulders, long effeminate fingers, and when he was bulding bombs, a steady nerve.

"What is the specific trouble that you are evidently incapable of dealing with on your own?" Khalil asked, his manner mild.

"Under normal cicumstances we would have killed the man."

"What's stopping you? He's a traitor; deal with him as you deal with all traitors."

"He's probably been sending information about our operation back to Paris for months. Since they know where we are, and yet have not moved against us, it can only mean that they do not consider us a threat to French security. Or at least not enough of a threat to send a strike force or launch missiles."

He had a point, Khalil thought. If they killed the spy, the French might reconsider the value of the camp and launch an attack.

As they headed directly south out of the city on the Medea Highway and up into the Hatatba Mountains, Khalil considered all the options. He'd been against bin Laden releasing the tape so soon after the failure to capture Shaw. Trying to rescue the former secretary of defense would have split the American forces, making it much more difficult for them to deal with the threat of another 9/11. As it was, they were even more highly motivated now, especially the CIA, and more acutely focused. Martial law in a country as vast and as open as the U.S. was mostly a joke, but no matter how slightly, it was increasing the risk that the martyrs for Allah would be caught.

Perhaps they needed a diversion, he thought. Something to refocus the French counterterrorism efforts and therefore make the Americans blink. Amar was dispensable, as were the thirty or forty mujahideen instructors and trainees at the old headquarters of the GIA that al-Quaida had taken over a couple of years ago. But the timing would have to be absolutely correct. If the French moved too late, as late as the same day of the attack of the martyrs in the U.S., the diversion would be useless. And if the attack came too soon, the French might realize it had been nothing more than a diversion.

"Tell me more about your French traitor. How did you first come to suspect him?"

"We found his satellite phone two days ago. Such devices are strictly forbidden, of course. But rather than confront the man, we watched him. He telephoned last night, and in French he gave a very complete report on all of our training activities for the previous twenty-four hours. That is when I sent the e-mail to you."

"At what time did he make his call?"

"Midnight. He was on guard duty; one of the instructors overhead him talking and managed to get close enough to hear everything."

"Will he be on guard duty again this evening?"

"Yes."

Khalil smiled. "You did the correct thing after all, my brother. We will turn the situation to our advantage tonight."

Amar was relieved. He shot a nervous glance at Khalil. "Will you interrogate him?"

Khalil shook his head dreamily. He was no longer irritated. He was looking forward to the pleasure of the kill. "It won't be necessary."

"He doesn't suspect that we're onto him—"

Khalil dismissed the comment with a wave of his hand. "That doesn't matter either, my friend." He smiled again, his eyes half-closed. "You'll see."

Was it not said that for the man who could bend like the willow in the wind would come victory?

French Service 5 Operative François Brousseau entered his contact number on the satellite phone's keypad with a shaking hand and waited for his call to Paris to go through. He stood on a rise behind the camp, looking down toward the Medea Highway in the distance. It was midnight, and there had been no lights on the highway for the past hour, which heightened his sense of isolation. For six weeks this place had operated as nothing more than a mujahideen training camp. Hand-to-hand combat, Stinger-missile dry-fire exercises, AK-47 live-fire practice, bomb making, infiltration and exfiltration lectures, and five times daily the prayers to Mecca.

Amar had driven away this evening, and three hours later he'd returned with Khalil himself. The second biggest prize of all behind bin Laden.

His call was answered. "*Oui.*"

"*Ici Hasni,*" he spoke softly, giving his code name. "Something new has developed. The king of spades—"

A dark presence loomed up behind him, and before Brousseau could react, something horribly sharp sliced deeply into the base of his neck where it attached to his right shoulder. His arm went instantly numb, and he dropped the phone.

Khalil pushed the French spy, stumbling nearly off-balance. "*Bonsoir, Monsieur Le Traître; maintenant, il est les temps pour votre mort,*" he said, and then he came at the man with the razor-sharp knife as if he were a hunter skinning the pelt from a wild animal, with no one to hear or care about the screams of the dying man.

THIRTY-SEVEN

McGarvey walked across the Place du Casino from his hotel and entered the soaring, marble-columned atrium of the Casino de Monte-Carlo a few minutes before ten on a balmy evening. The odor of money mingled in the air with cigarette smoke and expensive perfume.

He'd been in the principality since noon, but had kept a relatively low profile, waiting to see if his arrival had been noticed. But no one followed him when he took a walking tour around the harbor, nor had his room been searched while he was gone.

He found it odd that bin Laden's warning and the president's declaration of martial law were going all but unnoticed here. But as a waiter at a terrace café told him with a Gallic shrug, the world saw what America did after 9/11; this time, if it happens again, nothing will be different.

Nightlife was just getting into full swing, the streets packed with every style, from blue jeans and tee shirts off to play the slots; to micromini skirts and stiletto heels off to the discos; to jackets and demure cocktail dresses going to the roulette tables, international and English; and to people like McGarvey, dressed in evening clothes and heading for one-of-the-two Salles Privées, where only the well-heeled went to play mostly chemin de fer.

The newly remodeled casino had been brought back to all its Old-World magnificence, with soaring, ornately decorated ceilings from which hung massive crystal chandeliers; gold inlaid mahogany walls; rare paintings, sculptures, and other artwork, ranking the casino as an important gallery; handwoven, intricately patterned carpeting; and gilt mirrors in which patrons could admire themselves. But there were no clocks to remind them that it might be getting late.

There was no other gambling establishment like it anywhere in the world for sheer elegance. Even the best of Las Vegas or London couldn't compare. With four main gaming rooms in two wings—the Salon de l'Europe, Salle Blanche, Salle Touzet, and the Salle Médecin—plus the two

Salles Privées on a good evening when American movie stars came up from the film festival at Cannes or Arab oil sheiks were in town, tens of millions of euros would switch hands.

This evening, however, the only excitement was the presence of Prince Abdul Salman, whose 428-foot yacht MV *Bedouin Wanderer* had been brought by her crew up from Palma on the big island of Mallorca earlier in the day. Whenever that happened, it signaled that the prince was planning on making a miniseason on the Côte d'Azur, and this meant action, because money always attracted money and beautiful women. The combination was glittering.

McGarvey stopped at the *caisse* to confirm that CitiBank had followed up on his instructions to establish a line of credit with the casino under his work name of Robert Brewster in the amount of one million dollars. Rencke had suggested using CIA funds, but this was personal and McGarvey was no longer on the payroll.

The head *caissier*, all discreet smiles, had been expecting him. "Oui, Monsieur Brewster. Everything is in order. Do you wish to make a withdrawal?"

"Ten thousand," McGarvey said. "I'll be in the Salles Privées."

The *caissier* passed ten one-thousand-euro plaques across. "*Naturellement, Monsieur. Bonne fortune.*"

McGarvey pocketed his plaques, then sauntered across the atrium and into the Salon de l'Europe, very busy with gamblers at the roulette wheels and the *trente et quarante* tables. This was the very end of the European vacation season, and most of the casino patrons were dressed in blue jeans and sneakers or sandals. Someone hit their number at one of the roulette wheels, and a cheer went up.

Passing through the Salle Blanche with its noisy slot machines and video poker games, into the Salle Touzet with its raucous craps tables and relatively subdued blackjack games, he came to the much more discreet Salle Médecin, which until the remodeling had been the old Salle Privée, where the big money played.

This room was in the east wing of the building, and McGarvey stopped just inside the doorway for a moment before he angled across to the entrance into the two private gaming rooms. A velvet rope blocked the opening. A security officer dressed in a tuxedo smiled as McGarvey walked up.

"Good evening, Monsieur Brewster," he said, pleasantly, as he unhooked the rope and stood aside. "*Bon fortune.*"

"*Merci,*" McGarvey said, passing through directly into an ornately gilded and mirrored small room that could have been the interior of a jewel box.

The Salles Privées were arranged to the left and right, and they were busy this evening. A muted hum seemed to stay within the confines of the two rooms, as if the privileged class here did not want anyone outside their circle to hear what they were saying.

McGarvey caught a glimpse of Prince Salman seated at one of the chemin de fer tables in the left room. His pistol had come across in a sealed diplomatic package, which he hadn't opened until he'd arrived at the Hotel de Paris across the Place from the casino. Now that he'd confirmed Salman was here, he fought the urge to return to his hotel, get his gun, and come back to wait until the prince left the casino to take him out.

It would be easy. It would be swift and sure and, most of all, clean.

The patrons were dressed in evening clothes, most of the women young, very beautiful, and bedecked in diamonds and haute couture. All but two of the ten players seated around the prince's *tableau* were men, and there were no vacant seats.

McGarvey fixed a slight smile on his face, walked in, and took his place behind the brass rail at the fringe of the crowd. A waitress carrying a tray of champagne came by, and he took a glass as Salman said something and a murmur of approval arose from the onlookers.

"*La banque est cent mille,*" Salman announced. As the banker for the moment, the dealing shoe was in front of him. He had just announced that he would be the bank for one hundred thousand euros, about $125,000.

Twenty years ago, at the height of the Arab oil stranglehold on the world, such a bet would have been very conservative in a place like this. But nowadays even in the Salles Privées, bets above fifty thousand were increasingly rare, except at the very height of the season.

The game was played at a kidney-shaped table, the players seated on the outside rim across from the croupier, who raked in the cards. Seated behind him on a tall chair was the *chef de parti*, or umpire.

Salman had offered to play anyone or any combination of players around the table for up to the full amount of the bank. If someone wanted a piece of the action, he or she might push a pile of betting plaques forward. If a player wanted the entire bank, he or she would announce, "Banco." If it was too rich a bet, that hand would be canceled and a smaller bank offered.

An expectant hush fell over the table.

Salman was seated with his back to the door. A young woman wearing a dazzling white off-the-shoulder evening dress, a dozen carats of diamonds around her long slender neck and a matching bracelet around one wrist, stood behind him, one hand delicately placed on his shoulder. She bent down and whispered something in his ear; he looked up and she kissed the side of his face.

McGarvey put his champagne glass aside and moved past the onlookers and through the opening in the rail at the opposite end of the table from Salman. "Banco," he said. He nodded pleasantly to the chef de parti. "That is, if someone would relinquish a seat for me."

An older American woman, seated in the number two position next to a man who was probably her husband, looked up at McGarvey with a rueful smile. She was slender and put together as if she might have been a model sometime in the past. She had a very small stack of black plaques, which were worth a thousand euros each. She scooped them up. "Take my place," she offered. "The prince is just as lucky as he is charming."

"Thank you," McGarvey said, holding her chair, and when she got up he kissed her hand.

"Kill the smug bastard," she whispered in McGarvey's ear. Her husband started to get up too, but she waved him back. "Stick around; I'm just going to the ladies'."

McGarvey turned to face the prince for the first time, and for what seemed like a very long moment he had no idea who he was looking at. Salman had Khalil's eyes; though the prince's were pale brown and the terrorist's were jet black, they were the same shape, as were their faces and general build. Beyond that, McGarvey couldn't be sure that they were the same man.

The way Salman held himself, his attitude and the expression in his eyes and on his mouth were that of a Saudi royal: he expressed a vague, indifferent amusement, as if he considered himself at the center of the world and only those important enough to be noticed by him understood it. With a slackness that was almost effete, perhaps effeminate, he was the epitome of an ultrarich, bored playboy. The attitude was a studied one, but it was a badge of honor among a certain class.

Khalil had been intense, his movements and actions quick, precise, and sure. There'd been nothing vague about him. Nothing indifferent. The only attitude he'd seemed to share with the prince was the expectation that whoever he faced knew who was the center of the world, knew who was the superior intellect and the superior force.

All that passed through McGarvey's head in an instant, as he nodded pleasantly to Salman and then took the plushy upholstered seat still warm from the American woman.

"Good evening, Mr . . . Brewster," Salman said, languidly. "Did I hear you correctly—you have offered *banco?*"

McGarvey nodded, though he knew that his one-million-dollar line of credit would not pose any serious threat to the Saudi prince. At some point one flip of the cards could end it. This would have to be more a game of psychology than of cards. McGarvey turned to the *chef de parti*. "May I assume that the gentleman banker is good for the money?"

A gasp rose from the players and the onlookers who'd heard the gauche remark. McGarvey had been less than polite; he'd been insulting.

Salman's mouth tightened. "It is I who should be asking you the question."

"My credit is on file with the *caissier*. I don't believe anyone in Monaco would question my character or my honesty."

"You are an honest American here in Monaco then, doing what?"

"Hunting down rabid animals," McGarvey replied, sharply.

The *chef de parti* intervened before Salman could say anything else and thus escalate what already seemed to be unacceptable behavior for the *salle*. "Both gentlemen have sufficient funds to cover the bet. May we proceed?"

Salman slid four cards in quick succession from the shoe, slapping them on the table and turning them over for everyone to see. They were the discards: a king, a ten, a natural nine, and a three.

The croupier raked in the cards and placed them in a tray.

Salman slid two cards out of the shoe, which the croupier raked across to McGarvey, and then dealt himself two cards.

McGarvey glanced at his cards, then looked up at Salman and snorted derisively. *"Neuf,"* he said, flipping his cards face up. They were a jack and a nine, which was a natural win unless the banker also had a nine.

Salman turned his cards up. They were a five and a three.

McGarvey laughed again. "Close, but no cigar," he said boorishly. "Too bad."

The croupier raked in the cards, then started to slide ten plaques, each worth ten thousand euros, across the table, but McGarvey made a brushing motion with his hand. "Let's double it—that is, if the prince has the courage of his Bedouin ancestors."

Already word had begun to spread through the casino that something was going on in one of the Salles Privées, and the room was completely filled. Someone brought McGarvey a glass of champagne, but he ignored it, his eyes locked on Salman's, goading the man, and yet he still wasn't sure that the prince was Khalil.

Normally, the shoe would have passed to the player on the banker's right, but the *chef de parti* offered no objections when Salman passed it across to McGarvey.

"Deux cents milles," McGarvey said.

"Banco," Salman replied, immediately.

McGarvey slid two cards out of the shoe, which the croupier raked to Salman, then dealt himself two cards.

Salman smiled and flipped his cards over. They were a pair of fours, a natural eight that could be beaten only by a nine.

McGarvey flipped his cards over without taking his eyes off Salman. "They were a six and a deuce. A tie."

"Quatre cents milles," McGarvey announced even before the croupier had raked in the cards.

"Banco," Salman said. He gave McGarvey a forced smile. "It's a dangerous game you are playing, Mr. Brewster."

"Yes, it is," McGarvey agreed. "Someone could get hurt." Without looking down at the shoe, he dealt out two cards for Salman and two for himself.

McGarvey looked at his cards. He'd dealt himself a queen and a seven.

Salman looked at his cards, and shrugged. *"Carte,"* he said, which meant his hand totaled five or less.

McGarvey dealt the prince the six of hearts faceup.

Salman shrugged again, and he flipped his down cards over to show a jack and a king. His hand totaled six.

McGarvey threw his head back and laughed, then gave Salman a vicious look of satisfaction as he turned his cards over. "*Sept*," he said. "I win, you lose." He laughed. "Again."

The young woman with Salman reached down to kiss him on the cheek, but he brushed her away like she was an annoying insect. "Eight hundred thousand?" He directed his question to the *chef de parti*.

McGarvey shook his head, and slid the shoe to the man on his right. "I came looking for a challenge, not a slaughter."

Salman turned, his eyes narrow, a slight sardonic smile on his thin lips. "Perhaps another time, then? Another, more interesting game?"

"I'm looking forward to it." McGarvey got up, tossed two black plaques to the croupier and *chef de parti*, and walked out, the crowd parting respectfully for him.

The opening shot had been fired, and walking back to his hotel McGarvey found that he was actually looking forward to whatever came next. He wasn't yet certain that Salman and Khalil were one and the same, but he was certain that he would kill the man, and do it very soon.

THIRTY-EIGHT

McGarvey was having a late breakfast on the balcony in his suite when Salman's secretary telephoned at nine. "The prince would like you to join him aboard the yacht this morning to continue your conversation, then perhaps take a short cruise this afternoon."

McGarvey smiled. Salman was reacting exactly the way a man with an overinflated ego would act. "What time should I be there?"

"A car and driver are at the front door of your hotel now."

"Tell the prince I'd be happy to join him," McGarvey said, and he hung up the phone.

From where he sat, he could see Salman's yacht docked at the outer pier just inside the breakwater across the bay in La Condamine. A French Alouette helicopter was parked on the ship's afterdeck, but the distance was too great for McGarvey to make out much detail, except that the ship was very large and all her flags were flying as if the prince was celebrating something.

Which, McGarvey mused, *he was if he was the terrorist Khalil.*

McGarvey took his time finishing his coffee and croissants and the Herald Tribune before he took a leisurely shower and got dressed in white slacks, a soft yellow, light, V-neck sweater, and tasseled loafers without socks. He debated arming himself, but decided against it. This invitation to the yacht was too open and public a move for anything untoward to happen, unless it was an accident, for which a pistol would be no defense.

The car was a pearl-white Mercedes S500 with Spanish plates, and if the very large German driver was impatient for having been kept waiting, he did not show it as he opened the rear door.

"There was a pretty girl with the prince at the casino last night. Tall, blonde. Will she be aboard this morning?" McGarvey asked.

The driver nodded. "That would be Inge Poulsen, the prince's social secretary."

McGarvey snapped his fingers, as he'd forgotten something. "Give me a minute," he said, and he walked back into the hotel.

He went to the concierge, an attractive young woman in a light blue blazer with the hotel's crest on the breast pocket. She looked up, smiling. "Good morning, Monsieur Brewster. How may I be of service?"

"How soon can you have a dozen roses delivered to Prince Salman's yacht?"

"How soon would you like them delivered?"

"Within fifteen minutes."

Her smile broadened only slightly. "That won't be a problem, sir." She took a card from a drawer, and handed it and a pen across to McGarvey.

"They're to be delivered in person to Mademoiselle Inge Poulsen," McGarvey said. He wrote on the card as the concierge dialed a number. *From an admirer. Kirk.*

She said something into the phone, then nodded and hung up. "The flowers will be delivered to the yacht within fifteen minutes."

McGarvey handed her the card and a one-hundred-euro note, then put on his sunglasses and went back out to the car and driver Salman had sent for him. The docks were less than one thousand meters as the crow flies, but they had to skirt the bay, and traffic was heavy, so it took nearly ten minutes to get to the yacht.

The morning was warm. Only a slight breeze fluttered the flags that had been run up on halyards along the port and starboard and from the bow to the masthead above the bridge deck. The yacht was a Feadship, built in Holland. At 428 feet on deck, she was sleek, with a long tapering bow, a sharply sloping superstructure with sweeping curved lines, until the stern, where a wide sundeck overlooked an even wider helipad.

In the bright sunlight the brilliant white hull sparkled like a precious stone under a jeweler's lamp. No other yacht in the harbor came close to the splendor of the *Bedouin Wanderer*, and in fact, Salman's ship was larger than Adnan Khashoggi's before him, and even larger than the yacht on which Aristotle Onassis had hosted parties with his wife Jacqueline.

A ship's officer, dressed in an immaculate white uniform shirt and shorts, waited at the head of the boarding ladder, but McGarvey ignored him and sauntered down the dock to the stern of the yacht for a better look at the helicopter. It looked new, its registration numbers were Spanish, and although the rotors were still tied down, the windshield was not covered and the engine air intake ports were not blocked. Nor were the tips of the rotors sheathed, as they would be if the ship was preparing to sail this afternoon with the chopper on deck.

A florist's van pulled up behind the Mercedes, and the delivery boy brought a long flower box across to the yacht. He said something to the officer, who gave McGarvey a questioning look, and then led the boy aft and up to the sundeck above the helipad.

After a moment or two the delivery boy followed the officer back to the main deck and left the ship. In the meantime, Inge Poulsen, the beautiful woman from the night before, came to the rail of the sundeck. She wore only the thong bottom of a white bikini. Her breasts were small, her shoulders and neck narrow, her face tiny with high cheekbones, and when she lifted her sunglasses, McGarvey could see that her eyes were very large.

She had taken the roses out of the box and held them to her nose.

McGarvey raised his sunglasses. "Bon matin, Mademoiselle. Le parfum c'est agréable?"

"Très bien, merci. Mais vous êtes trop aimable."

"Not at all," McGarvey said. He nodded to her, then walked back to the gangway and boarded the yacht. "I believe that I'm expected," he told the officer who looked nervous, as if he was expecting trouble.

"The prince has been awaiting your arrival, sir. Are you familiar with the yacht?"

McGarvey glanced through the big windows into the main saloon, and shook his head. "Never been here before." He looked at the officer. "Where is everybody?"

"There are no guests this morning," the officer said. He pointed the way aft. "The prince is in the salle de gym. I'll show you."

McGarvey almost laughed. On a boat such as this, owned by a man such as Salman, there would not simply be an exercise room. He followed the officer beneath the stairs that led up to the helipad and sundeck, through a door, and down a short, plushly carpeted and expensively decorated passageway to a second door.

"Just here, Monsieur," the officer said, opening the door and stepping aside to allow McGarvey to pass.

Two figures dressed in white jackets and knickers, mesh masks covering their faces, were fencing in the large gymnasium that was located directly beneath the helipad. The port, starboard, and forward bulkheads were mirrored floor-to-ceiling, but the aft bulkhead was a solid sheet of floor-to-ceiling tinted glass that curved across the entire stern. Fencing blades and masks and other equipment were lined up on a rack against one wall, and state-of-the-art exercise equipment trimmed in gold was scattered here and there around the room, except for on the fencing strip that was two meters wide and ran the length of the gym. The effect was stunning; it was a hedonist's pleasure palace, like the yacht's exterior, very expensively done, but gaudy and without taste.

The taller, much bulkier fencer, who McGarvey took to be Salman, was much better than his opponent; his footwork was superior, his hand speed dazzling, and his technique of the blade very strong, very aggressive.

Twice the smaller fencer was forced backward under Salman's on-slaught, the second time stumbling and almost falling to the deck when Salman moved in with a counter six, viciously disarming his opponent and sending the épée clattering into a stationary bike.

Salman ripped off his mask and tossed it aside. His face was screwed up into a state of extreme disdain and anger, as if the person he'd just beaten was nothing more than an insignificant insect who'd had the audacity to challenge him. He said something sharp and harsh in Arabic.

His opponent stumbled back another step under the verbal onslaught, then slowly removed her mask to reveal that she was just a round-faced girl, probably no more than fifteen or sixteen. Her eyes filled with tears. She spotted McGarvey, and immediately turned away in embarrassment. She said something to Salman that sounded like an apology, then hurried away through a door on the opposite side of the gym.

The prince studied McGarvey's reflection in the mirrors, then turned, a wry smile on his handsome face, the épée held loosely in his right hand. "I expected you sooner."

McGarvey shrugged. "I was engaged, doing my sums."

The prince's smile widened. "It was only money."

Khalil wasn't a man who expected to lose, and McGarvey figured that was another point of similarity between the two men—if they were two. "There was that too." He nodded toward the door the young girl had left by. "Do you treat all your women that way?"

Salman's eyes narrowed. "What are you doing in Monaco undercover, Mr. McGarvey?"

McGarvey shrugged again. "Looking for some action, like last night."

Salman was amused. "Your luck would have turned, and you would have lost your million dollars."

"I don't think so. I'm not some young girl you can slap around and in-timidate." McGarvey grinned, trying to goad the man. "I fight back."

Salman was like a chameleon; none of the anger directed at the girl re-mained. His color had returned to normal, and his composure was nearly perfect, except that his fingers tightened on the épée handle. "If you must know, Sofia is my daughter. I am raising her to be strong."

McGarvey knew Salman had no daughter that age. "The Bedouin way with their girls, is that it? Raise them to be strong, or else leave them exposed in the desert to die. Better six weakling sons than one daughter, no matter how able."

Salman's jaw clenched very slightly. "I would have thought that a man of your position . . . and talents . . . would have remained on the job in Washington after what happened in Alaska, and then bin Laden's warning to your country."

"Perhaps I'm still on the job."

The prince snorted derisively. "You're desperate for our oil, and yet you continue to accuse us of financing terrorism. I've heard it all before, and frankly little men like you are becoming tiresome. I can understand why Haynes fired you."

For just a second McGarvey could almost believe that Salman was innocent. A man didn't have to be a gentleman to be not guilty. But all of the evidence that Otto had collected on Khalil and Salman's movements was too much to be nothing more than a fantastic run of coincidences. And looking into the man's eyes, talking to him now, seeing the slip in his self-control when he'd been angry with the young girl, his bearing and conceit, the way he held himself, the way he spoke, his words, his tone of voice—all of it was Khalil.

Yet McGarvey could not be certain his belief that Salman was Khalil was not just the product of his wishing it to be so.

Alaska weighed heavily on his mind. He could not erase the images of the young mother and her infant dying in the water, and of Khalil's hands on Katy.

"Actually I resigned," McGarvey said, realizing that he would have to push the prince into making a mistake before he could be sure.

Salman's expression darkened. He seemed to be on edge, his mood brittle. "You think that bin Laden is getting his money from Saudi Arabia, and that I'm brokering his connections?"

"He's run through his own fortune, and his family has cut him off. He's getting money from someone."

Salman nodded. "There are a lot of wealthy Arabs who aren't in love with America. Bin Laden has no lack of admirers. If he's still alive. But then your FBI has already identified many of his banking connections. So that can't be the real reason you've targeted me. So what could it be? Why *are* you here?"

"I'd have thought you would have figured that out by now," McGarvey said easily. "I'm here to kill you."

THIRTY-NINE

□

A look of wonderment crossed Salman's face. But the change of expression did not erase his arrogance or his amusement. "You have quite a reputation, but you're not armed at the moment, so unless you mean to tear me limb from limb with your bare hands, how do you propose doing it?"

"I can think of any number of methods," McGarvey said, his voice hard and flat. "A bullet in your brain tonight would work."

"Because you think I'm brokering money for bin Laden?"

"Because I think that you're the terrorist Khalil."

Salman turned suddenly and walked a few paces away toward the opposite end of the strip, his movements smooth, almost balletic. He tapped the point of his épée on the floor, making a small menacing noise like a creature scratching to get in, or the warning rattles of a diamondback. "I would have thought the man, if he exists and if he's still alive, would be in hiding with bin Laden in the Afghan mountains for the moment, considering their warning to America." He laughed. "But that's not the real reason you're here. To find a terrorist. You're here for revenge, aren't you?" He turned back. "You might as well admit it, you know. I had you figured out the moment you showed up at the casino last night and challenged my bank, then insulted me in front of my friends." He shook his head ruefully. "This is all about Washington—what was it, ten or twelve years ago when I made love to your wife?"

"You worked for the Russians then," McGarvey said, conversationally, though he wanted to rip the bastard's throat out. He walked over to the rack of fencing equipment and selected one of the épées. "KGB General Baranov," he said, over his shoulder. "An interesting man."

"He made love to your wife too," Salman said, matter-of-factly.

McGarvey had feared that one thing for a very long time, until he'd come to the conclusion that either it wasn't true, or if it was, it no longer mattered. "No," he said, turning back. "Just you and Darby." He flicked the blade with a strong motion of his wrist, as if the weapon were a steel bullwhip. It had a solid feel. An Olympic-class weapon. He looked up. Salman was watching him warily.

"Are you so sure?"

McGarvey nodded, "Yes. But you got part of why I'm here right." He walked back to the strip. "Revenge." He came to attention, his left foot at a ninety-degree angle directly behind his right foot, his left hand at his side, the épée pointed at the floor to his right.

Salman was mildly amused and it showed on his face. "Do you mean to fence me in street shoes?" he asked. He had a slight smile at the corners of his broad mouth. "No masks? Could be a dangerous game, if this is how you mean to kill me. I'm quite a good fencer."

McGarvey wasn't surprised that Salman was keeping up his act. He'd have to be good to have eluded detection all these years. "Actually my wife was in love with Darby Yarnell, or thought she was, and I suspect that you took advantage of her like you probably do with all your women. What do you prefer: booze, drugs, intimidation, rape?"

Salman's face darkened with a sudden anger that passed as quickly as it formed. He laughed. "You're trying to get me mad by insulting me." He shrugged. "That's a valid approach. Some fencers might fall for it. Get mad, make a mistake. But look here, are you sure that you don't want to at least put on some decent shoes? I'm sure we have your size."

McGarvey brought his épée straight up, the shiny bell guard just in front of his mouth, and then with a crisp movement snapped it to the right in the traditional salute before a bout. "I'm curious about how much your uncle, the crown prince, knows. The family has to be walking a very fine line between supplying us with oil while funding the terrorists trying to bring us down. If they go too easy on us, their neighbors will hate them, but they openly support scumbags like bin Laden. Riyadh might become our next Baghdad."

Salman returned the salute. "What do you have?" he asked. "Where's your proof?"

McGarvey moved his left foot back a half step, flexed his knees slightly, and brought his épée loosely on guard. "I know you. We faced each other when you tried to kidnap Don Shaw."

"I've never been to Alaska in my life," Salman said. He too came on guard, his stance relaxed, almost nonchalant.

"You were in Vancouver." McGarvey moved forward, feinting to the left. Salman moved back easily, not accepting the feint so when McGarvey presented his blade in six, Salman parried it lightly, not bothering to riposte.

"If you know that much, you must also know that all of my time was accounted for."

"There were gaps," McGarvey said. He leaped forward explosively in a perfectly executed advance ballestra, taking Salman's blade in a counter six. When the prince disengaged, he returned with a strong opposition in four in order to open a line of attack, but then retreated out of distance when Salman disengaged again with lightning speed.

Salman didn't bother to follow up with a counterattack. It was obvious that he was the superior fencer, or thought he was, because he was toying with McGarvey, not really taking the bout seriously.

"When I was in bed asleep," Salman said.

McGarvey moved to the left edge of the strip and lowered the tip of his blade as if he were angling for an attack to the foot, leaving his own unprotected face open. The épée tips were equipped with buttons that, when pressed against a target would close an electrical circuit, thus registering a score. The tips were not sharp, but they were small enough in area that the blades would easily penetrate an eyeball and stab a fatal wound six inches inside the brain. Or, with enough pressure, the tip could be forced through an unprotected throat.

"There were longer periods than that when you were unaccounted for."

"What am I accused of doing?" Salman asked mildly. "Sneaking out the back exit of my hotel, flying up to Alaska, perhaps parachuting down to the boat to face a couple hundred crew and passengers, plus you, and then when it was all over somehow fly back to Vancouver, sneak up to my hotel room, and order breakfast?"

With lightning fast speed, moving nothing but his hand and arm, he thrust his point at McGarvey's face, leaving his own left flank open, figuring that it wouldn't matter because even an extremely hard touch there would do him little or no harm.

It was exactly what McGarvey had hoped the superior fencer's arrogance would lead him to do. At the last possible moment, the épée less than an inch from his right eye, McGarvey reached up with his left hand, slapped the blade away, and drove his own épée upward to Salman's exposed neck, stopping just short of a penetrating thrust.

For several long moments the two men stood in tableau, neither moving, until finally Salman let his épée drop to the floor and slowly spread his hands. "It would seem that the director of Central Intelligence does not play by the rules. But what now? His hand is stayed. Why?"

McGarvey was back on the stern deck of the *Spirit*, and he could hear Khalil talking to Katy. *You will look good in black, madam.*

He'd been too formal, as if he hadn't known her, or hadn't remembered.

His voice had been different.

McGarvey stepped back, studied Salman's amused expression for a second, then saluted.

He wanted this. For the young mother and infant, for the other passengers and crew, for what had been done to Katy aboard the cruise ship and twelve years ago in Washington.

But he couldn't be sure.

Salman's sardonic grin widened. "What is it, Mr. McGarvey? Has your taste for blood left you? Or were the tales of your adventures in the Alaska wilds, coming to the rescue of women and children, mere public relations?"

"I owe you an apology," McGarvey said.

Salman laughed. "Get off my boat while you're still able. If ever we meet again, my hand will not be stayed. I will kill you."

McGarvey tossed his épée aside, and walked out the way he had come in, conscious that Salman had come to the door to watch him leave.

He couldn't be sure. Not one hundred percent.

Inge Poulsen, now wearing a sarong, a rose in her hair, waltzed down from the sundeck, her pretty face lit up in a bright smile that immediately faded when she spotted McGarvey at the gangway. "*Arrêtez.* You can't leave yet. I must know about the flowers."

McGarvey could see Salman at the door to the aft passageway, but the young woman could not. "*Je suis désolé, Mademoiselle.* But I must go."

"Non—" she protested, but Salman cut her off almost as if he were mildly reprimanding a naughty child.

"The *monsieur* is leaving, Inge. Now I want you to return to your cabin, like a good girl, or I'll have you tossed overboard tonight."

McGarvey turned slowly to look at Salman standing in the doorway. *Toss the woman and child overboard.* They were Khalil's words aboard the cruise ship. And now they were Salman's words. Same inflection, same voice.

FORTY

□

Day or night no longer had any significance for Liese, so that even now driving toward the chalet in the bright early afternoon, she was having trouble coming away from the erotic dreams she'd been having about Kirk. She could feel his body next to hers, hear his voice in her ear, feel his breath on her neck. She felt disconnected from reality.

The small boats with their brightly colored spinnakers were back on the lake, and as she came up the gravel driveway she spotted Gertner's car along with several others parked beside the chalet. It looked as if someone was throwing a party, or a conference, and the worry that something had happened to Kirk spiked.

Gertner's call had come a few minutes before noon while she has having lunch in her apartment. McGarvey was in Monaco. He and the prince had actually come face-to-face at the casino, where McGarvey publicly insulted the man. And this morning McGarvey was actually aboard the prince's yacht.

"How do you know this?" Liese had asked.

"The French are keeping an eye on things. As a favor."

"Then you have what you wanted," Liese said, tiredly. Gertner had fired her after her warning to Kirk, and she had gone home to try to divorce herself from caring. But that was impossible, and that's when the erotic dreams had begun in earnest. "It no longer concerns me."

"But it does," Gertner cried. "We need your help out here." He lowered his voice as if he was sharing a secret with her. "*Liebchen*, listen, I know that we've had our differences. It's only natural, with two strong-willed and . . . I admit it . . . bull-headed individuals to clash swords. But I need you, *Liebchen*. Kirk needs you."

"Has something happened to him?" Liese had demanded, but Gertner would tell her nothing further, except that she was back on the job. She had a second chance, which was a favor Gertner did not hand out every day.

She drove around to the south side of the chalet, out of sight from the Salman compound across the bay, and pulled up behind a Bureau of Technical Services van, the roof of which bristled with high-frequency communications antennae. In the past two days Gertner had called up a lot of support. This was important to him, and as he had explained to her ad nauseam, to Switzerland.

Ziegler was waiting for her at the kitchen door, his thick brown hair disheveled, his eyes red. He looked exhausted. "Thank God you're here. Maybe you can get him to calm down," he said, stepping aside for her.

"Has something happened to McGarvey? He wouldn't say on the phone."

Ziegler shook his head. "That's what he wants you to find out. But he keeps saying that we've finally got the bastard."

The kitchen was a filthy mess of dirty dishes and filled garbage bags stacked in a corner. The great room smelled of sweat, schnapps, and sweet pipe tobacco. Besides Gertner, LeFevre, and the translator, there were four other men she didn't recognize. And there was more electronic equipment stacked on the long table, on top of aluminum carrying cases, and on the odd chair placed here and there. Wires connecting the equipment with several computers crisscrossed the floor.

Gertner sat at one of the computer terminals, intently listening to something on headphones. One of the technicians motioned toward the door. Gertner turned, and when he spotted Liese in the hall, he tore off his headphones and jumped up. "What took you so long? You're not being followed, for heaven's sake, are you?"

Liese tried to gauge his mood, which seemed more mercurial than normal. He looked tired, as did Ziegler. They'd all apparently been going at it around the clock since she'd been kicked out two days earlier. But Gertner looked worried too, as if not everything was going his way. He had set himself to go up against Kirk McGarvey, using Prince Salman as bait. What he had not counted on was McGarvey's strength and the prince's apparent deviousness. *Gertner had been in over his head from the beginning, and he was finally starting to realize it.*

The translator, Sergeant Hoenecker, looked at Liese with a mild smirk, as if he'd known all along that she couldn't help herself from coming back any time Gertner snapped his fingers, because she was in love with Kirk McGarvey. It was a power that all of them held over her. And the bastards were right: she couldn't help herself, as stupid as it was.

"No, I'm not being followed," Liese said, stepping carefully over the wires. "What's going on here? What's the TMS van doing out back?"

"That was our big break," Gertner said. "I can tell you with all modesty that had I not thought of a satellite intercept, we wouldn't be at this point." He looked to the others for approval. Hoenecker gave him a nod.

"I'm here, like you asked. What piece of intelligence vital to Swiss national security have you turned up? And has something happened to McGarvey?"

"So far as we know, he and his friend are just dandy," Gertner said. "But I want you to know that I'm willing to bury the hatchet here. Let bygones be bygones. We have work to do, you and I, and yes, it is vital to Swiss national security." He shook his head as if he were saddened by the naughtiness of a little girl. "You are a capable police officer, *Liebchen*, but if you don't mind one piece of advice from an older, more experienced man to a rising, but impetuous star, you need to get in control of your emotions."

Liese winced inside. He was such a smarmy bastard, she could hardly stand to be in the same room with him, let alone have him for a boss. But she needed him if she was going to help Kirk. "It's a feminine thing," she said.

"Of course it is." Gertner agreed, wholeheartedly, as if he was relieved that she was finally beginning to see reason. "I'm glad you're here, because we need your help. It's a delicate situation."

Liese looked at the headphones Gertner was holding. "Is it another telephone intercept?"

"Yes, it is," Gertner said. "The prince is in Monaco, and so is your Mr. McGarvey, which you saw fit to insure. What you might not appreciate is that the prince is staying aboard his quite ostentatious yacht, and McGarvey has been there to visit."

"The Americans suspect that the prince might be the terrorist Khalil," Liese said. "McGarvey is there to investigate him."

Gertner smiled indulgently. "In what capacity? Certainly not as the director of Central Intelligence. Men in that lofty position do not carry on in the field. But of course he resigned or was fired, and yet he's aboard the prince's yacht. Curious, no?"

"Kirk is there to kill him."

Gertner gave her a wary nod, as if that idea had already occurred to him, but he wanted to see where she would take it.

"What about this call?" She asked.

"There were actually two of them from the yacht in the Monaco harbor within one minute of each other. The first was to his chief of security here at the lake house, informing his people that he might be gone longer than he had expected. In fact, he's sailing tonight for his house in Corsica. On the south shore near the village of Bonifacio. There was mention of his estates in the file I sent you."

"Did he mention Kirk?" Liese asked.

"Not by name. But he tells his contact that he may be entertaining an interesting guest." Gertner was perplexed. He shook his head. "The prince was being coy, and for the life of us we cannot fathom why. Nor can we fathom his next remarks." Gertner picked up a printout of the telephone intercept. " 'Have the compound made ready,' " Gertner read. "That's the prince talking. 'Have the compound made ready. Fully ready.' "

He looked up. "What do you suppose he meant by that last part?"

Liese's head was spinning. McGarvey was stalking Salman. He had traveled to Monaco to put a bullet in the man's brain. Apparently the prince knew about it and was setting up a trap at his Bonifacio compound. "The guest he's talking about may not be McGarvey."

"Perhaps not, unless you consider the possibility that McGarvey intends to go to Bonifacio with the prince, where the two of them will hunker down until this bin Laden insanity unfolds itself."

"He would expose himself as a traitor," Liese shot back. "Whatever you think of him, he is not stupid."

"Anything but," Gertner agreed. "After the attack on America, McGarvey could emerge a lone patriot who valiantly tried to stop the terrorists, but who failed in his mission."

"But why?" Liese practically screamed.

Gertner smiled. "That, *Liebchen*, is exactly what I want you to ask your Mr. McGarvey."

Ziegeler came over and handed Liese a cell phone. "He's staying at the Hotel de Paris under the name Robert Brewster. His number will dial automatically if you press one."

"Call him, *Liebchen*," Gertner prompted. "Perhaps you could suggest a visit. You know, old friends talking over old times. He respects you. Trusts you. After all, it was you who tipped him off about the prince coming to Monaco."

Now that she was clear in her mind about what Kirk was doing, she wasn't about to hinder him. Yet she was a Swiss federal cop, and she had responsibilities to her family, most of whom still lived down in Morges, near Lausanne. Her mother and sister didn't understand her, but her father and grandfather did. She was the first woman in the family to do something with her life other than have babies and maintain a household. *Watch your tongue scheibelpuf, and you'll stay out of trouble,* her father told her when she went off to the police academy in Bern. He was proud of her. *And always remember first and foremost that you are Swiss.*

She started to raise the phone when Gertner held her off.

"Understand something, Sergeant Fuelm. Should you take it upon yourself to favor this man over your duties, should you warn him that he is under investigation by this department, you will be subject to immediate arrest and prosecution under the Secrets Act."

Liese pressed "one" on the keypad, surprised at how frightened Gertner was. Proving Kirk was a traitor to his own country would make Gertner's career, and would satisfy his revenge for what happened to poor Marta, but if he was wrong he would lose everything. He would be guilty of poor judgment, a characteristic that the Swiss did not admire.

The call went through to the front desk of the hotel, and Liese asked to be connected to Monsieur Brewster's room. After a few seconds the operator came back.

"I am sorry, Mademoiselle, Monsieur Brewster does not answer his telephone. Would you care to leave a message?"

Gertner held one cup of the headset to an ear. He was monitoring the call. He gave Liese a warning look.

"Tell him that Liese telephoned and would like to talk to him about an old friend."

"Oui, Mademoiselle."

Liese disconnected and handed the cell phone to Ziegler, knowing that if Salman were leaving, Kirk would follow him. Monaco was far too public a venue, and the Monegasque police were famed for their ruthless efficiency with anyone breaking the sanctity of the principality. But Corsica was a different story. A man could fall to his death off one of the cliffs, and it might be days before the body was discovered. She turned to leave.

"What was that about an old friend?" Gertner demanded.

Liese turned back. "I was talking about Marta. He was in love with her, you know."

"Where are you going?"

Liese hoped that Kirk would understand her warning, but it was all she could do for him from here. "I'll be back in the morning. But for now you know where Kirk is."

Halfway back to her apartment in Lucerne, Liese used her cell phone to place a call to Emile Lescourt, an old friend in Bern. She had worked with him a few years ago when he was a young detective with the Kantonpolizei doing a brief stint in Lucerne. They were both single, he was good-looking, and they had naturally fallen in together.

They'd had a brief, interesting affair, and some of the best nights she remembered were not spent lovemaking but flying. Lescourt was an excellent pilot. He belonged to the Club Aeronautique Bern and had the use of any of the club's five lightplanes.

They were still the best of friends, even though he was now a police lieutenant and outranked her. He had married, but he got a nasty divorce after only three years, and from time to time he and Liese got together to fly and afterward make love. There was no longer anything frantic about their relationship, just mutual comfort.

It was his private number, and Lescourt answered on the first ring. "Oui."

"Emile, c'est moi, Liese," she said, keeping her voice light. "Bonjour."

"Ah, Liese, m'petite," he replied. "I was just thinking about you. I hope this isn't an official call." He sounded hopeful, and Liese figured he was going through another one of his lonely stages.

"I called because I need your help. I have to meet a friend of mine in Monaco as soon as possible. Could you fly me to Nice?"

Lescourt's tone was suddenly guarded. "What, this afternoon?"

"Yes. I could be at the airport in about an hour."

"Considering what I've heard you're doing up there, I have to ask if this is an official request, Liese. Because if it is, I'll have to hand it back to Gertner for his approval, but if it's not, I'll hang up and forget that you called."

"Wait, Emile, please. I beg you," Liese cried. She hated to do this to him, but driving to Monaco was out of the question, and taking a commercial flight, if one was still available this afternoon, would be far too public. Gertner would be on her before she buckled her seat belt. "I'm asking you as a woman who shares your bed, and your sadnesses. I've been there for you. Now I need your help."

Lescourt hesitated. For a second or two Liese thought he'd hung up. "Merde," he said. "I'll fly you there, but I will not wait. You will have to return home on your own."

"Thank you, Emile."

"And Liese," he said, solemnly, "this will end it between us."

F O R T Y — O N E

McGarvey slowly replaced the telephone on its cradle after listening to Liese's odd message. She had not traced him to this hotel to talk about Marta, the only mutual friend they'd ever shared. She had called to warn him about something. But that was five hours ago.

The clock was ticking on bin Laden's message, and he felt as if he was running out of time and running out of options.

He walked back to the balcony and looked out toward La Condamine. It was getting dark, and the prince's yacht was bathed in lights. Though he couldn't make out much detail at this distance, it did seem as if there was some activity on the dock. He could make out at least two delivery vans, and the white Mercedes.

His tuxedo had been sponged and pressed, ready for another evening in the casino, where he expected Salman to come for another chance at chemin de fer after his beating last night, and especially after what had happened this morning aboard the yacht.

It's what a man such as Khalil would do.

Liese had told him that Salman would come to Monaco.

She knew that McGarvey would come here too.

And she had called to warn him about what? Something she might have learned from her surveillance operation in Lucerne? The "old friend" was obviously a reference to Salman, made that way because someone was listening over her shoulder.

Shortly after 2:30, McGarvey had rented a BMW Z3, and he drove down to Nice for drinks and a late lunch at Hotel Negresco, watching his back to see if he was being followed.

But the prince had sent no one.

When he got back to Monte Carlo, he turned the car in, and then took a leisurely stroll over to the Rainier Palace on the Rock. From there he descended through the medieval alleys past the cathedral and finally to the

Musée Océanographique, which at one time had been directed by Jacques Cousteau.

He'd stopped often to study a piece of architecture or to take in the view. Several times he turned around abruptly as if he had suddenly remembered something, or as if he'd suddenly realized that he was lost, and retraced his steps.

When he passed shop windows, he watched for the reflection of someone behind him, or across the street. It was old tradecraft—cold war stuff—but effective.

He saw no one out of place in the fairly crowded streets and sidewalks. Even if he was being double- or triple-teamed, with shadows in vehicles as well as on foot, there would have been patterns. The same colored shirt, the same taxi or delivery van or plain dark sedan.

But there was nothing.

Nor could he spot anyone with binoculars or perhaps a small scope watching from any of the apartment balconies. All the rooflines he scanned as he walked through the principality were free of movement.

There should have been someone. After McGarvey's threat, Salman should have done something more than toss him off the yacht.

After the museum he even hiked over to the marina and walked out to where Salman's yacht was tied to the largest of the docks.

Here I am. What are you going to do about it?

The gangway was still down, but the white Mercedes was gone, and there didn't seem to be any activity on deck, nor could he see anyone topside on the bridge. No one came out to tell him to leave.

Not only that, but something was out of place. It was only a feeling, but looking at the yacht McGarvey thought he was missing something that was right there in front of him.

Now, coming back to the hotel and hearing Liese's warning, he suddenly knew what he'd missed.

The helicopter's air intake vents had been blocked, and the windshield and side windows covered. The yacht was being prepared for departure. Salman wasn't coming to the casino; he was leaving tonight.

McGarvey had pushed, but the prince had not pushed back.

Yet.

Now it appeared as if he was leaving town.

McGarvey turned, his gray-green eyes narrowed in thought. Liese was part of a Swiss investigation of Prince Salman. But she had been included on the case *because of her connection with the director of the CIA.* Whatever they were investigating was so explosive, so sensitive, that an official request for information through diplomatic channels could not be made.

The Swiss might suspect that because of his tenuous connection with Salman a dozen years ago, there might still be a connection. It wasn't that farfetched to believe that the director of the CIA was working with Saudi intelligence, and through them he was possibly working with al-Quaida in a roundabout way. In the eighties the CIA had supplied money and weapons, most notably Stinger handheld missiles, to bin Laden and his mujahideen, who were fighting to kick the Russians out of Afghanistan.

There were even a small number of political analysts who believed the Israeli Mossad had engineered 9/11 in order to mobilize America against Islam. And the CIA and Mossad had a very close relationship.

There were all sorts of theories.

From the Swiss point of view, McGarvey's actions in Alaska could have been a diversion, turning the CIA's attention away from bin Laden's announcement. Then McGarvey had come to Monaco and had made contact with Salman.

And Liese had called McGarvey to warn him about something. But her superiors would be watching over her shoulder, listening to her conversations, analyzing every word, depending on her emotions to control her, so he could not return her call to find out more.

She was in love with McGarvey, but she would not have taken the risk unless she felt that he was in grave danger. Which possibly meant that Salman was planning on hitting back sometime tonight and then sailing away aboard his yacht.

A narrow, cruel smile played at the corners of McGarvey's mouth. If that were the case, maybe he would make it easier for the prince by going back to the yacht and somehow getting aboard. If there was to be a fight, taking it out to sea would be much cleaner, with less backlash. Fifty miles off shore there would be no witnesses if the prince were to meet with an unfortunate accident. After all, he seemed to be fond of tossing people overboard. Maybe it was time for him to see how it felt.

He took his Walther out and checked the action, then slipped it back in the slim profile holster at the small of his back. He made certain that he had an extra magazine of ammunition, and donning the gray tweed jacket he'd worn on his tour this afternoon, he was headed for the door when the telephone rang.

The only people who knew that he was here under a work name were Liese and her people, and the prince. To everyone else he was Robert Brewster, a rich, ill-mannered American who was lucky at cards and who tipped to excess.

He went back and picked up the phone on the third ring. "Oui?"

"Kirk, thank God I'm in time. Has the prince invited you back to his yacht tonight?"

McGarvey's fingers tightened on the phone. It was Liese. She sounded out of breath, as if she had just run up a flight of stairs. But she was probably taking a very big risk calling him again, unless she was using a clean line. "Are you sure that you're not being monitored?"

"Absolutely," she said. "I'm calling from a house phone downstairs. Has the prince invited you back to his yacht tonight?"

It had taken no feat of rocket science to trace him here, but for her to leave Switzerland to come here in person could only mean that she was convinced he was in grave danger. He didn't think that she was setting him up. The Liese he'd known didn't operate that way. "No. As a matter of fact I think he's getting ready to sail."

"Yes, he is—to his compound on Corsica. I think he's going to invite you to go with him, and he'll kill you down there. Maybe make it look like an accident."

"How do you know all this?"

"We've been watching this guy for a couple of years. Even before 9/11. Kirk, he's Khalil; we're sure of it. May I come up?"

For now McGarvey wanted to maintain an arm's-length distance from Liese, if for no other reason than to reduce the trouble she was probably already in with her people. "No, stay where you are; I'll be right down. Better yet, there's a sidewalk café just to the left as you walk out the front doors. I'll meet you there in five minutes."

Liese's voice was suddenly guarded. "Bring your pistol. I think that you are in a great deal of danger here in Monaco, and right now. He might not wait to take you in Corsica."

FORTY-TWO

Khalil sat in the shadows at a sidewalk café across from the Hotel de Paris, sipping a milky *Pernod et eau minérale* as he watched the passersby. The Place de Casino was particularly busy this evening, even as the European holiday season wound down. Limousines, taxis, and tour buses came in a steady stream.

The lights and glitter were worlds apart from the calm serenity of the desert, but Monte Carlo, which was actually one of his favorite small towns, was as good a place for a righteous kill as any other place on earth. The British had discovered oil in Saudi Arabia, the Americans had exploited it, and as a result the Arabs had discovered and were exploiting the principality.

In time the oil would be pumped dry, the money would disappear, and the time of true *Dar el Islam* would return. In the meantime, there was the *jihad.*

Insha'allah.

Opening his laptop on the table, he switched it on and calmly waited until it booted up; then he established a wireless Internet connection. He wanted to be finished with his business and gone from the principality sometime tonight, preferably before midnight, which was less than four hours from now. And he felt a rising excitement even though Osama had taught him never to take his work personally.

Be detached. It will be your armor. This is a jihad for Allah not for man.

But this now was very much a personal thing for Khalil.

The only man he ever loved and respected was Osama bin Laden.

The only man he truly hated, besides his father, was Kirk McGarvey. Khalil had killed his father more than thirty years ago, and this evening he would kill McGarvey.

He brought up the Web site for the Hotel de Paris, then broke through its pitifully simple security system into the guest registry, which showed not only names, but also passport and credit card numbers. He eliminated all the European names, reducing the list of 205 guests to thirty-seven. He saved this list to a file, then opened a search engine that found passport numbers and matched them to names, dates, and places of birth.

McGarvey was possibly fifty, and he spoke with a flat midwestern accent, which Khalil placed somewhere in Kansas, Missouri, or Nebraska. He eliminated all the obvious mismatches, reducing the list to nineteen names. Of these he picked five likely possibilities, based mostly on instinct. McGarvey would be traveling under a work name that would be rock solid. Like the man himself.

Khalil connected with the U.S. State Department in Washington and hacked into the main passport database. The security blocks for this system were far more sophisticated than the hotel's. He had only a few seconds before various telltales would pop up and ask for additional passwords. He quickly ran the five passport numbers, immediately coming up with the information that three of the passports had been applied for at the passport agency in New Orleans, the fourth in New York, and the fifth in Washington.

He backed out of the program and went to the issuing agency in Washington, where he ran the single number. A copy of the actual passport came up, showing the photograph of a slender-faced man with blond hair.

Khalil considered the photo, but rejected it. Even with a good disguise McGarvey could not be made to look like the man in the photo.

Next he entered one of the numbers from the New Orleans agency, and when the record came up he was looking at a photograph of Kirk McGarvey, under the name Richard A. Brewster, Tampa, Florida.

Khalil quickly backed out of that program, and returned to the hotel's Web site, hacking into the switchboard. Next he used his cell phone to call the front desk.

"*Bonsoir*, Hotel de Paris. How may I direct your call?"

"I say, be a doll and connect me with Dick Brewster's room, would you?"

"*Moment, s'il vous plaît*," the operator said.

A couple of seconds later, the call came up on Khalil's computer screen at the same time he heard it ring over his cell phone. McGarvey was in suite 204.

The number rang five times, and the operator came back on. "Monsieur Brewster does not answer. Would you care to leave a message?"

"No, that's okay, darlin', I'll try later." Khalil broke the connection, and brought up the hotel switchboard's automated message service, which recorded all messages and telephone calls to or from numbers outside the hotel for which charges were levied.

McGarvey had received only one call since noon, and it was from a number in Lucerne.

Khalil brought up the recorded message. It was from a woman. She sounded young, and perhaps even frightened.

Tell him that Liese telephoned and would like to talk to him about an old friend.

Khalil raised his eyes and looked past the gaily lit pool and fountain toward the hotel. Besides the motor traffic, couples were strolling hand in hand in the balmy early evening air. There was always a sense of excitement in Monaco, yet with its grand promenades, the splendid hotels and restaurants, the magnificent palace, and the yacht-filled harbor, this was also a city for lovers. Was it as simple as the possibility that McGarvey had a mistress from Switzerland with whom he was having a rendez-vous?

After the events aboard the Alaskan cruise ship, Khalil would have thought that McGarvey was a man singularly dedicated to his wife. He had certainly gone to great lengths to come to her rescue.

The important fact at this moment, however, was that McGarvey was not in his suite.

Khalil shut down his computer, finished his Pernod, and paid the tab with a few coins. Then he got up and started across the Place to rent a room at the hotel, his computer case in one hand and a small leather overnight bag in the other.

No one noticed the tall, somewhat overweight man wearing a poorly cut, dark suit that looked as if it had been slept in, his dark hair mussed and his eyes red behind bottle-thick glasses, even though he moved with the fluid grace of a dancer—or perhaps a jungle animal on the hunt.

FORTY-THREE

□

McGarvey encountered no one in the corridor or in the emergency stair-well, which he took to the service level one floor below the lobby. This area of the hotel was busy with white-coated waiters, some pushing serv-ing carts for room-service suppers; maids in black with white frills; and supervisors in formal cutaways scurrying along the broad, unadorned corridors and using the several service elevators, some of them speaking urgently on walkie-talkies as the evening began to ramp up.

He had kept himself alive all these years in part because of his trade-craft, but in a large measure because he trusted almost no one. If some-one had been monitoring Liese's call, they might be waiting for him to emerge from the hotel's front doors. He would make an easy target.

He buttoned his jacket and stepped out of the stairwell. No one gave him a second look as he walked back to the large kitchen and passed directly to the pantry and delivery area that opened outside to the loading dock. The area behind the hotel was slightly below the level of the central plaza, and it was concealed from the street by a row of palm trees and a concrete wall on which grew a profusion of bougainvillea and other flowering vines.

He walked up the ramp, paused at the top as a cab sped past, then walked around to the Place and blended with the early evening crowd, all of his senses alert for any sign that something was out of place. If Liese was right about Salman extending an invitation to sail to Corsica, then McGarvey figured that the white Mercedes would be parked in front. But when he came around the corner the car wasn't there.

Crossing the street, he made a pass in front of the hotel and the side-walk café where Liese was supposed to be waiting. He didn't spot her at first—she was seated two tables from the sidewalk in relative darkness.

At the corner he waited for a break in the heavy traffic, and then skipped across the street, coming back to the café from the direction opposite to the one he would have come from had he left the hotel from the front.

Liese was sipping a glass of wine, her attention directed toward the hotel. She was wearing a black leather jacket over a white tee, her purse on the table in front of her. In profile her face was narrow, with high cheekbones and a delicately upturned nose; her blond hair was stylishly short and on just about any other woman would look masculine. But the past decade had been very kind to her. When McGarvey had left Switzerland for the last time, Liese had been a kid in her mid-twenties, with a big mouth, and the skin-and-bones figure of a runway model. From what he could see from where he stood twenty feet away, she had matured into a beautiful woman.

McGarvey studied the street scene for another moment or two, but he couldn't detect anyone lingering in front of the hotel; no one was seated in a parked car, no windowless van was in position.

When he turned back, Liese was staring at him, her face an expression of relief mixed with fear and something else. She nodded her head very slightly toward the hotel, asking if he thought he was being followed, and he shook his head no.

She half rose from her seat and raised her lips to him as McGarvey reached her. He kissed her lightly on the cheek and sat down next to her, his back to the interior of the café. Her scent was the same as it had been ten years ago, and it brought back instant memories of the young Liese Fuelm who'd thrown herself at him from the moment she'd been assigned by the Swiss Federal Police to keep watch on him. She'd never made it a secret that she was madly in love with him, and wanted nothing more in life than to have him make love to her.

At the time McGarvey had been living with Marta Fredericks, another Swiss watchdog sent to find out why a former CIA assassin had come to Switzerland. And even Marta had once suggested that the best thing might be for Mac to sleep with Liese. Maybe it would cure the girl of her puppy love.

McGarvey hadn't taken Marta up on the suggestion, and shortly after that he'd left Switzerland, and a year later Marta was dead. But looking into Liese's eyes now, he could see that nothing had changed; she was still in love with him, her feelings open and easy to read, her disappointment that he had merely kissed her on the cheek obvious.

"It's good to see you again, Kirk," Liese said. She touched his hand, and again it was as if the past ten years had never happened.

McGarvey withdrew his hand. "What are you doing here? You didn't

come in an official capacity. And by now you have to know that I resigned, so I'm not here officially."

Liese couldn't hide her disappointment. "I've come to warn you that
Prince Salman means to kill you."

"What do you think I'm doing here?"

"Obviously you believe that the prince and Khalil are the same man,
and you've come here to prove that, then to kill him not only for what he
did in Alaska, but also because he's almost certainly involved with the
new bin Laden threat." The waiter came. McGarvey ordered a *café express*,
and Liese ordered another glass of *vin blanc ordinaire*. "But there are people
in Switzerland who don't believe it's that simple."

McGarvey wasn't surprised. "Because of the Saudi oil connection."

Liese glanced over toward the hotel, and McGarvey followed her gaze.
But he still couldn't see anything out of the ordinary. She was waiting for
someone or something.

She looked back at him. "That, and the fact you missed in Alaska. You
don't have many friends in Switzerland, but everybody respects your abilities. And some of them are afraid of you."

"That's nothing I don't already know, Liese. Otto said that you
called while I was out of Washington, wanting to talk to me about
Salman. You're running a surveillance operation on him. Your people
think that he's Khalil. But that was *before* Alaska. Why did you try to
reach me?"

"Because it's not only the prince who we're investigating. You're a part
of it."

"Yes, because we need oil and the Saudis have it."

Liese's mouth compressed. She was frightened. "It's my immediate superior, Ernst Gertner. He's nothing more than a Kantonpolizei director,
but he has powerful friends and he considers you his enemy. He means to
destroy you any way he can."

This wasn't making any sense. McGarvey had never heard the name.
"Why does he have a beef with me?"

Liese lowered her eyes. "He was in love with Marta when you and she
were living together in Lausanne. He thought that when it was over he
would be there to pick up the pieces for her."

"But she came running after me in Paris and got herself killed," Mc-

Garvey said. "Is that it, Liese? He thinks I was responsible and now he's gunning for me?"

Liese nodded. Her eyes were moist. It was obvious she was frightened, and that she wanted McGarvey to take her into his arms and tell her everything would be fine. "That's part of it, but there's more." The waiter came with their order, and when he was gone, she squared her shoulders as if she had made a difficult decision. "He thinks he has proof that you and Salman are actually working together."

McGarvey was irritated. She was going around in circles. "The Saudi thing, you've already said that."

"I don't mean Salman as a Saudi royal; I mean Salman as Khalil the terrorist."

McGarvey had to laugh. "He can't be that stupid."

"Salman slept with your wife ten years ago, and yet you've done nothing about it," Liese blurted. "He thinks it's proof enough that you're protecting him. You didn't kill him in Alaska, and there are people from the cruise ship who said you could have done it at the end. And here you are now in Monaco. And you even went aboard his yacht this morning."

McGarvey's mind recoiled. He had to wonder how many people didn't know about his wife and Salman all those years ago. But that wasn't as important as the fact that Liese knew he'd been to the yacht. "How many people do you have here watching me?"

"I don't know. Probably none of our people. Gertner has a lot of friends with Interpol and the Sûreté. So it's probably the local cops on your tail."

"That's just great," McGarvey said. Because of the Swiss interference his hands were effectively tied here in Monaco and anywhere in France. He wasn't exactly a welcome guest of the French, who considered him a dangerous man. And any enemy of France was automatically an enemy of Monaco. As long as he was here under a work name and as long as he caused no trouble, his presence would be tolerated. But the moment he so much as sneezed in public without first covering his mouth, he would be arrested and put on the next flight back to the States. "How do you know Salman is going to Corsica?"

"We're monitoring his telephone calls. We've got a pretty good decryption team and Arab speakers. He's been talking to someone—we can't figure out who, just yet—in the royal palace in Riyadh. This morning he told his contact that he was going to his compound at Bonifacio. And he wanted it made *fully ready*. His words."

"Your boss is convinced that if I show up in Corsica it'll prove that Salman and I are working together?"

Liese nodded. "That's why I had to come here to warn you in person. Nobody thinks that bin Laden's threat is an empty warning. Al-Quaida will try to hit you just like 9/11, and not too long from now." She looked away for a moment. "That's the other reason I came." She turned back to face McGarvey, a defiant, resolute expression on her face. "I'll help you kill him. No one can say that both of us were here to protect him."

It was about what McGarvey figured she would say. He shook his head. "Not a chance, because nothing's going to happen here in Monaco. I'll take the ferry from Nice in the morning, and you're returning to Lucerne."

"I'm not going back."

"Don't be stupid, Liese. Gertner assigned you to investigate Salman and me, because you and I have a history. And you can bet that if Gertner has people watching me here, they've already told him that you showed up."

"He believes that I'm still in love with you. He'll think I'm here to throw myself at you."

"Then that's exactly what you're going to do," McGarvey said. He laid some money on the table to cover their drinks, then leaned over and kissed Liese on the lips. "We're leaving."

Liese's eyes were wide, her face flushed with pleasure. A dream for her had suddenly come true. "Where?"

"The hotel. You're staying with me tonight."

FORTY—FOUR

Khalil had hacked into the hotel's computer and downloaded the key code to McGarvey's suite onto the electronic card key he'd been issued for his own room on the third floor. Standing now at the door to room 204, the corridor empty for the moment, he reached inside his jacket for the handle of his SIG Sauer P226 pistol with his right hand, while with his left he slid the key card through the slot. The mechanism flashed green, and the lock released with an audible click.

If you come face-to-face with the man, kill him. He will not give you a second chance. Osama had been very specific. And very respectful.

Nothing stirred inside the suite as he eased the door open with his toe, nor were there any lights, except the lights from outside on the brightly lit Place filtering through the floor-to-ceiling French doors covered with diaphanous sheers.

The security chain wasn't in place, but a man such as McGarvey might not feel he needed the extra protection.

"*Service de chambre,*" Khalil called, pleasantly.

He waited for a moment, and when there was no reply from within, he checked over his shoulder to make sure no one had gotten off the elevator. Then he drew his pistol, pushed the door the rest of the way open, and stepped inside.

He checked behind the door, then closed it. To the right was a small half bath for guests. Straight ahead, past an elaborate wet bar on the left, the chamber opened to a large, expensively furnished sitting room. Moving through the shadows without noise, he crossed the sitting room and checked the equally expansive bedroom, dressing area, palatial bathroom with a sunken Jacuzzi on a raised platform, and separate shower-stall bathroom.

McGarvey's shaving things were laid out at the double sinks, and his tuxedo was neatly pressed and ready on the bed.

Khalil studied the arrangement for a second or two. McGarvey was planning on going to the casino tonight. But not until later. For some reason he'd left his room, perhaps to have a drink at the bar or an early supper, but he would be back to dress.

The tension that Khalil had initially felt—that somehow McGarvey knew that he was coming and had set a trap of his own—subsided. Walking back into the sitting room, he was slightly irritated with his foolish fears. McGarvey was simply one man. An imaginative and capable fighter, especially when he was defending his wife or trying to save women and children—people who Americans almost universally thought of as *innocents*—but for all of that one man who would be entering a killing chamber when he walked through the door.

He went to the double French doors, and careful to keep out of sight of anyone looking up from the Place, parted the curtains and studied the busy street scene. Nothing appeared to be out of the ordinary. Mostly tourists were going about their business; some of them he expected were Americans, enjoying themselves while Mohammed's sword once again hung over their country.

It amused him to wonder if any of them would feel the least bit of guilt for being here when the attacks happened in a few days. There'd been little or no media coverage about the Americans who'd been vacationing when the World Trade Center and the Pentagon were hit. Yet nearly every human being on the planet knew exactly where they were and what they had been doing that day.

They would remember again.

The French doors opened onto a narrow balustraded balcony. From this point there was no view of the street directly below because a palm tree came up almost even with the balcony, and the broad fronds were in the way.

He unlocked the doors and eased one of them open a crack. The sheers immediately billowed into the room, and he could hear the street sounds and smell the night sea air. He took a very brief look outside before he ducked back out of sight. The balconies off the rooms adjoining this suite were about two meters apart, a manageable distance. The hotel's stonework had joints that were deep enough and well placed so that a man, even in a hurry, could easily climb up to the floor above or even to the roof, if need be. And the palm tree was within reaching distance.

He closed the French doors, but left them unlocked.

He walked across the sitting room to the corridor door, then turned and looked into the room, seeing what McGarvey would see when he first walked in. Like anyone standing in front of the French doors, McGarvey would be silhouetted by the light from outside for just a moment before he reached for the light switch.

Khalil turned and examined the wall between the corridor door and the door to the half bath. There was a panel with three switches. One of them probably controlled the bathroom light, while the other two were for the entry hall light and probably one or more of the table lamps inside the sitting room.

McGarvey would come in, see or hear nothing out of the ordinary, then half turn to his right to turn on the lights.

At that point Khalil would shoot him dead from the shadows beside the French doors. It was a distance of perhaps twelve or fifteen meters. Not a difficult shot, especially since the target would be well lit.

Once McGarvey was down, Khalil would have two avenues of escape, the primary one being through the corridor, downstairs, and then out of the hotel. But if someone were in the corridor, he would leave via the balcony and make his escape either left, right, up, or down. The overnight bag he'd left in his room was empty, and he had sanitized his computer, trashing the hard disk and wiping the entire unit down for fingerprints, so there was nothing to go back for.

Khalil took the pistol out of his shoulder holster, and as he walked back to the French doors, he took the Vaime silencer from his jacket pocket and screwed it on the end of the Sig's threaded barrel.

Below on the Place the traffic was increasing. It was well after eight o'clock, and by ten, when the serious gambling and partying got into full swing, it would be like a carnival on the streets.

No one would hear or see a thing. And certainly no one would notice the pudgy man in the cheap dark suit going about his business, probably a minor functionary at the hotel on his way home after his shift.

FORTY-FIVE

Away from the sidewalk café, McGarvey led Liese across the street into the Place in the opposite direction from the hotel. She did not offer any objections or question the direction they were going. She was openly happy and content to be with him, even with the danger they both faced. They passed shops selling Louis Vuitton, Yves Saint-Laurent, Gucci, and Givenchy. Traffic was increasing, and every second car, it seemed, was a Rolls-Royce, Bentley, or Ferrari. Yet most of the people on foot wore casual clothes, some even shorts and sandals.

He wanted to put some time and distance away from the café before they headed back to the hotel in order to spot anyone tailing them. Now he was watching not only for someone on Salman's payroll, but also perhaps someone working for the Swiss.

Nothing had changed in the past ten years as far as Liese's infatuation with McGarvey went. If anything, he thought, her love had deepened, even though they had not seen or even spoken with each other until just a couple of days ago. It wasn't rational. "Look, nothing is going to happen tonight," he said.

Liese made it a point not to turn and look at him. But she looped her arm in his, as if they were lovers out for a stroll. "I know. Just let me indulge my fantasy for a little while."

It wasn't what McGarvey meant. "I'm not talking about what's not going to happen in my room tonight."

"What do you mean?"

"We're not going to make love, if that's what you're expecting. But I'm talking about Salman. He's not going to invite me to go to Corsica with him, and so far, unless his people are damned good, he's sent no one to follow me."

She shook her head and looked up at him. "I wouldn't count on it, Kirk. After all, he did have you aboard his yacht this morning."

"Only because I beat him at cards last night and then insulted him. According to him, he wanted to find out what the hell I was up to."

"He was the same guy you faced in Alaska, wasn't he?" Liese asked. "You did establish that?"

McGarvey had been asking himself the same question ever since he'd walked away from the yacht. He'd been sure then, but now he was having second thoughts. "What makes the Swiss Federal Police think that Salman is Khalil?"

"I'm not sure how it started, but it was one of Gertner's pet projects. He wants to become the director general someday and he's trying to make a name for himself. It started right after 9/11. The prince had apparently been traveling all over the place, but then he disappeared, the attacks occurred, and he suddenly showed up at his house in Lucerne and went into seclusion for the next few months."

It was one of the bits of circumstantial evidence that Otto had come up with. "A lot of Saudis ducked for cover. Osama bin Laden himself had cousins in Florida and Maryland. They went back to Riyadh, where they figured they'd be safe until things cooled down."

She shook her head. "That's the same argument I used when he first came to me. But Salman has disappeared just before almost every single act of al-Quaida terrorism. Everything from the first attack on the World Trade Center, to the *Cole*, to the embassies in Africa, and even the Khobar barracks right there in Riyadh. Gertner has the entire file."

"How'd he get onto you?"

"He had friends on the team that was keeping track of you." She looked down, obviously in pain. "It was pretty much an open secret that I was in love with you. Which was fine with Gertner. He figured that if I could seduce you away from Marta, he'd get her." She shook her head again. "Of course, it didn't work out that way."

"He sounds like a charmer," McGarvey said. They had reached the entrance to the casino just as a stretch Mercedes limo pulled up. A dozen paparazzi were there, roughly jostling into position, their cameras flashing as the driver came around and opened the rear door for a young, very thin, very beautiful blond woman. She waved to the photographers as a man dressed in a tuxedo got out behind her, and the two of them went inside.

It was nothing more than a moment of Riviera glitter, which McGarvey forgot as he and Liese headed back around to the hotel.

"You have to believe me, Kirk. I think he's convinced a lot of people that you and Salman have a long history. And if he can prove that Salman is Khalil, that would tie you to 9/11. Even the suspicion would be enough to bring you down."

McGarvey felt sorry for her. She had fallen for a man she could never have, and she was being manipulated because of it. The world was full of bastards. Not just the Osama bin Ladens and the Khalils, but ordinary bastards like Liese's boss who was willing to ruin her life to further his own ambitions. "All the more reason for you to go home tomorrow before you totally screw up your career."

She stopped, her eyes narrow, her lips puckered into a stubborn pout. "I'm not going back."

"If you want to help me, you can go home and keep Gertner busy. And you can keep Otto up to date." She was digging in her heels, and McGarvey was getting irritated. "Look, Liese, we don't have a lot of time here. I'm going after Salman in the morning, and it would be a good thing if someone was helping watch my back in case I don't make it. If he is Khalil, he'll be expecting me to come down there."

A look of incredulity came over her face. "If?" she said. "Are you saying that you're still not sure?"

"Not sure enough to put a bullet in his brain."

"Merde. What the hell did you talk about aboard his yacht? The weather?"

"I told him I had come to kill him. And he tossed me off his yacht. If he really was Khalil, I figured he would come after me. But so far that hasn't happened." McGarvey shrugged. "So I'm left with the same question as before, and less time in which to get it answered." He took Liese's arm and they started walking again. "That's why I'm following him to Corsica and you're going home."

They walked the rest of the way across the Place back to the hotel in silence, McGarvey trying to figure out how to insure that Liese actually went back to Switzerland in the morning. He wouldn't put it past her to follow him down to Corsica, which would all but tie his hands. He'd always tried to work alone, responsible for no one's safety but his own.

With Liese in Corsica he would be looking over his shoulder. Distractions like that could get them both killed.

He didn't think that Salman would try anything tonight. He'd know by now that McGarvey was aware of his plans, and he would wait in Corsica for the former DCI to show up. Like a spider spinning a web and waiting for its prey to get entangled.

They crossed the street to the front entrance of the hotel and were about to go inside when a small Peugeot pulled up to a screeching halt in the driveway behind them. They turned as a tall, lanky man with several cameras around his neck leaped out of the car and came running toward them.

McGarvey, working on pure instinct, disentangled his arm from Liese's, shoved her aside, and turned sideways to offer less of a target as he reached for his pistol.

The photographer pulled up short and began furiously snapping pictures, first of McGarvey and then of Liese.

McGarvey stayed his gun hand. He recognized the photographer as one of the paparazzi who had been at the casino entrance just a couple of minutes ago. Any assassin that Khalil might send would not act in such an open, brash manner. Heads were turning because of the commotion, something neither a gunman nor a French cop here to check up on McGarvey would want to happen.

Liese had opened her purse and was reaching for her pistol, but McGarvey turned back and took her arm, and together they started into the hotel.

"Mr. McGarvey," the cameraman shouted after them. His accent was French. "For the Agence France. What is the director of the CIA doing away from his desk in Washington? Why are you here?"

"Are you sure he's legitimate?" Liese whispered, urgently, as they entered the hotel.

"He was in the pack in front of the casino," McGarvey told her.

The photographer was right behind them, snapping pictures. The lobby was fairly busy at this hour of the evening, and everyone was looking at them trying to figure out who they were and what was going on.

"Mr. McGarvey," the cameraman shouted.

McGarvey and Liese angled directly across the lobby to the elevators. A car had just arrived, and they stepped aboard, the cameraman right on their heels.

McGarvey turned and gave the photographer a stern look. "Stay away from me."

The man started to say something, but then evidently thought better of it. As the elevator door closed, he raised his camera and snapped several shots.

FORTY-SIX

□

Khalil, his heart rate up, moved away from the French doors, where he had been watching the Place off and on for the past half hour, and took his position in the dark corner.

He had moved an easy chair one meter to the left and had unplugged the floor lamp. It gave him a perfectly dark spot with an excellent sight line to the door from which to make the kill.

His attention had been drawn to the casino entrance directly across from the hotel, where a commotion had erupted with the arrival of someone in a limousine. Cameras flashed, and for thirty seconds or so a mob of paparazzi flitted like flies around carrion. He'd almost turned away, but there was something about a couple walking away from the casino that piqued his curiosity.

They walked arm in arm like lovers out for an evening stroll, but even at a distance of more than one hundred meters in the imperfect light, Khalil was convinced there was something familiar about the man. The certainty that he knew who it was continued to grow, until just across the street the man glanced up.

Khalil's heart bumped, and a slow smile spread across his face.

It was McGarvey returning to the hotel, with a young, beautiful woman. He was typically Western after all, a man who professed love and devotion for his wife, while in a foreign city having no compunction against picking up a whore for the evening.

It is righteous to slay the infidel, the sinner, the unbeliever of Muhammad's teachings, and all those who have sinned with him.

Khalil picked up his pistol from the reading table next to the chair, cocked the hammer, and concentrated on settling his nerves. He was somewhat irritated with himself that he was having an attack of the jitters, like an anxious schoolboy. But since Alaska, he'd come to have a much better understanding of—and respect for—McGarvey. Osama's warnings were not overstated, as Khalil had first believed.

If it had not been for the tip from an informant that McGarvey had come to Monaco the day before, he would not have this chance.

The kill tonight would be beautiful.

FORTY-SEVEN

The situation was beginning to feel wrong to McGarvey.

Too many people knew that he was here. Liese knew, Salman knew, and now even the photographer knew. Not only that, but there'd been no activity aboard Salman's yacht. No parties. No people on the sundeck other than the one young woman. Yet Salman had the reputation as an international bon vivant. A party boy. According to the press, he never went anywhere without a crowd. Yet here in Monaco he'd been alone.

As the elevator stopped at the second floor and the door started to open, McGarvey drew his pistol, concealing it behind his right leg.

Liese was alarmed. "What is it?" she asked, softly.

No one was in the corridor. Directly across from the elevator was a gilt-framed mirror, beneath which was a Louis XIV table flanked by two chairs. The house phone, plain white without a keypad, was on the table.

"Something's not right," McGarvey said. He held the elevator door open with his left hand and stuck his head out, all of his senses alert for something, anything that might be out of place. He stood in rapt concentration for several seconds. So far as he could see, none of the room doors were ajar, nor was the emergency stairwell door at the end partially open as if someone were standing there ready to take a shot at anyone getting off the elevator.

"Do you think he's here?" Liese asked. She'd taken her pistol out of her purse. She thumbed the safety catch to the off position.

"Maybe," McGarvey said. There'd been no one out on the streets tailing him, and yet according to Liese somebody was feeding information back to her boss. Somebody had to be looking over his shoulder. The photographer downstairs could have been a distraction. And the girl at the casino last night with Salman and this morning aboard the yacht could have been a distraction too.

"What do you want to do?"

"Hold the elevator, but keep an eye on the stairwell door," McGarvey said. "I'll be just a minute." He stepped off the elevator and went to the house phone, where he called the concierge.

Liese stood half in and half out of the elevator, holding the door from closing with her hip, her head on a swivel watching the corridor in both directions. Her pistol pointed down and to her right, her trigger finger flat against the trigger guard. Very professional.

The same woman who'd helped McGarvey earlier with the flowers answered the phone. "Concierge."

"Good evening. I'm Robert Brewster. I received a telephone message this afternoon from Lucerne. Have there been any other messages or telephone calls since that one?"

"I'll be happy to check for you, Monsieur."

"Kirk," Liese called softly to him. "Someone is calling for the elevator."

"Ignore it," McGarvey said. A moment later the concierge was back.

"There was one further telephone call, from outside the hotel, at 20:05 but no message was left."

"Do you know where the call originated from?"

"No, sir. But apparently it was from outside Monaco."

"Was a name or number given?"

"*Malheureusement, non.*"

"*Merci,*" McGarvey said, and he hung up. Someone had tried to reach

him from a blind number, to talk, or merely to confirm that he was a registered guest of the hotel. But the call had come from outside Monaco less
than an hour ago. If it was Khalil and he meant to come here to get revenge for Alaska, he could have been calling from almost anywhere. It
was a reasonable assumption, however, that he would not have reached
Monaco in such a sort time. If he were planning on a hit, it would probably come in the middle of the night.

Anyone else, such as Katy back home, would have left a message. That it
was a blind number that did not show up on the hotel's telephone system
pointed toward Otto or perhaps Adkins at Langley.

It did not point toward Salman, unless the yacht was equipped with
the electronics to make blind calls. It was a trick that U.S. intelligence had
not seen any evidence of in al-Quaida intercepts.

"Who tried to call you?" Liese asked.

"The hotel doesn't know, but it came from outside Monaco," McGarvey said. He dragged one of the armchairs from beside the table across
the corridor and placed it in the path of the elevator door. "I don't want
anyone coming up behind us for the moment."

"Don't you trust the concierge?" Liese asked.

"I don't trust anyone," McGarvey replied, tightly. He'd seen Khalil's
handiwork up close and personal. He knew what the man was capable of
doing, because whatever else the man might be, he was very smart and
very ruthless.

He nodded toward the end of the corridor. "Check the stairwell," he
said. "I'll cover you from here. But be careful."

Liese hurried to the end of the corridor as McGarvey walked three
doors to his suite. They had been lucky so far that a housekeeping maid or
room-service waiter hadn't shown up to find two people scurrying
around the corridor with guns drawn. But he didn't expect their luck to
hold much longer.

He listened at his door for a sound from within the suite as he
watched Liese cautiously approach the stairwell door. He heard nothing.
Liese turned the door handle, and keeping to the side, eased the door
open a few inches with her foot. She took a quick look, glanced back at
McGarvey, then pushed the door the rest of the way open and rolled into
the stairwell, leading with her pistol in both hands.

A couple of seconds later she was back, shaking her head as she hurried up the corridor to him. "Someone is below, maybe on the ground floor," she reported, careful to keep her voice low. "Talking. A man and a woman."

McGarvey nodded. He was probably being paranoid, but over the years he'd learned to trust his instincts. Larry Danielle, who'd risen to deputy director of the CIA starting out as a young man with the OSS in World War II, had been McGarvey's mentor in the early days. "A dead field man is an operator who doesn't listen to his inner voice," he'd advised. "Develop your instincts, and then, for heaven's sake, trust them."

Danielle was long dead, but his words of wisdom were etched in the brain of every field officer he'd ever trained. The live ones.

The door opened inward to the left. McGarvey positioned Liese on the right, ran his key card through the slot, and when the light blinked green, eased the door open just a crack, keeping out of the way to the left.

He waited for a couple of seconds, then shoved the door the rest of the way open.

There was no sound or movement from inside the suite, but alarms were jangling all through McGarvey's nerves.

Something. He was missing something.

Cloves. Katy said the one odd thing she clearly remembered about Salman was the odor of the Indian clove cigarettes he smoked. It had been an offhand comment two days before, and now McGarvey thought he was smelling something from within the suite.

Something out of place. Something that hadn't been there earlier.

Liese gave him a questioning look.

He motioned to her that he was going in and she was to back him up, when he caught a movement outside the French doors. Out on the balcony. A momentary shadow blocking the light from the Place.

The bastard had come after all. He meant to wait in ambush outside, make the kill after McGarvey was in bed or had his back turned to the windows, and then leave before the body was found. After what had happened on the cruise ship and then this morning aboard his yacht, he had lost his stomach for a stand-up fight.

His only mistake was not keeping out of sight. He'd seen the corridor door opened, and when no one came through the door he apparently got spooked.

Liese had her pistol up at the ready, waiting for him to charge into the room.

"He's out on the balcony," McGarvey told her in a whisper.

"Did you see him?"

"I saw something. I want you to stay out here in the corridor. If anyone comes through the window, shoot him. But don't take any chances."

"What about you?"

"I'm going outside so I can get behind him. I don't think he'll want to risk a shootout in plain sight of half of Monte Carlo. I'm betting he'll try to get past you."

Liese nodded, a grim, expectant look in her eyes.

"Watch yourself," McGarvey warned her. "He won't give you a second chance."

She nodded again, and McGarvey turned on his heel, sprinted down the corridor to the stairwell door, and took the stairs two at a time to the ground. He had no intention of giving Khalil the chance to escape. The public be damned for the moment. The instant he had a clear ID on the man and a good sight line, he would take his shot.

He safetied his pistol and stuffed it in the waistband of his trousers before he burst out of the stairwell and raced across the busy lobby. Several heads turned his way, and the concierge got to her feet. She started to call out something to him, but he was out the door before she got it out.

Traffic was definitely beginning to pick up. In addition to several taxis and a limousine parked in front of the hotel, a Principality Police cruiser had just pulled up, and four uniformed cops were getting out.

McGarvey slowed his pace to a walk until he was away from the bright lights beneath the entryway. Making sure that he hadn't been noticed yet, he sprinted the rest of the way down the street until he was just below the balcony outside his room.

The fronds of the palm tree blocked much of his view, but after a moment he spotted a figure crouched in the relative darkness just to the left of the French doors.

McGarvey checked over his shoulder to make sure the cops hadn't spotted him. But they had gone into the hotel, and for the moment he hadn't attracted any notice.

He pulled out his pistol, thumbed the safety catch to the off position, and moved closer.

The man on the balcony was motionless. He back was turned to the street. But even with the bad angle and uncertain light, McGarvey began to get the feeling that the man was not Khalil. He was too slightly built. Khalil was much larger.

McGarvey raised his pistol. "You," he shouted up.

The figure jerked as if he had been startled, and he turned around. All at once, McGarvey could see the cameras hanging by straps around his neck. He was the photographer who'd accosted them in front of the hotel just a few minutes earlier.

It struck him suddenly that the odd smell upstairs *was* cloves after all. Khalil was in the suite, and the advantage was his because Liese thought he was outside on the balcony.

"Don't move," McGarvey shouted to the cameraman, but it was too late.

The man straightened up and stepped directly in front of the French doors. Almost immediately he was thrown forward, as if punched from behind. His chest erupted in a spray of blood, and he was pitched over the rail, shot from behind. But there'd not been the sound of a gunshot. Whoever had fired was using a silencer. It wasn't Liese.

McGarvey headed back up the street in a dead run even before the cameraman's body had reached the ground.

Apparently no one in the Place had seen or heard a thing. No one stopped or looked over to where the cameraman had fallen from the second-floor balcony.

McGarvey had made a bad decision leaving Liese alone outside the suite. The smart move would have been to call the police, and make sure that Khalil did not get out of there before the cops came.

But it had become personal aboard the cruise liner. Khalil had murdered innocent people, including the mother and her infant child. And he had laid his hands on Katy.

McGarvey reached the front entrance as two police cruisers, their blue lights flashing, sirens blaring, screeched to a halt.

They were in a big hurry, and McGarvey was getting the feeling that he'd been set up to take a fall. It was probably Gertner's friends here in Monaco reacting to Liese's chasing after him.

He pulled up short, stuffed the pistol back into his waistband, and as calmly as possible walked into the hotel lobby. He couldn't afford to be stopped now with Liese upstairs on her own. In no way was she a match for Khalil. She might hesitate to take the shot, but Khalil wouldn't.

The lobby was a scene of confusion. The cops who'd shown up as Mc-Garvey had left the hotel were talking with the concierge and a large man dressed in a dark suit, probably hotel security.

McGarvey tried to be as unobtrusive as possible, angling across to the stairway before someone looked over and recognized him.

There was a sudden commotion at the entry behind him.

"*Arrêtez!*" a man shouted.

McGarvey took two more steps as the cops standing with the concierge and security man turned his way.

"*Arrêtez!*" one of the cops behind him shouted even more urgently.

McGarvey turned and raised his hands in plain sight. Several of the cops had drawn their pistols. Some of the hotel guests and staff, realizing that something dangerous was happening, were scrambling for cover. The situation was on the verge of exploding into an uncontrolled shootout in which innocent people would get hurt.

"*There's a Swiss Federal cop and a killer on the second floor.*" McGarvey said, loudly, in French, so that there would be absolutely no misunderstanding.

At that moment everyone heard two gunshots from somewhere upstairs.

FORTY-EIGHT

Khalil slumped in a kneeling position beside the chair he had pushed aside, his head lolling on the chair seat, his eyes open and fixed on the corridor door, as if he were dead.

The situation was rapidly becoming critical for him, and he seethed with a barely controlled rage. He'd heard the police sirens outside, and if they had heard the two unsilenced shots they would be on their way now. It's why he had momentarily stepped into view to draw fire and then had pretended to be wounded. He wanted to lure the shooter in the corridor to show herself.

The woman whom McGarvey had come up with was in the corridor. She had to figure that her two shots had hit their mark. From her position she would be able to see him, unmoving.

She was hiding behind the door frame, taking only brief glimpses at him and then ducking back. She was obviously a cop or an intelligence officer, and not a prostitute as Khalil had first thought.

It was a stupid mistake on his part, just as shooting the idiot cameraman on the balcony had been a less than ideal move because of the attention it had apparently attracted. But having one of his critical avenues of escape denied him was totally unacceptable.

Khalil was almost sure that McGarvey had spotted the photographer in the windows, mistook him for an assassin, and had gone down to the street to catch him from behind.

Now he was in a bad situation. Unless the woman made her move before the police came up to investigate the shots or surrounded the hotel, he would not be able to make his escape.

His pistol was in his right hand, on the floor between his torso and the side of the chair. He had to raise it only a centimeter or two to have a clear shot at anyone coming through the doorway. Or if she came close enough, he could reach for his belt-buckle knife.

It would give him a great deal of pleasure to watch life leave her eyes as her blood pumped out of her body with each diminishing beat of her fading heart.

Khalil fluttered his eyes and took a big, blubbering breath as if he were gasping for air, fighting for his life. He had seen his victims do the same thing countless times. He was an excellent mimic.

The woman stepped into clear view, her pistol extended in both hands in front of her, her elbows slightly bent.

Khalil could not see her face clearly because she was backlit from the lights in the corridor, but he got the impression that she was probably pretty, and young. She held herself like a cop, though her mistake was exposing herself and not simply waiting for the police to show up. And he thought with amusement, she didn't know the proper narrow-profile sideways stance for approaching a downed, but possibly dangerous, assailant.

If there was more time, there were so many things that he could teach her. Women needed to be guided with a firm hand. Especially Western women who did not know their place in the historical sense.

She stood in the doorway, hesitating with indecision.

He could see that from the way she held herself. She was waiting for McGarvey to return. But she had enough respect for the man she thought she had shot and wounded to keep her distance.

Khalil raised his pistol very slowly, ready to take a snap shot if she spotted his movement.

But she remained in place, her gun pointed into the room.

Khalil's finger began to squeeze on the Sig's trigger.

The stairwell door at the end of the corridor opened with a tremendous bang. Liese turned her head toward the noise as uniformed cops, their guns drawn, burst through the door and immediately began to spread out.

"*Mademoiselle, put your weapon down now, and step back!*" one of them shouted, in French.

Liese hesitated. She glanced at the figure crumpled against the chair inside the suite. His movements had stopped. In all likelihood he was dead. Kirk was not going to be happy, because he had counted on capturing Khalil. He'd wanted to force the man into telling him about bin Laden's threat. The Americans were in desperate need of immediate information.

"*There will be no further warning!*" the cop shouted.

Liese had to wonder how Gertner was going to take the news that she'd been arrested in Monaco for shooting to death a Saudi prince she was supposed to be investigating.

Moving very slowly, she bent down, placed her pistol on the floor, then straightened up. Raising her hands above her head, she stepped away from the doorway.

"*Un terroriste du al-Quaida est ici,*" she said. She nodded toward the suite. "*Là,*" she said. "*Il est mort.*" He's dead.

More cops emerged from the stairwell as two rushed down the corridor to Liese. One of them kicked her weapon away, his pistol never leaving her, while the other turned her around, brought her hands behind her back, and cuffed her.

She didn't resist. She knew better than to give them any provocation, even though the one handcuffing her ran a hand over her ass. Anyway, it was finished. Khalil was dead. He wouldn't provide them any information, but there was one less very bad man on the streets. He would not kill again.

Even more cops had arrived on the scene, and suddenly Kirk came through the door, his hands cuffed behind him.

"He's dead," Liese called to him in English. "I shot him."

The cop, who had handcuffed her, moved her down the corridor, as two other cops, wearing vests, their weapons at the ready, flanked the door to the suite.

On signal, one of them rolled inside the room, sweeping his pistol left to right. A moment later the second cop entered the suite, while two others took up positions on either side of the door.

Someone took the chair away from the elevator, and the car started down. Other cops came from the opposite end of the corridor, guns drawn, but none of the hotel's guests had dared to open their doors to see what all the commotion was about. The two unsilenced shots had been enough to keep them inside. It was just as well, Liese thought. Khalil had shot the photographer on the balcony, and he would not have hesitated to kill anyone else who got in his way.

"Are you sure he's down—" McGarvey said, but a slightly built Frenchman in crumpled civilian clothes came through the door at that moment. His long narrow face and dark eyes were a blank slate, as if he were in the middle of a poker game and was hiding his emotions. He took a quick look at the scene in the corridor, then held his ID wallet in front of McGarvey's face.

"I am Lieutenant of Police Maurice Capretz. Why have you come to Monaco, Monsieur McGarvey? Why aren't you at home attending to your duties? Basking in the adulation of your countrymen who believe you are a hero?"

"I came to find the man who was responsible for the deaths in Alaska."

Capretz nodded, as if it was what he knew McGarvey was going to say. "Oui, Prince Salman is your prime suspect." He glanced at Liese. "And you are Sergeant Fuelm. We were warned about you as well. And here you are in the flesh, apparently having just done mischief."

One of the uniformed cops appeared at the suite's doorway. He had holstered his weapon. He shook his head. "Lieutenant, there is no body."

"But I shot him!" Liese shouted. This was all wrong. She'd seen him react to her two shots. He'd gone down. He was dead.

"No body, no blood," the cop said. "No one was there, though there are bullet holes in the windows."

"Perhaps you shot a fantôme, Mademoiselle," Capretz said. He seemed relieved. "But it is perhaps for the best. Had you actually shot and killed someone, you would not be returning to Switzerland quite as rapidement as you would like."

McGarvey had a resigned look on his face. Liese shook her head. "I'm sorry," she said. She had let him down when he'd counted on her.

"But there is a body," McGarvey said. "Just below on the street. I think that you'll discover he was shot with a silenced pistol. Probably a large caliber from the effect of the impact."

Capretz nodded to one of his men to check it out, but his eyes never left McGarvey's. "No doubt you are telling the truth. France has always had a great respect for you, though you will never be welcomed back. Would you care to explain to me what you are talking about, because I certainly hope that someone hasn't shot the prince. There would be no end to the political repercussions."

"He was a photographer trying to get a picture of Sergeant Fuelm and me, together. He tried to take our photo down on the street when we came back to the hotel earlier, but I sent him away. Apparently he found out what room I was in, and climbed up to my balcony. It cost him his life."

"The phantom in your suite shot him?"

"Someone did," McGarvey said. "I think your ballistics people will confirm that the bullet didn't come from either of our weapons. Which will leave you with something of a problem, compounded by the fact you're allowing an al-Quaida killer, who probably climbed down the tree outside my room, to walk away."

Capretz wasn't impressed. "Are you aware that the prince's yacht suddenly left La Condamine one hour ago?"

"Was Salman aboard?"

"I don't know," Capretz admitted.

"Then I think I would like to contact my government."

The police lieutenant's cell phone rang. He took it out of his pocket and answered the call. "Oui," he said. He glanced at Liese and then back at McGarvey, and nodded. "Bon. Merci."

Liese stared at McGarvey, trying to gauge his mood. Unless the French meant to put him in jail, he wasn't finished. He would continue going after the prince until one or the other of them was dead.

Bin Laden's threat was real. No one believed any differently. And the attack would happen very soon. No one had any doubt of that either. Nor was there any question that the strike would be every bit as big as 9/11.

Liese knew her career was almost certainly on the edge of disaster.

Capretz broke the connection and put the phone in his pocket. He turned to the cop who'd brought McGarvey up. "Did you examine his gun to see if it has been fired recently?"

"It did not appear to have been fired, sir. The magazine is full, and there is a round still in the chamber."

Capretz turned his attention back to Liese. "But you fired two shots— at your phantom. Can you explain why there is no body and no blood? Are you that terrible a marksman, Mademoiselle?"

Liese felt lightheaded. "I must have missed," she replied, evenly.

Capretz shrugged. "We'll see," he said. Once again he looked at McGarvey. "A representative from your Federal Bureau of Investigation is waiting downstairs. You will be turned over to him. There is a warrant for your arrest." He grunted. "Unless, of course, you wish to fight extradition."

McGarvey shook his head. "That was fast work," he said. "What about Sergeant Fuelm?"

Capretz shrugged. "A representative from her service is here as well. As soon as we finish our ballistics test to ensure that her weapon was not used in a crime of bodily injury, she will be returned to Switzerland."

"I suppose it would be useless to ask for help from Action?" McGarvey said.

Capretz shrugged again. "Totalement."

Liese felt miserable. It was obvious that she would have to do whatever she could to help Kirk, even if it meant first returning to Switzerland without creating a fuss to somehow make amends.

Looking at him, her resolve hardened.

Whatever it took, even if it meant sleeping with Gertner.

THE COUNTDOWN

□

Muhamed Abdallah sat on a plastic chair in the screened patio behind the trailer, letting his nerves wind down in the cool evening mountain air. Working with explosives was a tricky business. The Polish-made Semtex was in itself not unstable. In fact, the dead gray, puttylike substance could be thrown against a wall, struck with a hammer, or even put into a fire, and yet it would not explode.

It was the triggering mechanisms that were extremely delicate and dangerous.

A wrong move at this stage—when he was wiring the twenty kilos of bricks to a single trigger so that at the proper time the entire mass would explode at the same instant—would be disastrous.

He extended his right arm and raised his hand in front of his face so that it blocked a section of the not-so-distant mountains. When he spread his fingers, he could see strips of the highest, snowcapped peaks.

Mountains were power. Dear Osama had a perfect understanding of this when he first went to Afghanistan to drive the infidel Russians from the righteous land.

The jihad had taken ten long years. But what was that compared to the eternity of Paradise?

When the word came, the attack would take place in seventy-two hours. It would be a second blow against the Satan America. More important even than 9/11, as it was explained to Muhamed. This time they would strike at the heart of the people.

"It will be much the same as the Israeli attacks on our refugee camps in which our children are targeted," the man from Pakistan told them at the Nablus meeting.

He said his name was Ghulam, after the secretary to the former defense minister Aftab Mirani. No one believed it, of course, but it didn't matter. He had come to offer them certain salvation as soldiers of God.

"Take me," Muhamed had cried, his enthusiasm bubbling over. "I must go for my mother," he added, shyly.

No one in the small courtyard apartment in one of the few buildings that hadn't been damaged or destroyed by rocket attacks laughed. And Ghulam was patient with him.

"But you don't know what the mission is," the Pakistani mujahideen said, not unkindly. "It may be too difficult. Too terrible for you to contemplate, let alone carry out."

His eyes were kind and understanding. Much the same as Muhamed imagined Osama's eyes were. They had seen unimaginably horrible things, and yet al-Quaida's resolve was strong because the jihad was just and the men at the core were strong.

"What can be more terrible than what the Israelis are doing to us?" Muhamed said to the other young men gathered in the apartment. "They kill our soliders and old men, and now they even kill our children." Muhamed looked back to Ghulam. "What can be worse than that to contemplate?"

"Killing the infidel's children," the al-Quaida recruiter answered, quietly.

Muhamed was shaken. But just for a moment. He shook his head. "There can be no innocents in the battle for the will of Allah." He looked at the others now, none of their enthusiasm damped. "Insha'allah." He looked Ghulam directly in the eye, his own gaze steady. "Tell me what I can do for the jihad. My life for the cause."

They had driven north that night out of the West Bank and all the way across the border into Lebanon, passing through the Israeli checkpoints on the strength of Ghulam's credentials almost as if they were ghosts. During the two hundred-kilometer drive to Beirut, Muhamed learned that in return for his giving his life to Allah's cause, his parents would receive fifty thousand American dollars when the mission was completed. He was also told that his sacrifice would not take place in Israel or Palestine. In fact, he would never see those places again, nor would he see his family until they joined him in Paradise. But that would be as if only an eyeblink in time.

In Beirut, Muhamed was placed aboard a Liberian-registered freighter, where he was confined to his tiny cabin in the bowels of the ship for five days and nights until he was finally taken ashore in a small boat in the middle of the night.

"Welcome to Algeria, my brother," his guide welcomed him. "It is here that you will begin your journey."

His journey to Paradise.

Gazing up now at the Front Range above the college town of Fort Collins, Muhamed could feel his anxiety subsiding. His hands no longer shook. Nor did he suffer from the despair that had gripped him for many weeks after he had learned the true nature of his mission here in the U.S. He knew that he was not alone, that there were others who would be carrying out similar attacks at exactly the same moment.

But that knowledge had never given him any comfort.

Even now they would be doing the same things he was doing. They had seen their targets. They were preparing their explosives, which they would strap to their bodies. And they were preparing their minds for their deaths.

Muhamed had made lists in his mind of the things he would miss. His mother. His father and his brothers. A future in which he would be married and have beautiful sons of his own. Especially a future in which he and his family would live in a free Palestine.

He even allowed certain silly things to occupy his list. But only for a short time. Drinking *cha* and listening to the men talk while they played dominoes in the sidewalk cafés. Playing soccer with his friends. Someday seeing movies. Tasting ice cream. New clothes, especially white shirts.

Seyoum Noufal came out to the patio, a strange pinched expression on his long sad face. "Muhamed," he whispered, as if he were afraid that their nearest neighbor several hundred meters away might overhear him.

Muhamed looked up at him, and he knew what he had come out to say. "The message has come?"

"Yes."

Muhamed turned his gaze back to the vista of the mountains, the details washing out with the gathering dusk.

The Qur'an says that for every people there is a messenger; when their messenger comes, the issue between them is justly determined and they are not wronged.

His messenger had come, and he would not be wronged, for he had a passage to Paradise.

In three days, freshly shaved, the Semtex strapped to his body beneath his schoolboy clothes, he would enter Rocky Mountain High School as a student. At the very same moment others across the country were doing the same thing in similar small-town high schools, he would place himself in the middle of the school and activate the detonator.

It would be a blow against the infidel, worse in horror than 9/11.

Infinitely worse.

Insha'allah.

PART

THREE

FORTY-NINE

□

McGarvey had all but resigned himself to being too late, as the FBI's Gulf-stream executive jet touched down at Washington's Reagan Airport a few minutes before dawn, and their F/A-18 fighter/interceptor escort peeled off back to its station ten miles south.

He'd come back to the States like this, with a lot of heavy hitters lined up against him, more times than he cared to count. Yet he'd never had the mindset to simply turn his back on a problem and give up. Looking out the window now, the city across the river like an ancient Rome with its marble statues and granite monuments, he could only wonder at his own persistence.

Just run. Turn around and leave. Go. Give it up.

The city had become an armed fortress since the bin Laden tape. Any aircraft operating within the Washington terminal control area was escorted and would be shot out of the sky if the slightest thing seemed wrong. That included official aircraft.

The flight had been long, doubly so because the pair of FBI special agents who'd been sent over to bring him back to the States had refused to answer any of his questions, or allow him to use the aircraft's comms gear.

But they had handed him a CIA briefing package that had been rushed out to Reagan just before the Bureau plane had taken off for France. The file had been released on Adkins's signature, but it had obviously been put together by Otto Rencke. They were deferential to him, but their orders had been very specific.

"Whose orders?" McGarvey had asked at one point.

"Mr. Rudolph's," one of them said. "Now, sir, maybe we should all try to catch a few z's."

McGarvey had worked with Fred Rudolph off and on for the past ten years to narrow the gap between the Bureau and the Agency. Since 9/11 the two agencies had become even closer, especially since McGarvey had taken over as DCI and Rudolph had become the Bureau's deputy director. Between the two of them they had done good things.

Already in the thirty-six hours since McGarvey had left, the situation on the ground had changed. Coming in on final approach to landing, he'd seen armed personnel carriers or tanks at all the major bridges and highways into the city. In the distance he'd made out even heavier concentrations of military equipment stationed at the White House and the Capitol Building.

According to the slim, leather-bound briefing book, even if al-Quaida's attack never came, serious damage had already been done. The public's confidence in Washington's ability to protect them was almost nil. But instead of cowering in their homes, curtains drawn, lights out, people were at least going about their business. Schools had been closed for only one day before people began escorting their children back to classes. National Guard troops were stationed in front of the bigger schools across the country, though there weren't nearly enough troops to do an adequate job for even ten percent of the campuses in each state.

Absenteeism in the workforce had spiked the day after bin Laden's tape, but twenty-four hours later most people had gone back to work. But no one was spending money, and Wall Street had been thrown into a panic, both the DOW and NASDAQ losing nearly thirty percent of their values before computer-driven automatic controls dropped into place.

Though no public announcement was being made, the Fed was estimating that the U.S. economy was losing a billion dollars a day while the nation waited for the shoe to drop.

All of America's military units and civilian police forces, from the FBI down to the one-cop stations in small towns, had been mobilized.

Nuclear submarines and guided-missile frigates—in port from Newport and Jacksonville on the East Coast to San Diego and Honolulu in the west—recalled their crews, lit off their power plants, and set out to sea, ringing the entire continental United States plus Hawaii and Alaska with a curtain of steel capable of throwing more firepower, nuclear as well as conventional, than had been fired in all sides of all the wars ever fought on the planet.

The entire array of Keyhole, Jupiter, and other eye-in-the-sky satellites in the National Reconnaissance Office's suite of technical means were trained first on U.S. borders and areas of interests, and then on known or suspected hotbeds of terrorist activity, including training and staging areas in such places as Iran, Syria, Algeria, Saudi Arabia, and even the Upper Peninsula of Michigan and parts of Montana.

No one seemed to remember, or cared to mention, the Pentagon warning shortly after 9/11, when the U.S.-led war on terrorism was being launched, that all of America's nuclear might had been useless against the attacks on the World Trade Center and the Pentagon.

The briefing book included a summary of a meeting with the president and his security council that had taken place sometime the previous day. Even the Department of Homeland Security, which had raised the threat level to red at the same time bin Laden's tape had been leaked to the public, admitted to the president and the NSC that stopping an attack by a determined adversary was next to impossible, given the openness of our borders.

"Even Israel, with its stringent security measures, can't keep its citizens safe," Homeland Security's new director, Peter Townsend, reminded the group. All that was left to do, beside doubling-up on air marshals on all flights over U.S. airspace, was to ignore the ACLU and other human rights organizations and take profiling to new heights.

Most terrorist attacks against the U.S. and its interests had been carried out by Arab males between the ages of eighteen and forty-five. "They're our targets," said one of Townsend's deputy assistants, stating the obvious.

The president was remaining in Washington, though the vice president and a significant number of congressmen were in seclusion in rural Maryland. Air Force One was ready at Andrews, with its crew on standby 24/7 to whisk the president out of the area within minutes of notification. A Marine helicopter and crew stood by on the south grounds in sight of the West Wing. And the White House Secret Service detail was tripled, and supplemented by Marines and additional radar-guided Patriot missile launchers.

"We're facing one big problem," Townsend's deputy assistant warned. "We don't know if they're going to come at us with airliners again, or if they're going to hit us with a nuke, or a bioweapon, or a car bomb. We just don't know, Mr. President."

The Gulfstream got off the main runway, followed one of the taxiways across the airport from the main terminal building and past the maintenance hangars of several airlines, and was directed by a Follow Me pickup truck to an unmarked hangar.

Watching from the window, McGarvey spotted Adkins and a pair of men standing next to a Cadillac SUV with tinted windows. The two men, who were obviously security officers, were dressed in dark blue windbreakers and baseball caps, their Heckler & Koch M8s in the compact carbine version at the ready, their heads on swivels.

Fred Rudolph climbed out of a plain gray Chevy Impala, and as the Gulfstream came to a stop and its engines began to spool down, he went over to Adkins and they shook hands. Neither of them seemed to be particularly happy to be there.

Before the aircraft door was opened, one of the guys who had come to escort McGarvey back to the States handed him a padded envelope. "Your weapon, spare magazine, and cell phone, sir," he said. "We were instructed to give them back when we got here. Someone will grab your bags from the hold in a minute."

"I thought I was under arrest," McGarvey said, ripping open the envelope. He wasn't feeling charitable.

"That was just for the benefit of the French," the agent replied, evenly. He wasn't enjoying the exchange, but he had a job to do and he was doing it.

"Right," McGarvey said. He loaded his pistol, stuffed it in his belt, and pocketed his spare magazine and cell phone. He was tired and irascible. His chance to get to Khalil on Corsica had been blown. Coming back like this would be starting all over again. And he didn't know if there was enough time.

Last night, trying to get a couple of hours sleep, he had wondered if he should go on. If he should ignore the president's orders to back off.

The woman did not want to be rescued from the water without her baby. Her cries still pierced his heart. There had been no reason to kill them. No reason at all.

Backing off, he decided, had never been an option.

He tossed the envelope aside. "Did you guys have a surveillance set up on me?"

"No, sir. We were instructed to sit tight and wait until you got into trouble, then bail you out if we could."

The other agent was watching from the open door, a neutral expression on his features. Like his partner he had a job to do, and he was doing it. He only wanted McGarvey to get off the airplane and his job would be over.

McGarvey softened a little. "Okay, fellas, thanks for the lift. What do you say we try to catch the bad guys before they can hit us again?"

"Yes, sir."

McGarvey got off the airplane and walked across to where Rudolph and Adkins were waiting. "Your timing stinks, Fred."

Rudolph didn't offer his hand. "Nothing I could do about it, Mac. Weissman gave me no room to maneuver, and his orders came straight from the White House." He glanced at Adkins. "We're not screwing around here."

"Neither am I, Fred."

Rudolph was angry. "Goddammit, going after the Saudis won't help. We'll just get tangled up in money trails, nothing more."

From the beginning Rudolph had been caught between a rock and a hard place in his dealings with the CIA. This time it was worse because he and McGarvey had become friends. McGarvey nodded. "What's my situation? Am I under arrest?"

"The president wants you neutralized. And he's serious about it." Rudolph was apologetic. "Means house arrest." He glanced at Adkins again. "Why the hell did you have to quit in the middle of this?"

"Because I don't agree with Haynes. The Saudis were behind 9/11, and they're right up to their necks in this one. I had a chance to stop one of them in Corsica."

"If you're talking about Salman, he's not there. In fact, his jet landed at Dulles a couple of hours ago. He's here at the Saudi Embassy. If it makes you feel any better, we're keeping a watch on him."

For just an instant McGarvey was taken aback. Salman coming here was the last thing he'd expected. "Well, that's a real comfort, Fred," Mc-

Garvey said, meanly, to cover his racing thoughts. The arrogance of the Saudi bastard was awesome.

Rudolph turned away in frustration. "I'm not the enemy," he shouted.

McGarvey's muscles bunched. He was in Alaska. He couldn't get it out of his head. "Someone is," he barked, "and unless we get off our dead asses we're going to have another fucking 9/11 on our hands."

Rudolph lowered his head and shook it. He was silent for a second, and when he looked up he compressed his lips. "What happened to us, Mac? What the hell happened in the past ten years to make us the bad guys? I thought it was the Russians."

"Simpler times, Fred," McGarvey said. He turned to Adkins. "Take me home, would you, Dick?"

"Stay there, Mac," Rudolph said. "I don't want to arrest you."

FIFTY

□

Dennis Berndt put down the telephone, paused for a moment, then got up and went to the window that looked toward the Rose Garden. It was morning finally, after a long and difficult night. He rubbed his eyes and took a deep breath to relieve the pressure that had steadily built in his chest since he'd heard bin Laden's tape.

When he'd come down from Harvard at Haynes's behest to become the president's adviser on national security affairs, he had thought of the job in academic terms. He would work in the White House. He would be among the chosen few to actually *make* history and not simply live it, or react to it. He would conduct national security briefings on a daily basis. He would consult with the heads of the CIA, FBI, and National Security Agency. He would be among the privileged few who were privy to the nation's secrets. He would have the ear and the trust of the president of the United States.

But now his job wasn't so academic. He had a wife and two children, one in high school and the other at Princeton. It was his family that the bastards were targeting.

Government was no longer simply an intellectual exercise.

His secretary, who like most of the other White House staff was working 24/7, catching catnaps whenever possible, buzzed him. "The person from Langley you wanted to see is here."

"Send him in."

Otto Rencke, carrying a plain buff file folder, his red hair flying in all directions, his sneakers untied, his Moscow University sweatshirt stained with what might have been coffee or Coke, bounded in as if he were the March Hare with no time to spare. "Oh, wow, Mr. Berndt," he bubbled, "thanks for agreeing to see me."

Berndt motioned for his secretary to close the door. "Give us five minutes; I don't want to be disturbed."

"Yes, sir," she said, and she withdrew, closing the door behind her. This meeting was an unofficial one, and it would not be logged, except by security.

Rencke sat down cross-legged in a chair. "I thought you guys would dink around until we ran out of time. Your Homeland Security people mean well, ya know, but they're not doing any good. No time. No time. The bad dogs are already here, so sealing borders won't do, Jack. And blocking Washington won't do any good either. They're not attacking here, and they won't use airplanes again. We're safe. No one has to run for their hidey-holes."

Berndt had had dealings with Rencke on several occasions, but each time, like now, the experience was something new and novel. The man was a genius, but he was probably the most eccentric individual Berndt had ever met. "Has Mac gotten back from France yet?"

"About a half hour ago."

"Have you talked to him this morning?" Berndt asked. "About coming here?"

The crazy animation suddenly left Rencke's face. He no longer looked like some kid high on speed. "I understand your position, Mr. Berndt. We all do. But the name of the game is stopping the bad guys before they hit

us again. Mac is going to do his thing, no matter what the president orders or how hard the Bureau tries to stop him, because that's the way he
operates. In the meantime, the Company is there to serve the administration. Of which you are a senior member. Which is why I'm here." He
handed the file folder across to Berndt. "Prince Salman."

"Mac thinks that the prince and the terrorist Khalil are one and the
same man," Berndt said. "He told us about it, but the president doesn't
share his view."

"We have confidence that Mac might be right."

Berndt was skating on thin ice, going directly against a presidential order that the Saudis were strictly off limits. This was realpolitick. Oil was
power. Without it, the U.S. would all but cease to operate. Almost every
other consideration was secondary.

But the nation could not endure another 9/11. Especially not an attack on children,
who after all were one commodity that was more precious than anything pumped out of the
ground.

"How high a confidence?" Berndt asked. "One hundred percent?"

Rencke shook his head without hesitation. "Eighty percent. Our data
are mostly circumstantial."

It's what Berndt was afraid of. If he was going to make a successful
case to the president for going after Salman, he wanted more than that.
His career was on the line. The president had warned McGarvey that continuing on a collision course with the Saudi prince would possibly be
construed as treason. Berndt would be an accessory.

"Circumstantial evidence is a hard sell," Berndt observed.

"Not this stuff. You gotta listen, because no matter what's the truth,
Salman is here in Washington. And every time Salman shows up somewhere, Khalil is right there. Don't ya see? It doesn't matter if they're the
same dude; they're practically using the same travel bureau."

Berndt suddenly had a bad feeling that today was going to be one
hundred percent worse than yesterday, which had been no picnic.
"What's he doing here? Are they going to hit us in Washington?"

Rencke shook his head. "Khalil isn't here to direct the attack. He came
to face McGarvey. Something that would have happened in Corsica if the
FBI hadn't interfered in Monaco."

"McGarvey's under house arrest—"

"Yeah, right," Rencke interrupted. He got to his feet. "You'd better cross your fingers and hope he doesn't stay home like a good boy." At the door Rencke stopped and gave Berndt a baleful stare. "We've got another bloodbath coming our way, Mr. National Security Adviser. Do what you can to convince the president who's behind it. Short of that, don't tie our hands."

"Good luck."

"You, too," Rencke said, and he left.

Berndt opened the thick file folder that Rencke had brought him and began to read. After only two pages, he picked up the phone and called Calvin Beckett, the president's chief of staff. The call rolled over on the second ring to Beckett's cell phone. He was in his car just coming down West Executive Avenue.

"Good morning, Dennis. Did you spend the night?"

"Yeah. I wanted to see the overnights from State as they came from our embassies," Berndt said, tiredly. "We're getting plenty of sympathy but no offers of assistance. No one wants to be next on the list. They don't want to end up getting hit like they did in Madrid because they were our ally."

"From their standpoint, it makes sense," Beckett said, crossly. He sounded peckish. Like everyone else in the loop he was probably not getting much sleep. "What have you got?"

"McGarvey is back."

"Good," Beckett said. "No one was hurt, I presume. And I hope he'll listen to the good advice he's getting this time and stay the hell out of it."

Berndt looked at the timetables for Prince Salman and Khalil that Rencke had laid out like a spreadsheet. "There was a shooting, but apparently it was a photographer who got in the way." Berndt hesitated. He'd read that report from Paris at five this morning. Fred Rudolph over at the Bureau had been kind enough to fax him a copy. "But the shot wasn't fired from McGarvey's pistol or the gun the Swiss cop was carrying. Someone else was there."

Beckett was suddenly very interested. "So who was it?"

"Probably Khalil. He wants revenge for Alaska."

"Shoot-out at the OK Corral. At least it happened somewhere else—" Beckett stopped. "But that's not why you called."

"I'm calling a meeting for the NSC at ten. The president needs to know about this."

"He's coming down at seven-thirty. Tell him then," Beckett said.

Berndt glanced out the window. It promised to be a beautiful day. At least weatherwise. "There's a good possibility that Khalil is here in Washington. And that's not all. I think we finally have a convincing argument that the Saudis are up to their necks in this thing."

Beckett took a moment to answer. "When we were accused of being behind the curve on 9/11, there weren't a whole lot of people who knew even half of it," he said, resignedly. "We're under the same gun now."

"Ten o'clock?"

"Ten," Beckett said. "I just hope that you have some concrete suggestions in addition to your dark possibilities."

FIFTY-ONE

□

The elegant three-story brownstone off Thirty-second Street in Georgetown had belonged for five years to a Saudi business institute under the name Middle East Center for Advanced Studies. In the climate of Washington it had gone all but unnoticed by the FBI. In reality the house was used by Saudi intelligence for operations deemed too sensitive to be conducted out of the embassy.

Khalil got out of the Capitol City Cab a few minutes before eight and stood for a moment at the security gate savoring the idea of what was coming in the next seventy-two hours. Not only would another major blow be struck against the infidel, but Kirk McGarvey would die.

The man was everything Osama had warned him to be. Watching the life drain from McGarvey's eyes would be a pleasure of inestimable measure.

Under martial law Washington had turned into a fortress. Yet customs at Dulles didn't raise an eyebrow when he presented his British diplomatic passport in the name of Donald Baden Powell, nor were any questions asked. The authorities aboard the commercial flight from Hamilton and on the ground were looking for Arab males between the ages of eighteen and forty-five. A tall, well-dressed diplomat from the island of Bermuda did not fit the profile.

Traffic was heavy on the main thoroughfares, but back here on Scott Place there wasn't even pedestrian traffic for the moment. Once the cab left, he was alone, tasting the air in the enemy capital.

The house was set back fifteen meters from the street behind a tall wrought-iron fence. It was an armed camp in the middle of the infidels' headquarters. The windows were all blank, either curtained or silvered. Nothing could be seen through them, nor was there any activity in the driveway at the front.

After this blow, the search for bin Laden would intensify again, and sooner or later all his doubles would be captured or killed, and it would finally be his turn. No man was immortal. But even that didn't matter, Khalil thought, for the jihad had had a life of its own.

The struggle would go on despite any man's passing, be it bin Laden or McGarvey.

Khalil switched his leather overnight bag to his left hand, took a security pass card out of his pocket, and swiped it through the reader on the electric gate. The lock buzzed, and as the gates swung open he stepped inside the compound and started across the driveway to the front door.

Someone shouted something on the speaker above the card reader behind him, and as Khalil mounted the three steps to the entryway, the door opened and a very large man dressed in a Western business suit was there.

"*Good morning, brother,*" Khalil said, pleasantly, in Arabic. "*I'm here to see al-Kaseem.*"

The security officer wasn't impressed. He studied Khalil's face without recognition, glanced at the bag in his hand, then glanced over his shoulder at the electric wrought-iron gate, which was swinging shut.

"There are no visitors here. How did you get in?" he demanded.

Khalil held up the pass. "Take me to al-Kaseem, please."

The security officer reached for the pass, which was exactly what Khalil thought he might do. The fool.

Khalil moved his hand to the left, diverting the officer's attention; took a quick look over his shoulder to make sure they weren't being observed by someone passing on the street; then easily shouldered the man back into the stair hall and slashed the edge of the plastic card across the bridge of his nose, opening a small gash that immediately welled blood.

The guard roared something unintelligible as he struggled to regain his balance. He pulled out a boxy Glock semiautomatic, but Khalil stepped inside his reach, grabbed the man's arm under his own, and stepped sharply to the left.

The security officer's arm bent backward nearly to the breaking point before he dropped his pistol.

Two other security guards came up the hall from the rear of the house on the run, their pistols drawn.

"I'm going to step back," Khalil said, loudly enough for them to hear, and they pulled up short. "I don't want anybody to do something foolish that would make me cause further pain or suffering. I am a friend, and I come in peace. Rashid al-Kaseem will verify my identity."

A security officer behind a short counter to the left had risen and pulled out his pistol. He was pointing it at Khalil's head. "Take care that you do not reach for a weapon, or I will shoot you," he called out, in a steady voice. He was a professional.

"I am unarmed," Khalil said. He spread his arms and stepped back.

The security officer he'd damaged started for him, but someone at the head of the stairs shouted an order, and the officer stopped in his tracks.

Khalil looked up as Rashid al-Kaseem, chief of station for Washington Saudi intelligence, came down the stairs. He was a short, dapper man, dressed in a conservative British-cut tweed sport coat, gray slacks, and a club tie. He was bald except for a fringe of dark hair above his very large ears. He was only a very distant cousin in the royal family, but he had a lot of respect from the major princes. He knew things. He saw and heard things. One day he would rise to head all of Saudi intelligence, which was a very powerful position within the kingdom.

"Achmed, pick up your weapon, and see to your injury," al-Kaseem said. "If you need stitches, someone will drive you to the embassy. The rest of you, return to your duties. And there is blood on the floor. Clean it."

When the others were gone, he motioned for Khalil to follow him, and together they went upstairs and down the broad, expensively carpeted corridor to a small book-lined office at the rear of the building. A hum of muted conversations, a few voices raised in anger or frustration, came from behind closed doors. This place, like just about every other office in Washington, was on an emergency footing.

When they were alone, al-Kaseem turned on him. "What are you doing here, now of all times?" he demanded, harshly. He was one of very few men who knew Khalil by sight.

Khalil considered the possibility that the intelligence chief, who had entirely too high an opinion of himself, might beg for mercy as his life's blood drained from his body. The expression in his eyes at the end would be most interesting. "I have a job to do, and I require your assistance, here and at the embassy."

"That's impossible—"

"I'm going to set a trap, and the timing will be delicate. I'll need a van and at least two men plus a driver. I mean to kidnap the wife of the CIA director."

Al-Kaseem was struck dumb.

Khalil took four fat envelopes out of his pocket and handed them to the intelligence chief. "Place these in your safe for me. And see that they are not tampered with."

Ernst Gertner was at Zurich's Kloten Airport when Liese arrived on a charter flight from Marseille at four o'clock in the morning. The French authorities had held her until all the ballistics reports were completed, and to finish interrogating her about her relationship with Kirk McGarvey, a man who'd always been of great interest to them.

Gertner was in a higher-than-usual state of agitation, and he kept flapping his arms as if he were an ostrich trying to take off. "Goodness gracious, what am I supposed to do when one of my star officers simply goes off into the bush without a word, against all orders to the contrary, and then gets herself involved with a shooting death?"

Liese was beyond tired, and very worried about Kirk's reception back in Washington. He'd gone against his president's orders. Not only that, but Khalil wasn't finished. He would continue to go after McGarvey until one or both of them were dead.

She looked up at Gertner, almost feeling sorry for him. "Sorry, captain, I was following a lead. And we almost got Khalil." She looked away momentarily. "It was very close."

"The French are distressed—"

Liese turned back. "Are you going to fire me for good this time?" she asked. She felt alone and isolated, and frightened.

"As of this moment you're on administrative leave, but I'll expect you to stand it at the chalet."

Liese shook her head. "He's not guilty, you know."

"For heaven's sake." Gertner puffed up. "Then explain why he left you alone in the corridor to face Khalil while he went off gallivanting around outdoors?"

FIFTY-TWO

□

It had only been forty-eight hours since McGarvey left for Monaco. He'd promised Katy he would come back safely, and that he would deal with Khalil. It was unsettling to return home with his work left undone, and the danger to the U.S. worse than before he'd left.

Coming up the cul-de-sac from Connecticut Avenue to his house, he could see that the security detail was gone, but he said nothing to Adkins, who had ridden beside him in silence most of the way from the airport. There was nothing to say that they hadn't said to each other the morning McGarvey left headquarters. Adkins was directing the CIA's efforts to track down the al-Quaida terrorists before they struck. In that administrative task he was every bit as good, if not better, a DCI than McGarvey was.

Unspoken between them was that Adkins had withdrawn the Direc-

torate of Security detail from the house against his better judgment in order to give McGarvey the freedom to come and go without hindrance.

Adkins's driver parked in the driveway; then he and the bodyguard
grabbed the M8 carbines from their brackets on the transmission hump,
got out of the limo, and did a slow three-sixty scan of the neighborhood,
leaving the two men alone for a couple of moments.

"Your daughter spent the night with Kathleen," Adkins said. "I've put
her on administrative leave for the duration."

"Anyone else inside?" McGarvey asked, looking up at the front bedroom window. Liz was standing there.

"No. I didn't think you wanted anyone else. Under the circumstances."

"This close I don't think they'll bother coming after Katy," McGarvey
said. "How about Todd?"

"Your son-in-law is back at the Farm helping to get the student-
instructor crews out the door to work security around Washington." Adkins was clearly unhappy. "Listen here, Mac, the White House is in an
uproar over your stunt in Monaco. The French have lodged a protest
against you. The Saudis are screaming bloody murder, threatening to convince OPEC to cut oil production another seven or eight percent. And half
the people on the Hill think you might be guilty of treason, while the
other half think that at the very least you're a quitter. Depends on whether
they're Republicans or Democrats."

"Pretty quick turnaround for someone who was a national hero three
days ago," McGarvey said. "Is there any word on where Salman is staying
in Washington?"

"The Bureau had him at the embassy as of an hour ago. They promised
to let us know the instant he makes a move." Adkins looked at him. "I
suppose it'd be fruitless to ask you if you knew what you were doing. You
always do." He shook his head. "But Jesus, Mac, you're going head-to-
head with the president this time."

"How close is the Bureau watching Khalil?"

"I don't know," Adkins admitted. "But certainly close enough so that
he won't be able to pull off anything significant." He glanced at the
house. "Like coming here after Katy."

McGarvey had been thinking about that very possibility from the moment he'd learned Salman was in Washington. He didn't think Khalil would bother trying to inflict any collateral damage this late in the game, though why Salman, if he wasn't Kahlil, had come to Washington at this moment was a puzzlement. Unless he'd come to personally lodge a complaint with the president about McGarvey's behavior aboard his yacht. After all, the former director of the CIA had threatened to kill him.

Whatever the case the sheer arrogance of the Saudi prince was nothing short of awesome.

"It'll all be over in the next day or two, so just keep the Company on track in the meantime," McGarvey said.

"Unless al-Quaida postpones the hit."

McGarvey shook his head. "They're committed this time. If they back off, they'll lose too much face."

Adkins was studying him. "You're going after Salman, aren't you?"

"Don't ask," McGarvey said.

He gathered his two bags, got out of the limo, and without looking back went up to the house. The door opened and Katy was there, a worried but relieved expression on her narrow, pretty face. Dressed in a pair of designer jeans and a white tee, she looked like a model who hadn't slept since he'd left; her hair was a little mussed and her eyes were red, but she threw her arms around him once he stepped inside and put down his bags.

"God, am I glad to see you," she said, clinging tightly.

She felt good to McGarvey, even though he had not come in from the field yet. Only a small part of him was home with his wife in his arms. Most of his head—his concentration, and his awareness of his surroundings—was at a heightened, unnatural level. He was on the defensive, like a boxer with his guard up, while at the same time he was circling for the kill.

Katy caught this feeling immediately. She parted and looked up into his face. "Oh," she said, "it's not done."

"I missed him in Monaco, and now he's here in Washington," McGarvey told her. "Sorry, Katy. But I'm not going to miss this time."

"They wouldn't tell us why they were withdrawing security from the house," she said. "Even Dick wouldn't say, except that they thought the threat level against me personally was down. But they left Elizabeth."

"Hi, Daddy," Liz said, coming down from upstairs. She was dressed in khaki slacks and a soft yellow pullover, with a Walther PPK in a quick-draw holster at her left hip.

McGarvey looked up. "Hello, sweetheart. How're you doing?"

"Fine," she said. "But I just got word from Neal Julien that Salman left the Saudi embassy, and he thinks that the FBI might have lost him."

McGarvey nodded. He had been afraid of something like this. "He'll be back. Anywhere else in Washington will get too hot for him."

Liz's pale green eyes narrowed as she assimilated the information. "They're not making any real progress stopping these guys, so it looks as if it's going to be up to the CIA to nail Khalil and make him tell us what their plans are." She looked a little pale and drawn. Like everyone else in Washington, she'd not been getting much sleep since the bin Laden tape.

"I'll have to get to him first."

"Do you have any ideas, Daddy?" Liz asked. Her parents had divorced when she was just a little girl, so she had spent all of her teenage years without a father. Instead of hating him for his absence, though, she had put him in a fantasy world in which he was her knight in shining armor. Whenever she had a problem, she would ask herself what her father would do about it—what he would say, how he would react. When he'd finally come back into her life, she wasn't disappointed; in her mind he was even better than her fantasy version of him. Her adoration of her father sometimes was a bone of contention between Todd and her. But he too looked up to McGarvey, so he could never stay angry with his wife for very long.

"Getting Salman out of the embassy is going to be easier than getting me inside," McGarvey said. He had a couple of ideas, neither of which would make the White House happy. "If I can get him isolated, I'll need ten minutes."

Liz smiled wickedly. "That fast?"

McGarvey nodded. "He's a coward. Won't be pretty, but it'll be fast."

Kathleen was following all this closely. "I thought you were going to kill him," she said, an intensity in her voice. She had seen Khalil brutally gun down innocent passengers, and had been at his side when he'd ordered the young mother and her infant child thrown overboard.

"I am," he said gently. "But first I need to get to him, and then I need to get some answers."

McGarvey studied the expression on her face. She had changed since Alaska. All of them had. But in her the change had taken the form of a hardness around the edges of her personality. There was a certain recklessness in her attitude, as if she was impatient to get on with things and was willing to take whatever chances had to be taken; damn the consequences despite the baby.

Or perhaps because of the baby.

"Good," Kathleen said.

McGarvey turned back to his daughter. "Did you talk to Otto this morning?"

"He left the White House a few minutes ago. Berndt took the package, and at least agreed to look at it."

Rencke had laid out his plan in the briefing book he'd sent over with the FBI agents who'd gone to France to fetch McGarvey. No matter what might or might not have happened in Monaco, the White House had to be convinced that at least some members of the Saudi royal family had been involved in 9/11 and were almost certainly involved in the latest bin Laden threat. Rencke had gotten that information into the hands of the one man the president trusted most.

"One thing, Kirk," Kathleen said. "Are you sure that Salman and Khalil are the same man? Because I am. It was his eyes."

That was another question McGarvey had wrestled with since Monaco. Half the time he was sure they were one and the same, but the other half he just couldn't be sure. One thing was certain, he thought; ten minutes alone with the prince and he would find out.

"I think so," he told his wife. He turned back to his daughter again. "Where do Otto and I meet?"

"Right here, at the fifteenth fairway shelter." It was across the creek, next to the maintenance barn and access road. Liz looked at her watch. "He should be getting there in the next twenty minutes."

"It'll give me time to change," McGarvey said. "In the meantime I want you two to stick it out here. Anything comes your way, call for backup. But I think you'll be okay. It's me he wants now."

"What if someone calls for you?" Kathleen asked.

McGarvey grinned viciously. "Tell them I'm in the shower."

FIFTY-THREE

Kathleen McGarvey was fifty and pregnant, in her mind a sublimely ridiculous combination, but she was not an invalid. Her husband was off trying to find a key to lure Prince Salman into the open so he could be taken down, and she had an idea that she knew where to find it.

Kirk was only one man. That was Karen Shaw's take. And she was correct. Despite his abilities, despite his heart, he was one lone man against an organization that had brought down the World Trade Center towers. On top of that he did not have the active support of his own government.

After Kirk left to meet Otto, Kathleen had changed into a pale cream pants suit with a plain white blouse, brushed her hair, and put on some makeup. She was just finishing when Liz came to the bedroom door.

"You look nice, Mom, but what are you doing?" Liz said.

Kathleen put on a pair of small, gold hoop earrings as she watched her daughter's reflection in the dresser mirror. Elizabeth would be the toughest hurdle "Getting ready to go out."

"No," Liz blurted.

Kathleen turned to face her daughter with a look of mild amusement. "What did you say?"

"Dad wants us to stay put," Liz answered. She looked determined.

"Your father is out laying his life on the line. Once again. Your husband is helping with security. The FBI, the police, the National Guard are all out doing their duty, trying to stop the monsters. Yet you and I are simply going to sit here and do nothing?" Kathleen shook her head. "I don't think so, sweetheart." She smiled. "Is that what you want to do?"

"I think we should stay here," Liz replied, with a little less certainty.

"We're either going to be a part of the problem or a part of the solution. And I do not want to be in the former category." What she wanted to do was right; she was convinced of it. "You weren't on the cruise ship.

You didn't witness what those monsters are capable of doing. I did." She got her purse and went to her daughter.

"Goddammit, Mother."

Kathleen brushed a strand of hair off her daughter's forehead. "Don't swear, please; it's ugly. I simply want you to take a drive with me into Georgetown. I want to have a quick peek at something, and we'll come right back."

"At what?" Liz asked, crossly.

"Get a jacket or something to cover up your gun, and I'll tell you on the way," Kathleen said. She gave her daughter a peck on the cheek, then brushed past her. "We'll take my car. I'll drive and you can ride shotgun."

If the truth be told, Elizabeth much preferred doing something to sitting around the house guarding her mother from an attack that probably wasn't going to happen.

In any event, providing any real security against a determined attack at the house would be impossible to do alone. One gun was simply not enough of a deterrent.

The car was a smoked silver Mercedes 560SL, which Kathleen drove fast and impatiently. "We're going to take a quick look at Darby Yarnell's old house," she said.

"He's dead," Elizabeth said. "Somebody else owns it." She had seen the entire file a couple of years ago when she had gone looking into her father's past. But the business of her mother having an affair had not been included. She'd learned of it for the first time two days ago, and her gut still hadn't recovered from knowing that her mother was not perfect after all.

They headed out of Chevy Chase on Connecticut Avenue, crossing over to Wisconsin Avenue at Tenley Circle, traffic almost back to normal despite the bin Laden threat.

"Do you know who owns it?" Kathleen asked, glancing at her daughter. "The Saudi government," she said without waiting for a reply. "It's a think tank."

Elizabeth had not known that part. There was no reason for her to have gone looking. But it made sense, especially if Khalil was a Saudi. And all of a sudden it dawned on her what her mother was attempting to do, and her blood ran cold.

"Turn around now, Mother," she said. "We're going back home."

"No," Kathleen said. They were passing the U.S. Naval Observatory grounds on their left. The vice president lived there, and a pair of National Guard Armored Personnel Carriers were parked on the main driveway. Directly across the avenue were the embassies of Fiji and three other small countries.

"I'm serious. We are not going to Yarnell's old house, because I know what you want to do, and I'm not going to let you."

Kathleen was unfazed. "If you know that much, then you know why I have to do this for your father. Khalil might not come to the house after me, but if he sees me parked outside his front door, he might try something. The second anything starts to happen, we'll get out of there and let your father know."

"That's my point," Elizabeth said, frantically. This was sheer madness. "What am I supposed to do if they come out guns blazing?"

"They wouldn't do that in the middle of Georgetown in the middle of a sunny morning."

"Well, if they do, you could get us both killed," Elizabeth shouted. "All three of us," she added, bitterly, knowing whatever she could say was going to do no good.

"Somebody has to stop him before it's too late," Kathleen said. "At least we have to try."

Khalil was in the second-floor operations center, where a detailed street map of Chevy Chase was displayed on a wide-screen computer monitor, while on another, photographs of Kathleen McGarvey scrolled down the screen. With him were the four security officers who al-Kaseem had assigned to him for the kidnapping. At this moment their driver was parked in a garage around the block in a Comcast Cable truck that they would take to the McGarvey house. They would neutralize whatever security was in place and grab Kathleen McGarvey.

Key to the operation would be making sure that Kirk McGarvey wasn't home. Khalil did not want to go up against the man again, not without the leverage that holding the man's wife hostage would give him. They were working on the surveillance operation to do just that.

There could be no mistakes because McGarvey would move heaven and earth to protect her. He'd already demonstrated that. But if his wife were to be taken to an absolutely secure location, his effectiveness as a player in this little drama would be neutralized.

The revenge would be sweet. Especially after the attacks when Kathleen McGarvey would be returned to her husband. When her body would be returned.

The normally calm al-Kaseem appeared at the steel security door in a hurry; he was flushed. "She's here."

Khalil looked up. "What are you talking about?"

"Kathleen McGarvey and another woman are sitting in a Mercedes directly in front of this building. I recognized her from the photographs."

For a moment Khalil was unsure of himself. Someone had traced him here, and the woman had the audacity to show up and challenge him. McGarvey knew!

"I'm telling you to stop this before it gets totally out of hand," al-Kaseem said. It was an order he was not qualified to give. Khalil was of a higher rank within the royal family than al-Kaseem was. But the intelligence chief had his own orders, which were to keep a very low profile until whatever was going to happen was over with. Already more than eight hundred Saudi citizens had been airlifted back to Riyadh, where they would wait out the attack and the backlash that was expected to last a year or more. There were to be absolutely no incidents involving Saudi citizens in the U.S.

Khalil decided that whatever the reason the brave but empty-headed woman had come here, the advantage was his for the taking.

"We'll take her now," he said.

"You're not bringing her into this facility," al-Kaseem shouted.

Khalil looked at the intelligence officer as if he were an insect. "I'll take her wherever I please."

Elizabeth knew that this was all wrong, sitting in plain sight in front of the Saudi-owned building. Her mother's aim was to flush Khalil out of hiding, if this is where he was, using herself as bait. After Alaska, the terrorist had a strong incentive to hit back.

The problem was that her ruse might be successful. Without backup they would be sitting ducks out here.

"You've made your point, Mother," she said. She pointed to the closed-circuit cameras mounted behind the tall iron fence. "They know we're here. So let's go."

Katy seemed to be disappointed. "I thought someone would have come out to find out what we wanted."

"Be glad they didn't," Elizabeth said. She was getting seriously spooked.

A white panel van turned the corner on Thirty-second Street, and came up the narrow Scott Place. It moved slowly, as if the driver was looking for an address. Elizabeth could see no one in the passenger seat, but her muscles instinctively tightened. They were in a dead-end cul-de-sac with no room to maneuver. If they were cut off, they could be in trouble.

"Start the car, Mother," she said, urgently. She unsnapped the restraining strap on her pistol.

Katy was looking at the approaching van. She nodded. "I think you're right," she said, and she reached for the key.

The van glided slowly past them. The driver didn't look over, and for just a second Elizabeth breathed a sigh of relief, but then she stiffened. "No," she said. The van supposedly belonged to a cable TV company. But the driver was wearing a suit and tie. It was all wrong.

She drew her pistol and thumbed the safety catch to the off position, when her door was jerked open and the muzzle of a pistol, held by a very large, very determined man, was jammed into the side of her head.

"There is no reason for you to lose your life," he warned. His English was heavily accented. He was a Saudi. "We want her, not her bodyguard."

Elizabeth raged inside. Dumb. Dumb. She had been dumb. It was entirely her fault that they were in this situation. But she wasn't going to compound the trouble by making a stupid move. So far no shots had been fired.

She nodded.

The heavyset man reached in with his free hand and took her gun. He said something in Arabic over the top of the car.

Kathleen's door was opened by a large man in a dark business suit, a pistol in his hand. He reached in, shut off the car, took the ignition keys, and tossed them across the street. Kathleen turned to Liz and started to speak, but Liz cut her off.

"Do exactly as they say, Mrs. McGarvey. I'm sure they mean you no harm. They just want you as a hostage to neutralize your husband. Do you understand?"

For a long moment Kathleen looked as if she was on the verge of making a move against the man pointing the gun at her. But then she visibly relaxed and gave Liz a nod, a look of apology in her eyes.

The Saudi security officer checked to make sure that there was no oncoming traffic or pedestrians, no one to see what was going on; then he helped Kathleen out of the car and hustled her back to the Comcast van parked directly behind them.

"If you try to follow us or if our movements are hindered in any fashion, we will kill her," said the officer holding the pistol on Elizabeth. "Tell your boss to go home and stay there. His wife will be returned unharmed in two days."

There it was, Liz thought. The man had made a mistake. He knew the timetable for the attack. Two days.

FIFTY-FOUR

□

Whatever the outcome of the latest threat to America, McGarvey figured that he would never be welcomed back to any job in U.S. intelligence. Even if he could somehow avoid jail time, his career was over. And it felt odd to him after more than twenty-five years to be branded a pariah, and by none other than the president himself.

McGarvey didn't want his friends to be tainted by association. In the face of martial law anyone perceived to be a threat to the nation could be shot. Yet he needed help.

"What I want to do will probably blow up in our faces," McGarvey told Otto Rencke. They stood facing each other in the shelter hut in the woods between the fifteenth fairway and the golf-course maintenance barn. No one was on the course this morning. Some things had not gotten back to normal.

"Boy oh boy, Mac, the shit has truly hit the fan over Monaco," Rencke hooted. He was hopping from one foot to the other. It was a little shuffle he did when he was nervous or excited.

"I know. Dick filled me in on the way back from Andrews. He told me that you managed to get to Berndt. What was his reaction?"

"He took the stuff, and he wished me good luck," Rencke said. "It's something, ya know. He's a good guy. If anyone can convince the president, he can. But everybody's coming up with zip. Nada. The bad guys are here, and we're making arrests. But all the wrong guys."

McGarvey had seen this coming well before 9/11. Because of sky-jackings in the seventies the U.S. had put air marshals on most commercial airliners. The skyjackings finally stopped, in large measure because of the sky marshals. But instead of continuing with the program, the budget was cut, sky marshals were taken off the airlines, and 9/11 occurred. Now the sky marshals were back, and al-Quaida wasn't going to use skyjackings again, and yet that was Homeland Security's main area of concentration.

No one was seeing the facts for what they were. To stop the attacks we had to go to the sources of the money. Which were certain members of the Saudi royal family.

"Do you have anything new on Khalil?"

"Salman showed up at the embassy this morning. And the FBI sent a surveillance team over to keep watch. But when he left a couple of hours later, they lost him." Rencke spread his hands in wonderment. "I don't think their hearts were in it. Nobody believes he's one of the bad guys."

That too was about what McGarvey expected. "Have they found him yet?"

"Not as of a half hour ago."

That didn't make sense to McGarvey. Salman had come to the U.S. so that he would be in plain sight when the attacks came. For him to shake his FBI tail and disappear somewhere in Washington was just the opposite of what he had done before. But, if Salman was Khalil, he might have slipped out of sight because he had something to do concerning the attacks, perhaps send a signal that would start the clock ticking.

Or he had gone hunting.

McGarvey had left his cell phone at the house. He did not want to be traced. Not with what he was going to do, contrary to direct orders from the president. He stepped around Rencke and gazed across the fairway toward his house. He could see a corner of the roof and the chimney, but nothing else. Still there was no one else in sight. Nor were there any sounds: no lawn mowers, no barking dogs, sirens. *No sounds of gunfire or cries for help.* The country was holding its breath. Waiting.

Rencke was closely watching him. "What is it, Mac?" he asked. "What's wrong?"

"Call my house."

"Okay," Rencke said. He took out his cell phone and hit the speed dial. "Who do you want to talk to?"

"Whoever answers."

"It's ringing," Rencke said.

McGarvey turned back, snapshots of what Khalil and his people had done on the cruise ship flashing in his head. He could still hear the mother's screams for her infant in the freezing water.

Rencke shook his head, a frightened expression in his eyes. "It's your answering machine. No one's picking up."

At that moment they both heard a car coming very fast up the gravel road to the maintenance barn. McGarvey drew his gun, flicked the safety catch off, and motioned for Rencke to drop down out of sight.

Let it be Khalil, he told himself. *Let it end here and now.*

Elizabeth hauled her mother's Mercedes around the maintenance barn to the cart path leading to the fifteenth fairway and jammed on the brakes, sending gravel and loose dirt flying. She'd been continuously on the phone to the Watch officer at Langley, who'd put out an APB to Washington Metro Police and the FBI to look for the Comcast maintenance van. She gave the license number, and made sure the Watch officer understood that under no circumstances was the van to be stopped.

By the time she had retrieved the car keys, the van was long gone, so she hadn't even tried to go after it, relying on the Watch officer to get it right.

Two minutes ago the FBI surveillance unit in front of the Saudi Embassy on New Hampshire Avenue, just off Juarez Circle, reported the van entering the parking garage at the rear of the building.

Elizabeth her heart in her throat, leaped out of the car and raced up the path through the woods to the shelter hut, hoping that she wasn't too late to catch her father and Otto. No one was around. In fact the maintenance area was deserted. But not many people were out playing golf when the country was on red alert.

She saw the fairway and then the hut at the same moment a figure moved in the relative darkness inside. "Shit," she said under her breath, and she reached for her pistol. Something had gone wrong here.

Before she could veer off the path and get her pistol out, her father stepped out of the hut. "Liz, what are you doing here?" He had his gun out. Otto was right behind him.

"They've got Mother," she cried, reaching them. "It was my fault. I shouldn't have let her leave the house. We shouldn't have gone to Yarnell's. It was a set-up, like they were waiting for us." She said it all in a rush.

McGarvey holstered his pistol, controlled anger in the set of his features. "Slow down, Liz. Who has her?"

"It was the Saudis. They had a gun to my head, and told me that she wouldn't be hurt, provided that you stayed out of the way. And they said that she'd be released in two days."

"Oh, wow, that's the timetable," Rencke said.

"Were you able to follow them?" McGarvey asked, his tone still reasonable.

"They were too fast, so I had the Watch officer call DC Metro and the Bureau," Elizabeth said. "They spotted the van going into the Saudi Embassy just a few minutes ago." She tried to gauge her father's mood. He was like a volcano on the verge of exploding. She'd read his missions files, and had seen him in action more than once. He never went off halfcocked, but when he moved it was awesome.

"This has to go to the president," Rencke said. "He can put pressure on the Saudi ambassador."

McGarvey shook his head, his jaw set. "You can try, but the Saudis will deny they have her."

"They didn't hurt her, Daddy," Elizabeth said. Tears welled in her eyes. She hated to cry. It was weak. "I'm sorry. It was my fault. But I did exactly what they told me to do so that no one would get hurt. I didn't want that." She closed her eyes. "Oh, God."

McGarvey took her in his arms. "Take it easy. It's not your fault. You didn't kidnap her. And I know you did your best."

Elizabeth opened her eyes and looked up into her father's face. "We'll get her back, Daddy," she said. "You'll get her back, won't you?"

"Count on it, sweetheart," McGarvey said, his gray-green eyes already seeing beyond her.

FIFTY-FIVE

□

The Saudi deputy ambassador to the United States, Mamdouh Nuaimi, was deep in thought looking out the window of his office toward the Watergate Hotel complex when his secretary buzzed him. These were troubling times, and he wished that he were just about anywhere except here in Washington.

"Prince Salman has returned, Your Excellency," the male secretary said.

Girding himself for a potentially difficult encounter Nuaimi keyed the intercom. "Please ask the prince to come in."

"Yes, sir."

Nuaimi got to his feet and adjusted his tie as Prince Salman, also wearing a Western business suit, with a correctly knotted silk tie, walked in, a scowl on his dark features. Nuaimi came from around his desk, and embraced the prince.

"You honor me by coming here," Nuaimi said, his Arabic formal, as befitted a man of the prince's wealth and position of power. "Will you have tea?"

"The honor is mine, Deputy Ambassador," Salman responded, correctly, if somewhat brusquely. "I have no time for tea. I was summoned and here I am. What do you want?"

"It's a matter of some delicacy that the ambassador asked me to handle," Nuaimi said, choosing his words with care. The prince was not a man to be offended by a careless remark. And although Nuaimi, whose brother was the oil minister Ali Nuaimi, had wealth and power, it was nothing in comparison to Salman's. "It is the troubling time we find ourselves in at the moment."

A brief smile crossed Salman's thick lips. "It will serve the bastards right, another 9/11. They haven't awakened to the real world, even yet."

"Pakistan is cooperating—"

Salman dismissed Nuaimi with a flick of his hand, as if he were shooing away an annoying but ineffectual insect. He was obviously in an extremely foul mood. "Make your point, Mr. Deputy Ambassador," he demanded, rudely.

Nuaimi smiled, ignoring the insult. "As you wish. The ambassador would like to know if there is anything he can do to enhance your current visit, considering the difficult moment we find ourselves in. If an al-Quaida attack were to occur, there would certainly be a problematic backlash. We merely wish to provide good advice and security for our citizens."

"You want me to leave?"

Nuaimi spread his hands in a gesture of peace and conciliation. "We understood there was an unpleasantness in Monaco between you and the former director of the CIA. You were on your way to Corsica. Perhaps you should go there now. Or perhaps return to your family in Switzerland."

Salman flared. "Only Crown Prince Abdullah himself can order me to leave," he shouted.

"Please, no one is ordering you to do anything against your will." Nuaimi said. "Not I, not the ambassador. We are merely suggesting that for your personal safety you might wish to leave the U.S. as soon as possible."

"My safety is exactly why I'm here," Salman said. "The madman threatened to kill me."

It was in the dispatch the ambassador had received from Monaco. Saudi intelligence had an agent aboard the prince's yacht. "That's fantastic, Your Excellency. But why would he make such a threat against you?"

"As I said, he's mad, and I'll take this to the president—"

"No," Nuaimi said, flatly. He'd been warned that the prince might want to do exactly that, and it wasn't to be allowed under any circumstances. But since Salman was such a powerful man, one that even Crown Prince Abdullah did not want to cross, the job of stopping the man fell on Nuaimi's shoulders. If Salman retaliated, the only man to be damaged would be the deputy ambassador, which was a perfectly acceptable loss under the circumstances.

"What did you say to me?" Salman demanded, his voice scarcely above a whisper.

"You will not attempt to contact anyone within the U.S. government at this time, not without the express approval of this embassy," Nuaimi said. He was thinking about his wives and children, whom he'd sent back to Riyadh yesterday. He was glad they were gone. "I will need your word of honor on the issue, or else, regrettably, I will have to place you under arrest until your return to Riyadh can be arranged."

"You don't have the authority."

"In this, I assure you that I do, Your Excellency," Nuaimi said. For an instant he thought Salman was actually going to lay hands on him, do him physical harm. But then it passed. "Do I have your word, sir?"

Salman continued to glare at Nuaimi for a long second or two, then turned on his heel and left the office.

Nuaimi considered calling security to prevent the prince from leaving the embassy, but decided against it. Dealing with the royal family was always fraught with danger, for the simple reason, in his estimation, that most of them were insane or on the edge of insanity.

Kathleen sat on the edge of a narrow cot in a small windowless room, feeling despondent that she had been so stupid. Because of her insistence on playing amateur sleuth, people were going to get hurt. She'd not only put herself in danger, but she'd endangered the lives of her daughter and her husband. Elizabeth had been allowed to go unharmed. By now she would have told her father what had happened, and Kirk would be going into action.

A hood had been placed ever Kathleen's head as soon as they'd turned the corner on Thirty-second Street, so she had no idea where they had taken her. Nor was there any clue in the room as to her whereabouts, which could only ever have but one use—as a jail cell. There was a toilet without seat or lid, and a small, stainless steel sink with only a cold-water tap. There were no mirrors, no covering on the bare concrete floor, and only a single dim light in a ceiling recess, protected by steel mesh.

Besides her stupidity, the other thing that bothered her the more she thought about it was the stains on the concrete floor. They looked like rust, but she suspected they might be blood.

For the first time since Alaska, she was truly and deeply frightened.

Two days, her captors had told her, and then she would be released provided her husband cooperated and stayed out of it.

But if Khalil was here and had engineered her kidnapping, she did not think she would get out of this one unscathed no matter what Kirk did or didn't do.

Someone was at the door, turning the lock. The tiny viewing window was blocked so Kathleen could not see who was coming, but she knew who it was, and she shuddered in anticipation.

The door opened and a tall man came in; he was wearing an expensive, dove-gray business suit, a white silk shirt and tie, and a bland expression, one almost of indifference, on his long handsome face. He looked at Kathleen for a few seconds, as if he were studying some interesting specimen in a test tube, then gently closed the door.

Kathleen's throat constricted, and she was sick to her stomach. He looked familiar, but she couldn't be sure. *She wouldn't give the bastard the satisfaction of seeing her terror.* "I thought that I detected your unpleasant odor. You couldn't beat my husband, so now you've come to take your revenge on me." She laughed. "Is that it?"

Khalil smiled faintly. He took off his suit coat and hung it on the doorknob. "Why, yes," he said, his voice gentle, as if he were talking to an animal or a small child and didn't want to spook it.

Kathleen's heart skipped a beat. She recognized the voice from Alaska.

Khalil loosened his tie, then rolled up his shirtsleeves.

Kathleen realized with an intensely sick feeling that the man was insane, and that he meant to hurt her. "I don't care as much for my own safety right now, as I do for the baby that I'm carrying," she said.

He shrugged indifferently and started for her.

Kathleen leaped up from the cot, doubled up her fist, and smashed it into his face with every ounce of her strength. His head rocked back, but then he punched her in her stomach just below her rib cage, sending her sprawling backward on the cot, her head smashing into the concrete wall.

She saw spots in front of her eyes, and bile burned at the back of her throat, making her gag.

Khalil was right there, over her. He grabbed her by the front of her blouse, dragging her to her feet and ripping the thin material to shreds. Holding her arm with his left hand, he backhanded her in the face with his other. Her nose gushed blood, but the cobwebs suddenly lifted from her brain.

"Bastard," she cried, as she drove her knee into his groin.

He grunted in pain, but continued to hold her with one hand while slapping her with the other.

She tried to knee him again, but he deflected her blow with his leg. He looked into her eyes, still with a frighteningly bland expression on his face, doubled up his fist, and struck her very hard in her left breast.

The pain was instant and incredible. Her knees buckled, and the room went hot and dim.

Khalil struck her again in her breast, then in her stomach, and he slammed his knee into her groin.

She could not fight back, nor could she feel more than a dull pain throughout her entire body. But she felt a wetness in her panties, and she despaired that she would lose Elizabeth's baby.

There had been so much suffering in their family. So much loss. Not this, she cried inside. *Please, God, not this.*

The last thing she was aware of was Kahlil's fist connecting with her face.

FIFTY-SIX

McGarvey stood beside the front bedroom window looking down at the cul-de-sac as Liz, driving her mother's Mercedes, pulled into the driveway; Otto, in his battered Mercedes diesel sedan, was right behind her.

McGarvey had trotted over from the fifteenth fairway and entered the house through the pool-deck door to make sure that neither the Bureau nor anyone else had shown up to look for him. Sooner or later they would be coming in response to Kathleen's kidnapping. But he figured there was still time for him to make his preparations.

He was not angry. He was beyond that. At this point he was in his hunt-find-kill mode, and no power on earth could stop him from doing what he was going to do to find his wife and damage her captors.

Khalil had been at Yarnell's old house, possibly hoping that McGarvey would make the connection and come looking for him. Instead it had been Kathleen, and the Saudi terrorist had taken her.

She was the bait that would draw McGarvey into a trap. What Kahlil could not guess was just how eager McGarvey was to comply.

What made no sense to McGarvey were the Saudi ambassador and embassy staff. The royal family was walking a tightrope, continuing to sell oil to the U.S. while funding and even encouraging terrorism. Kidnapping the wife of an important American government figure and then holding her hostage at the embassy was risky.

Too risky for the Saudis? Or was he missing something?

He went to the closet, where he stripped off his shirt and khaki trousers, changing into dark slacks, dark blue sneakers, and a black pullover that covered the pistol holstered at the small of his back. He also donned a lightweight reversal windbreaker—dark on one side and white on the other—that had several zippered pockets.

"Dad?" Elizabeth called from the front hall.

"It's okay; I'm changing," he called back. "Be right down." He opened a secret compartment in the floor of the closet, which contained his escape kit: six clean passports under six different names from the U.S., Great Britain, Australia, and Canada; credit cards and other bits of identification to match; twenty-five thousand dollars in cash, mostly in U.S. currency, but some in British pounds and a fair amount in euros; hair dyes; lock picks; a spare Walther PPK with several magazines of 9mm ammunition; a custom-made Austrian silencer; a stiletto; several small bundles, each the size of a package of cigarettes, that contained blocks of Semtex explosives and securely protected acid fuses; and a few other odds and ends.

The cache was an old habit of his. Whenever he landed somewhere, one of his first tasks was to establish an escape kit against the day he might be required to step outside the establishment and suddenly go to ground.

Like now, he thought. *On his own for the most part. Beholden to no one, following no orders other than his own, on a single-purpose mission.*

He taped the spare Walther to his left calf, strapped the stiletto in its leather sheath to his chest beneath his windbreaker, and pocketed a small mag light with red and white lenses, two spare magazines, the silencer, and three of the Semtex packages.

He left everything else. He had no need for the passports or the money, because when this was over he wasn't going to run. And he decided he wouldn't need the lock picks. What he was going to do would not require stealth. He had the Semtex for any locked gate or door he might encounter.

For just a moment he stood over the compartment staring at the envelope of cash and identification documents. His first instinct had always been to run. It was a survival tactic he had learned in the jungles of Vietnam. Plus he'd always wanted to distance himself from the people he loved so that they would not come into harm's way because of him.

No running this time, he thought, closing and securing the compartment. *Not now. Never again.*

Downstairs Elizabeth was in the kitchen drinking from a bottle of Evian. When McGarvey came in, her eyes were round and worried and still apologetic for a situation she felt was largely her fault.

"Where's Otto?" McGarvey asked.

"In your study. He's trying to get to Dennis Berndt, to tell him about mother." Elizabeth hung her head. "The dirty bastards. I pretended to be her bodyguard. If they'd known I was her daughter, they would have taken me too." She looked up at her father. "But I didn't know what else to do, Daddy."

"You did the right thing, sweetheart," McGarvey assured her. In all likelihood they might have killed her and left her body to be identified. It would have been an even more powerful incentive for McGarvey to rush into the trap, blinded not only by fear for his wife's safety, but also by grief over his child's death.

"You're going after her, but how are you going to get in?" Elizabeth asked. "The Saudis aren't just going to let you come up to the gate and invite you in."

"You and Otto are going to create a diversion," he said. "But not until tonight, after midnight. And in the meantime we've got a lot to do. I want to make them nervous. Maybe the Saudi ambassador will put pressure on Khalil to give it up, at least release your mother. Stranger things have happened, and I don't think they want that kind of political trouble, especially not right now." Something else suddenly occurred to him, and he looked away.

"Daddy?" Elizabeth asked. "What is it?"

Men like bin Laden and Khalil and their followers firmly believed they were in a war for their very existence, and they believed that there were no innocents in the war. Every Christian and Jewish man, woman, and child was not only fair game in the jihad, they were also the prime targets. It was a view 180 degrees out of sync with what McGarvey had always believed. Minimize the risk to the noncombatants. Minimize the collateral damage.

The woman desperately screamed for her baby, but there'd been no hope. Khalil had known it, as he had known McGarvey would try to save them anyway. The dark water aft of the cruise liner had become a killing ground, the woman and child the bait.

Just as Katy was the bait. And just as Kahlil had picked out another killing ground.

Rencke came from the study. "I got to Berndt, and he's agreed to take this to the president—" He looked from McGarvey to Liz. "What've I missed?"

"I just thought of something," McGarvey said. "But I'm going to need an untraceable cell phone. Is that possible?"

Rencke shrugged. "Sure. Where's yours?"

"Out on the hall table."

Rencke went to fetch it, and when he came back he was entering a series of numbers. He pressed the pound key, and then Send. A code came up, and he entered a second series of long numbers and letters, pressing the pound key and Send again. Another code appeared on the display, and Rencke looked up, grinning. "You'll keep the same number, but all your calls in and out will be routed through a redialer in Amsterdam." He handed the phone to McGarvey. "It'll drive anybody monitoring you nuts trying to figure out how you got outta Dodge so fast."

"What are you going to do?" Elizabeth asked.

"Play Khalil at his own game." McGarvey said, pulling up a number from his cell phone's memory. He pressed Send. "Give him something that he'll understand."

It was after lunch and Liese Fuelm was getting ready to pull the pin and head back to her apartment in town when her cell phone vibrated at her hip. She was accomplishing nothing out here on the lake. They had learned that Salman was in Washington, probably stalking Kirk, but that's all she'd been told. Gertner wanted her here, where keeping an eye on her would be easy. *The hell with him.*

The caller ID showed a U.S. area code and number, but the call was coming from Amsterdam. "Oui?"

"Hello, Liese, is your phone being monitored?" McGarvey asked.

Liese's stomach gave a little lurch. Ziegler was upstairs getting some sleep, and LeFevre was in the kitchen finishing his lunch. For the moment no one was seated at the equipment table. "Just a minute." She went over to the recording machines and pressed the Pause button. "It's okay now, Kirk. Are you really in Amsterdam?"

"No. I want you to do something for me."

Liese was thrilled. "Yes, of course. Anything."

"Don't be so fast to agree. What I'm asking will be dangerous. Could get you hurt, and at the very least get you fired."

"I don't care—" Liese protested. The man she was in love with had asked for her help. There could be only one answer.

"You're still in love with me, aren't you?"

Liese closed her eyes. She nodded. "I've never stopped loving you, Kirk."

"Nothing can ever come of it," McGarvey said, gently.

"I know."

"Khalil is here and he's kidnapped my wife, and what I want you to do for me might help to save her life, and possibly stop the terrorists before they hit us."

"My God, I'm sorry," Liese said, and she was sincere. She wanted Kirk, but not that way. Not at the expense of his wife's life. "Tell me what you want me to do."

There was a short silence. "Will your badge get you into Prince Salman's compound sometime today?"

Liese was startled. "Of course. There's a house staff over there, including bodyguards, but they wouldn't turn away a Swiss Federal cop. Getting in would be easy, but the instant I approach the gate my surveillance crew will pick up on it and inform Gertner."

This time when he spoke, McGarvey sounded cautious. "Are you able to monitor conversations inside the house?"

"Yes. At least in most of the apartments," Liese said. She could hear LeFevre rattling around in the kitchen. "Whatever I say or do once I'm in will be recorded here."

"Good. Then there'll be no mistakes. No one will rush in with guns blazing."

"What are you talking about?"

"I want you to get inside the compound, and hold Salman's wife at gunpoint."

A jolt of electricity shot through Liese's body. "She's not involved in any of this. I'm not going to hurt an innocent woman."

"Listen to me, Liese. I don't want anybody hurt. If something doesn't go right, then get the hell out of there. Or put your pistol on the floor and raise your hands. Your people will bail you out. No matter what happens, there'll be no shooting."

All at once Liese understood what Kirk was trying to do. By taking

Salman's wife hostage, a possible trade could be made for Kathleen Mc-
Garvey. That was crystal clear, and it might work if nothing went wrong
here. But what was also perfectly clear in Liese's mind was just how
deeply Kirk loved his wife. There was no hope after all. Liese closed her
eyes again to squeeze away the tears. "When do you want me to do it?"
she asked.

"Within the next few hours," McGarvey said. "Call me when you're in."

"Then what?"

"Then I'm going after Khalil."

"Kirk—"

"Yes?"

"Be careful," she whispered. *My darling.*

McGarvey's voice softened. "You too."

"Oh, wow," Rencke said, hopping back and forth. "Do you think she'll
pull it off? Do it, ya know?"

McGarvey was looking at his daughter, who had an odd, hurt expression on her face. "I think so."

"If somebody gets hurt, especially the man's wife or his kids, we're
going to be the bad guys."

He didn't know how he could live with himself if something did happen. But he didn't
know anything else that would get to a man such as Khalil, except by
threatening his family. It was a universal language, the one point of com-
monality between the terrorists and us. Except that the terrorists were
perfectly willing to target innocent women and children, while up until
now the Americans were not.

"Were you in love with her?" Elizabeth asked. She was obviously having trouble saying the words.

McGarvey understood his daughter's fear. He had left her once, and
she didn't want to lose him again. He shook his head. "No, I was never in
love with any woman except your mother. Then or now," he added.

Elizabeth took several seconds to digest her father's answer. "Okay,
Daddy, what do you want us to do?"

"Three things. First, I want a major surveillance operation on the
Saudi Embassy started as soon as possible. Vans, cars, foot patrols, chop-

pers, the whole works. I want to saturate the entire area one block out from the building, and I want them to know that we're doing it."

Rencke's eyes narrowed. "The Bureau will want to know what's going on, and the Saudis will start screaming bloody murder the moment they spot us," he warned. "Won't take long till someone over at the White House orders us to pull the pin."

"Communications will be very bad this afternoon and tonight," Mc-Garvey said. "I'll need just a few more hours, no longer. And as for the Saudis, I want them to start making noises as soon as possible. Maybe even create an incident. Maybe DC Metro would have to be called in, especially if there's trouble on the streets *outside* Saudi territory."

"I'll call Todd; he can bring some people out from the Farm," Elizabeth said. "What next?"

"I want you and Otto to find a way to get into the place. Maybe there's a storm-sewer tunnel under the building, something that opens inside the compound. Maybe a cable and heating conduit. When you get it figured out, I want you to fax the information to me here at the house."

Rencke caught on to McGarvey's plan; it was plain by his expression, but Elizabeth was confused.

"We'll have to sweep the phones first," she said. "Make sure they're secure. Hasn't been done since before you left for Alaska."

"Oh, boy, let's hope that they're dirty," Rencke said. He was excited. "And even if there isn't a way to get inside, I'll make one up and fax the plans here." He grinned. "Soon as you give me word, we'll cut all the utilities to the building. Electricity, water, phones, and cable."

Elizabeth objected. "They'll lock that place up tighter than a drum," she said. "They'll know they're under attack, and they'll shoot at anything that moves."

"That's right," Rencke said. He suddenly stopped hopping. "Mrs. M isn't there, and neither will your father be."

"But the Comcast van was spotted going into the embassy compound."

"That's right, sweetheart," McGarvey told his daughter. "Exactly what Khalil wanted us to see. It's why his people didn't take you with them. They wanted you to yell bloody murder so that someone would look for the van. But it took time to organize the search. No one picked up the van until it showed up at the Saudi Embassy. Nobody actually followed it from Georgetown. It could have gone someplace else first, dropped your mother off, and then headed over to the embassy."

Elizabeth saw it all at once. "She could be almost anywhere in the city." Suddenly her eyes lit up. "Darby Yarnell's old house. My God, they doubled back after I'd left."

McGarvey nodded. He was seeing Khalil's hands on Katy. He could see the man's gun pointed at her head, and his jaw tightened.

"They don't have diplomatic immunity over there," Elizabeth said. "We can get a search warrant and let the Bureau handle it—"

"They might kill her first," Rencke suggested, softly.

"No search warrant," McGarvey said, and he shivered inside at the depth of his anger and resolve to take the fight to Khalil on the man's own terms. "I'm going in. No one else. Just me."

FIFTY-SEVEN

As Berndt headed for the Oval Office, the West Wing was a beehive of activity, even more than it usually was on a weekday morning. Rencke's telephone call coming so close on the heels of his earlier visit was frightening. He clutched the CIA file close to his chest, as if he expected someone to grab the explosive material from him.

Kathleen McGarvey had been kidnapped and was being held hostage. By the Saudis.

At first Berndt had not wanted to believe Rencke. The implications were too stunning for him to take the story seriously. But the more he thought about it, the more it made a kind of twisted sense. McGarvey was the only man in town who believed Kahlil and Prince Salman were the same man. They had kidnapped McGarvey's wife in an attempt to make him stop his pursuit.

But they had no idea of what McGarvey was capable of doing to them.

And at stake now was more than bin Laden's threat, or the safety of the ex-CIA director's wife. At issue was the stability of the entire Middle East and all the oil there; it could make the difference between an America that continued to be strong and prosperous and an oil-poor America that could sink to the level of a third world nation.

Before that was allowed to come to pass, we would go to war, Berndt thought. And fighting to take control of Saudi Arabia would be one hundred times the nightmare that Iraq had been. All of the Middle East would be against us.

Berndt entered the Oval Office, as the president, standing behind his desk, was on the phone. Secretaries and staffers came and went in a continuous stream. The four television sets were tuned to the three major networks plus CNN. "We have a problem, Mr. President."

Haynes looked at him. "I'll get back to you," he said, and he put down the telephone. "What is it, Dennis?"

"It's Khalil and the Saudis," Berndt said. He was sick at heart thinking about what they faced. Nothing like this had been on his mind when he'd accepted the president's call to become the NSA.

The president's chief of staff, Calvin Beckett, walked in. "What have I missed?"

"Get everybody out of here," Haynes ordered, his eyes not leaving Berndt's. "Give us a couple of minutes."

"Shall I stay?" Beckett asked.

"You'd better," Berndt said before the president could speak.

Haynes nodded after a beat, but said nothing until Beckett had ushered out the other staffers and closed the door. "Okay, what about Khalil and the Saudis?"

"We have the timetable for the attack. It happens in two days."

"You have my attention," the president said. "Do you know this for a fact? What's your source?" He eyed the buff folder with orange diagonal stripes that the CIA used to hold classified documents with a Q rating, which was a step higher than top secret.

When Berndt was growing up in the midwest and involved with school politics and the history and social sciences clubs, it was the last era in which becoming president of the United States was considered to be a noble, worthy goal. That was no longer the case, he thought, sadly. Anyone wanting the job immediately came under the same close public scrutiny as a career criminal might. Something was wrong with you if you wanted to be president.

"Kirk McGarvey's wife was kidnapped this morning at gunpoint and taken to the Saudi Embassy. The men who did it told her daughter they'd hold her mother for only two days, if Kirk were to withdraw from his investigation of Khalil."

Haynes sat down. "God in heaven," he said, at a momentary loss. But then he looked up, anger coloring his face. "That's insane. Do you believe her?"

"Actually I got it from Otto Rencke, he's McGarvey's chief of Special Operations—"

"I know who he is," the president interjected, angrily. "Is that his report?"

Berndt decided that no matter how this crisis turned out, he would leave Washington and return to academia. Working in this place could kill a man. "There's more," he said. He handed the folder to the president. "Rencke brought this over to me a couple of hours ago. Pretty well nails Khalil and Prince Salman as being the same man." Berndt glanced over at Beckett, who looked skeptical. In this town it was usually the bearer of the bad news who was the first to fall. "From what I can gather, the evidence is mostly circumstantial—there're no DNA matches or anything like that—but there's a lot of it. And what they've come up with seems convincing."

"Goddammit, I won't have this," the president shouted. "I warned him to stay out of it."

Berndt girded himself. "Whatever we might have believed about the Saudis has changed. They took Kathleen McGarvey against her will, and they're holding her in their embassy. Mr. President, we might be able to ignore the circumstantial evidence that the CIA has gathered on Khalil and the prince, but we cannot ignore this."

"Where was she when they grabbed her?" Beckett asked. Like the president, he seemed to be having a hard time getting a handle on this latest development. "Not at home?"

Berndt shook his head. Rencke hadn't been exactly clear where the kidnapping took place, just that it had happened. "Somewhere in George-town, I think. The men were driving a Comcast Cable TV van. Her daugh-ter got the tag number and immediately called the Bureau and DC Metro. But by the time they found the van it was just going into the Saudi Em-bassy, so they had to back off."

"Where's McGarvey?" Beckett asked.

Berndt had asked Rencke the same question. "At home for the time being," he said. But he didn't believe it for one minute.

"Bring him in," the president told Berndt. He managed a wry smile. "*Ask* him to come in." He called his secretary. "I want to speak to Prince Bandar bin Sultan." Prince Sultan, the son of the Saudi defense minister, was the ambassador to the U.S., and had been since 1983. He was a moderate.

The call went through to the embassy, and the president put it on the speakerphone "Prince?"

"I'm sorry, Mr. President, this is Mamdouh Nuaimi. The prince is out of the country at the moment. May I be of some assistance?"

"When do you expect the prince's return?" Haynes said.

"Not for several days, I'm very sorry to report, Mr. President," the deputy ambassador said. "Now, sir, is there something I may deal with?"

"Have the prince call me as soon as possible," the president said, and he broke the connection. He got his secretary again. "I want to speak with Crown Prince Abdullah, and I don't care what time it is in Riyadh."

Beckett got on another phone and had his secretary dial McGarvey's home.

"Tell him that we've been informed about his wife, and that I want to see him this morning," Haynes told his chief of staff. He gave Berndt a bleak, angry look. "This could turn out very bad for us."

"Yes, Mr. President," Berndt agreed.

Much worse than 9/11, with further reaching consequences. If they kept hitting us, sooner or later we could lose our national will to fight back. It had happened in Vietnam, and if the liberals had their way, we would get out of Iraq and step away from everything we'd worked for.

Beckett looked up and shook his head. "I got his answering machine. Either he's not home or he's not picking up."

"Goddammit," Haynes said, through clenched teeth. "Get Dick Adkins over at Langley, and find out what the hell McGarvey thinks he's doing."

The president's secretary buzzed him, and Haynes put the call on the speakerphone. "Crown Prince Abdullah, good afternoon."

"Mr. President, I am the crown prince's personal secretary," a man said. His English was heavily accented. "Unfortunately, His Excellency is in meetings. But he will be informed of your important call, and I am quite certain that he will arrange to speak with you at the first opportunity."

The president hesitated, and it struck Berndt as an ominous sign from a man who was known for his decisiveness.

"Very well, I'll wait for his call," Haynes said, and broke the connection.

He sat back, looking at his national security adviser as if he were waiting for some advice. But for once Berndt was at a loss.

"There's not much we can do about them," the president said. "Not unless somebody finds us a new source of oil, pronto." He shook his head. "God help the bastards if these attacks actually happen and if we can prove that Saudi Arabia was involved." His jaw tightened. "I would ask Congress for a formal declaration of war."

Berndt let out the breath he was holding. "In the meantime we still have to deal with the issue of McGarvey's wife. He will try to rescue her, and as you say, Mr. President, God help the poor bastards who try to stand in his way."

Beckett had his hand over the phone. "Mr. Adkins is in a staff meeting. Do you want me to call him out of it?"

"Yes," Haynes said. "I want him here within the hour. Then get Herb Weissman and Frank Hoover." Hoover was chief of DC police. "Between the three of them I want to know what the hell we can do to get the Saudis to release McGarvey's wife before he blows up the place and starts a war all by himself."

If she was inside the Saudi Embassy, there wasn't much that any of them could do, except try to hold McGarvey back and wait it out, Berndt thought. And neither was a very good option at the moment.

FIFTY-EIGHT

□

"Am I going to lose the baby?" Kathleen asked the young Saudi doctor who'd come to tend to her injuries. He'd given her an injection for the terrible pain, and she wanted to float. But she was still frightened to the core. "Please tell me."

The doctor looked like a teenager, with a long, narrow, sad face, and a heavy six o'clock shadow. He listened to her heart. And when he was finished he sat back. "I do not know," he told her. "You have a broken rib, and there will be much bruising." He shook his head. "Beyond that we would need to see X-rays, and you would need a gynecological exam. Very soon."

He had brought a pair of dark cotton pajamas for her and a Kotex pad, as well as soap, a washcloth, and a towel so she could clean up. But he had stepped outside while she changed, and he'd refused to give her more than a cursory examination.

Not out of some religious modesty that forbade him to see a naked woman who was not his wife, Kathleen reasoned. It was because he was frightened of getting involved. If he treated her and she died, it would be on his head.

And that was the most frightening part. She knew that she could die here for lack of medical attention. The bleeding from her vagina hadn't worsened, but it had not stopped.

"I'm still bleeding."

"How far are you along?" he asked.

"Four weeks."

The tight expression around his eyes softened a little. "Sometimes there is bleeding in the first month. It may mean nothing—"

"*Nothing?*" Kathleen screeched. "The bastard beat me unconscious. What kind of fucking monsters are you people? You're in the goddamned Stone Age." She felt what little control she had slipping away from her. She was on pain medication, but she felt as if she were going insane. "Do you have a wife? Is this how you would like a man to treat her?"

Kathleen half rose from the cot, and the doctor gently helped her to sit back. "Please, madam. It will do no good for you to become hysterical."

She slowly came back from the brink. She could see that the doctor was nearly as frightened as she was. "So far, being reasonable hasn't seemed to work for me. What else do you suggest?"

"That you cooperate with these people," the young doctor recommended, in a reasonable tone. He was dressed in a shirt and tie, with khaki slacks but no jacket, as if he had been hastily summoned from a clinic somewhere. He'd brought the few things for her along with his doctor's bag, but nothing else.

"That man means to kill me," Kathleen said, her own words sending a chill through her body. She shivered involuntarily. "Then God help you, because my husband will surely come down on you like the hand of God, and destroy you all."

The doctor's eyes had grown wide. He hastily stuffed his stethoscope in his bag and went to the door. "Do as they say, madam. And you will come out of this alive. It's your only hope."

"Remember what has happened here, doctor," Kathleen said, foggily. "If I should manage to survive, I will not forget you."

Someone was out in the corridor. When the doctor left, Khalil and another man, who carried a video camera, came into the cell. Kathleen shrank back against the concrete wall, her fear spiking.

"The doctor gave you good advice," Khalil said.

She didn't think she could stand another beating. She decided that if he tried to hit her again, she would gouge his eyes out with her fingers or rip his throat apart with her teeth. Anything to stop the monster.

"Your husband doesn't know where you are," Khalil said, "but even if he should figure out where you are, it will be too late for you. You're going to make a statement for the six o'clock news."

"Or else what?" Kathleen asked. "You're going to kill me?" She was surprised at how steady her voice sounded. She had no spit left.

"If it comes to that," Khalil said, shrugging. He held out a sheet of paper to her. "You're going to read this aloud."

"What is it?" Kathleen asked, trying to shrink back even farther, but there was no place in which to retreat, except to think about Kirk. Especially his eyes: kind, understanding, patient, confident.

A faint smile crossed Khalil's full lips. "I believe you call such a thing a propaganda statement. Harmless, but it's part of the dance."

Kathleen shook her head. The pain medication was taking her down. "If it's harmless, then you don't need me to read it."

Khalil seemed to consider her refusal. He nodded. "Perhaps I could offer you an inducement," he said, blandly.

"Fuck you."

"I could call the doctor back. He's a loyal servant who does as he is told. He has the instruments and the skill to perform a simple procedure on you. An abortion."

There had been so much pain in their lives. This thing that she had done for Elizabeth had been meant to set the scale back into balance. To bring some small measure of joy and happiness to them.

As children we'd been led to believe that monsters didn't really exist. But 9/11 had changed that. And bin Laden's al-Quaida wanted to do it to us again.

She reached up and took the single sheet of paper on which was typed perhaps twenty lines in fairly large print. But it took Kathleen a few seconds to get her eyes to focus so that she could make sense of what she was supposed to read for the video camera.

She read it once, and then a second time. The message was as simple as it was chilling, because it was nothing more than a repetition of the same demands bin Laden had been making all along for something that was impossible. Al-Quaida freedom fighters wanted Saudi Arabia. They wanted every westerner off the peninsula, they wanted the dissolution of the Saudi royal family as a ruling power, and they wanted control of the oil fields. Oil would be for friends of Dar al-Islam.

It is no different than in 1776 when the valiant American freedom fighters forced their oppressive masters off the land. And today America and England are partners.

All of a sudden it struck her. She looked up into Khalil's eyes. On the cruise ship he'd worn a balaclava to hide his features. He didn't want his face known.

But here he had allowed her to see him.

She would not leave this place alive.

From the first he had planned on killing her. The tape was to be nothing more than a goad for Kirk to walk into a trap.

She didn't know what to do.

⊏ I ⊏ T ⅄ – ⊓ I ⊓ ⪢

□

It was noon by the time the cabby dropped McGarvey off at the corner of Thirty-second and Q streets in Georgetown and he made the rest of his way on foot to the Boynton Towers apartments. The place had been modern ten years ago, but though it had aged, the eight-story building was still an elegant address and the apartment rents had skyrocketed.

He took the elevator to the top floor, and using the lock pick set he'd taken after all, he spent a half minute opening the door to 8B, and let himself in.

The small, neatly furnished apartment smelled slightly musty. The CIA had owned it for ten years, using it first in a surveillance operation against Darby Yarnell, and since then as a safe house for the occasional clandestine meeting.

So far as Otto Rencke had been able to find out, the place hadn't been used for nearly thirteen months. Nobody had been here to clean or to check on the place. The rent was paid on time every month by housekeeping at Langley, and so far as the neighbors were concerned the renter was likely a government employee of some sort, off on another long foreign posting.

McGarvey moved slowly across the living room and down the corridor to the back bedroom. The window blinds were partially drawn allowing sunlight to cast stripes on the pale gray carpeted floor. Keeping to one side, he eased one of the slats upward and peered across at Yarnell's old house. An instant rush of memories came back at him.

Lorraine, the field officer with the *Sommersprosse* who'd been on the team that had come for him in Lausanne, had been up here. So had a couple of Trotter's people, a man whose name might have been Sheets, or something like that, and another named Gonzales. They thought that Yarnell was a spy for the Soviet government, and they were watching the comings and goings at his house.

The apartment had been filled with surveillance equipment, including a big Starlight scope on a sturdy tripod.

Tell them I came, and no one answered, that I kept my word.

It was the same bit of de la Mare that had come to him then. The listeners, waiting for the lone rider to bang on the door, find that no one was home and then leave again.

Gonzales had been on the Starlight. "Maybe you want to take a look; maybe you don't." He nodded toward the scope. "But it's something."

A man and a woman stood locked in an embrace next to a four-poster bed in an upstairs bedroom. The man's back was toward the window. When they parted, McGarvey was looking into Kathleen's face. She was flushed. Then the man half turned, giving McGarvey a clear view of him. Yarnell.

Oh, Kathleen! he'd thought then and now. She'd always played dangerous games, but she hadn't known just how precarious her position really was. And here she was again.

The street below was quiet, and there were no sounds in the apartment. It was as if this part of the capital city was holding its collective breath, which in a way it was.

The waiting had always been the hardest part. And now it was made infinitely more difficult because it was Katy over there again.

McGarvey slowly lowered the slat back into place, and then adjusted the blinds so that he could see outside. Taking off his jacket, he laid it on the bed, then took the small lamp off the nightstand and pulled the little table over to the window. He pulled the easy chair from the corner and positioned it next to the table so that when he was seated he could look out the window and see the street and front entrance to Yarnell's old house.

Katy would be frightened but defiant. By now Khalil would be figuring out how to let McGarvey know where he had her. That would take time, during which Katy would be relatively safe.

Hold on, darling, he thought.

He used his cell phone to call Liese in Switzerland. She answered out of breath on the first ring.

"Oui."

"Are you ready?"

"Very nearly," she answered. "Within the hour."

"Be careful," McGarvey said. He broke the connection and called Rencke, who also answered on the first ring as if he too had been expecting the call.

"There's a storm sewer that opens at the rear of the embassy. You can get into the tunnel on G Street just off Juarez Circle."

"Have you faxed that on an open line to my house yet?" McGarvey asked.

"It's set to go by fax and by unencrypted e-mail to the house," Rencke said. "I want to make it real easy for them."

"Do it," McGarvey said. "Then keep your head down; there'll be a lot of heat."

Rencke laughed, but it sounded vicious. "They don't know what heat is if they hurt Mrs. M."

"Nobody knows where I am."

"Right," Rencke said.

A Mercedes pulled up in front of Yarnell's old house. A slightly built man in a shirt and tie but no jacket, carrying what looked to be a small briefcase, came out of the Arab Center, passed through the gate, and got into the car, which immediately departed.

McGarvey got the impression that the briefcase might have been a doctor's bag, but he didn't want to take that thought any further. For the moment he was doing everything he could.

He telephoned his daughter, and she answered immediately.

"Daddy, are you ready?" she asked. There were traffic sounds in the background.

"I'm in position," McGarvey told her. "Where are you?"

"In front of the embassy, and there are a lot of nervous-looking people over there. Soon as I pulled up and started taking pictures, three guards came out. They're there right now, taking pictures of me."

It was what McGarvey had expected would happen. Now he wanted to ratchet up the pressure. "How many people have you got over there?"

"Just me for now," Elizabeth said. "But Todd is on the way with three surveillance teams and vans. They should be here any minute, and we'll hit them with everything we've got."

"No gunplay," McGarvey warned. "If it seems to be heading that way, call DC Metro and get the hell out of there."

"Soon as Mom's free."

"What about their utilities?"

"Their water goes off in about five minutes, and Otto gave me a computer program to cut electricity. Soon as you give me the word, it's a done deal."

Down on the street another black Mercedes passed in front of the Arab Center, but did not stop.

"Thirty minutes, sweetheart," McGarvey told his daughter. "Don't do anything stupid."

"No," she promised. "We're just going to make the bastards real nervous."

McGarvey broke the connection, laid the telephone on the small table, then unholstered his pistol, placed it next to the phone, and sat back to wait.

SIXTY

Inside the embassy an extremely nervous Nuaimi finished his difficult phone call to Riyadh. Neither the ambassador nor Crown Prince Abdullah had offered to help with what was escalating into an impossible situation. They were leaving the problem to him.

No matter what happened he would take the blame. In the end he would be recalled home in disgrace.

His telephone rang, but it was Ali bin Besharati, chief of embassy security. "In addition to the car there are now four vans across the street. They are bombarding us with electronic and laser pulses."

"Get rid of them," Nuaimi shouted.

"I'm sorry, but that's impossible. They are on a public street and are breaking no American laws. I can direct one of my people to walk over and ask them to leave."

Nuaimi tried to get himself together. He lowered his voice. "No, that's not advisable. Just have your people hold their posts. No one is to be allowed in or out of the building for the time being."

"I understand," bin Besharati said.

You don't understand anything, you fool. "See to it."

"Yes, Your Excellency. But there is another problem, and it may be somehow related."

"What is it?" Nuaimi demanded, impatiently.

"Our water has stopped flowing."

"What are you talking about?" Nuaimi practically shouted. What was happening? His entire career was blowing away like a bit of cloth in a wind.

"All the water faucets and toilets in the building have ceased to function. Our engineer believes that there may be a problem with the water main out on the street."

"Get it fixed——" Nuaimi said, but then stopped. His eyes went to the lamp on his desk. He flipped the switch and it came on. Whatever U.S. agency was outside spying on them—probably the FBI—had not shut off the utilities to isolate the embassy. The water was just an annoying problem. "Call the city or whatever agency supplies our water service, and report the problem."

"Yes, Your Excellency," bin Besharati said.

Nuaimi buzzed his secretary. "Where is al-Kaseem?"

"I don't know, Your Excellency. Shall I find him for you?"

"Yes, immediately."

"Prince Salman has returned, sir. He would like just a moment of your time."

For a fleeting moment Nuaimi wondered if the prince's trouble in Monaco with the former director of the CIA was connected to what was happening across the street. But then he dismissed the notion as melodramatic. Americans were cowboys, but the government did not operate in such a fashion.

"Send him in, but as soon as you locate al-Kaseem I want to speak with him."

"Yes, sir."

Nuaimi had risen to the post of deputy ambassador to the most important nation on earth not because of his family name, but because he was a skilled diplomat. He had worked in various capacities at embassies around the world, from Moscow to London and from Damascus to Tokyo, where he'd learned the business. In this situation, with another bin Laden attack against the U.S. on the verge of happening, he was in the most precarious position of his career. If he did nothing he would be finished. Which, he begin to realize, actually gave him the power to do whatever he wanted. Within reason.

One small step at a time. That was the diplomat's credo, Nuaimi thought, as prince Salman came in. *And perhaps the prince could be the first step.*

"I've reconsidered," Salman said. "I don't think Washington is the place for me to be at this moment. So I'm going home."

Nuaimi's spirits sank. He'd had the vague thought of using the prince as an emissary to the White House. At the very least he might be able to learn why the embassy had become the target of a surveillance operation. "Perhaps I was being too hasty, suggesting you leave."

Salman was amused. "Not at all," he said. "Is your telephone secure?"

Nuaimi was confused by the question. "Normally I would say yes, but considering what is happening across the street, I could not guarantee it."

"Good," Salman said. "In that case I would like to use it to let my staff in Lucerne know that I am returning. I want to make sure that when I walk out the front door I will be expected. Considering the climate in Washington, it would not do to make a sudden, unexpected move." He gave Nuaimi a sly look. "I don't think my presence here is wanted. Calling from your desk might be worth something for you."

"Of course," Nuaimi said, and he sat back as Salman came around the desk and direct-dialed his compound on the Swiss lake.

He spoke for only a half minute, informing his people that he would be returning no later than sometime the next day, his work here nearly finished.

"Thank you," he told Nuaimi after he'd hung up. "When I return, I'll speak to my uncle about you."

"That is very kind, Your Excellency," Nuaimi said, and Salman walked out. *What work had he come here to do that was nearly finished?* Nuaimi wondered.

His secretary called. "Mr. al-Kaseem does not answer his page, sir. No one has seen him since earlier this morning."

Nuaimi felt a sense of fatalism. He was the deputy ambassador. He was a diplomat. It was time to live up to his position, because he no longer had anything to lose. "Get me the White House. I wish to speak to President Haynes about why we are being surveilled contrary to international conventions."

Khalil and the cameraman had left the cell to give Kathleen time to think over the threat to abort the baby, but in the fifteen minutes since they left she was no closer to making a decision. She was frightened, and she didn't know what to do.

She sat on the cot, her back against the wall, tightly hugging herself for warmth and to stop from shaking. She wanted to cry, but the tears wouldn't come, and her mouth was still dry. It was as if her entire body was drying out. Even the bleeding seemed to have diminished. Nor was she in much pain now that the injection the doctor had given her had kicked in.

She didn't want to die. Not here, not like this, without ever having a chance to see Kirk again. Just one more time she wanted to look into his face, feel his arms around her.

It had been a stupid act of vanity driving down here and showing herself in front of Yarnell's old house. Elizabeth would have told her father by now, and God only knew what Kirk was in the act of doing. People were probably going to die because of her stupid pride. She was the wife of the former director of the CIA, one of the Company's top agents ever. News of her kidnapping had probably reached the White House by now. It was another bit of trouble in an already deeply troubling time.

It had been her plan to find out if Khalil was staying at the Arab Center by driving up and parking across the street. If he was inside and he spotted her sitting there, he might worry that Kirk would be coming after him and Khalil would do something foolish, like bolt. But she realized now that she'd never had the real measure of the man. After his failure in Alaska, he'd become like a cornered animal, fighting for its life.

Kathleen looked up, another thought coming to the forefront. *She was alive.* They hadn't killed her yet. And just like in Alaska, on the fantail of the cruise ship, in the cold and dark when she didn't think she would survive, something happened. Kirk happened. Lovely, strong, impossible man.

She owed him now. For Kirk and the baby and Elizabeth and Todd, she had to remain alive, had to keep the baby safe.

She got shakily to her feet and staggered to the door. She pounded on it. "Hey," she shouted, her voice weak. "Hey. I'll make the tape. Come back."

Someone was outside the door. She stepped well back, and then straightened her pajama top and fluffed her hair as best she could without a mirror.

The door opened, and the cameraman, short, thick-necked, was there. "What is it?" he demanded. His accent was harsh.

"I've changed my mind," Kathleen said, careful to keep her voice steady. "I'll read the statement."

"I'll tell him," the cameraman said, and he started to close the door.

"Wait!" Kathleen shouted. "May I have a glass of water, please?"

The man laughed and closed the door.

Kathleen closed her eyes for a moment. *I will be strong. I will survive.* She went back to the cot and picked up the script Khalil had given her. She didn't know for sure where she was, but she thought it was possible they'd brought her to the Saudi Embassy. As she read the message she was supposed to read for the camera, she tried to figure out a way to indicate where she was. She didn't know Morse code, so she couldn't blink out a message, but there had to be a way, and she was determined to figure it out.

The door opened again and Khalil came in. "You have decided to co-operate?"

She looked into his cobra eyes, and the words stuck in her throat. She nodded.

SIXTY-ONE

☐

There was no traffic on the lake road, the sun low behind the mountains to the west, and Liese drove recklessly, on her way into a situation that would not only get her fired, but could also send her to jail or even to her grave. Her eyes were full and her heart ached, but she felt no fear.

This was for Kirk, even though she finally knew that she would never have him.

Prince Salman's call to the compound had come up on one of the monitors, and Ziegler had recorded it along with Sergeant Hoenecker's simultaneous translation just as Liese was getting set to head out. She had no idea what it meant that Salman was suddenly leaving Washington. It made no sense if he'd gone there in the first place to confront McGarvey, and if he had kidnapped Kirk's wife.

But the prince was returning to Switzerland, and before Liese had left the chalet, Hoenecker was on the phone to Gertner, the one man that Liese did not want to speak to.

Her telephone buzzed against her hip. It was Gertner already trying to reach her. She had told no one she was leaving, or where she was going. She had just slipped out of the chalet and driven off.

She let the call roll over to the answering machine in her apartment. They wouldn't have long to wait before they found out where she had gone, and then the clock would start. It was possible she would not be able to get in, and it was equally possible that seeing what she was up to, Gertner might order a raid on the compound. Not to rescue her, but to arrest her.

Liese wanted to pull over to the side of the road and close her eyes and her mind to the world around her. But that had become impossible on the very first day she had laid eyes on Kirk, and had instantly fallen head over heels in love. Marta had called it a schoolgirl crush, an infatuation, but now more than ten years later she still felt the same. She was miserable.

Taking her pistol out of her purse, she stuck it in the waistband of her jeans and pulled her jacket down so that it was hidden. Any time a weapon was introduced into a situation, there was a danger that someone would get hurt. But she was a professional, and so were the security people at the prince's compound, which reduced the odds of an accident. The last thing she wanted was to hurt the prince's wife or his children. He might be a terrorist, but they were innocent.

Do it now, she thought, *before Gertner sends someone.*

A cool breeze came down from the mountain passes, and the sailing fleet was back on the lake, the spinnakers ballooned out as they raced toward the downwind mark. She caught glimpses of them through the trees as she drove around the bay and then headed back up the private road to the Salman compound at the end of the narrow peninsula jutting out into the lake.

Peaceful. It was the only word Liese could think of. And it stuck in her mind how far away this place was from America, which was facing another 9/11. The Swiss had always been the neutrals. But not this time, she thought.

And for that there would be a scapegoat.

Prince Salman's compound consisted of the main sprawling chalet with two separate living wings one for the prince and the other for his wife and children. There were several outbuildings, including two garages, living quarters for the security and house staff, a maintenance shed, a boathouse, and a long dock at the foot of the shallow hill.

Most of the year it was only the wife and the staff who were in residence. The children were normally away at boarding school, and the prince himself came home only a few times each year, usually to stay no longer than a week or two.

Except during the major terrorist strikes. Each time he withdrew his children from school and hunkered down with his family for a month or more. They would play on the lake aboard one of several powerboats and sailboats, or go into town to the theater or to dinner. Sometimes they even left the compound to take trips up into the mountain resort towns, just like ordinary tourists.

Not a terrorist and his family. Not a monster who the world feared and loathed. Not bin Laden's number-one lieutenant and killer.

A couple of hundred meters down from the house, which was hidden from view by the trees, the road was blocked by a security gate with a closed-circuit television camera and intercom system. Liese pulled up, took her police wallet with badge and ID card out of her purse, lowered her window, and pushed the intercom button. She held up the open wallet to the camera.

Almost immediately a man's voice, speaking heavily accented French, came from the grille. "Good afternoon, Officer Fuelm. What is the business of the Swiss police here?"

"I have a message for Mrs. Salman," Liese said. She could imagine the confusion now among her colleagues across the bay. Hoenecker would be on the phone to Gertner.

"Give me the message. I will make sure that madam receives it."

"I don't know who you are, though I'm assuming that you're one of her security people. But this message is for her alone, and I have been instructed to give it only to her." The only chance she had of pulling this off in the time Kirk wanted was to get through the gate and up to the house. If this failed, her only other option would be to come back tonight after dark and either breach the perimeter fence, or approach the compound from the water. Kirk would understand.

"That's quite impossible, Sergeant. The Madam is not at home—"

"She's not only at home, but her children were recalled from school and are there with her. In addition, her husband, the prince, will very soon be en route from Washington. I must speak with her right now."

The security staff personnel were all Saudi private contractors, ex-military or intelligence officers, who understood that their presence on Swiss soil with weapons was strictly illegal. The authorities turned a blind eye to this disregard for Swiss law because of Prince Salman's political and financial importance, and only so long as there were no incidents. They also understood now, if they didn't know before, that the comings and goings at the compound were being monitored.

In the past there had been no trouble, and the staff had very probably been ordered to be cooperative. Liese was counting on it. Just as she was counting on them not to make any show of force. Most of the staff would be out of sight.

The speaker grille was silent for several seconds.

"Very well," the security officer said. "The princess will receive you."

"I will need to see the children as well," Liese said. "This is a matter concerning the school."

There was another brief pause.

"Very well. Do not stop or deviate from the road, s'il vous plaît."

The electric gate swung inward, and Liese started up the driveway to the house, her gut tied in a knot. This situation had all the earmarks of a disaster in the making. But she had come this far and she would see it through. And considering what Kirk was facing in Washington and what the entire U.S. was staring down the barrel at, this move could work to avert another tremendous disaster.

As the road came out of the woods and the main house came into view, Liese glanced across the bay. LeFevre would be at the spotter scope looking at her face. She tried to will him a message not to let Gertner do anything stupid. All she needed was a few minutes. Once she was in and had control of the situation, there was little any of them could do.

Kirk had promised that he would need only a few hours. It would be up to her to hold out that long, and make sure that no one got hurt.

She pulled up directly in front of the main house, in plain view not only of someone inside, but of LeFevre and the others. As she got out of the car and walked up, the chalet's front door opened, and a very large man stood there, in black slacks and a dark short-sleeved pullover that was tight across his thick shoulders. If he was carrying, it was not obvious.

"The princess and the children will be down momentarily," the security officer said. His thick accent was the same as that of the man she'd spoken to over the intercom. He wasn't smiling. He held out his hand. "Your identification."

She opened her ID wallet and held it up for him to see.

He took it, and carefully inspected the badge and then the photograph, comparing it to her face. He grunted. "I'll keep this until you leave."

This was the first test of who would be controlling the situation. Liese shook her head and held out her hand. "No," she said, emphatically.

The security officer scowled. But he handed over the wallet, which she put back in her purse.

"Are you armed?"

Liese looked up, returning his scowl. "Most Swiss Federal Polizei do not carry firearms. They do not see the necessity. What is your name and position here?"

The security officer didn't flinch. "My name is Sayyid Salah. I am the butler."

Liese stifled a laugh. "Very well, Mr. Salah. The sooner I can speak with the princess and children, the sooner I'll be gone."

The security officer stepped aside to allow Liese to enter, and then he directed her through the short entry hall, with its heavily carved wooden coat rack and mirror, into the great room, just as Salman's wife, the Princess Sofia, came down the stairs, followed by four children. The princess was a diminutive woman, with a tiny round face and very large, very dark eyes. She was not dressed in traditional Muslim garb. Like her three girls and one boy she wore blue jeans, a tee shirt, and sneakers. The children ranged in age from seven to thirteen, and except for their dark coloration and Semitic noses they could have been typical Swiss kids. They smiled uncertainly.

Liese felt absolutely rotten for being here like this. She could understand Mac's reasoning, and yet this was all wrong in her mind. She wasn't going to harm them, but they would not know it. Once she pulled out her pistol they would be terrified.

"*Bonjour, Mademoiselle,*" the princess said. Her voice was mellifluous, her French accent good. "I am Sofia Salman, and these are my children."

Liese wanted to apologize, say there had been a mistake, and get the hell out of there. But beyond doing this for Kirk, she had a clear vision of the television images from 9/11 in New York and Washington and Pennsylvania. Especially the World Trade Center towers coming down. Of couples hand in hand leaping to their deaths from the buildings to escape the horrible flames.

Bin Laden had been the spiritual leader for that horrible day, but Khalil had been the major planner, the guiding force. The concept for the attacks had come from his warped brain. And so had whatever was going to happen in America next. More people would die, unless he was stopped. This time bin Laden promised to strike at children.

"*Mademoiselle?*" the princess prompted.

They stood in tableau for a second, the princess and her children at the foot of the sweeping staircase that led to the upper floor, the security officer at the entry hall three meters behind Liese's left shoulder.

"*Je suis desolée, Madame,*" Liese said. She pulled out her pistol, as she turned left toward the security officer to present less of herself as a target.

The man reached for something at the small of his back.

"Do not go for your weapon," Liese ordered, sharply. "I mean the princess and her children no harm, but I will shoot you!"

The security officer hesitated for just a second, then slowly brought both hands up and away from his body. There was a calculating look in his eyes. He was a pro. He would be patient and wait for her to make a mistake.

Liese glanced at the princess, who had gathered her girls, but the ten-year-old boy stood defiantly in front of his mother and sisters, ready like a good Bedouin man to defend his womenfolk. Liese felt horrible.

The security officer had begun to lower his right hand.

"Goddamn you son of a bitch, I'll blow your fucking head off if you don't turn this instant and get out of here," Liese shouted.

Another man, dressed in a Western business suit, appeared from the back of the house from the opposite side of the great room, and stopped. His hands were in plain sight, but Liese was now caught in the middle of the two men. From a defensive stance she was in a very bad position. She could not cover both of them.

She switched her aim to the princess. "Do nothing foolish and we'll all walk away from this. I mean nobody any harm. I promise you." She tried to make the princess and her children see that she was telling the truth, but it was not possible. A crazy woman was holding a gun on them.

"Lower your weapon, and you will be allowed to leave here," the man from the far end of the room told her, reasonably. "No one will interfere with you."

"I can't do that," Liese replied. "I want both of you out of here now."

"What do you want here, Sergeant Fuelm?" the security officer in the suit asked. "Or should we telephone your superiors and let them talk to you?"

"I wouldn't advise that," Liese said. "I'm only going to need a few hours."

"Why shouldn't we inform your superiors?"

"Because then the Kantonpolizei would *officially* know that Prince Salman's actual identity is that of the terrorist we call Khalil."

The princess gasped. She said something to the security officer in the business suit.

"I don't know what fantasy you have deduced that from, but you are wrong, Mademoiselle," the security officer said. "Your error could very well cost you your life before this day is done." The man was maddeningly calm. He could have been discussing the weather. "You have one last opportunity to lower your weapon and leave in peace. If you do not, we will be forced to kill you."

"*Insha'allah*," Liese said.

The boy started to say something, but Liese looked directly into the princess's eyes and drew back the Walther's hammer. The princess pulled her son to her.

"Very well," the security officer said. "We will get out of your way. And we will do as you wish and not call your superiors—though by now I suspect you must understand that because of Prince Salman's position within the royal family we will have to inform Riyadh. What might happen after that will be out of my control."

"Leave," Liese told him, "and nobody gets hurt."

"As you wish." The security officer said something to the princess, and then he and the man who'd answered the door withdrew.

"What do you want with us?" the princess said. "You're crazy if you think my husband is a terrorist. He is a playboy, not a murderer."

Liese nodded. "I sincerely hope that you're right." She motioned toward the grouping of furniture in front of the huge, freestanding fireplace. "Sit down, please. If you'd like, call someone to bring you something to drink, eat."

The princess straightened up. "We will sit as you order, since it is you holding a weapon pointed at me and my children. But we will not eat or drink, nor will you be given refreshments." The woman's left eyebrow arched. "Unless, of course, you mean to slaughter us all for a glass of water."

What had happened to them all in the past ten years? The Soviet Union had disintegrated. The cold war had been won by the West. Then the world had begun sinking into utter chaos.

The princess herded her children to the modernistic white leather couch, and the youngest girl, with long dark hair and big eyes just like her mother, began to cry. Her mother said something to her and then gathered her up.

Keeping her pistol trained on the princess, Liese took her cell phone out of her purse and speed-dialed McGarvey's number. It answered on the first ring.

"Are you in?"

"Yes."

"Has anyone been hurt?" McGarvey asked, and Liese could hear the genuine concern in his voice. It was reassuring.

"Everyone is fine. Frightened, but okay," she said. "But this is bad, Kirk."

"I know," he said, "but we didn't create the situation. They did. Just give me a couple of hours. I'll call when we're set here with the answers."

"Kirk? They deny it."

McGarvey hesitated. "They might not know, Liese. They're innocents." He hesitated again. "That's the difference between us. It'll always be the difference. We don't harm innocent people to make political statements."

Except now, Liese thought.

SIXTY-TWO

☐

Sitting in her mother's car directly across the tree-lined street from the front entrance to the Saudi Embassy, Elizabeth waited for the signal from her husband that the street from the Watergate Hotel and apartments had been blocked to traffic. So far they'd not been interfered with. Though by now DC Metro would have been informed that something was going on down here. And the Bureau would be getting into the act soon because somebody from the embassy was probably raising hell.

Besides Elizabeth's car, CIA surveillance teams were working from four vans—one parked directly behind her, one at each end of the street, and one at the rear of the Saudi compound across from the loading ramp, which led down into the basement parking garage. In the past ten minutes two limos with smoked windows had left the embassy.

Todd's voice came into her earpiece. "We're in place. Nobody else is leaving for now."

"Copy," Elizabeth spoke into her lapel mike. "Any sign of the cops or the federales at your end?"

"Not yet, Liz. But they're coming."

Elizabeth looked in her door mirror. She could see the tail end of

Todd's van, but there didn't seem to be any activity up there. "Have you picked up something on DC Metro's Tac One?" It was the FM radio channel that police dispatch used to communicate with its units on the streets.

"No. But Adkins called my cell phone and wanted to know what the hell we were doing, and was your dad down here with us."

"What'd you tell him?" Elizabeth demanded.

"That we were putting pressure on the embassy to flush your mother out. That your dad wasn't here and so far as we knew he was at home where he should be."

"Did he buy it?" Elizabeth asked. All her father wanted was a couple of hours.

Todd chuckled. "No way. But he didn't press me. He just warned me that Fred Rudolph was raising holy hell, and that the Bureau was probably coming our way."

"It's going to get real interesting around here with DC Metro and the Bureau trying to figure out what we're up to."

"That'll take at least a couple of hours, don't you think, darling?" Todd asked.

Elizabeth smiled wickedly. "At least," she said. "Okay, boys and girls, stand by. It's showtime." Her laptop was connected to the CIA's mainframe via the Internet. The program she was tapped into had been created less than an hour ago by Rencke; it could take control of the electrical power grid for the entire city and the surrounding areas out to, but not including, Dulles International. Otto had isolated the area of the Saudi Embassy.

Elizabeth clicked on that line. When it was highlighted, she hit Enter.

It would take ten seconds for the proper relays to be opened, and then the lights would go out. After that it was anyone's guess what would happen. But the pressure would be on.

She speed-dialed her father's cell phone. He answered immediately.
"Yes."

"Less than ten seconds," she told him.

"Anything from the Bureau yet?"

"No, but they're on the way. Rudolph is putting the squeeze on Adkins."
There was a pause for just a moment.

"Okay, sweetheart, nobody gets hurt down there," McGarvey said. "Do you understand what I'm saying? If there's even a hint of trouble coming your way, I want you and the others to immediately bail out. No grand-standing. Your mother's not in the embassy in any event. All you guys are doing is providing me with a diversion."

But Elizabeth knew that people *were* going to get hurt, probably killed, though not here at the embassy. "When are you going in?"

"I have one phone call to make that could put an end to this business right now," McGarvey said. "It's worth a try."

Elizabeth closed her eyes for a second. She had read her father's file. *The complete file.* She knew what he was capable of, just as she knew that like any really good soldier or field officer, he always did everything in his power to *avoid* conflict.

She opened her eyes as electricity to the entire block went off. The red lights on the security cameras in front of the embassy winked out, and the traffic signals at the end of the street went dead.

"The power's off," she told her father.

"Stall them as long as you can, sweetheart," McGarvey said.

"Good luck, Daddy," Elizabeth said, but her father was already gone, and in the distance she could hear the first of the police sirens.

Across the street in his fifth-floor office, Nuaimi had just gotten through to Dennis Berndt over at the White House when his telephone went dead. At first he thought that, as incredible as it seemed, the president's national security adviser had actually hung up on him. But when he tried to buzz his secretary to call again, he realized that the buttons on his phone console were all dead.

He slammed down the phone and switched on his light. But it too was dead. The faulty plumbing was not an isolated incident after all. Someone had cut their water, and now the electricity was off.

Pushing away from his desk, Nuaimi went to the door and threw it open. His secretary, startled, looked up. "The electricity has failed, Your Excellency."

"Get me Besharati—" Nuaimi said, just as his chief of security walked through the door.

"The water was no coincidence," the man said. He was tall, and lean as a greyhound, and he made most people he came into contact with nervous. Nuaimi thought of him as a Nazi, but he was very capable at his job. "Apparently we're under assault. I'd suggest that you place a call to the secretary of state and demand an explanation."

"The phones are dead."

Besharati handed him a cell phone. "Make the call now, Your Excellency, before the situation gets out of hand." His attitude was demeaning, and peremptory.

Nuaimi took immediate offense because he stupidly had not thought of using a cell phone. "Who do you think you are?" he demanded, sharply.

"I'm sorry, Your Excellency. I was merely trying to assist you—"

"Then take a dozen of your men, with arms, and surround this building as a show of force."

Besharati looked amused. "I do not think that is advisable—"

"I didn't ask for your opinion," Nuaimi said. "I gave you an order, and I expect that you will carry it out immediately."

Besharati lowered his eyes and nodded. "As you wish, Your Excellency." He turned and walked out, leaving Nuaimi wondering what in Allah's name bin Laden's people could be thinking. It was common knowledge that members of the Saudi royal family had been supplying the terrorist with money all along. But after the terrible attacks of 9/11, he thought Crown Prince Abdullah might have reined them in.

Apparently not.

SIXTY-THREE

It was ten o'clock in the evening in Riyadh when McGarvey reached the direct line to Prince Muhamed bin Abdul Aziz, head of the Saudi Secret Intelligence Service. The number was known to only a few members of the Royal family as well as the heads of a number of friendly intelligence agencies around the world. The CIA was one of them.

"This cannot be Richard Adkins calling from Amsterdam. So it must be Kirk McGarvey calling from a redialer service," Prince Muhamed said. "Good evening."

"I'll get right to the point," McGarvey said. "You have a lot of trouble heading your way that can be avoided if we can come to an understanding." He had worked with the prince on several occasions, but he'd never been able to read the man behind the dark glasses and flowing robes.

"Yes, the situation is very delicate," Prince Muhamed replied. He sounded like a man without a care in the world, but it was the attitude he always projected. No one in the West had ever witnessed his anger. "But under the circumstances I have nothing to gain by talking with you."

"Are you aware of the present situation here in Washington?" McGarvey asked.

"I am aware of many situations."

"Let's cut the bullshit, Muhamed," McGarvey shot back. "You know we're facing another attack, and it's due to happen in less than forty-eight hours. You also know that I resigned as DCI, and I'm on my own. So I'm not going to screw around with you. I called you merely as a courtesy. Maybe you and I can avoid a serious amount of bloodshed. If you'll cooperate this time."

The line was silent for a moment.

By now McGarvey figured that the prince had rolled the call over to his technical services to try to identify the redialer server so that they could pinpoint McGarvey's location. But Rencke had set it up so Saudi intelligence was wasting its time and resources.

"I'm listening, Mr. McGarvey," Prince Muhamed said.

"The CIA has gathered a reasonable amount of evidence to suggest that Prince Abdul Salman and the al-Quaida terrorist Khalil are the same man."

Prince Muhamed laughed softly "Yes, I understand that may have precipitated your resignation, and was the reason you drove the poor man out of Monaco. But you are wrong, of course."

McGarvey hadn't expected any other answer at this point. "It's what you would have to say out of loyalty to the family. But there's more."

"Of course there is."

"The prince is here in Washington," McGarvey said.

"He thought it would provide him a safe haven, being close to President Haynes, two men with mutual respect and admiration for each other."

"Khalil is here as well."

"If he is, then it must be a coincidence," Prince Muhamed said. "We have no connection with al-Quaida, a fact that must be apparent. Goodness, we have suffered our share of casualties. Their attacks are not confined to your country." The prince's voice had not risen at all, though McGarvey could hear his anger. "How much blood must we shed, and how much oil must we pump to supply your love of SUVs, for you to finally understand that Saudi Arabia is a friend to the U.S. and always has been? Without our oil your country would be nothing."

"Without our money, you would all go back to living on the desert in tents. Without our technical help even your water would stop flowing. And without our military you would have been invaded years ago by the Soviets, or maybe Saddam Hussein would have gone directly from Kuwait City to Riyadh."

The prince was silent again.

"Was it also a coincidence that when Khalil was attempting to kidnap our former secretary of defense from a cruise ship in Canadian waters that Prince Salman was in Canada? The west coast of Canada?"

"I know the prince personally," Prince Muhamed said. "In fact, we are related. Distantly. He is a deal maker and a playboy, arrogant and headstrong, a gambler and a womanizer. But he is not a terrorist. I give you my word, Mr. McGarvey."

"He has kidnapped my wife, and I have arranged the kidnapping of his family in Switzerland. Right now they're being held as hostages."

"It was you," the prince said, and this time he sounded shook. "What are you trying to do, get an innocent woman and her children harmed? Prince Salman's chief of security called me from Lucerne with the wild story that a Swiss Federal Police officer barged in, gun drawn, and took Princess Sofia and her four children."

"I believe you call such acts collateral damage," McGarvey said, coldly.

"This is monstrous—"

"So were the 9/11 attacks on our people," McGarvey interrupted.

"Tell your friend to walk away from the prince's home without causing any harm to the princess and her children, and she will be allowed to leave the compound alive," Prince Muhamed said. "Otherwise I will authorize the use of deadly force. The women and her children are innocents—"

"There are no innocents," McGarvey interrupted again, coming down hard on the prince. "I got that directly from bin Laden himself."

"We are not involved with al-Quaida," the prince shouted.

"Bullshit!" McGarvey shouted back. "Pure, unadulterated bullshit. Now, you listen to me, Muhamed. You're a bright man, and you have connections and influence. One, I want the immediate withdrawal of the terrorists here in my country. Two, I want an immediate exchange of hostages, my wife for Prince Salman's wife and children."

"Do you actually believe that your wife is being held at our embassy? Is that why it's under siege?"

"Do it now, Muhamed, and no one need get hurt. Except for Khalil. He's mine," McGarvey said. "I want your word."

"I cannot give my word for something outside my abilities," Prince Muhamed replied, heavily. "This is a very bad business between us. Your attack on our embassy will not be perceived well in the Arab world. And should some harm come to a member of the royal family, relations between our two countries will be strained even further. Perhaps to the breaking point."

"Where was the outrage in the Arab world over 9/11?" McGarvey asked. He had hoped to gain something from the prince, but he wasn't surprised that he'd been stonewalled. "The princess and her children will be released in two hours. Tell the security people there not to do anything foolish in the meantime."

"It is you who is being the fool," Prince Muhamed said.

"Continue to attack us and we will strike back," McGarvey said. "Afghanistan and Iraq were just the first." He broke the connection.

Pocketing his cell phone, McGarvey hoped he had at least bought Liese some time. Prince Muhamed was a powerful man within the royal family, and he would have a great deal of influence on the security people at Salman's Lucerne compound. McGarvey got up, holstered his pistol, and checked out the window. There was no activity across the street, and only the occasional car driving past.

He checked the blocks of Semtex and fuses, pulled on his jacket, and left the apartment, taking the elevator all the way down to the basement where he could leave the building from the loading area in the rear.

If he could reach the back entrance to Yarnell's old house without being detected, he would have the advantage of surprise for the first several seconds. Enough, he thought, to get him inside.

For Katy. For the woman and child they'd tossed off the cruise ship. For 9/11. For every other horror men like bin Laden and his fanatical followers had done and were threatening to do.

Payback time started now.

SIXTY-FOUR

☐

Khalil had just reached the communications room with the video disk of Kathleen McGarvey's statement when al-Kaseem, out of breath and with an angry scowl on his bland features, caught up with him. Khalil thought the man looked ill, on the verge of a stroke.

Definitely the wrong sort to head up Saudi intelligence's U.S. operations.

"I just got off the satellite phone with Prince Muhamed," al-Kaseem practically shouted. "A friend of McGarvey's is holding Princess Sofia and the children at gunpoint outside Lucerne."

Khalil considered this news for a moment, then shrugged. "If they die, they will become martyrs."

Al-Kaseem's eyes widened. "You cold bastard, you don't know what you've started."

"I know very well."

"I demand that you leave immediately."

"You don't have that authority," Khalil told him, contemptuously. "But in any event you'll get your wish soon. Less than forty-eight hours."

Al-Kaseem threw up his hands, a very rude gesture for an Arab. "The situation here will not last that long, you idiot."

The man had gone too far. Khalil shoved him up against the wall, pulled out his stiletto, and brought the blade to al-Kaseem's face, the razor-sharp point less than an inch from the intelligence chief's left eye.

"I find your lack of respect and bad manners irritating."

Al-Kaseem was not cowed. "McGarvey called Prince Muhamed a few minutes ago. Offered to trade his wife for the princess and the children."

It was something new. Khalil had not thought men of McGarvey's ilk were capable of such interesting, and certainly logical, acts, not with all their foolish talk about innocents. "What else did he tell the prince?"

"He said he was coming after you. No one else need get hurt, except for you." Al-Kaseem reached up and eased the stiletto blade away from his face. "He's very close, because he promised Prince Muhamed that the princess and children would be released in two hours."

They were in the third-story corridor on the southwest side of the building, directly below the west-facing satellite dish on the roof. Khalil cocked an ear to listen. The building seemed quieter than it had earlier in the day. Al-Kaseem was watching him, a mixture of disgust and even contempt in his eyes.

"If he finds out where you are, he'll come after you," al-Kaseem said.

"I think he already has it figured out," Khalil said. "How many people are left in the building besides us?"

"Everyone's here. We've just suspended most operations until the situation is resolved."

Khalil nodded toward the door to the communications room. "Have you shut down the satellite feed as well?"

"Not yet," al-Kaseem said.

"Good, I have a video to send." Khalil released his hold on the chief of station, then sheathed his stiletto.

"What video? Where are you sending it?"

"You'll see," Khalil said. He opened the communication center's door with an electronic key card and went in.

The equipment-filled room was small, not much larger than a master bedroom in a large house. Two technicians were seated at computer terminals, the monitors blank. They looked up, surprised. The communications and computer center was the most classified section of the building, and very few people were authorized entry. Khalil wasn't one of them.

One of the technicians reached for a pistol in a drawer, when al-Kaseem came in and waved him off. "He's here on my authorization."

"Yes, sir," the young man said.

"In fact, I want both of you to leave us. Get a cup of tea. We'll only be a few minutes."

The two men got up and left.

Al-Kaseem held out his hand for the video disk. "I assume this is Mc-Garvey's wife. Where are you sending it?"

"Al Jazeera," Khalil said.

Al-Kaseem shook his head. "I'll say it again: You're a cold bastard. You'll get us all killed. If McGarvey can't get to you today, he won't ever stop once he sees whatever it is you've made her say."

"In two days it won't matter," Khalil said.

Al-Kaseem gave him a hard look. "You and the woman need to be long gone from here before then. I will take this to Crown Prince Abdullah. There is much more at stake here than you can know. Political stakes."

Khalil gave the disk to al-Kaseem, who put it in the CD tray of one of the computers, brought that drive up, and double-clicked the Video icon. The image showed Kathleen, dressed in the same type of cotton pajamas that the Afghani and Iraqi prisoners of war had been made to wear, seated on the edge of a narrow cot, her hands folded together in her lap.

The camera zoomed forward, her face filling the screen. She had been beaten. Her eyes were already blackening, and the right side of her jaw was red and swollen. For all that, al-Kaseem thought she was a strikingly handsome woman, for whom her husband would commit murder.

"My name is Kathleen McGarvey, and I have a message for all the mothers and fathers of all the children in the great Satan nation, the United States."

"How long is this recording?" al-Kaseem asked.

"Two minutes. It was enough."

"Another blow for freedom will soon be struck against our children, but it need not happen. President Haynes must go before the United Nations today, and make the following declarations before the world. All U.S. and allied forces will make immediate preparations to leave Afghanistan, Iraq, and South Korea. In addition, all U.S. military forces, as well as all Christians, must immediately leave the Arabian Peninsula."

"That will never happen as long as they need our oil," al-Kaseem said. "No matter how many blows are struck against them. They learned their lesson from Vietnam."

A faint smile crossed Khalil's lips. He sincerely hoped that the demands were not met in his lifetime. This struggle was the very thing he had been born for. The only thing for which he lived. Without it he would be nothing.

"*It is no different than in 1776 when the valiant American freedom fighters forced their oppressive masters off the land,*" Kathleen continued. "*And today America and England are partners.*"

Watching the video, Khalil was struck again by the woman's strength, and once again he resolved to bring her back to the Saudi desert with him, no matter how impossible that idea was. He wanted first to kill her husband, and then he wanted to spend time with this woman. He wanted to teach her humility. He wanted to see her crawl on her knees to him, to beg his forgiveness, to grovel like an animal in the dust in front of him. He smiled inwardly. She would wash his feet before each prayer, and then prepare and serve his meals.

Her death, he decided, would be a particularly fruitful event.

Kathleen continued to read the words that Khalil had written for her, but he was no longer listening. There had to be a way to get her out of the country before the attacks, because afterward the U.S. borders would be sealed tight. The only other alternative was to find a place inside the country where he could be safe until the initial furor died down. Oklahoma City, perhaps. There was a very active al-Quaida cell there.

Al-Kaseem was looking at him. "If you order me to send this video to Al Jazeera, I'll do it. But then you will have to leave within twenty-four hours."

Khalil decided not to kill the man yet. But it was going to give him pleasure when he did. The chief of station had lived for too long in the West. He had practically become one of them.

"Send it," Khalil said. "I'll leave tonight."

Al-Kaseem hesitated for a moment, his jaw set, but then he nodded. "As you wish." He sat down at the computer, brought up the Internet, went to the Al Jazeera Web site, and attached the video file. He glanced up at Khalil, then turned back and hit the Send Now icon.

At that moment there was a small explosion somewhere directly below them.

"McGarvey," the chief of station said. "He's here already. The embassy attack was just a ruse."

Khalil headed for the door. "No one is to kill him. He's mine."

"What shall we do?" al-Kaseem demanded.

"Let him find his wife, of course."

SIXTY−FIVE

□

Dennis Berndt had attended numerous National Security Council meetings and other crisis gatherings, but never before had he seen a roomful of people with so much fear, anger, and confusion on their faces.

Herb Weissman was the first to arrive at the White House from his office in the J. Edgar Hoover Building, followed by Dick Adkins from Langley, Frank Hoover from downtown, and Crawford Anderson, from his office in the Old Executive Office Building. He was chief of DC operations for Homeland Security.

They gathered in the basement situation room, and Berndt was in charge until the president, running late, came down with his chief of staff.

"We need to figure out what we can do, and we don't have much time to come up with a recommendation," Berndt told them. There had been no need to go over the specifics with any of them; they were all in the loop. They'd had the better part of an hour to ponder the facts.

"Has anybody located McGarvey?" Weissman asked. "Fred Rudolph is in charge over at the embassy. As of fifteen minutes ago McGarvey had not surfaced, and his daughter isn't talking." He glanced at Adkins. "It's your surveillance teams over there who started all this, for God's sake. They won't back down."

"They won't until Mac's wife is released," Adkins said.

"If they're ordered, will they disobey?" Berndt asked, although he expected that he already knew the answer. All of them in the room did. As young as she was, Elizabeth Van Buren had already gained the reputation as a tough, capable field officer who in many respects was following in her father's footsteps. It was possible that if she continued on her present path, she would someday become deputy director of operations, a position no other woman had ever risen to.

"Frankly, I wouldn't want to give the order, Dennis."

Berndt was instantly angry. "We're in a no-win situation here, Dick. If the president orders them to stand down and they refuse, they would be subject to arrest. All of them."

Adkins shook his head. "You know better than that."

"I wouldn't care to send my people to do it," Weissman said. "Somebody could get hurt, and anyway we'd be playing right into the Saudis' hands. If they've got McGarvey's wife over there, they don't have a moral or diplomatic leg to stand on. If we start fighting among ourselves, they can claim anything they want." He looked around the table. "Hell, they could even admit they have her, but are concerned about her safety." He smiled ironically. "Fact is, she might be in the safest place in Washington right now."

The others agreed. "Which leaves us with McGarvey, because we sure as hell can't storm into somebody's embassy with the National Guard, guns drawn, and demand they turn over someone they may or may not be holding prisoner," Berndt said. "Where is he, Dick?"

"I honestly don't know."

"Well, somebody does," President Haynes said, entering the room. He moved fast, reaching the center chair around the table and sitting down before everyone else could get to their feet. He was clearly seething with anger.

"Mr. President, we were just—"

"Never mind that for the moment," Haynes said. He fixed each of them with a baleful look. "I'm late because Crown Prince Abdullah finally called me about two situations. The one at the embassy angers him the most." The president's jaw tightened. "The son of a bitch actually threatened to cut off oil shipments to us for thirty days if I didn't do something immediately."

Berndt had been afraid of just this from the moment he'd been informed about the developing situation at the Saudi Embassy. As the president's adviser on national security affairs, he should have been in on the call.

Haynes anticipated Berndt's concern. "I was just leaving the Oval Office when his call came through. Sorry, Dennis, you were already down here and there was no time to get you back upstairs." The president seemed to look inward for a moment, as if he was girding himself for some difficult decisions. "He flatly denied that Kathleen McGarvey was being held prisoner at the embassy." The president looked pointedly at Adkins. "He gave me his word, Dick." Haynes shook his head. "I couldn't very well call him a liar."

"No, Mr. President," Adkins said.

Thank God for that much, Berndt thought. "I don't believe that Saudi Arabia can afford to cut off our oil, Mr. President. They're in desperate need of money, and our surveilling their embassy, no matter how vigorously, would not give them sufficient cause."

"Exactly," the president shot back. "But there was a second situation he wanted to know about, the one that puzzles him most, happening at this moment outside Lucerne. A Swiss federal cop by the name of Liese Fuelm has taken Prince Salman's wife and four children hostage in their own home." Again he directed his attention to Adkins. "Does that name ring any bells?"

Adkins nodded. "Kirk knows her."

It was obviously the answer Haynes expected to hear. "Despite my warning, he's directing a full-scale assault on the prince, who, so far as I know, is at the embassy now, and on his family in Switzerland. A neutral country."

"The Saudis kidnapped McGarvey's wife, Mr. President," Berndt suggested, as gingerly as he could. "In his mind he has cause."

"Do you know this for a fact, Dennis?" the president demanded.

"I got it from Otto Rencke, his special projects director, who got it from Mac's daughter," Berndt said. "She was in Georgetown when they grabbed her mother. The kidnappers told her that they would keep Mrs. McGarvey for two days, and nothing would happen to her if Mac backed off. They drove off in a cable television van, which the DC police spotted entering the Saudi Embassy parking garage beneath the building."

"We're using that as our operational timetable, Mr. President," Anderson, the Homeland Security DC chief said, but the president held up a hand, cutting him off. "I know who can reach him," Haynes said.

Berndt knew as well. "He might have his hands full," he said.

But Haynes was having none of it. "Get Rencke on the speakerphone now," he ordered. "I'm going to end this standoff so that we can concentrate on stopping the bastards from hitting us again."

Which was exactly what McGarvey was trying to do, Berndt thought. But he didn't give voice to it.

"We've got forty-eight hours, give or take," the president said. "We ought to be able to find them by then." It was wishful thinking.

Using the president's telephone console, Berndt dialed the emergency number Rencke had left for him. It was answered on the first ring.

"Oh wow, Mr. Berndt, am I glad you called. I've got some good dope on the Saudis. I'm following their financial trails. At least one line of money goes from several Swiss accounts into one in Trinidad. And you'll never guess who the payer and the payee are. You'll never guess, not in a zillion years!"

Berndt looked at the president, who nodded for him to go ahead. "No, Mr. Rencke, who?" he asked.

"The Swiss accounts belong to none other than our old friend Prince Abdul Salman," Rencke gushed, excitedly, "and the Trinidad account belongs to him as well." Rencke laughed. "But do you guys want to hear the kicker, Mr. President, do ya?"

Berndt looked at the president again. Rencke was a frightening man. Somehow he was able to trace a supposedly untraceable telephone circuit to the console in the White House situation room. The president was very likely to be there in this time of national crisis.

"Yes, Mr. Rencke, I would like to hear the kicker," Haynes said.

"A businessman by the name of Thomas Isherwood arrived at the Juneau airport from Vancouver two days before Shaw almost went down. He took a cab to an air charter company where he had booked a flight to a fishing resort on Kuiu Island on the Inside Passage." Rencke suddenly dropped the little-boy enthusiasm from his voice. Now he was a professional intelligence officer passing crucial information to the president of the United States. "He was supposed to stay for a week, fishing with friends. But when the charter pilot flew back for the pickup, no one was there." Rencke paused for a second. "No one alive. The resort owner, his wife, and his daughter had all been gunned down."

"We know most of that, Otto," Adkins said. "What else have you come up with?"

"Oh wow, Mr. Adkins. Guess where Thomas Isherwood was from? Port of Spain, Trinidad."

No one said anything.

"Do you get it, Mr. President? Saudi royal family money—Prince Salman's money—has been transferred on a regular basis to Trinidad. The man traveling from Trinidad to Juneau via Vancouver was the terrorist Khalil. And at that very same moment Prince Salman himself was in Vancouver, supposedly on business." Rencke laughed. "Bingo!"

"Good work, Mr. Rencke," Haynes said. "I'll want you to carry your investigation as far as you can. In the meantime I want to speak with Mr. McGarvey. I suspect that you know where he is at the moment."

"But Mr. President, there can't be any doubt that Khalil and the prince are the same guy. Gosh—"

"It's an order, Mr. Rencke," the president said. "I'm trying to save lives—his, his wife's, and possibly a lot of innocent Americans. The attack is coming in less than two days. We don't have much time to stop it."

"No, sir, we do not," Rencke said. "But it's too late to reach Mac."

Berndt's stomach did a slow roll. "Why, Otto?" he asked. "Why is it too late?"

"He's already inside."

"That's impossible," Weissman sputtered. "We're watching the place along with your people."

"Nevertheless it's true," Rencke said. "I saw him go in just a couple of minutes—" Rencke stopped in midsentence.

For a moment Berndt thought that they'd lost the connection. But sounds were coming from the speakerphone. A woman's voice perhaps, and then a man's. But Berndt couldn't make out any of the words.

"Otto?" Berndt prompted.

Still there was nothing.

"Mr. Rencke," Haynes said.

"Power up your monitor, Mr. President; I'll send you something that I've just picked up from one of our satellite intercept programs," Rencke said. His voice sounded strangled, as if he had swallowed something bad.

A flat-panel computer monitor in front of the president's position was already on, the image of some Hawaiian beach on its screen wallpaper.

Haynes turned it so that the others could see the screen. "Go ahead, Mr. Rencke; we're ready."

The image of a battered Kathleen McGarvey came up. Dressed in what looked like cotton pajamas, she was sitting on the edge of a cot. Her face was bruised, and it was obvious she had been beaten. But she seemed to be alert and even defiant.

God help the sorry bastard who did this when McGarvey finds out, Berndt thought. He shuddered.

"My name is Kathleen McGarvey, and I have a message for all the mothers and fathers of all the children in the great Satan nation, the United States."

"Where did it come from?" Adkins asked.

"It's from a Saudi intel transmitter here in town," Rencke said.

"Where did they send it?" Berndt asked.

"Al Jazeera's main studio in Doha," Rencke said. He was choked up, as they all were, watching McGarvey's wife read from a prepared statement.

Her eyes were flitting all over the place, and Berndt suspected she was trying to tell them something, but for the life of him he didn't know what it might be. "Otto, is she trying to signal us?"

"It looks like it, but it ain't Morse code," Rencke said over her voice. "But I'm on it." The telephone connection was broken.

"There's not a damned thing we can do now, except storm the embassy," the president said, his eyes glued to the monitor. "And we definitely can't do that."

SIXTY-SIX

☐

His pistol in hand, McGarvey held up just inside what had been a pantry beyond the mudroom down a short corridor from the rear entrance. It had taken him less than two minutes to blow the lock on the rear security gate, cross the narrow parking area filled with a half dozen cars, and let himself in.

He'd been prepared to blow the rear door or take down anyone who came to investigate, but the door had been unlocked and no one had shown up.

The storeroom was dark and smelled musty. It was filled with locked file cabinets, and shelves holding hundreds of what appeared to be U.S. government bulletins, documents, and at least five years' worth of the *Congressional Record* pulp publication.

This was a trap. All his senses were superalert. No one had come to investigate the explosion at the back security gate, nor had the loading-entrance door been locked.

Where were the security people?

There were closed-circuit television cameras on the gate, outside the back door, and where the corridor opened into the large kitchen. They knew that he was in the building. Yet no one was rushing to intercept the intruder. It was very much unlike any Saudi operation he'd ever seen. Even their think tanks had tighter security.

Khalil wanted him to come here.

This was a large building with more than two dozen rooms. McGarvey had spent some of the morning trying to remember the layout. He'd only ever been inside once, after Yarnell's death, and he supposed that the Saudis might have changed things around to suit their purposes. But Katy could be anywhere, and even without interference it might take a long time to find her. No matter what Khalil's purpose was, the Saudis weren't about to let an American stay here very long.

Khalil was here, though, he was sure of it. He could almost smell the man's scent. "Here I am," he murmured. "I'm coming."

No one was in the industrial kitchen, nor did it look as if it had been used to cook a meal in a long time. There didn't appear to be any food-stuffs, and the three gas stoves were pristine; there weren't any pots or pans hanging on the hooks, nor plates or glasses on the shelves.

McGarvey stopped again and cocked an ear to listen. The house was dead quiet. Yet people were here.

A pair of swinging doors led to what had been a dining room large enough to seat thirty people. McGarvey eased one of the doors open and cautiously peered through the crack.

Nobody was there.

The large table was still in place, but it was laid out with glasses, water carafes, and lined tablets and pens at each position. At one end was a complicated-looking, multiline telephone console, and beside it a red phone without push buttons. The room was apparently used for conferences.

But this wasn't the headquarters of any Middle Eastern trade association. The Bureau had long suspected that Saudi intelligence was operating out of a safe house somewhere in the city that was independent of the embassy. McGarvey had a hunch that he'd just stumbled onto it.

The closed-circuit television camera mounted high on the wall on the other side of the room came to life and tracked McGarvey as he left the kitchen, hurried around the table, and made his way to the tall, ornately paneled sliding doors, which opened, as he remembered, directly onto the main stair hall.

If there was a security detail here, someone would be stationed in the front hall to screen incoming staff and visitors.

McGarvey put his ear to the doors, but there were no sounds. He eased one of them open slightly and looked out.

The large hall was empty, as was the railed second-floor corridor leading from the head of the stairs. Middle Eastern paintings and tapestries and long, curving scimitars decorated the walls. Persian rugs were scattered on the highly polished wooden floor. To the right a heavy wooden door with an oval, etched glass window led to a small vestibule. Directly across from the dining room was a counter about eight feet long. It was the security post. He could see the reflection of a monitor screen in the door glass.

McGarvey looked over his shoulder, but the way behind was clear. He was being led into a trap, but he had no options that he wanted to consider. Katy and Kahlil were here, and he was going to find both of them.

What bothered him most was not that Khalil had snatched Katy, but why he had not taken Liz as well and disappeared into the woodwork with both of them. If he were one of the al-Quaida leaders, he would be hunkering down now until the attack, and probably for the long haul. They had to know that the pressure to find them would be ten times what it had been after 9/11.

But Khalil had allowed Liz to leave, even telling her the timetable for the attacks.

For just a moment McGarvey felt a flash of self-doubt. Perhaps the cable television van transporting Katy had not doubled back here to drop her off before showing up at the Saudi Embassy. It was possible she was over there and not here after all.

He shook his head.

It was Khalil's ego driving him now. After his failure in Alaska, he was willing to go to any lengths, take any risks to hit back. His actions had nothing to do with al-Quaida or striking a blow against the West; this was personal between them.

They were watching his every move. Khalil wouldn't want to kill him at first, just disable him, bring him down. For that McGarvey would have to come out into the open where they could have a clear shot at him.

Which was exactly what he was going to give them.

He started to turn around, as if he had decided against continuing, but then he flung the doors open and darted out into the stair hall, sweeping his pistol left to right, covering the corners and then the upstairs landing for any sign of movement.

He was across the hall in a few long strides, where he levered himself over the counter and ducked down behind it.

He was somewhat exposed to anyone on the upstairs landing, but it couldn't be helped. In any event he planned only staying long enough to find Katy.

Keeping one eye toward the landing, he quickly studied the security board. In addition to a telephone console and what appeared to be the controls for the front and back gates, there were two monitors. One of them showed the corridor between the kitchen and the rear entrance. The other was an outside view, at the front gate.

Beneath each monitor was a double row of switches that controlled which camera was displayed. And lying on the console was a floor plan of the building, the camera positions marked and numbered.

McGarvey glanced at the upstairs landing, then flipped the first switch. The view in that monitor changed from the kitchen corridor, to the rear gate.

Katy could be anywhere in the house, possibly in an upstairs bedroom, but more likely she was somewhere in the basement, where there were no windows from which she might attempt to escape, or signal for help.

He started with the cameras in the basement rooms. The first showed a view down a dimly lit corridor. The second and third showed empty rooms, both of which could have been used as interrogation cells.

He found Katy in the fourth, a room at the end of the corridor, and his heart leapt into his throat. She was seated on a narrow cot, her knees drawn up to her chest. He couldn't see her face very clearly, but by the way she held herself he knew that she had been hurt.

For a second a monstrous dark rage welled up inside of him, threatening to block out all sanity. He looked up at the second-floor corridor, everything in his soul wishing for Kahlil to be there. Right now. Just the two of them.

But then he came down.

Katy was alone in the cell, and she didn't appear to be in any immediate danger. He found the room location on the floor plan. The entrance to the basement was just off the rear corridor the way he had come in.

His eyes went to the monitor showing the front gate. A black Mercedes with heavily smoked windows had pulled up. The rear door opened and a man stepped out.

He looked familiar.

McGarvey checked the upstairs landing again, and when he turned back to the monitor the man from the limo was at the front gate, pressing the buzzer, looking up at the television camera.

Suddenly McGarvey was no longer sure of anything. He was looking into the face of a man who should not have been outside this building. Katy was here, and so should this man have been. Unless everything he believed was wrong.

Or unless something else was going on. Something to do with the al-Quaida attacks in less than two days.

And he was afraid for Liese's safety because he had sent her on a dangerous wild-goose chase.

"Let me in at once." The voice of Prince Salman came from the speaker next to the monitor, and McGarvey pressed the button to open the gate.

SIXTY-SEVEN

□

The large living room of Prince Salman's chalet was silent and getting dark because storm clouds had blown in from the west, covering the late afternoon sky. Liese sat with her knees together, pistol in hand, across from Princess Sofia and the children.

She laid the gun on her lap, and brushed a strand of hair off her forehead. She hadn't even gotten through the first hour, and yet it seemed as if she had been here forever. But Kirk would call when he was in the clear, so she would have to hold on until then.

The first few minutes had been the worst, because she'd expected the security guards to try to take her by surprise. She'd been startled by every little sound, by every movement the princess or one of the children made. At one point a phone rang in another room, and for a couple of seconds she had the silly notion that it might be Kirk calling the security staff to let her go.

But no one came to talk to her, and gradually the house settled down until there were no noises. She wished she was almost anywhere else but here. In Kirk's arms, she daydreamed, even though she knew that would never be possible.

"Sergeant, my daughter has to use the WC," Princess Sofia said. The youngest girl had been fidgeting for the past five minutes.

Liese shook her head. "It will only be another hour. I'm sorry, but she'll have to wait."

The little girl's eyes were very wide, coal black, her complexion a beautiful olive, her long dark hair in a single braid. She sat nearest to her mother, her tiny hands in her lap. Her tee shirt had Minnie Mouse embroidered on the front, from Euro Disney outside Paris.

"She's only seven; she doesn't understand these things," the princess said.

"I'm sorry."

"Do you have children, Sergeant?"

The question was like a sharp dagger in an open, festering wound. Liese's breath momentarily caught in her throat. She shook her head again. "I'm not married."

The princess laughed disdainfully. "Of course you're not. You're Swiss, and you're too efficient to understand about having a husband who gives you children."

At least the man I'm in love with is not an assassin, Liese wanted to say. But even that wasn't true. *Was hers a life wasted?* she often asked herself. At this particular moment she was more confused than she'd ever been, and she had no idea what the answer was, or if she knew how to find it.

"Can she go alone?" Liese asked.

"Yes, of course," Princes Sofia said. "Anyway you'll still have me and the other three under the barrel of your gun." She said something in Arabic to the little girl, who hesitated for a moment, then climbed off the couch, and keeping a wary eye on Liese, left the room.

"She is a very pretty child," Liese said, in an effort to be pleasant.

Princess Sofia flared. "You have no right to say that to me. Keep your stupid, meaningless compliments to yourself. Better yet, put away that ridiculous gun and get out of my house."

"Your Highness, no one believes that you are involved in any way. And I have not come here to offer you any harm. You have my word as a Swiss officer of the law on that."

The princess was about to say something, when she looked beyond Liese to the left in the direction her daughter had gone and her eyes widened slightly.

"What—" Liese said, turning. A man stood on the other side of the stairs, some sort of a short-barreled rifle in his hand. Liese thought it might be an M16, she wasn't sure. But the laser sight targeted her left eye.

Oh, Kirk, the fleeting thought crossed her mind. *It wasn't supposed to turn out this way.*

She managed to turn her head and start to move left, when a tremendous thunderclap burst inside her skull and the lights went out.

SIXTY—EIGHT

☐

Khalil waited in the second-floor operations center directly across the corridor from the stairs, watching a bank of television monitors, an overwhelming fury threatening to blot out his self-control. The stupid, arrogant bastard coming here, now of all times and completely out in the open, was beyond belief.

Most of the twenty-two intelligence staffers were gathered here on al-Kaseem's orders, to stay out of the way until the situation resolved itself. This was one of the few rooms in the building without a closed-circuit television camera. They sat around the big table, at desks and on chairs pulled from other offices.

From the moment they'd heard the explosion at the rear gate until now, McGarvey had done exactly what Khalil had wanted him to do. He'd made his way to the ground-floor security post, had figured out the monitoring system from the floor plan that had been left for him, and had located his wife in her cell. Next he should have gone to her, which would have been his death sentence.

The downstairs corridor was narrow, ill lit, and very confined. When Darby Yarnell owned the house, that basement corridor had led back to his extensive wine cellar. It would have been a perfect place to corner the man. There was nowhere for him to run and hide, no room in which to maneuver.

Al-Kaseem walked over to where Khalil was standing, just out of earshot from most of the others. "This tears everything," he said, seething with anger. "Did you know he was coming here?"

"No, of course not," Khalil said, taking care to keep his voice even. He switched one of the monitors to Kathleen McGarvey's cell. She sat huddled on the cot, hugging her knees to her chest. Then he switched to the basement corridor.

"What are you going to do, damn you?" al-Kaseem demanded. "Your coming here like this will likely shut down our entire North American operation. All because you wanted revenge for your botched operation in Alaska."

"What are you talking about?"

"McGarvey, you fool. He didn't break in here without a plan for getting back out."

Khalil's eyes were on the monitors showing the view outside and the view inside the stair hall; he was fascinated despite the problem the man's presence created. McGarvey was good, but he *was* only one man, and he would now have the handicap not only of his wife, but also of the prince.

Prince Salman had gotten through the gate and was marching up to the front door. McGarvey had come back over the counter, and stood in the shadows beside the stairs, his pistol still in hand.

"I expect I will have to kill all three of them," Khalil said. "You can make the arrangements to dispose of their bodies. In two days they'll simply become additional casualties in the attack."

None of the staff could hear their conversation, but a number of them watched the outside monitor and took furtive glances toward Khalil.

"What about my people?" al-Kaseem whispered, urgently. "They've seen you. They're making the connection."

Prince Salman had reached the front door and was coming into the building.

Khalil turned his hooded eyes to al-Kaseem. "If you cannot control your officers, I can."

Al-Kaseem stepped back, struck dumb for the moment. He glanced at the monitor. "This has to end, or we're all dead," he said.

The prince had entered the vestibule, and he was opening the inner door.

SIXTY-NINE

As Prince Salman came through the door, McGarvey stood well back beside the soaring stairs so that he was hidden from anyone upstairs. It took everything within his power not to immediately shoot the man dead.

The arrogant bastard had been driving around Washington as if he were immune from the consequences of his actions.

Salman stopped at the counter and looked at the television monitors. He looked up toward the head of the stairs, but then he spotted McGarvey standing in the shadows, and he reared back. "You."

"You should not have come back here," McGarvey said. His gun hand was shaking with the effort not to pull the trigger. A small bead of sweat appeared on his forehead.

"What do you mean, *come back* here?" Salman demanded. "I've never been to this place in my life." He glanced toward the head of the stairs again. "What the hell are you doing here?"

"You kidnapped my wife, you son of a bitch," McGarvey said. It was becoming increasingly difficult to stay on track. They had stripped Katy, making her change into pajamas. And they had hurt her. "You wanted me to come here."

Salman was shaking his head. "I don't know what the hell you're talking about."

"You put your hands on her, like you did in Alaska, and I warned you then that I would kill you."

Sudden understanding dawned in the prince's eyes. "It's your people in front of our embassy." He stepped back. "You're crazy; do you know that? I think you *deserve* another 9/11."

It was the same voice that McGarvey had heard in Alaska. Or was it? After hearing Salman's voice in Monaco, his exact memory of how Khalil had sounded on the cruise liner was blurred. But Otto's evidence was nearly overwhelming. Whenever a terrorist attack had taken place in the past ten years in which Khalil could be placed in the vicinity, Salman was there as well. That was more than mere coincidence.

Katy had been kidnapped and she was here. So was Salman.

McGarvey motioned with his pistol toward the corridor that led to the back of the house. "Move."

Salman stepped back a pace and shook his head. "I'm not going anywhere with you," he said, haughtily. "You think that I'm a terrorist, and you're not bluffing. You *are* going to kill me. Well, I'm not going to the slaughter like a lamb. If you want to do it, you'll have to shoot me in the back."

Salman glanced at the closed-circuit monitors behind the counter, one showing the front entrance, and the other, Katy in her cell. He looked back at McGarvey. His eyes had narrowed, and a crafty, calculating expression had come into his face.

"We're going downstairs to get her," McGarvey said. "And then the three of us will leave here together."

"I didn't do this," Salman protested. But his words didn't ring true.

"I'm not going to kill you, as much as I want to, but you are coming with me," McGarvey said. "I'll turn you over to the FBI and let them deal with you. Either that or you'll die right here."

Salman seemed to think about it, but he shook his head again. "I don't think so," he said. "You're here and so is your wife, which means you probably know what this place really is. No use me trying to lie about it. Fact is I came here looking for help to get you off my back. The chief of intelligence operations is a family friend."

"Where are they?" McGarvey asked.

A moment of uncertainty crossed Salman's features. "Most likely waiting for you to come to your senses and leave without bloodshed."

"Not without my wife or you," McGarvey said. "Nobody's coming to rescue you, because you're an embarrassment to the royal family."

"You're insane."

"You got caught, and when you tell us what targets al-Quaida will hit in two days, your own government will cut you loose the same as they did to bin Laden."

Salman laughed disdainfully. "You are a naïve man for the director of Central Intelligence—or should I have said, *former* director? But in case you didn't already know it, President Haynes is a close personal friend. So are a number of your key officials."

"They'll be disappointed," McGarvey said. "Get going now, or I'll shoot you."

"Harm me and you'll go to jail."

This was not what he expected. None of it. This place was most likely a Saudi intelligence operational center, and Khalil's capture here of all places would be a serious embarrassment to the royal family. So would Katy's kidnapping and imprisonment here create a major international incident. U.S.-Saudi relations would probably never be the same, oil money or not.

But no one was coming to stop what could turn into a major disaster for Riyadh.

The only way in which any of this made sense was if someone very high in the royal family had finally decided to cut its recent losses and totally withdraw its support for the terrorists, just as Libya's Qaddafi had done. McGarvey didn't believe it, but in the face of bin Laden's new threat, maybe Crown Prince Abdullah had finally had enough.

Whatever was going on, he needed to get Katy out of here right now.

McGarvey crossed the stair hall in four strides. Salman grabbed for the telephone behind the counter, but before he could reach it McGarvey shoved him back against the door frame and jammed the muzzle of his pistol into the side of the man's head.

"Give me the slightest excuse to put a bullet into your brain and I'll do it, I swear to Christ," McGarvey said.

"I'll enjoy coming to your trial for treason," Salman said, immediately giving up the struggle. His face was inches from McGarvey's. He smiled. "Let's go fetch your wife, if that's what you want. And if we're allowed to leave, I'll go with you to the FBI. I won't cause you any further trouble."

McGarvey backed off, and glanced up at the second-floor corridor. No one was there, and everything in his being told him he was walking into a trap. But he had no other choice. "Lead the way."

Salman shook his head. "As I told you, I've never been here. I don't know where she is."

McGarvey roughly shoved him toward the corridor. Together they headed toward the back of the house, past the open door of what in Yarnell's day had been the library, but that was now a large functional room jammed with a half dozen desks and file cabinets. Heavy drapes were drawn over the windows, but the lights had not been switched off. It looked as if whoever had been working in here had suddenly dropped what he was doing and scurried off somewhere to hole up. On one long wall was a large map of the world with Arabic markings and lines drawn in red. This was probably where their analysts worked.

The door to the basement was across from the pantry where McGarvey had come in. He directed Salman to open it. Dim lights illuminated the stairway and the corridor below.

McGarvey glanced over his shoulder at the closed-circuit television camera mounted on the wall just below the ceiling. Its red light was on, indicating it was functioning, and it was tracking them.

Someone was watching. But what were they waiting for?

Salman started down the stairs first, McGarvey directly behind him. From what he remembered, there was no way in or out of the basement except for this door. *It's not a cellar; it's a redoubt,* Otto had remarked at the time. *Kept the philistines from stealing Darby's wine.*

Every nerve end in McGarvey's body tingled. The basement corridor could very well turn into a shooting range. It would all hinge on the timing.

They held up at the bottom. Four doors opened off the narrow corridor that ran only thirty feet from the back of the house toward the front. The end door led to Yarnell's wine cellar, which had taken up nearly one-fourth of the entire basement, extending from one side of the house to the other. The other doors opened onto storerooms and the big area where the furnace and utilities were located. Katy was being held in the last room next to the wine cellar. Its door, unlike the others, was made of steel.

All the doors were closed, but the television camera on the ceiling had swiveled from the spot McGarvey had observed upstairs at the monitor, to the stairs. Trouble, McGarvey decided, would come from the kitchen above, unless they actually meant to allow him to leave in peace with his wife now that he had Salman.

"What now?" Salman asked.

McGarvey pulled out his stiletto, reached up over his shoulder with his free hand, and cut the wires to the camera. Its red light went out.

"Won't matter," Salman said. "If they don't want you to leave, they'll just wait upstairs, and there'll be no way of getting past them."

"In that case we'll find out how good a negotiator you really are," McGarvey said. He prodded the prince in the back. "At the end."

Two small bulbs in the ceiling provided the only illumination except for the light that filtered down from the open pantry hall door. Except for McGarvey's and Salman's footfalls on the bare concrete floor, there were no noises. No machinery running, no water in the pipes, no traffic outside, nothing. The house and the entire neighborhood could have been deserted.

When they reached the steel door to Katy's cell, McGarvey tried the latch, but it was locked. He directed Salman to go another ten feet to the very end of the corridor. "Sit down and cover your head; I'm going to blow the door."

"Very dramatic," Salman said, languidly. But he shrugged and did as he was told.

When the prince was safely out of harm's reach, McGarvey slid the cover away from the small viewing port in the door. Katy was still seated on the cot, her knees hunched up.

"Katy," he called to her.

Her head snapped up and her eyes went wide. "Kirk? My God, is that you?"

"It's me, sweetheart. Are you okay?"

Katy got up and hobbled to the door. She was obviously in a great deal of pain. The side of her face was swollen and bruised, and there was some blood on her pajama bottoms. "I'm afraid for the baby," she cried. "Get me out of here, darling. Please."

McGarvey looked at Salman, who was watching him with an inscrutable expression in his hooded eyes. It took every ounce of will in McGarvey's body not to put one round into the man's forehead. End it here and now, so that no matter what else happened the bastard would be dead.

But in less than forty-eight hours al-Quaida would hit us again.

Only Khalil knew exactly when and where the strike or strikes were going to take place.

He turned back to the viewing port. "Listen to me, Katy. I have to blow the door. I want you to turn the cot over on its side and get behind the mattress. When you're set, I'll do it."

"Okay," she said, and she turned away.

"I did not kidnap your wife," Salman said. "I was at my embassy the entire time, and I can prove it."

McGarvey stuffed his pistol in his belt. "Move and I will shoot you," he said. He took out a Semtex packet, and quickly molded the small block of plastic explosive around the door lock and latch handle, while keeping a cautious eye on the prince.

The fuse was set for five seconds from the moment he cracked the acid cylinder.

He looked through the viewing port. Katy had the cot over on its side, and she was huddling down behind the mattress. "Are you ready?" he called to her.

She looked up over the edge of the cot. "Yes," she shouted.

"Keep your head down," McGarvey said. He cracked the fuse, then stepped a few feet away from the door, flattening himself against the wall and turning his face away.

The Semtex went off with an impressive bang, an eight-inch-wide piece of the door and its latch clattering off the corridor wall.

McGarvey pulled out his pistol, went back to Katy's cell, and pulled the door open. "It's okay now; you can come out," he told her.

Salman raised his head. "May I get up?"

"Just a minute," McGarvey told him. Katy was having trouble getting out from under the cot. "Stay put," he warned Salman. He went into the cell, pulled the cot and mattress away, and helped his wife to her feet.

Katy came into his arms, shivering. He wanted nothing more than to hold her until she calmed down, but there was no time.

"We have to get out of here right now," he told her. "Can you walk?"

She looked up into his eyes, and nodded. "Yes, I think so."

"On your feet," McGarvey called out to Salman as he helped Katy to the door.

"Who is it?" she asked.

"Kahlil, the bastard who did this to you."

At the door Katy looked at Salman as he got to his feet. Then she turned back to her husband. "I don't understand," she said.

"What do you mean, Katy?" McGarvey asked. "It's him. The man from the cruise ship, the one who brought you here, did this—"

Katy was shaking her head. She looked at Salman again. "Darling, I recognize the man, of course. He's Prince Salman. He could practically be Khalil's twin. But he's not the one who beat me up. The one from Alaska. I know it for a fact, because he was just here not more than an hour ago."

At that moment McGarvey realized the enormity of the trap he had walked into, because of nothing more than his ego, pitted against that of another man.

SEVENTY

□

Across the street in the CIA's Boynton Towers safe house, Otto Rencke was on the phone with Elizabeth and Todd, who were racing over from the Saudi Embassy. He had called them the moment Prince Salman had driven up in the Mercedes and gone inside.

None of them knew what it meant, except that there was a very real possibility that he and Khalil were not the same person after all.

"What else is going on over there?" Liz shouted.

Rencke was having trouble grasping how he could have been so wrong. The data he'd gathered had been circumstantial, but there'd been so much of it. There'd been a long-term consistency.

"Nothing," he said. He'd watched the front of the house through the standard-issue, mil specs, Steiner binoculars he'd drawn from one of the Covert Ops guys, who'd known better than to ask the special projects director any questions.

Except for Prince Salman's arrival, there had been no activity over there. The window curtains were drawn, and there was no sign of any security guards within the gated area, yet by now the Saudis inside knew that McGarvey had gotten in.

The silence combined with his confusion put him off-balance.

"Have you tried my dad's cell phone?" Liz asked, and Rencke could hear the traffic noises in the background.

"The Saudis have the building shielded. Nothing will get through."

"Are you sure he got inside?"

Rencke swung the binoculars to the narrow side street that ran to the rear of the house, but he was unable to see the rear entrance from here. "I'm pretty sure; otherwise he would have come back here by now."

"Then he's got some kind of plan to get back out. But he's been in there too long. I think he needs help."

"I think so too."

"Just a minute," Liz shouted. Todd was saying something to her.

Rencke had loitered at the end of the block, waiting for McGarvey to emerge from the apartment building, and then had come up to keep watch. If something went wrong across the street or if Rencke figured McGarvey was taking too long, he was going to call for help.

"Otto, I need to know if my dad still carries the cigarette lighter my mother gave to him," Liz said.

Rencke lowered the binoculars. McGarvey had quit smoking several years ago, so he had no need for a flame. But maybe he'd kept Katy's present. Rencke tried to remember if he'd seen Mac with it recently. Maybe taking it out of his pocket and looking at it. Playing with it. "I think so, Liz, but I'm not one hundred percent sure."

"That's good enough," Liz said. "I didn't think he'd toss it in a drawer someplace." She said something away from the phone, her voice muffled, then she came back. "Do you have your laptop with you?"

"Sure."

"Can you tap into whatever computer controls the electricity over there, just like you did with the embassy?"

"Yeah, no problem," Rencke said. "Do you want me to shut them off?"

"Yes, but give us five minutes to get over there," Liz said. "Then call the fire department; tell them there's a major blaze and a lot of people are trapped inside and are going to burn to death."

Rencke caught her idea immediately. She was Mac's daughter, and she was getting good at seeing into her father's tradecraft. They were going to send McGarvey a signal that they were here to back him up.

Unless it was already too late.

SEVENTY-ONE

Khalil stood at the head of the basement stairs, with the Heckler & Koch M8 compact NATO carbine he'd gotten from the security people upstairs in hand. A long silencer was screwed to the end of the barrel. Although he wanted to take the woman with him, there would be a certain symmetry to killing her and her husband together.

What was most vexing, however, was Prince Salman's barging in. He was going to have to die here today, shot to death by McGarvey. Afterward it would be up to al-Kaseem's people to clean up the mess.

There were other Prince Salmans in the royal family. Playboys who were willing to fund al-Quaida in the hope that when the Islamic revolution finally hit Saudi Arabia with full force, there would be a place for them in the new government.

As he'd done with Salman, Khalil would change his appearance and time his moves to match those of his new prince. The cover had worked for a very long time, and from the beginning he'd only hoped to have a few years, moving in Salman's shadow. But he'd picked well, and Western intelligence agencies had inadvertently helped by concentrating on the prince. They had bought into the fiction, and yet had been unable to do much of anything because of Salman's relationship with the last three White House administrations.

But it had to be done now, before al-Kaseem finally mustered the courage to do something foolish.

"McGarvey," Khalil called down to the basement. "You must know by now that you have made a mistake. Would you like to make a deal?"

"Thank Allah you've finally come," Prince Salman shouted. "He's armed with a pistol and a knife."

Khalil wondered how the fiction had held up for so long with such an idiot. Even more amazing was Salman's friendship with the past three American presidents. But it was about to end. "Yes, I know, which is why I am making him this offer."

"I'm listening," McGarvey said.

"You are a very inventive, persistent man," Khalil said. "Is Prince Salman unharmed?"

"Yes, so far."

"Then release him, and I will allow him to leave the building," Khalil said. "He is an innocent man, of no use to either of us. Although after Monaco he cannot be your friend."

"He stays," McGarvey said.

Khalil's gorge rose. "He's nothing more than a playboy."

"At the very least he probably supplies you with money, and you've been masking your movements behind his for years. You *wanted* us to believe that he was a terrorist. The FBI will be interested in him."

Khalil was momentarily taken aback. How could they know that? Unless Salman had talked about the Trinidad banking connection. All the careful planning was beginning to unravel because of one man. And they were so close to something that would be an even bigger blow to Americans than 9/11. "As you wish, keep him. But you must realize that there is no way out for you. You're going to die down there."

"Sorry, pal, but you've got it wrong," McGarvey called from the basement, his voice maddeningly calm. "You're going to die for what you did in Alaska, and for what you did to my wife down here. And your death won't be a pleasant one."

Khalil's nerves were jumping all over the place. He wanted to open up with the M8 and spray the corridor. Maybe he would get lucky and at least hit one of them with shrapnel. But suddenly a calmness descended upon him like a soothing mist. Al-Kaseem was wrong. McGarvey had no plan. He'd just bulled his way into the building with only one thought in his head: to rescue his wife.

"Just you and me, then," he said. "You can keep Salman or kill him, whatever you want to do. But at least let your wife leave. I suspect she needs medical attention."

McGarvey's wife said something. Although Khalil couldn't make out the words, he could detect the urgency in her voice.

"You'd have to kill her," McGarvey said. "At this point you don't have any choice. She's seen your face."

"I give you my word as a Saudi prince that I will allow her to leave this place unharmed—"

McGarvey laughed. "Why don't you come down here where I can see you? Then we'll let both of them go."

"You would shoot me the moment I reached the bottom of the stairs."

"No, I wouldn't," McGarvey said. "I give you my word as an American gentlemen."

Khalil shivered in anticipation. The killing was going to be very good.

Khalil reached into his pocket for one of the stun grenades he'd gotten from the Security section's armory, when al-Kaseem hurried down the corridor from the front hall, a determined look on his face. "We heard an explosion, but the monitor is out so we couldn't see a thing."

"He's rescued his wife," Khalil said. "From her cell. But they won't get out of the basement alive. And neither will the prince. Now leave me to finish the job."

"I talked to the deputy ambassador on his cell phone and outlined what was going on over here," al-Kaseem said.

Khalil smiled inwardly, though he was irritated. He'd always considered al-Kaseem to be at least competent. But the man was buckling under the pressure. Making stupid mistakes. "Was that wise? Talking on an unencrypted line?"

"I didn't have to go into detail," al-Kaseem said. "He understands the situation that you have put us in. We won't participate in another 9/11. The retributions will be much worse."

"I agree," Khalil said. "This will be much worse than 9/11. So it's up to us to clean up this particular mess, no matter whose fault it is."

"He's going to speak with Crown Prince Abdullah—"

"Abdullah will not be in for his call. Nor will Prince Bandar." Khalil was tiring of the arguments. "Nuaimi is to be the scapegoat. His career is dead. And when he returns to Riyadh in the aftermath of the attacks, he will probably be shot. Take care that you do not join him."

"First you need to get out of this building, and then out of Washington," al-Kaseem said, angrily. "Take care that I don't withdraw my support. You would find that your escape would be much more difficult without me."

Khalil looked at him as a snake might look at a mouse. "Rashid, are you threatening me?"

"I'm trying to talk some sense into you."

"Leave me to attend to this business, and I will soon be gone."

"Perhaps I'll shoot you myself and turn your body and the letters in my safe over to the FBI," al-Kaseem said. "I could end this madness."

"Yes, you could," Khalil said. He casually raised his carbine, thumbed the safety selector to semiautomatic, and squeezed off two rounds, the first catching the intelligence officer in his neck, destroying his windpipe, and the second entering beneath his chin, the round spiraling up into his brain and exiting the back of his head in a spray of blood and tissue.

He looked up at the camera. *"I am in charge for now,"* he said in Arabic. *"Leave me alone and none of you need die."*

He turned back to the stairway. "Listen to me, Mr. McGarvey. It is just us now. There will be no further interference. I'm giving you one last chance to send your wife and Salman out of there. Otherwise all three of you will die."

Another sharp explosion came from the corridor below.

"McGarvey!" Khalil shouted. He pulled one of the British flash-bang grenades out of his pocket, yanked the pin, and tossed it down the stairs.

SEVENTY-TWO

□

Rencke's fingers flew over the keyboard as he hacked his way into the Potomac Electric Power Company's mainframe computer on Pennsylvania Avenue. The only way in which to shut off an individual building's electricity was to physically pull the plug at the meter. With the computer the entire block would have to go down, which would include power to the Boynton Towers and its elevators.

The system controlling the area around the Saudi Embassy, the Watergate Hotel, and the Kennedy Center had been modernized, but the system for most of Georgetown was still of the old style. So although he got in with ease, it took him several minutes to figure out the antiquated system.

He was frustrated with himself not only because of the precious minutes he was wasting chasing after old computer codes, but because he had been so terribly wrong about Khalil and Salman. "Bad, bad, bad dog," he muttered. He wished his wife were here. She would understand his frustration, and help him through it.

The apartment door burst open, and he heard Liz and Todd racing down the hall, but he was almost there with the right computer line so he didn't look up.

Suddenly Liz was over his shoulder. "Did you shut it off?" she demanded, out of breath.

Todd grabbed the binoculars and went to the window.

"I'm on it," Rencke told her.

"Did you call the fire department?"

"Not until I find the right line—" Rencke said. Then it came up: the cross-reference that isolated Scott Place off Thirty-second "I got it. Call them."

Elizabeth dialed 911. "How long will it take?" she asked Rencke.

"I don't know. Thirty seconds, maybe longer."

"Do it," Liz said. "I want to report a fire," she told the emergency operator.

Rencke highlighted the line and hit Enter. Soon power to the entire block would shut down; then it would be up to Mac.

"It's the Middle East Center for Advanced Studies," Elizabeth said. "Just off Thirty-second Street in Georgetown. Scott Place." She went over to the window. "Anything yet?" she asked her husband.

"Nothing," Todd said.

"There's not much smoke, but there are a lot of people who might be trapped inside, so hurry," she told the operator. She broke the connection and speed-dialed another number. "Call our guys at the embassy and get them over here," she told Rencke. "I'm calling the Bureau. And get DC Metro too."

"I'm on it," Rencke said. He speed-dialed The Watch, which was the operations center over at Langley. When the shit started hitting the fan, they would need all the help they could get.

And all the witnesses.

SEVENTY-THREE

There were no bottles left in Yarnell's old wine cellar, but the racks that had held several thousand different vintages in a climate-controlled environment were still in rows and columns like shelves in a library. The four-inch-thick, solid oak door had held up well under the small Semtex charge, but the modern electronic lock had not.

McGarvey's ears were still ringing from what he figured was a flash-bang grenade that had gone off about halfway up the corridor. He'd been last through the door into the old wine cellar behind Katy and the prince, so he had taken the brunt of the blast. But for the moment they were safe here.

"What's he trying to do?" Salman demanded, shrilly. "Kill us all?" He wasn't so arrogant now.

"That's exactly what he means to do," McGarvey said. Katy had stumbled when he shoved her through the open door, and he had to help her to her feet. She was shaky on her legs, and she held her gut with one hand while steadying herself against her husband with the other.

"If you mean to get us out of here, darling, right now would be as good a time as any," she said.

McGarvey was frightened. "Is it the baby?"

She looked up at him, her eyes round and bright in the dim light from the corridor. She appeared frail and vulnerable. She nodded. "Maybe," she said. "He hit me in the stomach, and I was bleeding for a while."

For a second he was almost as afraid for his own sanity as he was for Katy and the baby. Afraid that he would do something in a stupid rage that would get them all killed. But he'd never lost his head before, and it wasn't about to happen now. This was no longer only about Khalil.

He and Katy were on one side of the open door, while Salman was crouched in the darkness on the other side. "You stupid American bastard," the prince said, his voice low, menacing. He looked like a wild animal ready to spring. "You brought this down on yourself. You all did." He took a quick look out into the corridor.

"Go out there and he'll kill you," McGarvey warned.

"It's never been personal. But with you it's different. Ever since you disgraced Osama and blasphemed the name of Allah."

"Al-Quaida wants to get rid of your government, and yet you people help them," McGarvey said.

"You don't get it," Salman practically shouted. "The Arabian Peninsula is for Arabians. Not infidels."

"Then tell us to leave."

"Not until the oil is gone," Khalil shouted from the end of the corridor.

McGarvey grabbed Katy's arm and fell back with her, away from the doorway, shielding her with his body an instant before Khalil sprayed the corridor with automatic weapon fire. Bullets slammed through the empty wine racks, ricocheting off the concrete walls, fragments flying everywhere.

McGarvey was hit low in the left shoulder. He grunted with the shock of impact.

"Kirk, my God, you're hit," Katy cried.

"It's okay," he whispered, urgently. He shoved her away and went to the doorway, where he stuck his gun around the corner and fired six shots into the corridor before he pulled back. He ejected the spent magazine, slapped another in its place, and cycled the slide.

Salman was watching him, wide-eyed.

"You'll have to do better than that," Khalil taunted. He fired a second short burst, but then the lights went out, plunging them into nearly complete darkness.

The basement was utterly silent for just a moment, until something moved across from McGarvey. It was Salman.

"It's me," he shouted. "I'm coming out. Don't shoot! Don't shoot!"

"Don't do it," McGarvey shouted, but it was too late. The light was too dim to see anything, but he heard the prince bolting out the door and into the corridor.

Khalil let him get only a few steps outside the wine cellar before he fired. Salman's body was flung back into the wine cellar, crashing into one of the wine racks.

McGarvey immediately stuck his gun around the door frame and fired four shots as fast as he could pull them off. He thought he heard a muffled cry of pain, but he couldn't be sure.

"One down, two to go." Khalil's voice came out of the darkness. "Unless, of course, you want to send your wife out. It'll just be you and me. I promise I won't hurt her—again."

McGarvey figured that the terrorist was in one of the rooms off the corridor, out of the line of fire. "Turn the lights back on, and I'll send her out," he called.

Katy whimpered something, but he reached back with his free hand and touched her cheek. She quieted immediately.

"I didn't turn the lights—" Khalil cut himself off in midsentence. He had made a mistake.

McGarvey seized on it immediately. Otto was across the street. He had sent a message. Liz was probably over there too. She would have been the one to figure out his plan of escape, which depended for its success on Darby Yarnell's paranoia about his wine collection. The man had installed not only climate-control equipment down here, but he had also installed an alarm system.

And a fire suppression system. Sprinklers.

McGarvey thought he heard a siren very faintly, but it was there. If the fire department had already been called, they wouldn't come inside unless an alarm in the building went off.

He reached around the door frame, fired off a couple of shots, then grabbed Katy and hauled her farther away from the door.

Khalil did not return the fire.

McGarvey took out his cigarette lighter, lit the flame, and held it up toward the ceiling, providing a small circle of light.

Katy was alarmed. "What are you doing?" she demanded. Her eyes darted to the doorway. "He can see us."

McGarvey found one of the sprinkler heads. He moved over to it and held the lighter's flame directly beneath the heat sensor. "The fire department is outside. I'm giving them a reason to break in and rescue us."

Something metallic clattered on the concrete floor just outside the doorway and rolled into the wine cellar at the same moment the sprinkler system went off, spraying water everywhere.

McGarvey extinguished his lighter and tossed it aside. In one smooth motion he gathered his wife and bodily propelled her farther into the room, putting two solid-oak wine-storage racks between them and the doorway before he shoved her to the floor and laid on top of her.

He knew he had hurt her, but before she had a chance to cry out, the grenade that Khalil had tossed down the corridor went off with a tremendous bang, sending thousands of coil-spring fragments flying in a thirty-foot radius.

McGarvey was hit in his legs and in the soles of his feet, the razor-sharp pieces of wire slicing easily through the leather of his shoes.

He rolled off Katy and painfully scrambled up on one knee, his pistol trained in the general direction of the open door, though in the darkness and with the noise of spraying water it would be nearly impossible to hear or see anything.

Suddenly the building's battery-backup fire-alarm system came on with a deafening shriek, and a red emergency lantern lit up at the end of corridor.

"Stay here; help is coming," McGarvey told his wife.

Kathleen grabbed his sleeve. "Don't leave me," she cried, in desperation.

"You'll be okay here for now," he told her. "But I can't let him escape again."

"It doesn't matter what he did to me—"

"He knows where the terrorists are going to hit us," McGarvey tried to explain. "I have to get to him before it's too late." He looked into his wife's eyes, willing her to understand what he had to do. "This is our last chance, Katy."

She was struggling with herself; McGarvey could see it in her face. But she finally released his sleeve and nodded uncertainly. "Go. Do it," she said. "Stop him once and for all."

McGarvey brushed a kiss on her cheek, then got up. He fell to his knees before he took one step, the sharp pain from the fragments embedded in his feet impossible to bear.

"Kirk," Katy cried.

Not this. Not now. He wasn't going to let the bastard get away.

With Kathleen clutching at him, he laid his pistol down and tore off his shredded shoes and socks. The bottoms of his feet looked like hamburger-patty pincushions, with a dozen or more wire fragments sticking out. Blood splattered everywhere under the spray from the sprinkler head just above them.

Keeping one eye on the doorway lest Khalil was ignoring the fire alarm and would press his attack, McGarvey started pulling bits of wire out of his feet. Katy, seeing what he was doing, helped him, her tears mingling with the sprinkler water.

It took less than a minute before he picked up his gun and got back to his feet with Katy's help. The pain was bad, but it was bearable.

"No matter what happens, stay here. Hide somewhere until either I come for you or someone from the fire rescue team gets down here. They'll be searching the building."

"Oh, God," Katy said. Blood was everywhere around McGarvey's chewed-up feet. "Can you walk?"

He gave her a thin smile and nodded. "It looks worse than it is," he told her. "Now find someplace to hide."

He turned and headed for the corridor door, painfully crawling over the shattered remains of several wine racks that the grenade had destroyed.

Nothing on the face of the earth would stop him this time. Khalil was going to die.

SEVENTY-FOUR

□

Khalil reached the front stair hall in a black rage.

He'd had absolutely no idea that McGarvey would come up with such a move. Water flew everywhere, soaking carpets and paintings. Fifteen or twenty security analysts, translators, and communications people were scrambling down the stairs and across the hall to the front door to get away from a nonexistent fire.

Fools. They were like sheep being led to the slaughter.

For just a second he was stopped in his tracks. Unless McGarvey had been killed or seriously hurt in the blast, he would have been coming up from the basement when he realized that the attack had been abandoned. He was a resourceful man, for whom Khalil had finally developed a healthy respect.

There was a great deal of commotion outside the front gate. Fire trucks, police cars, and ambulances jammed the street. A crowd was already gathering. It would be the same in the back.

It suddenly struck Khalil that the fire department had been called *before* McGarvey had set off the sprinkler system. By a CIA team somewhere nearby. The same team that had cut the electricity to the building as a signal to McGarvey.

He had to admire the ingenuity. But the letters to the families of the four martyrs had to be saved, or destroyed, at all costs.

Which left him two problems: getting into al-Kaseem's safe, and then making his escape before McGarvey caught up with him.

The first staffers had reached the front gate and opened it, allowing the firefighters into the compound. At least two civilians, one of them a woman, were right there with them.

They were CIA; there was little doubt in Khalil's mind. But he was out of time now.

Khalil glanced over his shoulder to make sure that McGarvey wasn't there, then sprinted across the stair hall and pushed past the last few of al-Kaseem's staffers coming down the stairs.

No one tried to stop Khalil as he raced to the head of the stairs and rushed down the corridor to al-Kaseem's office at the rear of the building. The door was open, and two security officers were hastily shredding documents from the safe.

They looked up when Khalil appeared in the doorway. One of them reached for his pistol, but before he could get it out of his shoulder holster, Khalil raised the M8 and fired two shots, both hitting the man in the chest and knocking him back from the shredder, where he collapsed in a bloody heap.

The other security officer stood clear of the safe and spread his hands away from his sides. The sprinkler head in this room was not working. In a fire, Saudi intelligence *wanted* any stray documents left out—to be burned up.

"We don't have much time before the American authorities reach this room," he told Khalil, with some urgency. "I must be allowed to finish—"

"I gave Rashid four envelopes to keep in his safe. Have they been destroyed yet?" There were a great many people in the stair hall downstairs.

The security officer glanced at the desk. The four thick manila envelopes—each containing a death letter, a personal note from bin Laden himself, and fifty thousand in U.S. hundred-dollar bills—were in a neat stack. *Out in the open. The bastard had not safeguarded them. Al-Kaseem's intention all along was to hinder the operation, not help it.*

Khalil's rage spiked. He fired four shots into the security officer's chest, driving the man against the wall.

SEVENTY-FIVE

McGarvey cautiously peered around the door frame into the pantry hall, his pistol at the ready. Water cascaded down the stairs into the basement, and even through the din of the fire alarm he could hear a commotion at the front of the house. The fire department had arrived.

A body of a man was sprawled on its side in the corner. He had been shot under his chin, the back of his head half blown away. McGarvey had no idea who it was, but he was pretty sure who had killed him.

The man had gotten in Khalil's way and had lost his life for the mistake. It was possible that the terrorist had slipped out of the building and in the confusion had made his escape. But McGarvey doubted he'd had the time. And Liz and Otto would have been watching for just that. Everyone who was evacuated from the building would be held until they could be identified.

Elizabeth came down the corridor in a dead run, her gun drawn. She spotted her father through the spray, and immediately brought her pistol up as she pulled up short and dropped into a shooter's stance.

"It's me," McGarvey shouted.

For a second she held her position, covering the pantry hall, but then she eased up, raising her pistol. "Daddy?" she called.

McGarvey came up the last step into the hall and showed himself. "Did Todd come with you?" He was running out of time if he wanted to catch Kahlil one-on-one. He had to hurry.

Elizabeth's shoulders sagged in relief. She said something into her lapel mike, but then she saw that he was wounded, and she gave a little cry and went to him. "You're hurt."

"Never mind that," McGarvey said. "Is Todd with you?"

"Yes, he's in the front hall making sure all the Saudis are getting out. Otto told us to watch for Salman or anyone who looked like him. But we haven't seen him." She glanced at the body. "Who's that?"

"I don't know, but Khalil probably killed the poor bastard, and I think there's a good chance he's still in the building somewhere," McGarvey said. "I want the fire department out of here right now. Tell them it was a false alarm, anything, but no one else is to get out of here."

"We set up a perimeter. The Bureau and some of our people are on it," Elizabeth said. "What about Mother?" she demanded, and McGarvey could see the fear in her eyes as she girded herself for bad news.

"She's downstairs in the room at the end of the hall. As soon as you get the building secured, I want you to get her out." His jaw tightened thinking of Katy huddled in a corner in the dark. But he didn't want her moved until he was sure it was safe to do so. Khalil could spring up around any corner.

"Is she okay?"

"He beat her up," McGarvey said, tight-lipped. "She needs to get to the hospital as soon as possible."

"The dirty bastard," Elizabeth said. "She would have told him that she was pregnant. But it didn't make any difference."

Looking into his daughter's angry eyes, he realized that this had nothing to do with revenge. Or it should not. It would give him a great deal of pleasure to kill the terrorist for what he had done in Alaska and here, and for all the 9/11s in the past and yet to come.

McGarvey wanted to see the expression on the man's face when he knew that he was dying. Would he be defiant, angry, frightened, remorseful?

But Khalil had to be captured alive if at all possible, no matter how badly McGarvey wanted to kill him, because he was the key to stopping al-Quaida's attack in less than forty-eight hours.

McGarvey touched his daughter's cheek in the downpour. "Get Todd on it, and then get your mother out of here. I won't be much longer," he told her.

"Be careful, Daddy," Elizabeth said.

At that moment the sprinkler system shut down, followed by the fire alarm. In the sudden silence, McGarvey started for the stair hall, all of his senses alert for Khalil's presence. Behind him, Elizabeth was urgently issuing orders to her husband to clear the building, and then she went down into the basement.

Soon there would be nobody left except him and Kahlil.

It was exactly what he wanted.

Upstairs, Khalil came to the door as the water stopped and the fire alarm was silenced. Two firemen had just reached the head of the stairs, and he pulled back.

Killing them would be meaningless, though Kahlil had to admit to himself that he wanted to lash out at this moment, hurt someone, damage their confidence by his savagery. Firemen had been the heroes of

9/11. There would be a certain symmetry to destroying these two men.

He had his letters. He would leave now, evacuated with the others. Once outside he could slip away.

But he wanted McGarvey, which meant he would have to remain in the building a little longer, no matter how dangerous for him it would be.

But suddenly he knew the solution, as simple as it was satisfying.

Khalil leaned the M8 up against the wall, took out his stiletto, and holding it out of sight behind his leg, stepped out into the corridor. The two firemen were heading back to the stairs. "Don't go," he called to them. He allowed a note of desperation in his voice.

They turned, startled. He couldn't see their faces behind their masks, which was exactly how he wanted it.

"Get out of there," one of them said, gesturing for Khalil to come. "The building's being evacuated."

"I can't," Khalil said softly, as if he were afraid. "My friends—" He looked back in al-Kaseem's office. "They're hurt. I need help. Please."

The firemen hurried back, and Khalil stepped aside to let them enter the office.

The first one pulled up short when he saw the bodies of the two security officers and all the blood. Khalil swiveled into the second fireman, and slipped the stiletto under the lip of his helmet, driving it into the base of the man's skull, killing him instantly.

As the fireman collapsed, Khalil withdrew his stiletto and turned to the first man, who had spun on his heel and was pawing at the microphone on his shoulder. But he was too late. Khalil yanked the fireman's air mask off his face, and drove the stiletto up under his chin, angling it inward, burying it in his brain.

The fireman reared back in horror, a terrible gagging noise at the back of his throat, but then his eyes slowly went blank, and he sank to the floor as if he had been deflated.

For just a moment Khalil savored the man's death. It was a pleasure to watch. Almost sexual.

It was the ultimate expression of intimacy between two men, between the killer and his victim, and Khalil never wanted to rush the climax.

But this time had to be different if he was going to escape.

He bent over the second fireman and fumbled with the straps holding the compressed-air cylinder on the man's body. But the buckles had become tangled, so he sliced the harness away and pulled the tank off.

The house had become silent again, though as he hurriedly removed the fireman's helmet, then his coat, boots, and fire trousers, he could hear a great deal of commotion outside—more sirens, police radios, engines on the ladder trucks, and the many voices of the crowd that had gathered.

In the confusion he would simply be another fireman whom no one would notice. His only regret was his unfinished business with McGarvey and the man's wife. She was fascinating, a woman unlike any other he'd ever met. He would have enjoyed teaching her humility, and especially watching her eyes as her life faded.

Khalil pulled on the fireman's trousers and boots, then stuffed the four manila envelopes into the bib of the coveralls. He donned the heavy yellow coat, but not the gloves. He wanted his hands free in case there was to be a fight.

In a rush now, anxious to be away, he took the seventeen-round Glock from one of the dead security officers, checked to make sure the magazine was full, then stuffed it in his coat pocket.

He cut the hose from the tank, strapped the air mask on his face, then put on the helmet. There was no way now that anyone would recognize him. He pocketed the stiletto.

And who could say for certain what events would conspire to bring McGarvey and him together one last time? It was a day to look forward to.

McGarvey reached the head of the stairs as a fireman came out of a doorway at the end of the corridor.

His wounds and loss of blood had sapped his strength more than he realized, and he was winded from just coming up the stairs. There was a great deal of activity outside on the street. Todd and Otto were out there, watching for someone to come out of the building. Him or Khalil.

But he had not counted on a fireman still being here. He concealed the pistol behind his leg. "Is there anyone else up here on this floor?"

"No," the fireman said, advancing down the corridor. "And you don't belong here. Get out." His voice was oddly strangled.

Something was wrong. Out of place. But it seemed as if a fog was starting to engulf McGarvey's brain. He shook his head. The approaching fireman seemed to waver out of focus.

"You're hurt," the man said. His voice was distant. Yet it was somehow familiar.

"Someone might still be in the building," McGarvey argued. The words were thick in his mouth. "The third floor. Has anyone checked up there?"

The fireman spotted the pistol in McGarvey's hand. He stopped a couple of yards away. "Who is it that you think you're going to shoot?"

"Is there anyone on the third floor?" McGarvey demanded. Every second spent here was a second longer for Khalil to make his escape. But it wasn't going to happen this time. Not like in Alaska. Not after what he'd done to Katy. *The terrorist had laid his hands on her. He had hurt her. Inflicted pain on her. Frightened her.*

Khalil would pay for his crimes on this day.

The fireman glanced down at the empty stair hall. His radio came to life. "Donnelly, Lee, where are you guys?" He turned back to McGarvey and hesitated for a long moment.

There was something about the man that McGarvey couldn't put a finger on. A familiarity that was just out of his grasp in the fog. Something else. There was something wrong. He should know what it was.

The fireman put his right hand in his coat pocket, but then hesitated. He shook his head. "I'm not going to deal with an armed man," he said. "Stay and search the whole building if you must." He brushed past and started down the stairs.

McGarvey turned to watch the retreating figure. The name stenciled on the back of the fireman's coat was Donnelly. But he hadn't answered the radio call. He wasn't wearing gloves. And although he was wearing a breathing mask, he was not carrying an air tank, and the hose dangled over his shoulder.

The fireman stopped halfway down the stairs, and looked back up.

McGarvey started to raise his pistol, his arm impossibly heavy. "Khalil," he said.

Khalil pulled a bloody stiletto out of his pocket, and in one smooth powerful motion threw it underhanded.

The razor-sharp blade sliced into McGarvey's right shoulder just below his collarbone, the pain immediate and intense. His entire right side went numb, and as he fell back, a tremendous wave of nausea overcoming him, he dropped his pistol.

Not like this, the single thought crystallized in his brain.

Khalil reached in the same pocket and was pulling out a pistol, when McGarvey yanked the stiletto out of his shoulder and launched himself down on top of the terrorist.

He hit Khalil in the chest, and together they crashed down the stairs into the hall, the terrorist's gun going off with a huge boom next to McGarvey's ear.

A great many people were right outside. Someone was shouting something, and McGarvey thought it might be Liz's voice, but he was focused on Khalil, who had lost his air mask.

McGarvey was looking directly into the killer's black eyes, bottomless, cold, indifferent, completely without emotion even now.

Blood pumped from the wound in his shoulder, and McGarvey knew that he would not remain conscious much longer.

There was something wrong with Khalil's left arm, but he grabbed McGarvey by the throat with his right hand, and his powerful fingers began to clamp down.

"Bastard!" The single thought crossed McGarvey's brain as his world started to go dim. With the last of his strength he raised the bloody stiletto to Khalil's face, and before the terrorist could deflect the blade, he drove it to the hilt into the man's right eye.

The terrorist's body convulsed once, and then lay still, the light going out of his other eye.

A great tiredness overcame McGarvey, and he let himself go with it, only vaguely aware that his daughter and wife were at his side, calling his name, until his world went dark.

THE JIHAD

□

The morning was chilly, with thick dew on the grass as Muhamed Abdallah got out of the dark blue Toyota SUV two blocks from Rocky Mountain High School. Workday traffic was normal for this hour. No one was armed, none of the storefronts in the city were boarded up, there were no bars on windows, nor were there police or soldiers stationed at the intersections.

The laxity was nothing sort of amazing to him. But after today no one would ever ignore the *fatwahs* of Osama bin Laden again.

Ever since he'd gotten word, a gentle peace had come over him, descending like the veils of Muhammad's wives. It was a blasphemous thought, one that he did not share with his hosts Seyoum and Mustafa, but it was comforting.

Paradise will soon be mine. Even now my black-eyed wife awaits me.

"Are you okay?" Seyoum asked, respectfully, through the open passenger window.

Muhamed opened his eyes to him and to Mustafa sitting behind the wheel, and his heart suddenly filled with love for them. *Rejoice, O my brothers, for I go first to heaven to prepare the way.* He nodded, but he could not trust himself to speak. All his spit had dried up.

"Then you know the way? It is only two blocks—"

Muhamed turned and walked off. He would never see his two brothers on earth again, but that did not matter. He smiled. He was finally on his jihad, and no power on earth could stay his hand.

Insha'allah.

I profess that there is no God but the One God, and that Muhammad is the messenger of God.

Rising before dawn this morning, Muhamed had bathed and had taken great care with his shaving. Like many young Muslim men, he preferred to maintain a four-or five-day growth; it was a matter of style. But not here. High school students in the U.S. were generally clean-shaven.

He began taping the twenty kilos of plastic explosives to his naked body at 5 A.M., molding the puttylike material first to his legs, then around his abdomen and his chest, even his back, though that had been extremely awkward to do. Finally he'd taped long slender strips of the Semtex to his arms from a few centimeters above his wrists to his shoulders.

He left his feet, his knees, and his elbows free so he would be able to walk and gesture normally, but Semtex was taped to every other square centimeter of his body that would be covered by his jeans and LA Lakers sweatshirt.

In the mirror he looked like some otherworldly monster whose hide seemed to be made of large gray scales.

Finished by 7 A.M., he took great care to connect the electrical wires that would send a current to the firing pins in each block of Semtex. When he got dressed, the wires would lead from a hole in his jeans pocket to the detonator that had been fashioned from a cell phone.

At the right moment, after he was inside the school, perhaps in the cafeteria or in the central corridor between class periods, he would reach in his pocket and press any key.

He would wait then, long enough for a brief prayer, and then press any second key, which would send the current.

"You will feel no pain," his recruiter in Nablus had promised him, although no suicide bomber had ever returned to give witness to the claim. "One moment you will be of this earth, and in the next you will be in Paradise."

"Insha'allah," Muhamed whispered, lost in his thoughts as he turned the corner onto Rocky Mountain Avenue, one block from the school.

The morning was suddenly deathly still. Where before the traffic flowed along Swallow, nothing moved here.

Muhamed pulled up short, realizing that something was wrong. He looked around. There was no traffic. No trucks or cars on the street. Not one person on the sidewalks. No kids in front of the school. No school buses.

He was alone, and suddenly conscious of how difficult it was to walk with twenty kilos of Semtex strapped to his body.

Even the McDonald's across the street seemed to be deserted. At this time of day the drive-in lane should have been filled.

It came to him all at once that he had failed.

A pair of police cars appeared at the end of the street and stopped in the middle of the intersection. Their lights were flashing but there were no sirens.

Muhamed stepped back and turned around. Police cars, lights flashing, were blocking the way he had come.

The Qur'an says that for every people there is a messenger. Muhamed knew the words well. His messenger had come for him, but the issue between them could not be justly determined now. Somehow the authorities had found out he was coming here.

He put his hand in his right pocket and pressed a key on the cell phone, and then held his breath, waiting for bullets to slam into his body.

No shots were fired.

He turned back in time to see at least a dozen sharpshooters suddenly appear on the high school's roof. They were dressed in the same kind of camos that the Israeli soldiers wore when they came into the camps on hit-and-run operations.

It came to him that they had also failed, and he breathed a little easier. If their mission was to stop him from detonating his bomb, they were too late. His finger was on the key. Even if they shot him, he would press it as his life left his body.

None of the infidels would be hurt. But Osama's message that America still was not safe, that al-Quaida and its brave mujahideen and brave Muslims everywhere were willing to give their lives for the cause of justice, would be made perfectly clear.

A heavily armored bomb-disposal truck lumbered from behind the school and headed across the parking lot toward him, stopping about fifty meters away.

Muhamed was no longer frightened. Even without success he knew that his path to Paradise was assured, for wasn't he promised that every son or daughter of the one true faith who lost their lives in the jihad were of the pure of spirit?

"Lay face down on the street," an amplified voice boomed from a speaker on the bomb disposal unit.

Muhamed took a step forward, surprised at how steady his legs had become.

"*Thou must lie face down on the street.*" The order came again, but this time it was in Arabic.

Muhamed took another step forward.

One of the sharpshooters on the roof rose up.

Muhamed closed his eyes. He could see his mother's precious, loving face. Scolding him sometimes, but always with love.

"*Allah O Akbar,*" he whispered, *God is great,* and he pressed the key.

PART

SEVENTY-SIX

☐

It was three o'clock in the afternoon of the next day when the Swiss ambassador, Helmuth Schmidt, left Dennis Berndt's office in the West Wing. Their meeting had been as short as it had been surprising to the president's national security adviser.

But then, he thought as he gathered his files and headed down the corridor to the Oval Office, this had been nothing short of a stunning few days. We'd dodged another bullet, largely because of Kirk McGarvey's actions. At the very least, Haynes was going to win the next election by a landslide, and Americans had gained a new confidence in their government that had been badly shaken by 9/11.

The fact was that although the terrorist Khalil and Prince Salman were not the same man, they in effect had been partners. Khalil set up the attacks, and Salman funneled him the money through a bank in Trinidad. Schmidt had been very precise about his facts. His government had been investigating the prince for nearly two years, and among other items of interest they had uncovered was that most, but not all, of Khalil's money had come from the prince. Several hundred thousand euros and other hard currencies had been transferred to Kahlil's account by Salman's wife, Princess Sofia.

In many respects she was even more devious than her husband. As far as the Swiss could figure, not one person in the Saudi government knew about her involvement, though there were some at the highest levels who knew about her husband's financial dealings with al-Quaida.

Schmidt described her as a loose cannon, who not only knew of her husband's involvement with bin Laden, but who also encouraged him to travel at certain odd times. On this point the Swiss federal authorities were a little less clear; they had not come up with any solid evidence. But it was believed there was a strong likelihood that Khalil had even given her instructions to help coordinate his moves with Prince Salman's.

It would make her an accessory to acts of terrorism and murder.

"We can't prove it, yet," Schmidt admitted, "but our evidence is strong enough to deport her." The ambassador was an older man, with thick white hair and impeccable Swiss formality. "We thought that your government should be made aware of our investigation in light of the recent events at the Salman compound outside Lucerne."

"Thank you, Mr. Ambassador," Berndt had said. "But what about Khalil? Do you know who he is? His DNA and fingerprints are not on any of our databases, nor has Interpol been able to help."

Schmidt shook his head. "For a time it was thought that he was a resident of Trinidad and Tobago. This morning I was sent word that our inquiries there have so far turned up nothing."

"He was an elusive man," Berndt observed.

"Yes," the ambassador said, rising. He took an accordion file folder secured with a string out of his attaché case and handed it across. "This is a précis of our investigation. Perhaps it will aid you in your hunt for bin Laden." He shook his head. "This ugly business must be stopped."

Indeed, Berndt thought, as the uniformed guards outside the Oval Office nodded to him. It would never be over until bin Laden was caught or killed. And even then, he had to wonder if there would be peace, or if some new Islamic fanatic with the same intelligence, charisma, and power would rise up. The war between Islam, Christianity, and Judaism had been going on for a very long time.

The Oval Office was abuzz with staffers coming and going, some of them on telephones or laptop computers, getting ready for the president's talk to the nation this evening.

Haynes was sitting at his desk talking to someone on the phone and looking out the windows toward the Rose Garden. Secretary of State Eugene Carpenter sat next to the president, a handset to his ear.

Beckett spotted Berndt at the doorway and went over. He was animated. "How'd your meeting with Schmidt go?" he asked. "Did you manage to pour oil on troubled waters?"

Berndt smiled faintly. "I'm a persuasive man." He nodded toward the president. "Who's he talking to?"

"Prince Abdullah, the last big hurdle," Beckett said. "Called to congratulate us on our victory."

"Big of him, since Saudi money financed the operation," Berndt said sharply. We had beat the bastards this time, but there would be others. He was getting too old for this. Once the dust settled, he was going to resign and return to academia. It was a decision he'd made some days ago, but now in light of the compromises that everyone was rushing to make, he found that he was sick of the business, and he didn't know if he could or even should wait that long.

Beckett's expression darkened. "We've already gone over that, Dennis. We don't have the proof—"

"We do now," Berndt said, holding up the Swiss file. "Salman *and* his wife have been pumping royal family money to Khalil for years. Couldn't have been done without Prince Abdullah's knowledge and at least his tacit approval."

"You got that from Schmidt?"

"Yeah," Berndt said, tiredly. "But they won't do a thing except to deport Salman's wife and children. The Saudi money is too important to them to upset the applecart by making what Schmidt called 'wild accusations.' "

"It's the same thing a spokesman for the Rainier family told us," Beckett said. "And the French. It's the real world."

"Yes, it is."

Beckett smiled. "The good news is that no one got hurt, except for the kid in Colorado who blew himself up. But it was close."

Berndt really looked at Beckett, and then at the others doing their thing around the president of the United States. They were happy and excited, of course. They *had* dodged a bullet that would have been even larger than 9/11. But the president's staffers were behaving as if it were they who had stopped the suicide bombers. They lived in an isolated environment here. No matter how often they traveled with or for the president around the country or around the world, they were still tethered to this one place.

"Dennis?" Beckett prompted.

"It wouldn't have been so close if we'd listened to McGarvey in the first place."

Beckett nodded. "And the president is willing to forgive his insubordination. There'll be a Senate investigation, of course, but the president will stand behind him." Beckett lowered his voice. "Maybe even give him the Presidential Medal of Freedom. It would put a nice cap on Mac's career."

"Yes, it would," President Haynes said, finished with his phone call. He got to his feet, a warm smile on his face. "And the Saudis have agreed to cooperate with us. We'll drop the issue of Prince Salman's money, and in turn there'll be no formal protests over the damage we caused at their embassy and think tank."

Berndt was struck dumb.

"How are our Mr. McGarvey and his wife?" the president asked.

"Recovering," Berndt said. "But what are we supposed to say to the families of the two firemen whom a Saudi citizen murdered?"

"We don't know that he was a Saudi," Haynes replied, mildly. "But be that as it may, those two men are heroes. They blocked Khalil's escape long enough for McGarvey to reach him. Their families can be proud that they didn't die in vain. And I'll tell that to the nation this evening."

"Yes, they were heroes," Berndt mumbled. Beckett's assessment of the real world politik was on the mark. This was political expediency in just about its most aggressive form. Oil for dollars. It had been all about that, even before World War II. It's why the politicians had divided the Middle East not along ethnic or religious lines, but along oil deposits.

Haynes was watching him. "Are you okay, Dennis?"

Berndt realized that he'd been wool gathering, something he'd been doing a lot of lately. And his disappointment probably showed on his face. He nodded. "Just tired, Mr. President. It's been a hectic few days."

"That it has," Haynes said. "I'm going to need you until we go on the air tonight, and then I think that you and Joyce should get away for a few days or a week. Linda and I are taking Deb out to Keystone. Maybe I'll catch a few trout."

"It's not over yet," Berndt said. "They'll try again." If he resigned he would be deserting his president at a very difficult time. He didn't know if he could do that. He was torn with indecision, something that had never seemed to bother McGarvey.

"They most certainly will," Haynes said, "which is why I'm going to form a task force to deal specifically with finding and capturing or killing al-Quaida's top leadership anywhere in the world they choose to hide. Just like we did in Iraq. And when McGarvey recovers, I'm going to ask him to head it."

"I don't know if he'll take the job——"

The famous Haynes campaign smile lit his face. "I think I'll be able to convince him, especially if we can hand him bin Laden's head on a platter."

Berndt felt a little thrill in his stomach. "Do we have a new lead?"

"Weissman's people did a quick sweep of the Saudi think tank in Georgetown before they had to let the Saudis back in. They found some credible documents pointing to a very specific area on Pakistan's border with Afghanistan."

"We've suspected all along that he's been hiding out up there," Berndt said, "but it's a tough place to operate in without Pakistani support."

"Well, we've got it now," Beckett said. "Musharraf has agreed to let us in on an all-out manhunt."

"Which is getting under way within the next twenty-four hours," the president said. "This time we'll get the bastard."

Berndt nodded uncertainly. He didn't share the president's optimism, and even if we did capture or kill the man, the terrorism probably wouldn't stop. "All we can do is try, Mr. President," he said. That's all any of them could do.

SEVENTY-SEVEN

Kathleen McGarvey stood at the window in her husband's hospital room and stared out toward the city that was coming alive with the dawn. The entire nation had breathed a sigh of relief, and she could feel it.

There had been a steady stream of visitors ever since Mac had been moved down from the ICU. He was a national hero once again, and half of Washington wanted to shake his hand. But Kathleen had managed to hold most of them off. He had lost a lot of blood, especially from the knife wound in his shoulder. There would be no lasting damage other than a new set of scars, but he was still weak, and the shrapnel wounds to the bottoms of his feet were causing him a lot of pain.

Kathleen had been treated and immediately released, and since then she had not left her husband's side. Except for a chipped tooth, a couple of broken ribs, and a lot of bruising, she'd not been seriously hurt. No damage had been done to the baby; as the Saudi doctor had told her, the bleeding had not been a result of her beating, but she'd been very frightened.

She felt her husband's eyes on her, and she turned around.

"Good morning," he said. He'd fallen asleep after Dick Adkins had left last night with the news that the president wanted him back, and he had not awakened the entire night.

"Good morning, darling," Kathleen said, kissing his cheek. "How are you feeling?"

McGarvey took a moment or two to answer. "Better," he said. "Hungry."

For the first time since the incident he seemed to be his old self. Alert, not so groggy and disconnected around the edges. "Breakfast is in an hour, unless you want something now. I can get it from the cafeteria—"

He shook his head. "Don't leave. I can wait." He seemed to study her face as if he hadn't seen it for a very long while. "How about you?"

"Sore as hell, but the baby's going to be okay." He had asked the same question a dozen times since he'd come out of surgery, and each time he was visibly relieved; the muscles around his mouth and eyes relaxing, he smiled. She wasn't tired of giving him the same answer.

"That's good to hear," he said. "I was worried about you."

Katy squeezed his hand, and a surge of emotions, from love to thankfulness for his presence in her life, filled her heart. She didn't want to go through this sort of thing ever again. She didn't know how she could take it. "Do you remember Dick being here last night?"

McGarvey nodded. "Do you remember what I told him?"

"Did you mean it?"

"Hundred percent, Katy," he said. "I'm quit and I'm staying quit."

She searched his eyes for any hint that he might be regretting his decision, that he might just be telling her what she wanted to hear. But she saw only warmth, and sincerity and love. Again her emotions surged, and her eyes wanted to fill, but she fought back the tears. "That's fine, darling," she said. "Really fine."

The door was open and the hospital was coming up to speed for the morning, nurses and orderlies passing in the hall. Katy hated hospitals, and the sooner she could get her husband home, the sooner they could start putting their lives back together. It would be a month or two before he could walk without crutches, and by then he would be irascible because of the enforced inaction, but she found that she was actually looking forward to his mood swings.

"When do I get out of here?" he asked.

"They said this afternoon, if you're up to it. But you're going to be on crutches."

"I figured as much," he said. "After breakfast I want to see Otto, and at some point my secretary, and probably Dick again." He smiled. "I don't think I had it completely together last night."

Something clutched at Kathleen's stomach, but it wasn't the baby. "Do you remember the president's speech? The Pakistanis think they've got bin Laden cornered, and they've asked for our help this time."

"That's why I want to see Dick and Otto. I've got a few ideas." He smiled at his wife. "Don't worry, Katy; I'm not going back. But I'll have to be debriefed, and that's probably going to take a couple of weeks, and there are a few loose ends I'll have to take care of. Including apologizing to the president."

His words were music to Kathleen's ears. "Don Shaw called; he's doing fine now. He and Karen want to have us to their house for dinner as soon as you're up for it. And of course the media have been camped outside from day one, wanting to interview you as soon as the doctors gave the okay. But I told them no, for now."

"I'm not talking to anybody."

Kathleen smiled. "You're not going to get away with it for long," she said. He started to protest, but she held him off. "You're a national hero, practically a saint. Not only did you rescue Shaw and the rest of us from the *Spirit*, you stopped the suicide bombers. No children were hurt. There isn't a parent in the country who isn't grateful as hell to you, and all of them want to thank you personally. Otto said he'd gotten word that there was going to be a Senate Intelligence Committee hearing on what you did. They wanted something to give the Saudis, but they wouldn't dare now. Besides, Haynes is behind you all the way."

McGarvey looked past his wife to the window. "We were wrong about Salman."

"That's the point; you weren't *completely* wrong," Kathleen said. "He wasn't a terrorist, but he and his wife were funding Khalil. Otto figures they'd probably supported others too, and maybe even fed money directly to bin Laden."

McGarvey's mood deepened.

Kathleen knew what he was thinking, but it no longer bothered her. "Liese was badly wounded, but she'll come out of it okay." It's what Otto had told them last night, and Mac was still beating himself up over what could have been a tragedy.

"I screwed up," he said, softly.

"We all do from time to time. But you did the best you could with the information you had." She wanted to make it better for him, even though she knew he would have to work out his guilt for himself. "In a few days you can give her a call, see how she's doing. I think it'll mean a lot to her."

He looked away again. "She's in love with me, and I used her."

"Yes, you did. And now you have to live with it," Kathleen said. "No one was killed, and she *will* recover. And think about what you and she together prevented. You stopped Khalil."

"A smart man," McGarvey said.

"But not as smart as you."

McGarvey laughed. "You're prejudiced."

"Yes, I am," Kathleen said, and she finally knew for a fact that everything was going to turn out fine. Just fine.

She kissed her husband, this time deeply and with a hundred years of love and passion and friendship, because he was finally coming home.

SEVENTY-EIGHT

□

Liese awoke to bright sunlight streaming through her hospital window, a terrific pain pounding at the back of her heavily bandaged head. Raising a hand to her face, she blocked the sun so she could see what kind of day it was. Only a few puffy summer clouds, but they were beautiful to her.

She had survived. By dumb, blind luck, according to Claude LeFevre, who'd come up to see her yesterday afternoon. Had the bullet entered her head one centimeter to the left, she would have been killed.

"We were picking up everything, but Gertner wouldn't let us go for the rescue," LeFevre said. "Not until we heard the gunshot. Then we *had* to get you out."

Liese tried to smile, but the effort sent a sharp pain through the middle of her head.

"Take it easy, Sarge. The docs say you'll come out of this with nothing more than a scar in your thick skull."

"And a lot of years behind bars to think about what I did," she'd told him. "I'm sure Gertner is beside himself with joy that he's finally able to get rid of me."

LeFevre shook his head. "You're wrong about that. Your Kirk McGarvey killed Khalil, stopped the al-Quaida attacks, and we got the proof that Salman *and* his wife were part of the money behind bin Laden. Wouldn't have been possible without your help. You're Gertner's star pupil."

She didn't want to believe it. "What about Salman?"

"Khalil killed him."

"How about the princess and the children?"

"They've been deported," LeFevre said. "But why don't you ask me about McGarvey?"

She hardened her heart for the bad news.

"He's okay, Sarge. He was hurt, but he'll pull through."

Liese closed her eyes for a moment, relief washing through her body.

It was finally over. No matter what happened now, this was behind them. Time to go forward.

LeFevre touched her arm. "Hey, are you okay?"

She opened her eyes and managed a small smile. "Do me a favor, would you, Claude? Don't call me Sarge. I don't like it. My name is Liese."

"Anything you'd like, Liese."

Time to go forward, she told herself again. But she was tired. "Would you stay a little longer? I don't want to be alone."

"I will," LeFevre said, a warm, honest smile creasing the corners of his eyes.

It was the last thing she had remembered from the previous night: his eyes. Someone came into the room, and she turned slowly to see who it was.

LeFevre, all smiles, carrying a vase of pretty flowers, came around the bed to her. "You had a good night's sleep?" he asked. He set the flowers on the broad windowsill. "I wanted to get these up here before you woke up, so they'd be the first thing you saw." He looked closely at her. "They're okay?"

"Just fine, Claude," Liese said, and for a moment, looking at LeFevre and the flowers he'd brought her, she couldn't bring a clear image of Mc-Garvey's face to mind.

She didn't know what that meant, because she had dreamed about Kirk every night for the past ten years, but she was willing to accept it.

THE ONLY ONE

"For God gave His only son,"
this we understand,
not as a child under the gun,
but whispered wishes upon clasped hands.

We hold these to be truths
because they are removed from us,
history soothes
allowing comfort and trust.

Someone, somewhere
has given that held most dear,
a sacrifice we selfishly try to share,
one many humans revere.

But if it were you, you
who must offer,
no, must ask your child to do,
would you?

Could you see,
in all your passion and poverty,
the greater we,
the presence of deity?

Well, I, speaking only for myself,
could see nothing but my only son,
my single source of wealth,
my only rising sun.

I will not call him to arms,
to feed the family,
to wrap himself in bombs
and do so happily.

I am simple and selfish,
basking in the light of my son,
I have but only one wish:
he'll never know anything of being the one.

GINA HAGBERG-BALLINGER